ALSO BY JAMES NOLL

Tales of the Weird

A Knife in the Back
You Will Be Safe Here
Burn All The Bodies
Mad Tales (Compendium)
Don't Turn Around (Illustrated Compendium)
Thirteen Tales (Short Story Compilation)

The Bonesaw Trilogy

The Rabbit, The Jaguar, & The Snake

The Topher Trilogy (Novels):

Raleigh's Prep
Tracker's Travail
Topher's Ton
The Topher Trilogy (Omnibus)

Audio Books

A Knife in the Back
Thirteen Tales
The Hive: Seasons 1-4
Raleigh's Prep

The Hive

JAMES NOLL

PULP!

Horror, Post-Apocalyptic, and Science Fiction

This is a work of fiction. Names, characters, places, and incidents either are products of the author's imagination or are used fictitiously and are not to be construed as real. Any resemblance to actual events, locales, organizations, or persons, living or dead, is entirely coincidental. I tell you true

 PULP books may be purchased for educational, business, or sales promotional use. For information, visit www.jamesnoll.net

Book Design by James Noll

Cover Art and Design by Grant Ervin

Author Photo by Haley Noll

ISBN: 9781733744317 (PULP!)

For Sasha. Best Dog I Ever Had

CONTENTS

THE HIVE

SEASON 1

BEST DOG I EVER HAD

When most people think of an alien invasion, they think of the dumb movies Hollywood pumps out every summer. Robots and spacesuits. Lasers and spaceships. What they don't think of is the thing that dropped onto our neighbor Mr. Gomez's farm and smashed his barn to smithereens, along with his horses, his pigs, his goats, and probably about a zillion rats. We didn't see it happen, Daddy and me, but we felt it. It was seven o'clock on a Wednesday morning, and I was laid up with a broken leg on the couch, dozing in and out while I watched sitcom reruns on the TV. *Hogan's Heroes. Gilligan's Island. The Love Boat.*

The broken leg came courtesy of Ruth Grace Hogg, starting fullback for the Caroline Cavaliers' Varsity Girl's Field Hockey team. I played forward for the Spotsylvania Knights, and for good reason, too. I lived in Spotsy, for one, and I was fleet and fast and good with my stick. Unfortunately, I didn't weigh much more than a hundred pounds. Ruth Grace Hogg tipped the scales at about a buck ninety.

I had legs like a colt. She had arms like a gorilla.

When she saw little old me cutting up her team, she knew what she was about. She ran up to me, cocked them big hairy arms of hers, and whacked my leg like it was a piñata. Two hours later I was laid up at home on the couch, two pins in my femur and forty mgs of Vicodin in my head.

"Ain't you going to do something about it, Daddy?"

Daddy was in the kitchen, sipping a cup of coffee.

"Like what?"

"I don't know. Complain to the school board. Call the president."

"I'll get on my personal line to him directly."

"It's rude to tease an invalid. Can't you talk to her parents?"

Daddy looked like someone had just asked him to solve a calculus problem with a fish.

"Why'd I want to do something like that?"

"Because I'm your daughter. And she broke my leg. On purpose."

Daddy chuckled and shook his head.

"'Manda, you know I love you, right?"

"I'm starting to question the depths of that love."

"Well I do. But let me ask you something. You do know how much Ruth Grace Hogg weighs, right?"

"Who don't? The whole county shakes when she gets out of bed in the morning."

"And you know how much you weigh, right?"

I waited a long time before I answered.

"Yeah."

"I couldn't be more proud of you. You had you a job and you didn't let nothing back you down. But you did try to run down someone nearly twice your size, and you lost. So let that be a lesson to you."

"I thought you said you were proud of me?"

"I am."

"So why're you telling me to back off the next time?"

"I didn't say that."

I ever tell you Daddy could be infuriating? I sighed, took a deep breath, and said, "You mind telling me what you are telling me, then?"

"Next time," he said. "Run faster."

So anyway, the invasion.

It was late summer, and school hadn't even started yet. The August heat and humidity weighed down on everything like a wet blanket. Our house was built in 1921, as

Daddy was fond of telling just about everybody who cared to listen. To him, that was an accomplishment. To me, it meant that nearly everything was broken or breaking down. The pipes froze every winter, the windows were like sieves, and in the summer we didn't have air conditioning. Oh, Daddy did his best. He planted a couple of recycled, wheezing window units in the windows, kept them alive with a healthy application of duct tape and freon, but all they did was make a racket while blowing not-really-cold air a few feet into the house.

Daddy'd just come in from loading Sparkles up into his truck, Sparkles being an old dog of his he'd gotten stuffed. It was a sad day for the old girl. The years had been unkind, and she'd started to smell. Daddy brought her to his regular taxidermist to fix the issue, but she gave him some sorry news: old Sparkles was rotting.

"Well no shit, she's rotting," Daddy said. "She's been dead fifteen years."

Apparently pointing out the obvious didn't improve Sparkles' condition. It was finally time to lay her to rest, and Daddy was going to do it Spotsy style. He got himself ahold of a remote-controlled detonator and some explosives—cherry bombs and fertilizer and the like—and stuffed her full to the brim. The plan was simple. He and his friends were going to drive Sparkles out to the country, set her up in a field, get drunk, and blow her up.

Daddy showed me the detonator as if seeing it would make me want to go.

"You sure you don't want to come?"

"No thanks."

"Alright then."

He put it in his back pocket and went over to fill his thermos up with coffee. That's when I felt this horrible pressure build in the air. It pushed down on me, like the atmosphere itself had gone feral and decided to attack. I held my hands to my ears, but the pressure kept building and building. I opened my mouth to scream but couldn't hear anything at all. Then it released and I could hear again. A sonic boom thundered in the distance, and the house shook and rattled and nearly jumped off the foundation. I thought it was an earthquake. Or maybe Ruth Grace Hogg having a fit. I almost fell off the couch. Plates and cups clattered in the cabinets, and Daddy's ham radio fell over and cracked on the floor. Then it fell quiet and still. I pulled myself into sitting position.

"What the hell was that?"

Daddy was kind of squatting down, hands out, looking like he was waiting for another blast. His overalls were covered in coffee.

"I dunno. And don't say hell."

"You say it all the time."

The phone rang and I gasped. I could tell he wanted to chew me out, but something big had just happened, and when the phone rang after something big had just happened, you answer it.

"Aw hell," he said and snatched it off its cradle. "Yeah? Yeah, Gomez, I felt it."

He covered the mouthpiece and mouthed "It's Gomez" to me like I couldn't hear. Gomer Gomez. Our next-door neighbor. (Out here a next-door neighbor could live ten miles away.) I turned my attention back to the TV. We didn't have a remote. Not that I minded. We was lucky to even get a signal at all. I struggled off the couch and hopped over to change the channels. I was looking to see if any of the local news stations were making a special broadcast. Channel 4, nothing. Channel 7, nothing. Channel 9, nothing. Daddy kept jawing away in the kitchen.

"Calm down, Gomez. I can't understand a word you're . . . Uh-huh. Your whole barn? Uh-huh. You get a look at . . . no, I wouldn't go out there. It'd be best if you didn't. I can't,

I got 'Manda here and she's got a—" Gomez screamed something and Daddy pulled the phone away from his ear with a grimace. "Gomez? You there? Damn." And he hung up the phone.

"What's wrong with Mr. Gomez?"

"Says a spaceship landed on his barn."

Daddy went over to his gun safe and started dialing in the combination.

"Spaceship?"

"Uh-huh."

"Out here?"

"Uh-huh."

"Damn."

"Dammit, 'Manda."

"He say what it looks like?"

"Uh-huh."

"You mind telling me?"

"Said it looked like a big wasp's nest."

The gun safe unlocked with a click, and he pulled it open and started grabbing boxes of ammo. Then he took out his favorite Remington .30 .06 and slung it over his shoulder and put a couple of .357's in a bag.

"You gonna kill it?"

"Gonna try."

"Can I come?"

"You're gonna stay right here, young lady."

"Why?"

"Because you're all busted up. And if there really is a spaceship out there that looks like a wasp's nest, there ain't much you'll be able to do."

"I can shoot one of them .357s."

"I know."

"Aren't you the one who always said its better to have a man on your six?"

"Yeah, I did say that."

Daddy was already putting on his jacket and hat. He was halfway out the door.

"You really think Mr. Gomez's gonna have yours?"

That made him stop. Daddy wasn't that much of a thinker. I don't mean he was dumb because he wasn't. I mean that when a decision needed to be made, he liked to make it fast. Just like that, he said, "If you can get out to the car before I leave, you can come with me."

Mr. Gomez's farm was down Brock Road a stretch, just past Todd's Tavern. Take a few turns back toward Locust Grove, a few back roads, and there it was. Fifty acres smack dab in the middle of Spotsylvania County Virginia, the northernmost southern county in the whole damn state.

Daddy turned up the long gravel drive that led to the house, sending rocks clattering in the wheel wells and dust clouding in our wake. I bounced around in the front seat like a baby in a bucket, hoping the rifle on the rack didn't accidentally go off. Or the .357's in the bag, for that matter.

"Slow down, Daddy! You wanna break my other leg?"

He didn't reply. He had a way about him when he got set on something. He called it 'Enthusiastic Designation.' I called it 'Acting Like A Jerk'. I knew better than to bring it up. He just got cranky if I did.

He ganked the wheel and skidded to the right, steering around the side of Gomez's worn out farmhouse. Gomez was the type who liked to keep all sorts of things in his yard. Old tires. Rusted out tractors. Landscape drags and farming tillers. Daddy slalomed through it all like he was an expert, tearing up the grass, finally slowing down when he made it to the pond a few hundred yards behind the house.

Mr. Gomez's barn was just off to the side. Or it used to be. Now it was scattered all over the field like it'd been blown to bits from the inside out. In its place was something that I don't even know how to begin to describe, but

I'll say this: Either Mr. Gomez'd never seen a wasp's nest in his life, or he was the stupidest man on God's green earth. The thing that landed on his barn was round and greenish-brown with spikes sticking out all over the surface. Looked more like a sweet-gum ball than a wasp's nest.

Steam or smoke or something poured off the top, and there was a crack at the bottom—an opening or a door or something—with a warm, orange light pulsing from deep inside and green stuff oozing out. And boy did it stink. Hit us full on even with the windows rolled up. I couldn't think of anything worse I'd ever smelled.

Daddy, in his usual way, summed it up nicely.

"Smells like roasted goat shit."

Mr. Gomez's neighbors were already standing in the field between the barn and the house. Mr. Sokolov and his boy, Vlad, and old Mrs. Freeman, who looked as spry as ever in her work jeans and red flannel. Mr. Gomez's sons, Gomez and Gomer, Jr, were in the middle of trying to restrain their mother who kept pulling away from them. Daddy pulled up to Mr. Sokolov's truck and put it in park.

"You stay here and watch Sparkles."

"Seriously?"

He got out without another word, leaving his door open and the keys in the ignition. I ain't one for whining, and I'm sure he was just trying to protect me, but the day I'm compared to a stuffed dog and come out equal will be the day I can fly and shoot bullets out of my nose. I wrenched the passenger side door open, hopped out, and grabbed my crutches. It was hard going, but Daddy didn't raise no bleater, and I caught him just as he tipped his hat at Mr. Sokolov.

"Hey, Skip." (Mr. Sokolov's name was Viktor). "What's going on?"

"That thing lands on Gomez barn. Gomez, he's sucked inside."

"Sucked inside?"

"Sucked inside."

Mrs. Gomez, or should I say the Widow Mrs. Gomez, seen us, pulled herself free of her sons, and came galloping over.

"Bill! Bill, please! You've got to do something! That thing has my Gomez!"

She collapsed into Daddy's arms sobbing and carrying on, and I never saw Daddy so uncomfortable. He was not a man to show his emotions. I think they embarrassed him. And if he wasn't already embarrassed enough by his own emotions, he was damn well mortified by other people's. He patted Mrs.

Gomez on the back a few times and then peeled her off and held her at arm's length.

"Okay, Mrs. Gomez. I need to you calm down and tell me what happened."

She nodded and tried to get herself together, and after a few deep breaths, she was finally able to talk.

"Gomez went about bonkers when that thing fell on our barn. After he made a couple of phone calls, he jumped in his truck and went speeding on down here, tearing up the lawn and my peonies."

Her eyes wandered back to the house.

"I told him not to go, that this was an issue for the president, but he wouldn't listen. You know how crazy he gets about the government."

"Yes, ma'am, I do."

"He wouldn't let me go with him, neither. Me or the boys. So we watched from the kitchen window. He drove his truck right up to that thing, got out with his hunting rifle, and started shooting."

"Don't look like he did much damage."

"None at all. And then as God as my witness, when he started to reload, that crack opened up, and a tentacle slithered out, wrapped him up, and dragged him in. I don't remember what happened after that. I was too busy screaming."

Daddy looked around at everyone, seeing if he could muster them up to do something, but they toed the ground and refused to meet his gaze. Mrs. Gomez worried the front of her dress, her face reddening when she realized that nobody was going to do anything.

"If you all ain't man enough to anything, I am!"

And she marched off across the field, her sons right behind her, calling out "Momma! Momma, wait!" I tell you what, Mrs. Gomez'd worked herself up into a state. She was screaming and yelling (what exactly she was saying, I couldn't tell) tearing at her hair, jamming her finger into the air. None of us moved a muscle. She was going to do what she was going to do, whether it was good for her or not.

Daddy said, "Y'all think we should call the president?"

Mrs. Freeman spat on the ground.

"I ain't too sure what Slick Willie'll be able to do about this."

The Gomez boys did their best to stop her. Gomer jumped on his momma's back and Gomez, Jr. latched onto her legs, and they all got to screaming and yelling and clapperclawing. It might've gone on like that forever, but I guess that spiky ball'd had enough because three tentacles shot out of it, wrapped around each of the surviving members of the Family Gomez, and started reeling them in. That seemed to be enough for Daddy.

"Aw hell," he said and marched right back to the truck. He grabbed the .30 .06 off the rack and the .357's out of his bag and started loading them. "Y'all bring yours?"

He needn't have asked. Mrs. Freeman already had her shotgun out, Mr. Sokolov had a .30 .30, and Vlad'd gotten himself a machete for some reason.

Daddy, Mr. Sokolov, and Mrs. Freeman positioned themselves in a line facing the thing and started shooting. Bam! Bam! Bam! Bam! Round after round. Bullets thunked into the thing's meat, but other than a little more smoke and what looked like green syrup pouring out of its side, they did about as much harm as a squirrel chewing on an elephant.

When they were done, the air smelled like goat shit and gunpowder, but it didn't do a thing to stop the tentacles. All we could do was watch as Mrs. Gomez and her boys were sucked inside with a syrupy slurp. Daddy waited a tic before he made his final assessment of their work.

"Well, crap."

And that's when the tentacles shot out again. Four this time.

The first one grabbed Mr. Sokolov and heaved him off his feet. Another one grabbed Mrs. Freeman. The third whipped out and snatched Daddy around the waist. The last one tried to get Vlad, but he sliced it off at the tip with his machete. The tentacle went wild, spraying purple gunk all over him that burned and sizzled. Vlad fell to the ground, screaming. Daddy fixed his eyes on mine.

"'Manda," he said. "Sparkles."

Oh yeah.

Sparkles the stuffed dog. Stuffed with explosives.

I don't know if any of you ever tried to run on crutches, but it ain't like pulling a string out of a cat's ass. Hurts your armpits, too. So I dropped one and hopped back to the truck, jumped in, and turned the key. The old thing cranked to life and I slammed it into gear and stepped on the gas, aiming straight for the hive.

That old hive must've known something was up because it shot three more tentacles at me as I sped toward it. One crashed through the windshield. Another hit the grill. The third missed entirely, but swung back around and grabbed the truck by the rear bumper. It yanked sideways, and I realized I didn't even need to drive no more. The only thing I had to concentrate on was getting out before it pulled me into them slimy green and yellow guts.

I forced the driver's side door open, but one of the tentacles slammed it closed again. Another swung at me through the busted windshield and I threw myself onto the bench seat. It smashed the driver's side window and wrapped around the frame, breaking off hunks of metal. Purple ooze splattered onto the dashboard and started to eat through it. I scrambled across the seat for the passenger side door and managed to get it open, and right when I was going to dive out, praying I didn't break my neck when I landed, my broken leg exploded with pain.

It was another one of them tentacles. Damn thing'd wrapped itself around my cast and got to squeezing.

If breaking my leg was the most excruciating thing I'd ever felt, squeezing it when it was already broke ran a close second. The vision in the corners of my eyes went black and I felt like I was going to vomit. The thing yanked again, and I felt something give in my knee. I was in so much agony that I couldn't even think straight. Another squeeze, another yank. I slapped around for something, anything I could use as a weapon, and happened upon a nice, long, hunk of the metal frame.

My body was halfway out the door, and I could see the opening of the hive, pulsing and squelching as we drew near. With a scream, I sat up and stabbed that tentacle with that hunk of metal. It pulled back, ripping my cast off and sending me tumbling ass over elbows out of the truck. I flipped once and landed strange, and then I was laying on my back in Gomez's field. Next thing I heard was an explosion, and a ball of fire filled the air.

One week later, both me and Daddy were sitting on the couch eating ice cream and watching *M*A*S*H* reruns. His arm was wrapped tight to his chest and he was wearing a neck brace. He didn't like it very much, and I didn't blame him. August in Virginia was hot enough in shorts and a t-shirt without adding a neck brace. I kept catching him in the middle of taking it off, saying it "cramped his style."

"Daddy, you try to take that thing off again, I'm going to sprain your other neck."

"I don't know what that means, but message received."

My new cast was even bigger and thicker than the one before, and the itching drove me nuts, and since I wasn't allowed to take a shower, and since Daddy told me that under no circumstances was he going to give me a sponge bath, I was starting to get a little ripe. He would, though, spring for ice cream.

"I personally like me some praline myself," he said, scooping a spoonful into his mouth.

"Yuck."

I took a bite of mine, trusty, dusty Neapolitan, and watched the TV. Hawkeye and Trapper John was in the middle of fixing a prank on that old stick-in-the-mud Frank Burns again.

"Well one thing's for certain," I said. "I'm glad that old stuffed dog's finally out of the house."

Daddy gave me a playful slap.

"Don't you talk about Sparkles like that. Sparkles saved the world. Best dog I ever had."

THE HIVE

Fall in the country was a beautiful thing. The leaves turned to gold and brown and red and yellow, the temperature dropped below fifty every night, and everything felt like it was hunkering down. By late September my leg was healing up good, even after it almost got broke a second time. My second cast was off, but I still had a boot on and had to walk with a cane. I was worried, though, because I needed physical therapy to get back to normal, and physical therapy cost a lot of money—a lot of money we didn't have.

Daddy didn't want to hear it.

"You're getting PT," he said.

He was sitting in his chair in front of the fireplace, sharping his knife, a big Bowie he'd had since he was a kid. I liked the sound it made as he scraped it against the sharpening stone.

"How? You gonna sell your new truck?"

"No. But I will plant some winter pot."

"I thought you said that was dangerous? Don't the feds have them thermal cameras?"

"We'll be fine. It's just this one time."

I gave him my best disapproving look, but he wasn't swayed.

"'Manda, you break a bone, it don't ever heal complete. Without PT it just gets worse. Look."

He held his left thumb up at me like it was the crown jewels. Daddy'd been using it as evidence of the frailty of the human body since I was in Kindergarten. Stub a toe? Better watch out this don't happen to you. Bruise a rib? I bet it looks like this.

It did look pretty gross. Damn thing was crooked as a senator. It twisted to the left and almost ran straight into his pointer finger before it straightened out again. And there was a notch in it down at the bottom, like whatever happened had created a new knuckle. He could've gotten it fixed, but he said he liked it that way, mainly because he could dislocate it at will. It was his favorite party trick: tie his wrists together, pop his thumb out of joint, and slip out of the bind.

"Fine," I said. "But if you get busted, I better not hear no complaints."

"If I get busted, you won't hear a thing from me. I'll be in the federal pen."

A few nights later, a goat-drowner rolled through the country. I was jolted out of sleep by a clap of thunder so loud that it shook the whole house. I started to freak out a little bit, but before it could get out of control, Daddy poked his head in my room and said, "Don't sweat it, sugar-booger. It's just a thunderstorm."

"Don't call me sugar-booger."

"Okay."

I went back to sleep to the soothing sound of sheets of rain punctuated by Daddy's startled muttering every time lightning struck.

The next morning was calm and clear. The house was still when I woke up, and when I shuffled into the kitchen, I saw the note Daddy left on the counter.

"Blue's," it said in his typically verbose style.

Blue was a former Marine. He owned a guns and ammo store in Partlow. He and Daddy had an arrangement. Daddy kept him in as much pot as he could smoke, and Blue kept Daddy in as many bullets as he could fire.

Doctor said I should be walking around as much as I could, at least until it began to hurt, so after breakfast, I decided to head out to the yard to do some chores and clean up. The storm had downed a few trees on the edge of the fields, and a handful of shingles had blown off the barn roof, but other than that, everything was basically fine.

I'd just sat down on the back step with a cup of coffee when a boy came walking out of the woods. Number 22, one of the barn cats who thought he was a house cat, rubbed himself against my leg and I pet him and he meowed. I pointed my mug at the kid who was now walking across my backyard.

"Look there, Number 22. That's little Seb Mack."

Seb Mack walked right up to me as if we had a date and said, "I'm Seb Mack and something's wrong with my Mama."

Seb Mack didn't have to walk the ten miles from his broke-down trailer to my back step to provide me with that information. Everybody in Spotsy knew who his mama was, and everybody in Spotsy knew there was something wrong with her. Hell, there was something wrong with the entire Mack family, fathers, mothers, uncles, cousins, grandparents, probably even some distant relations we ain't never met.

"I know who you are, Seb Mack. What's wrong with your mama this time?"

"She ain't right."

Then the weirdest thing happened. Number 22 hopped up on the rail behind me, took one look at Seb Mack, flattened his ears, and took to hissing and growling. Seb Mack locked eyes with him and glared. That's when I noticed the deep black bags under his eyes and how pale his face looked.

Mama Mack preferred her chemicals and alcohol to the feeding and maintenance of her offspring, but none of them ever looked as sick and malnourished as Seb Mack did right at that moment. I could see the bones of his cheeks, and the skin around his forehead looked clenched and thin like it'd been torqued tight with a socket wrench.

He took what looked like an involuntary step toward the cat, his arm partially raised, and Number 22 leaped off the rail and sprinted away, nearly running right into Daddy as he came around the corner carrying a new flat of plants. My leg was getting tight, so I stretched it out in front of me.

"Hey Daddy."

"Hey."

"How're your errands?"

"Got 'er done." He brought the flat over to the steel bulkhead that led to the cellar and put it down on the grass.

"What's he want?" he asked, fishing his keys out of his pocket.

"You wanna tell him, Seb Mack?"

"I'm Seb Mack and something's wrong with my mama."

Daddy kneeled down and unlocked the bulkhead, pulling it open with a squeal.

"Hell, boy. You didn't have to walk all the way over here to tell me that."

"Daddy, stop. Look at him."

"'Manda, I ain't got time to deal with Macks today."

"Just come here and look at him."

Daddy sighed and came over. Held the boy's chin and turned his head from side to side.

"What's she got into now, boy?" Number 22 sauntered over as if nothing had happened, and Seb's eyes locked onto him. "She been beating you? Feeding you? When's the last time you had a bath?"

Seb followed the cat, and his hands started to flex and relax, flex and relax. He kept doing that until Daddy snapped in front of the boy's eyes.

"Hey! Seb Mack! You hear me?"

"Mama got the infection."

"Infection? What infection?"

"She gave it to Amaryl and Brindle."

Amaryl and Brindle were Seb Mack's little sisters.

"Your mama got your sisters sick?"

"She made them sick. Fed them to the hive."

Daddy stood up and put his hands on his hips. I knew what he was thinking. Damn. That hive again.

"'Manda—"

"I'll go get your guns."

Seb Mack sat between Daddy and me on the drive over. Daddy tried to press him for more information about the hive—how big it was, what it looked like, why it ate kids, why his mama was feeding it kids—but Seb refused to answer. Daddy grit his teeth.

"Anybody ever tell you it's rude to ignore people?"

It was noon by the time we made it out to the Mack's place. They lived in a trailer about a mile back off Post Oak, close to Brokenburg. The entrance to their property wasn't marked, but my family had been in Spotsy for five generations; none of us needed no sign to show us where they lived. The driveway ran through thick forest, all two miles of it, dead-ending at what looked like a setting from a horror movie.

Seb Mack's mama's trailer stood in the middle of a clearing. The roof was blanketed with leaves, and the foundation had sunk about a foot into the soft dirt underneath. The siding was so covered with moss and grime that it blended in with its surroundings. At first I thought the condition of the trailer, not to mention the various rusty car parts, appliances, and trash scattered around the front, was just another expression of typical Mack laziness, but then I realized it might have been a strategy. Blend in enough with your surroundings and nobody'll ever bother you.

Daddy stopped about fifty yards from the trailer, and put his truck into park, leaving the keys in the ignition like he always did.

"You need to go farther," Seb Mack said.

"No can do, son."

"You need to go farther in."

Daddy pointed out the windshield.

"You see them trees? They're leaning against each other. With last night's rain, they're like to fall and block the way out."

Seb Mack looked stunned. He hadn't considered that.

Daddy chose to kick the bottom of the trailer door rather than touch any part of it with his exposed skin.

"Mama Mack! It's Bill Jett. I got your boy Seb Mack out here." He waited a minute before kicking again. "Mama Mack?" Nothing.

He looked down at the boy. "You sure she's home?"

Seb Mack nodded solemnly.

The woods were quiet. No birds flitting around in the trees. No squirrels skittering around the leaves. I didn't expect a scene from a Disney movie, but we were out in the middle of the woods. There should've at least been a coon waddling around. Of course, the Macks were hunters. They could've picked the area clean already, which would've been stupid, seeing as though it was only the beginning of fall and all. Daddy shrugged his rifle off his shoulder.

"'Manda, you wait here."

"What? No. You remember how that worked out last time?"

"Good point. Here." He pulled a sidearm out of his pocket and handed it to me. "Safety's on."

I checked the chamber. Checked the magazine. Loaded and full.

"Wouldn't have expected anything else."

Daddy went in first and immediately stepped in something gross. He lifted up his foot, stretching long strings of thick, gooey slime stuck to the bottom of his shoe and the tacky tile in the little square entry. It was pretty disgusting.

"What the hell is that?" I asked.

"How many times I tell you not to say 'hell'."

"A lot. I don't know why you're so hung up on it."

Daddy took a step back and shook his leg, trying to break the slimy string.

"It's . . . unlady—aw hell, I stepped in some more."

He tiptoed over to the living room to wipe his shoes off on the carpet, and I took a look around the place. The kitchen was a proper mess. Dishes piled up in the sink. Counter covered in all kinds of muck: red sauce, dried spaghetti, open cans of half-eaten beefaroni. Fruit flies crawled all over a rotting bunch of bananas hanging under an equally rotten (and fly-covered) handful of tomatoes.

And the smell. I hadn't smelled anything like it, and I grew up raising goats and pigs. It reminded me of the time a hunting dog got into our pig pen and gutted one of our sows and all her piglets.

Something thumped in the back room, and Daddy and I shared a look.

"'Manda," he said, and then the front door slammed shut.

I went over and tried to pull it open, but it wouldn't budge. I yanked and yanked, and it gave a little before slamming shut again.

"Seb Mack you open this door right now!"

He didn't reply.

"Seb Mack, I swear to God I'm gonna shoot this thing to bits if you don't let go!"

I had no intention of doing so, but he was just a kid, so it didn't hurt to try and scare him. I was about to threaten him again when his face popped up in the window next to the door.

"Seb Mack! You open this door!"

He stared back at me. Then another face showed up, and another, and another. Faces popped up in all of the windows, in the one over the sink, the two in the living room. Macks. All of them. It looked like the entire clan had showed up. Seb's uncles and aunts, brothers, sisters, cousins. And if that wasn't creepy enough, they all started banging on the side of the trailer. The trailer wasn't exactly professionally anchored to any real foundation, so you can imagine the effect that had. Glasses fell and broke on the tile. The velvet posters of dogs playing poker, and Elvis, and skeletons at a feast, too. I backed away to the middle of the living room and stood back to back with Daddy.

"Let's go," he said.

"Where we going?"

"Maybe there's a way out the back."

"You gonna punch a hole in the wall?"

"Might already be one there."

The hallway to the back was so narrow that we had to walk single file, Daddy first, then me. This was where the bedrooms were. Daddy pulled the sliding door of the first one aside, but it was empty. Judging by the crayon drawings and the decapitated dolls, it was where little Amaryl and Brindle slept. Or performed voodoo ceremonies. I didn't need to see the cut-out magazine covers of football players scattered all over the floor to know the next one was Seb Mack's. Both of them had windows, and both them windows was filled with Macks.

That left the master. Unlike the others, it had a door with hinges, but it was shut and locked tight.

Daddy said, "Give me some space."

I did, and he leaned back and leveled a powerful kick at the door. If he'd kicked the handle, he might have gotten the result he was aiming for, but this was a hollow core door, about as solid as a balloon, and his foot crashed right through and got caught on the other side.

"Aw hell," he said, yanking it out.

I leaned over to look through the hole me made.

The room was predictably depressing. It had just enough space to fit a queen-sized bed and a little chest of drawers at the end. I was about to say I didn't see anything when Mama Mack's face shot up on the other side. She was red-eyed and green-skinned, and something was bulging in her cheeks.

"Jesus!"

Before I could pull away, she coughed and a green cloud shot right into my face. I fell back, retching and hacking as the green cloud slicked down my throat and into my lungs. I could hear Daddy screaming my name, and the door to Mama Mack's room explode. Then it sounded like the windows all over the trailer burst in at the same time, and my head was filled with a roar and a fury.

I'd like to say I passed out. That would've been nice. But I was awake through the whole thing. I saw Daddy shoot Mama Mack. I saw Mama Mack jerk like she'd been pinched with a pea shooter, not clobbered with a .30 .06. I saw the hallway flood with people. Daddy got off a few more rounds before they took him down. Then Mama Mack burst out of her room and jumped on him, leaned over his face, and heaved out a thick cloud of that green stuff.

Everything went kind of herky-jerky after that. They tied our feet together with rope, did the same to our hands, laying them on our chests, making sure to cinch Daddy's up extra-tight. Then they carried us out into the woods. Must have walked for at least a mile, up and down hills, deeper and deeper into the darkest part of Spotsylvania I never wanted to see.

They lugged us all the way to a clearing in the middle of the woods where another hive was waiting, laid us out next to two other unconscious people, and stood in a semi-circle. Seb Mack tramped up behind, looking ridiculous with Daddy's rifle strapped over his shoulder and my gun jammed into his belt.

The green haze started to wear off, and I was finally able to think clearly. Problem was, thinking put me in a panic, and panicking didn't do nothing to help. Then I smelled it. The rot. Worse than in Mama Mack's trailer. Worse than that time our pigs got killed. I sat up and looked around. Bodies. At least a dozen. All of them with their feet and wrists tied tight with rope. All of them in various stages of decomposition. All of them with a hole the size of a bowling ball in their chests.

If I thought I was panicking before, I didn't know what the word meant.

"Who the fuck are you?"

It was the guy on the other side of Daddy. He'd come around, too. He was wearing city clothes, jeans and a button up, and his face was pale and his lips were blue, but he was alive. At the sound of his voice, Daddy's eyes popped open.

"Daddy!" I said. He didn't move. "Daddy, wake up!"

All of the Macks but Seb started to sing, and it was a horrible noise, deep and guttural, filled with weird dissonance. My chorus teacher played us a song once that sounded like it. I can't remember the composer, but it was some old German guy. It was terrible music, and the noise coming out of the throats of the things around us sounded exactly like it. The city boy didn't like it too much either.

"What the fuck is this?" he yelled. "What fuck is wrong with you fucking rednecks?"

The hive in the clearing cracked open, and those stupid tentacles slithered out again, four of them. One slid through the leaves toward a woman on my right and wound its way up her leg. She stirred and moaned, and when the tentacle tightened around her thigh, she sat up, screaming. One of the Macks stomped through the leaves, grabbed her by the shoulders, and slammed her back to the ground.

"Let me go!" the woman yelled, but the Mack clamped on tighter.

Then the tentacle wound into the air, button-hooked over her chest, and slammed down into it. She was dead before the last breath left her body. The tentacle started to undulate and pulse, and her corpse seemed to deflate.

"Holy shit!" my city friend screamed.

He rolled onto his side and pushed himself off the ground. Them bound up feet didn't allow for much more than desperate hopping, but he did his level best. Seb Mack pulled my gun out of his belt, closed one eye shut, tracking him as he ran past his singing brothers. He aimed and fired, but the city boy ducked right before Seb pulled the trigger, and Seb's bullet hit one of the other Macks right in the chest. I think it was his brother, Mack. Mack went down in a heap, dead.

I swear, if I hadn't turned my head when he fired, I would've missed something important. But I did turn my head, and when Mack Mack went down, the tentacle squirming through the forest floor toward me stopped moving. Just up and went dormant.

I heard another shot and turned back just in time to see the city boy jumping full-steam at Seb Mack. Seb Mack fired again, and City Boy, who had to have outweighed him by at least a hundred pounds, didn't just fall on Seb Mack, he engulfed the kid.

We wasn't out of the woods yet. The other Macks kept singing, and the other tentacles kept coming on. "'Manda," Daddy gasped. His eyes were still wide and dilated, but he was wiggling his fingers. "Crack it."

"What?"

He wiggled his fingers again.

"Crack it."

And then I understood. I rolled over, got to my knees, and grabbed his jacked-up thumb.

"I'm gonna count to three, okay?"

"Okay."

"Here we go. One—"

And I popped it out of joint.

The scream that erupted from his mouth was louder and uglier than anything any of them Macks could ever produce. He sat straight up, pulling his hand out of the rope, and popped his thumb back into joint. As if it knew what had happened, his tentacle skipped the winding around the legs part and went right to the button-hooking and the plunging.

At the same time, the Mack it belonged to stomped through the leaves toward us. I took it upon myself to get to my feet and take it on. I don't know what I was going to do. My foot was screaming in that boot, and the Mack outweighed me more than Ruth Grace Hogg, but unlike that mismatch, I had the advantage. Ruth Grace had at least a little intelligence. That Mack looked like it had the mind of a vegetable.

My plan was simple. I hopped right up to it like I was going to take it down with a big hug but dropped at the last second and took it out at the knees. Chop block. The Mack went down face first. Its head hit the ground at a weird angle, and it jerked once and fell still. The tentacle hovering over Daddy went limp and landed next to him.

Daddy didn't waste any time. He popped up off the ground and jumped on the last Mack. Wrapped his rope around its neck and choked it out. Then he limped over to me, winded.

"Give me your hands."

He untied them.

"You okay?" he asked, working on my feet.

"No."

"Me nei—"

A shot rang out and he went down to one knee. Seb Mack had managed to scramble out from under the bulk of that city boy.

Daddy winced. A flower of blood blossomed on his shoulder. "Just a stinger."

Another shot rang out and Daddy stifled a yelp.

"Left leg."

He got my rope untied, and I jumped up and sprinted for Seb Mack. Maybe sprinted isn't the right word. I galloped and weaved, my boot making me lean to the left a little bit. Worked out in my favor, though. Seb was an okay shot if you stayed completely still and had your back to him. But I was a moving target. He managed to fire off two rounds before I hit him right in the chest and brought him down. Ripping my .357 out of his hands was easy.

"Fire at me with my own gun!" I yelled, and pistol-whipped him. His head snapped back and he gnashed his teeth at me. I bashed him in the nose. I stove in his temple. I knocked out his teeth.

Seb Mack's eyes stayed wide open the whole time, the cords in his neck standing out. He slapped at my face, but I kept hitting him until his skull cracked open and I saw something pink and green and white spill out. I didn't stop then, not even after his arms went limp. I kept hitting him, over and over, mashing his face into pulp. I would've kept going if Daddy hadn't caught my arm.

"'Manda, it's enough. You did enough."

Daddy was right about them trees. They'd fallen into the road at some point during the day, and if our truck had been there, well, we wouldn't have had a truck no more. Neither of us spoke very much on the way back, and even though my boot was near to falling off and my leg ached something terrible, I didn't feel like complaining. We were about halfway home when I saw the blood from his shoulder had nearly soaked through his shirt.

"You're bleeding too much," I said.

He covered the wound with his left hand, kept driving with the right.

"I'm fine."

"Take your hand off it and let me see."

"'Manda—"

"What've you always told me? 'Just because you're tough don't mean you're stupid'."

He shot me a quick, meaningful glance and took his hand away. There was a hole in his shirt where the bullet hit. I ripped it open a little wider and he sucked in his breath.

"It didn't come out. You're gonna need a doctor."

"I can do it myself."

"You can get a bullet out of your arm by yourself?"

"Maybe."

He turned east onto Post Oak instead of west. We rode in silence a little while longer. Every now and then I looked out the back window, sure I'd see a pod of Macks on our tail.

"This ain't over, is it?" I asked.

"Nope."

"What're we going to do?"

He didn't say anything. He drove into Partlow, past Cross Creek, staying quiet all the way to Blue's Custom Guns. Then he parked and got out.

"Hand me my Army bag, will you 'Manda."

He didn't have to explain anything after that.

A PLACE FOR EVERYTHING

One day when I was eleven, Daddy came busting into the house covering his eye with one hand and holding a pitchfork in the other.

"'Manda! How many times have I told you to put your tools away when you're done with them?"

"Daddy, I—"

"Don't 'Daddy, I' me. Damn near poked my eye out. You realize how dangerous it is to leave this thing lying around?"

It wasn't no use arguing. He was right and I couldn't lie. We were the only two people who lived on the farm, and I was the one mucking out the stalls in the barn. I didn't remember leaving it out, though. Must've leaned it up against something when I was done and later on it fell over.

"Sorry, Daddy."

"Yeah, well, you'll be real sorry if I ever impale myself."

I thought that was a bit melodramatic, even if I didn't know what 'melodramatic' meant at the time. Daddy always was a little theatrical. Got it from his crazy Appalachian mama.

Wasn't nothing else I could do or say, so I just repeated myself.

"Sorry, Daddy."

That's what I kept saying over and over again as I took that bullet out of his arm.

"Sorry, Daddy!"

"Stop saying sorry and get the damn thing out!"

"Okay! Sorry!"

"Dammit, 'Manda!"

I bit my tongue, literally, and focused.

First bullet was easy. Went clean through his leg and was poking out the other side. All I had to do was cut the skin and yank on it with a pair of needle-nose pliers, which was about as fancy as we got out here on the farm. (Did I mention I have no formal medical training?)

But the second one was buried in his shoulder. Not too deep. I could see it wedged into his meat as I spotlighted his arm with the flashlight I was holding between my teeth. Daddy took another slug from a bottle of Dewers, the closest thing to anesthesia we had. He'd already killed half a fifth and was busy working on the rest. I hoped maybe if I took long enough he'd pass out and stop yelling at me. Would've made my job a hell of a lot easier.

"Would you stop squirming?"

"Pardon me, 'Manda, if I'm bothering you. But if you haven't noticed, I got a bullet in my arm."

That was it. I'd had enough. I pushed the pliers in, got myself a firm grip on the shell, and started yanking. Daddy reacted predictable. He screamed.

"Aaaaaaaaaaahhhhhhhhhh!"

I joined in as I pulled the bullet out and held it up in the air.

"Haaaaaaa! I did it!"

Daddy slammed his chest with his fist and made several uncharitable references I am not inclined to repeat. I guess that didn't do much to stop the pain because he slugged down a whole bunch more whiskey. Then he started mumbling. Then he passed out.

I know what you're thinking. You're thinking, "Why didn't they go to the hospital?"

We studied on it, but Daddy had a thing against going to hospitals. Said people died in hospitals all the time, which I guess was technically true.

I know what else you're thinking. "Why didn't they call the authorities?"

We did. Daddy did, anyway. Told me all about it. After he sobered up, he called the sheriff and told him that the Mack family'd gone even more feral than before, leaving out the part about the alien hive and the tentacles and all that on account that it'd probably diminish his credibility. As it turns out, the sheriff didn't need him to leave out nothing.

"They try to sacrifice you to that tentacle thing?" he asked.

"You know about that?"

"Yeah. You're not the first."

"How long they been at it? Don't you think that's something you might want to tell people?"

"Calm down, Bill. It popped up on our radar about three hours ago."

"Oh. Then I guess you don't know about Gomer Gomez?"

"They get him, too?"

"Maybe? I'm not sure of the timeline."

"Huh. Thanks for the intel."

"Is that it? Aren't you—"

"It's happening everywhere, Bill. You hunker down there on the farm. Unlock your gun safe. Got enough ammo?"

"Already on it."

"Alright then. Good luck."

And he hung up.

In the week that followed, I watched the news for any word of what happened. Were there hives forming in other parts of the state? The country? The world? Nothing popped up. Just the usual stories of kids dying in apartment fires and people getting shot. Then one day the stations shut down. All three of them. The power went out a day later. We were truly out on our own.

We were in the living room when it happened. We sat there, quietly contemplating the meaning of it. Then Daddy said, "Time to visit Maurice."

Let me explain.

Living with a man like my daddy could be infuriating. Half the time I didn't know why he did the things he did. The other half I understood but didn't think they were particularly good ideas. He seemed to be guided by an inner navigator that didn't truly understand the compass of the world—south was east, north was west and all that. Yet every offbeat project, crazy contraption, or pointless hobby always turned out to have a greater use that nobody, not even Daddy and his crack-brained navigator, could have predicted.

Like Maurice.

Out on the farm, everything gets used and everything gets recycled. That ain't so unusual. But Daddy took his salvaging to the extreme.

He was so crazy about it that he often took junk from other people that he didn't need "just in case." He said he drew the line at dumpster diving, but I had a feeling that he'd crossed it more than once. That's why we had two barns. One he built natural. That's to say he bought wood, nails, screws, and roofing intended for the construction of a barn. We housed all our animals and tools and hay in that one. The second barn he took on as a challenge. I imagine the conversation that went on in his head went something like this:

"Hey."

"Yeah?"

"I bet you can't make a barn out of all that crap you got piled up over there."

"I bet I can."

And that's why we got ourselves a barn made out of particle board, scrap metal, old doors, bald tires, half-chipped cinder blocks and just about anything else you could imagine. I think I even saw some of my old stuffed animals shoved into holes or filling up gaps. My favorite thing was what he did with about fifty antique chests of drawers, chifforobes, and other bedroom furniture. Took them all apart and jointed back together to make the prettiest sliding door I ever did see.

He called that barn "Maurice" for some reason. Used it to store all the new junk he was always bringing home. It was filled up with just about everything useful that'd ever been thrown away. Electronics, batteries, rebar, solar panels, barrels, bricks, insulated wire, shoes, weights, furniture, screws, nails, tires, inner-tubes, sheets of metal, spools of cable. Organized the crap out of it, too. Wasn't a thing lying around for no reason.

So when the tv stopped broadcasting and the power went out and he said, "Time to visit Maurice," I knew something interesting was afoot.

"What're you going to build now?"

Daddy was already up, limping toward the back door.

"We. What are we going to build now."

"I thought you said you wanted me to finish pitching hay."

"This is more important."

"Fine. What are 'we' building."

"Electric fence."

"Simple as that?"

"Simple as that."

And that's how we almost got ourselves killed.

It took us about three weeks to get it all done. Daddy had enough insulated wire to run two lines around three square acres. I was watching him hook the battery up to the solar panel in the west field when a man came bursting out of the woods, screaming "Hey! Hey! Help us!"

Daddy picked up the rifle he'd leaned against an apple tree, aimed, and fired. A chunk of earth exploded in front of our new friend, who skidded to a halt.

"That's far enough," Daddy said. "Keep them hands up. You got him, sugar-bo—'Manda?"

See, I already had my gun up, too. I closed one eye to get a better bead on my target. "Yeah."

I don't know about you, but people who have two guns pointed at them tend to lose control of their bladders. Not this guy. He kept his hands up, but he looked angry about it.

"You've got to help us."

"We don't have to do nothing."

"There's a woman out in the woods."

"I expect so."

"Her name is Lynn. She's pregnant. She needs help."

"Uh-huh."

The man put his hands down.

"You don't believe me."

"I believe you better put your hands back up."

"I'm telling the truth. Do I look like one of those things?"

Daddy grunted.

I knew what he was thinking. Seb Mack didn't look like one of those things. Neither did the rest of his family. (Except Mama Mack, I guess.) Daddy kept his finger off the trigger the whole time they were talking, but when the man didn't put his hands back up, he saw fit to do so. The man saw it, too. I saw him see it. But did he put his hands up then? Not a chance. He shook his head, looking back and forth between the two of us.

"You're not going to help us."

"Nothing personal."

"Is there any other place nearby?"

"Nope."

We stood there like that for a full minute, two guns trained on one unarmed man. My shoulder was getting tired so I let it drop.

"You can leave anytime, mister," I said.

"My name's Leo."

"Okay."

"And I'm not leaving. You can either come out here and help us or shoot me because we're as good as dead otherwise."

"Daddy."

"'Manda. Don't."

"What if he's telling the truth?"

If the look Daddy gave me could have spoke, it would have said, "Ain't she precious." Instead, he said, "What if he's not?"

I squinted against the sun, looking at Leo and trying to come up with a gentle way to say what I was going to say next. When I couldn't, I said, "We'll shoot him."

I don't know if I was going to shoot anybody or not. I would have if I needed to, but as it turns out, I didn't. And there was more than just a pregnant lady out there. There was another lady (Charlene) and the pregnant lady's boyfriend, Dez.

Daddy just about had a minor stroke when he saw them all. And Lynn was more than just pregnant. She was pregnant pregnant. Full to the brim. I'm not saying Daddy's a mathematical genius because he ain't, but he didn't need to be to figure out that taking four-soon-to-be-five extra people on our farm was going to stretch our resources way past thin. But he wasn't no murderer neither, and all it took was one shared look between us for the decision to be made.

"Alright then," he said.

There was more than enough room for everyone at the house. I might have been an only child, but Daddy had four siblings, three older sisters and a younger brother, and each of them had their own room. Now they sat dusty and dormant, and Daddy told me to take all the sheets and pillows outside and beat them clean, a task I did not relish at all.

"I'll help," Leo said, giving Dez a look. "You should lay down."

That's the first time I noticed how sick Dez was. He looked pale, almost green, with dark circles under his eyes and a light sheen of sweat on his skin.

"It's okay, Charlene and I—"

Charlene was already shaking her head.

"I'm not going out there, not right now. This will be the first time I've slept indoors in a week."

"Charlene—"

"Charlene nothing. I'm tired and I've got a headache."

And then she went into her room and shut the door. A second later, we heard the lock click. Leo looked apologetically at me and Daddy.

"It's been difficult."

"You don't have to explain," Daddy said.

I found plenty of old wash line in Maurice, and me and Leo strung it up between the old poles in the backyard. They hadn't been used since the fifties, I imagine, when Granddaddy finally wired the house for electricity. They were rusty and listing but sturdy. Leo found us a few dead branches and we commenced to swatting the sheets and pillows so hard that soon our hair and eyebrows were frosted with dust. Leo got to coughing so hard that he almost threw up, so we took a break and sat down on the back stoop.

"That didn't seem to bother you at all," he said.

"Country life's full of dust. I'm used to it."

"Maybe we should spray them down instead?"

"Still won't get rid of the dust. And you won't have no sheets or pillows."

"As long as I have a bed, I'll be happy."

"I bet."

We sat there for a while, enjoying the quiet. It was chillier than usual for October, and the air cooled the sweat on my skin. I looked over at Leo and saw that he'd turned his face up to the sun. His eyes were closed and he was actually smiling a little. I thought maybe he hadn't been able to relax like that in a while.

"Is it as bad as I think it is?" I asked. He nodded. "How long you been out there?"

"Two weeks."

"That's a long time to be out on your own. Lynn and Charlene and Dez. They friends of yours?"

"No."

"How long you been with them?"

"Couple of days. Met Lynn and Dez running out of Culpepper. We found Charlene wandering around here yesterday."

I was about to ask him where he saw her when someone screamed upstairs. Either Charlene or Lynn. Me and Leo exchanged a look.

We made it inside in time to see Daddy limp upstairs, rifle in hand.

"Stay down there, 'Manda!"

"Fat chance!"

We gimped up to the second floor and down the hall, Daddy, me, and Leo. The screaming was coming from Lyn and Dez's room. Daddy rammed it with his shoulder over and over until the lock busted and we all piled in.

Lynn was curled up in the corner, screaming and crying, ducking her face under her arm. She was still dressed but had taken off her shoes, and she was holding the bedside lamp in her hands. The shade was wrecked and spattered with blood. Dez was on the ground on the other side of the room, his head stove in. That didn't bother me as much as the green stuff oozing out of his skull. That and the fuzzy branch of fungus that split it in two. Daddy moved toward him.

"Daddy, don't," I said.

"It's okay."

Keeping his rifle trained on the dead man, he went over and nudged his leg. Dez didn't move. Daddy nudged him again. Nothing.

"Well, looks like—"

And that's when Dez pushed himself off the ground with a grunt.

"Look out!" I yelled.

Daddy fired off a wild shot, and Dez got to his knees, drool and blood spilling out of his open mouth. He lunged forward and Daddy fired three times, hitting him in the chest and head.

Daddy wanted to kick them all out right then and there.

"Daddy, you can't."

"I can't nothing, 'Manda. They're infected."

"You don't know that. It could have just been him."

"If they stay, we'll all be dead by morning."

"If you kick them off the farm, you'll be responsible for what happens to them after."

"Don't say that, 'Manda."

"It's true."

Daddy studied the weight of his decision.

"Fine. They can stay. But they're not staying in the house. We're locking them up in the barn."

"Daddy—"

"We're locking them up in the barn, 'Manda. That's final."

So that's what we did. Marched them out of the house at gunpoint and locked them up in the barn.

I slept so bad that night that I shouldn't have even tried. Every time I'd get close, I'd see Dez's face blow up or the green fungus coming out of the crack in his skull. I finally gave up around six thirty, throwing off the covers with a sigh. The sky was still dark.

Down in the kitchen, it was too dark out to see anything and too dark to go rummaging through the drawers for candles and matches. Daddy said we needed to save them anyway. We did have a battery-powered lantern, though. Used it for camping and hunting. Daddy left it out on the counter, so I turned it on and shined it around. There was a basket of apples sitting on the counter fresh from the picking the day before, so I took one off the top. After a bite and a think, I put three in my pockets, two in the front and one in the back, and set out for the barn.

The frosty grass crunched under my boots. I stopped at the barn door, wondering if I was doing the right thing. Daddy would kill me if he knew I was out there, but I couldn't let them starve, and Lynn being pregnant? I turned around, half-hoping I'd see Daddy coming out the door so I could stop, but he didn't. The house was a black form against the lightening sky. With a sigh, I checked the .357's magazine. Seven bullets. I tucked it in my belt and entered the padlock combo. The door slid aside with a screech.

The barn was dark and foreboding, and fear welled up inside my chest. What if they had turned? What if they were crouching in the dark, waiting for me? I could hear Daddy's voice in my head.

Well, 'Manda, if they are, you think leaving the door open's the best idea?

As usual, he was right, so I slid it shut and shined the lantern around, my hand resting on my gun.

"You guys awake?"

Nothing but the sound of the animals, stirring in the dark, a lone cricket singing in the corner. I brought the lantern up to Lucky, my favorite dray, and he nickered at me. I stroked his muzzle.

"Hey, Lucky. You're alive, at least."

"You can't keep us in here forever."

It was Leo. His voice had come from behind me. I held the lantern up as I headed in his direction and saw him up in one of the lofts. He was sitting on the edge, swinging his legs.

"You take the ladder up there with you?"

"Not taking any chances."

"Smart."

He laughed and shook his head.

"I guess."

"You hungry? I've got apples."

"Amanda. You know this isn't right."

"I know."

"Then let us go."

"I can't." I took the apple out of my back pocket and held it up to him. "You want one or not."

"Sure."

I tossed it up and he caught it and took a bite.

"Thanks."

"You know where the other two are?"

He shook his head.

"I've been up here all night."

I found Charlene sleeping in an empty stall. Nudged her awake with my foot. She rose up on her elbow.

"What?"

"I brought some food."

I tossed her the apple. She bobbled it, and it fell in the hay around her.

"You seen Lynn?"

"No. Are you going to let us out?"

"Help me find her."

Her face hardened. In the lamplight, she looked gaunt and hollow-eyed. She coughed.

"Why?"

"I want to give her an apple. She's got to be starving."

"Such a magnanimous gesture." When I didn't say anything, she added, "Magnanimous means—"

"I know what it means. You gonna help me or not?"

"Fine."

We searched every corner, every stall, but it wasn't until the sun started to rise and some real light filtered into the barn that we finally found her. She'd covered herself up with horse blankets and straw, her foot sticking out at one end, her head out of the other.

The fungus had gotten her, too. Erupted out of her skull. Blood leaked out of the corners of her eyes, running down her cheeks in little streams. I heard a little gasp behind me. Charlene must have been crying. I edged closer to Lynn's body, holding the lantern up. It flickered on and off, on and off, then went out right when I got it up to her face. I smacked it, and the lights turned on, and Lynn's fixed eyes shifted and focused on me.

"Aw hell!" I cried, jumping back.

She convulsed, shaking off the straw and blankets, and sat straight up, her arms reaching for me. I stumbled back over something and fell on my ass and the lantern went out again. The light of pre-dawn sifted through the slats in the barn walls, painting everything in a stark, gray gauze. I could hear her, it, the thing that used to be Lynn, shuffling out of the hay, the hiss of its breath.

I scrambled to my feet and drew my gun. I don't know what my plan was. I guess if something loomed up in front of me, I'd kill it. What I should have been doing was backing my way to the barn door, sliding it open, and getting the hell out of there, but adrenaline does crazy things to the brain.

My breath came in quick gasps. I swirled around at every sound, keeping my finger off the trigger, needing to save every last bullet. I was still holding up the lantern for some reason. Maybe somewhere in the back of my mind I thought that it would come back on. Something crunched in the hay to my left, and I swung around and fired. Something else crunched in the hay to my right, and I swung around and fired. After that, nothing. But I knew it was out there, the Lynn monster, and it was coming for me. Then I backed into something soft, a body, I think, and two arms clamped down around my shoulders.

I broke free and spun around with a scream, brandishing the lantern. It flickered to life and there was Charlene. A stalk of fungus had cracked through her skull just like Dez and Lynn, and the whites of her eyes were green. She opened her mouth and a nest of tentacles poured out. I must have pulled the trigger three times before I knew what I was doing, missing with each shot.

Down to my last two.

I tried to remember what Daddy taught me about shooting.

"You've got to do it calm, 'Manda. Take a deep breath. Aim, exhale, fire."

So I did it. I squinted one eye closed. Exhaled. Pulled the trigger. It hit her in the shoulder, and she stumbled back a few steps. One shot left. I aimed for her head. Took a deep breath. Let it go. Fired again.

Her head whipped back and she went down in a heap.

I didn't have time to celebrate or relax, though, because as soon as she hit the ground, the thing that used to be Lynn was on me. Took me down from the side. The lantern bounced away when I hit the ground. The thing was on top of me, its hands reaching for my throat, its mouth open. I brained it with the butt of the gun, cracked it's cracked skull even more, but that didn't stop it. Its mouth grew closer and closer, and no matter how hard I tried, I couldn't push it off.

As I was panicking, not doing nothing to help myself other than whine and wheedle, the door squealed open and morning light flooded the barn. I turned my head to avoid the thing's snapping teeth and that's when I saw it plain as day in the new morning sun.

The pitchfork.

I'd left it out again.

It was laying on the ground, its sharp tines sticking up out of the straw right in front of Lucky's stall. The Lynn-thing was heavy and round and awkward, and I wasn't no bull myself, but I was farm-strong. I pushed it up and off of me with a grunt, holding it out at arm's length, and rolled to my right, using the momentum to throw it as far as I could, which wasn't very far, but far enough. It landed half on the pitchfork handle, which didn't help, but the back of its head thunked into two of the tines, spattering blood and pus and green stuff. It shook once and went still.

I lay on my back, exhausted.

That was not at all how I'd hoped my morning was going to go.

After a while, I realized that the barn door was still open. Wind blew the leaves in. I got up and looked at the loft, knowing what I'd see. The ladder was back up again. Leo was nowhere to be found.

Daddy was awake when I limped into the kitchen from the back door. I should have noticed how pale and gaunt he looked, how his hair was matted to his forehead, but I don't think anybody would blame me for not. I was exhausted, covered in slime and blood and gook. Hay was sticking out of my hair, my jeans were ripped, and my boot was about to fall off again. He went from surprised to angry to concerned all in the space of about ten seconds. I sat down at the kitchen table and stretched my leg out in front of me and took a deep breath.

"You okay?" he asked.

"Yeah."

"Hungry?"

"Yeah."

I heard him banging around with the wood stove, and I thought I should help out, but all I could do was stare at the table. After a while, he put a steaming mug of tea in front of me. Blueberry. My favorite. He sat down on the other side and sipped from his own mug.

"You're going to be okay, 'Manda."

"I know."

"You need to sleep?"

"Maybe. Yeah, actually. I do."

"Okay. Go ahead. Maybe later you can help me finish that fence."

"Yeah. I kind of think we have to."

GOTTA HAVE HOPE

My Nana was never one to complain about the many difficulties that the world sent her way. When hardship reared its ugly face and menaced her with its nasty claws, Nana's first instinct was to grab them claws and break them in two. Sometimes it worked out in her favor. Most of the time it didn't. Always did seem a little thickheaded to me. She was just as like to use a shotgun on a weevil as she was on a bear. At least she was tough.

It used to drive me crazy, though. Why'd she always have to be so mean all the time? Daddy tried to explain it to me. Said Nana came from a long line of Scots-Irish who settled in the Appalachians in 1847. They were tough, contrary people. Fought the Union and the Confederates during the Civil War. After the war, they were so disgusted with the taxes their own state tried to levy on them that they left the mountains and settled in Spotsylvania. Never looked back.

"She ain't mean for meanness sake," he said. "It was just her way of getting things done."

"Yeah, well mean is mean. What do you think gets adopted first, a kitten or a hornet?"

Daddy laughed at that.

"What?" I asked.

"Pot meet kettle."

"You trying to say I'm mean?"

He studied on it.

"No. You ain't mean. Not as mean as her, at least."

"Well, it ain't fair. She was my Nana. Nanas are supposed to be sweet."

"C'mon, 'Manda. You know life ain't fair."

Worked out that way for Nana, too. All her meanness didn't help her one bit when she got cancer. Happened when I was thirteen. She tried to scare it by working herself to death, but that's where her natural inclinations butted heads with reality.

Disease don't care about your personality. It don't care about your life goals, your family, or what you planned on eating for lunch. Disease cares about one thing and one thing only: survival. Ironic, ain't it? The one thing it cares about is the one thing that kills it, but hey, ain't nobody said science was empathetic. It's just what happens.

I guess you could say it was my Nana in me that made me respond the way I did to Daddy getting sick. When his skin turned gray-green and he developed those dark circles under his eyes, did I break down? Did I fall apart? Nope. I strapped Daddy's rifle to my back, holstered up my gun, and packed his Army backpack full of ammo.

Daddy watched, bleary-eyed, from his spot on the couch. He'd used up all the tissues (I wouldn't let him touch our stock of toilet paper) and had moved on to a few of his chammy shirts.

"Where you think you're going?"

"Daddy, you're burning up. You need, I dunno, penicillin or something."

He coughed into the crook of his elbow and hawked up a lunger into the trashcan by the couch.

"I'm fine."

"Uh-huh. I'm going into town."

"'Manda, you can't know it'll help."

"Don't say that."

"I'm not going to let you go."

"You're not in any position to tell me what I can and can't do." I shouldered the backpack. It was heavy, but it wasn't nothing I couldn't handle. "I'll be back before it gets dark. Keep drinking that water, and . . . what do you think you're doing?"

He cast off his blanket and started making these little rocking motions like he was trying to build up enough momentum to stand.

"I'm coming with you."

"No you most certainly are not."

"You'll need someone on your six."

"Maybe so, but if that someone's you, you'll hold me up more than you'll help. Then I'll have to deal with the Macks and the hives and you, and that doesn't sound like a workable plan to me."

He opened his mouth to argue, but a series of wet coughs came out instead. He fell back on the couch.

"Don't die before I get back," I said.

"I'll try not to."

To tell the truth, I was scared. He'd been sick for three days already, and it was only getting worse. He was turning into one of those things. I knew it. But like I said, I had to try something. I wouldn't ever be able to forgive myself if I didn't.

I checked the fences before I left. Little Seb Mack had walked up onto our property as easy as he pleased four months before, but he'd be hard-pressed to do so now. First thing we did after we burned Lynn and Charlene's bodies was build a wall to surround the house and the barns. This one was tall. Eight feet tall. Took weeks to put it up and nearly emptied out Maurice in the process, but when it was done, between it and the electrified perimeter . . . well, I wouldn't say we were completely safe, but we were a far stretch safer than anybody else in the county. The weakest point in the whole thing was the gate, I suppose. Anytime you cut a hole in a structure it weakens it, but there wasn't much we could do about that.

Before all this, before the Macks and them weird hives, I could make the drive from our house to Brock Road in a half an hour, but we hadn't been able to replace the gravel in the worst part of the driveway since we built the fences, and navigating around the washed out parts added extra time.

At least the road was empty when I got there. I think I'd have lost my mind if I saw another car out there. I pulled out onto it, making sure to take it slow, and when I was positive them Macks weren't going to come running out of the woods at me or send a tree falling in my path, I tried the radio. It was all static. This didn't surprise me. Even Daddy's ham radio didn't pick up any signals anymore.

I remember the last time he tried it. He'd been listening for an hour, using up the last of the batteries, before slapping the table in disgust.

"Damn."

"Think they're all dead?" I asked.

"Probably."

"Then what's the point of listening?"

The radio waves wound up and down and through the static. Daddy turned the volume down.

"Gotta have hope," he said.

I repeated that to myself as I drove down the road: Gotta have hope.

I was about to cut the radio off when I thought I heard something. A human voice. Even though Daddy's truck was new when we bought it, he didn't like to pay for no frills. Manual transmission for him, thank you very much, and do I have to have seat belts? The radio must have been built in 1948. Turning the dial was a workout. I floated the red line over the part where I thought I heard the noise and . . . there! The signal came in a little rusty, fading in and out of the static with a whine, but I heard it.

". . . see that [garbled]? . . . yeah, lit up all [garbled] going too fast . . . whole bunch of them on Brock at [garbled] . . . everywhere . . ."

Then I lost it. I beat my fist on the dashboard.

"No!"

There was a bend up ahead, so I downshifted, keeping both hands on the wheel, and when I rounded it, there in the middle of the road was a tree. A huge tree. Must've been from the Paleolithic Age. I jammed my feet down on the breaks. The truck squealed and shuddered and I tried to turn into the skid, but the bend was too sharp and I was going to fast and I slammed right into the damn thing. I heard a crack and my head hit the steering wheel.

I came around to the white static of the radio. My vision was blurry, and something wet and slick was running down my face. I sat up, groaning at the pain in my neck and the back of my skull. It felt like . . . well, it felt exactly like slamming your head into a steering wheel is supposed to feel. Hurt like hell.

That wasn't the worst part, though. The worst part was what I saw standing in the middle of the road. Looked like a person but my head was so fuzzy that it could have been just about anything. I blacked out again, and when I came around the second time, my vision had cleared.

It was a Mack.

And it coming closer.

I slapped around on the bench seat for my gun but it wasn't there. Must have fell to the floor, but I couldn't see it there either and oh my head felt like it was split open and maybe the gun slipped between the bench and the passenger door, but I couldn't reach that far because the seat belt and . . . I peered out the windshield.

The Mack was maybe twenty feet away, and it looked terrible, all sunken eyes, concave cheeks, sticks for wrists. Its clothes hung off it in strips, and it looked like its ribs were sticking out of its skin. It reminded me of the pictures of the Holocaust victims I'd seen in history class.

It stared at me, head dipped forward, a weird, flat expression on its face. Panicked, I released the seat belt and lunged to the other side of the cab, frantically fishing for my gun. I shot up to see where the Mack was, but it had disappeared. I slapped my hand on the pushbutton lock, slid to the other side and did the same. All I could hear was my hurried breathing filling the cab. Something moved to my right. I whipped my head that way. Nothing. Now it was on my left. Again, nothing.

Then slowly, very slowly, I brought my eyes up to the rearview. It was askew, and when I adjusted it, the face of the Mack filled the whole mirror. It slammed its fist through the cab window and grabbed me by the throat.

That smell, that terrible smell of rot, filled the cabin. The skin on its hand was gray and covered in dark, purple bruises, and it sloughed off when I clawed at it. Its other fist punched through the glass, and a forearm pressed back on my forehead.

Then I heard machine gun fire. The windows and windshield shattered and showered glass down all over me. The driver's side door was wrenched open and I felt someone clamp down on my leg and pull. I reached out to grab something, anything, but I was too late. I flew out of the cab and my head smacked against the flung open door and then I was being dragged off the road and into the woods.

"Get her out of here!" someone yelled.

I was a little woozy but still managed to draw my free leg back and kick as hard as I could. I connected with something soft and heard a whoof of breath. Whoever it was hit me in the face. Twice.

"Jesus, Toni. Take it easy."

"Shut up, Ray."

I scrabbled to my feet and lunged around, swinging both fists. I couldn't see very good with all the blood and sweat and hair in my face, but I could make out two figures, two figures dressed in camouflage and toting automatics. Army? Guard? Survivalist wannabes?

"Whoa, whoa, whoa," one of them said. Must have been Ray. "We're just trying to help."

I stopped swinging and brushed the hair out of my face, wiped the blood away with the back of my hand.

"You got a funny way of showing it."

"There's a whole herd of skinnys out here. We have to move fast."

"Skinnys?"

"That's what we call them."

"I get it."

I staggered back to Daddy's truck. If wrecking into that tree hadn't killed it, the barrage of bullets did. The Mack was splayed out in back, its skull mashed to a pulp, its body riddled and leaking green. I rested my forehead on the frame and closed my eyes. Daddy, if he lived through this, was going to kill me.

"You all alone out here?"

Toni.

"Yeah. No. It's me and Daddy."

"Your daddy around here?"

"No. He's laid up sick. I'm heading into town. Gotta find some penicillin."

"Town? You mean Fredericksburg?"

"You know any other town nearby?"

"You don't want to go in there. Place is dead."

"The hospital then."

"Even worse."

"How?"

"How do you think? Those things. They're all over it."

I thought wildly for a second, but no response, no solution came to mind.

"Look," I said. "I don't care about you or what you're doing. If I don't get some medicine, he's going to die and . . . . So I've got to go."

Toni shook her head.

"There's no point. Penicillin doesn't work. Nothing works. Once you're sick—"

"Shut up! Shut your mouth!" I said, making to push past her. She grabbed my arm, but I yanked it free. Got about ten steps away when she lit up the ground around me. I stopped.

"I can't let you do that," she said.

I turned around.

"So what? You're gonna shoot me?"

Toni bristled, and I could tell she didn't like being talked to like that. She was in charge, or she thought of herself that way.

"You're coming with us."

"The hell I am!"

Then we heard it. The Mack's song. That terrible song. They were near.

Toni shrugged.

"Us or them," she said.

I stumbled along between them, Toni in front, Ray behind. They was strapped. Gotta give them credit for it. Full-on military gear: camo, boots, helmets, machine guns, utility belt, knives, body armor. Toni had a coiled, white wire trailing out of her shirt and into her ear, and whispers of a radio transmission trickled out as we walked along.

Everything on me hurt, especially my head, which had thankfully stopped bleeding. I got to limping, too, not that I'd broke my leg again (I hadn't), but because all the trauma made me weak, made my bones ache like there was an invisible line where old cracks ran. Daddy's voice echoed in my mind. "You break a bone, it don't ever heal complete," and not for the last time did I curse his experience.

We kept Brock to our right, heading north-northwest, so at least I didn't feel like I was backtracking. Toni made sure to march us through the woods to stay out of sight. Whenever we came across a house or a driveway, she steered us around it. Every now and then she put her hand to her earpiece to listen to the chatter. Other than that, we didn't speak a word.

They stopped after about an hour, and Ray handed me his canteen. I was so thirsty that I upended it, but before I even got a mouthful, Toni snatched it out of my hands.

"Sip it," she snapped. "Think that stuff comes easy?"

"Okay, okay."

She gave it back to me, begrudgingly, and set to munching on some kind of energy bar. I watched her isolate herself like she summoned an invisible bubble. Made it easier to, I don't know, dream about killing kittens. Ray handed me a chunk of his energy bar.

"I'm Ray."

He held out his hand, and I looked at it for a second before shaking it.

"I know."

"Then you've got one on me. What's your name?"

"Amanda."

"Nice to meet you, Amanda."

Toni balled up her wrapper and threw it on the ground.

"No time for chit-chat, you two. Time to boogie."

Then she got up and left. Didn't even wait for us. Ray stood up, finishing what was left of his bar.

"She's really not that bad."

"Could've fooled me."

It was gone noon when Toni stopped and knelt to the ground, waving for us to follow. I guess I didn't move fast enough because Ray grabbed me by the shoulder and yanked me down.

"What's up?" he whispered.

Toni held up a finger. She was listening to her earpiece a little too intently. Suddenly she hissed and yanked it out.

"What?" Ray asked.

"Zero's down."

"Oh shit. Maggie—"

"Would you shut up about her?" Toni hissed.

"What's Zero?" I asked.

Toni clicked the safety off her machine gun, scanning the woods around us.

"Toni," I said. "What's—"

"Shut up."

Ray filled me in.

"It's our farthest outpost. It's where we were heading."

"Both of you stop talking," Toni said. "They've breached Brock Road."

I assumed that was bad. Toni kept scanning the woods like something was going to jump out at us any minute.

"Ray, take off your pack."

Ray obeyed immediately. He threw it on the ground between them and unzipped it. It was filled with magazines. Three hundred rounders. When Toni seemed satisfied that the coast was clear, she turned to us to say something and her eyes widened.

"Shit!"

She raised her machine gun and started firing. I hit the ground and covered my ears. Had the Macks found us? I was wrapped up in a ball, machine gun fire deafening my ears. I heard a squealing sound, and then the smell hit me. The same smell from Gomez's farm, the same smell from the Mack's trailer, the same smell from the Mack that just tried to get me.

I opened my eyes.

It was a hive. Half-buried in the forest floor about twenty feet behind us. It wasn't there before. Must have boiled up while we were passing by. I watched it surface as Ray and Toni emptied their magazines. They paused to reload, and it cracked open, sending its tentacles whipping toward us.

One grabbed Ray by the feet and upended him. He yelled and dropped his machine gun as the tentacle dragged him toward the pink and green pulp pulsing inside. He took out his tactical knife and tried to hack away at it, but it tightened and he screamed again. Toni popped another magazine into her M16. She was about to fire when another tentacle shot out and knocked it away.

"Behind you!" Ray cried.

A third tentacle wrapped around Toni's leg. She whipped out her sidearm and emptied the clip into it. Then a tentacle swooped in out of nowhere and thunked into her chest. Another one smashed through her belly. A third took her head. They waved her in the air in triumph, her body deflating as they drained her dry.

Ray was still fighting. He'd managed to get one foot free and was slashing at the tentacles swarming for him.

"Help!" he yelled.

He slashed at one, cutting off the tip. Green stuff sprayed his chest, burning through his camo. He screamed. Another swept his legs out from under him.

I looked at the ammo bag. I looked at Toni's machine gun. I looked at Ray. I thought about Daddy lying on the couch, waiting for me, and I remembered what he said about Nana.

"I can't," I said.

I snatched up the gun and the ammo bag, and I ran.

It took longer than I thought to walk into town. Much longer. First I had to backtrack to the truck and find my gun. It was probably a pretty stupid idea, but the .357 was Daddy's and he let me use it and there was no way I was going to leave it there. It was jammed down between the bench seat and the door, just like I thought.

Had myself a moment when I couldn't find it, fishing around with a machine gun strapped to my back, totally vulnerable to whatever Mack or skinny or whatever you wanted to call them happened upon me. Gave my belly an icy feeling, and I kept looking over my shoulder, which made it take longer to find the dang thing. But then my fingers traced the grip, and, still looking over my shoulder, I snagged it up and then I had it in my hands. Felt a little little compared to the weight of the machine gun, but a bullet don't care where it came from.

It was as nice a day as anybody could ask for. No clouds but no sun, neither. Couldn't have been but a pinch under fifty degrees. Only thing that shivered my nerves was the sound the leaves made as I walked. And the sticks and branches, too. Between the crunching and the cracking, I probably announced myself to anybody within a half-mile radius.

I avoided the main roads as much as possible, cut across Gordon rather than take Route 3, and used the bike path that connected to Cowan to cut to Route 1. Toni's words kept popping back into my head.

"It won't work. Once they're sick . . ."

I wanted to ignore them, but I couldn't. I had to try. I had to.

The CVS by the college was a bust. So was the one down by the hospital. Found plenty of painkillers, aspirin and ibuprofen and the like, but nothing with "cillin" in it.

By four o'clock in the afternoon, the sun was starting to go down, and I didn't have a thing. Hadn't seen no Macks nowhere, hadn't needed to fire a shot, but I didn't have anything to show for all my effort. Rt. 1 was as empty as my stomach, so I ducked into the

Weis and looted me some food. Nothing nourishing. A bag of potato chips. A chocolate bar. Gave me a burst of energy, brought up my mood.

There was a tattoo parlor next to the Subway. On a hunch, I broke the window and rummaged around in every drawer I could see. Didn't find nothing but rubbing alcohol and sterilized needles and some skunk weed in a crinkled baggie. And that was it.

All I could think about was my poor daddy, sweating and suffering on our couch. He was going to die because I couldn't get my shit together. I didn't know what to do. I couldn't think of any other place to go. I couldn't go house to house, rummaging around in medicine cabinets. Who knew how long that would take or what I'd run into. I went out on to the sidewalk and sat down on the curb.

I didn't want to make the long walk home. I didn't want to go home at all. I knew what would be waiting for me when I got there.

MAKE THE HIVE GREAT AGAIN

Daddy didn't like to use dogs for hunting. Said it took the sport out of it. It wasn't like we didn't like pets. Daddy had Sparkles. I had Number 22 on occasion. I understood why people fawned all over theirs. I liked playing with my friends' dogs, man's best friend and all that. But more than half of running a farm included taking care of animals, and when the day was done and we'd taken off our boots and hung up our overalls, minding a pack of hounds or a litter of cats was a sure-fire way to drive yourself insane.

At least until the day I met Maggie May. This is the story of when I went back in time and was saved by a dog.

Best thing about living in the country during the apocalypse was not having to rely on the county. Need clean water? Dig a well. Want to pee indoors? Fix you up a septic system. Want to cook with gas? You're out of luck. We did have us a wood burning stove at least.

It wasn't all butterflies and puppies. When the power went out, we lost about a month's worth of fresh meat, and I couldn't watch TV anymore. I didn't miss it all that much, but every now and then I got the urge to catch an episode of *Star Trek* or watch the news. One time, I went right up to the set, pushed the on the button, and stared at the blank screen for a full minute wondering why nothing was happening before I realized what I'd done. Old habits was hard to break, I guess.

One morning about a month after Daddy got sick, I woke up early to make breakfast. I stocked the fireplace with oak logs and mesquite chips and brought the flames up, let it get the cooking surface nice and hot. When the water I flicked at the pan sizzled, I poured some hemp oil on and got to cooking breakfast. Daddy liked his eggs sunny side up. I liked the opposite.

I opened the stove door when I was done, let it warm the cold night away, and ate my eggs in silence. When I was done, I put my fork down and wiped my mouth with the back of my hand and sat there looking at the empty seat on the other side of the table.

Daddy's knife was sitting in its sheath where his plate should have been. I picked it up and took it out, running my finger along its edge.

He'd kept it primed and ready to go. I tried to imagine what he would have wanted to do that day.

"'Manda, we should check on the fence. Make sure it's still up and working."

"You think it's broken?"

"I dunno. That's the point. You take the west field. I'll take the east."

"Don't you think we should stick together? All things considered."

"Yeah, well, we need to get her done fast and get her done faster. This ain't the only chore we got to do today."

"Aw, Daddy."

"'Aw Daddy' nothing. You go ahead and get your gun and get dressed and get out there."

Back then I would have grumbled my way through the morning. Now I'd give anything to have that conversation again.

An hour later, I was out in the west field, limping along the fence, checking for breaks in the line, checking the posts, checking the terminals. I came prepared. My gun was holstered on my belt on one side, Daddy's knife in its sheath on the other. It had been a wet summer and an even wetter fall, and the ground was soft and dangerous, filled with dips and holes. I nearly wrenched my ankle in one of them, and the third time I slipped on a slick of grass, I started to worry about my executive decision making abilities. I needn't have worried. The wet weather made my leg ache and my ankle throb, but other than that, nothing else was amiss.

When we put that fence up, Daddy was only thinking about the Macks coming to get us. The threat was real, and the fence was a great way to cut it down. It didn't matter how many tentacles they spewed out of their mouths, nothing fried a body better than a jolt of juice. But now I came to understand that the Macks weren't our only problem. What if a hive decided to make an appearance? We thought they were dropping in from the sky, but it turns out they were also coming up from the ground. There wasn't enough voltage in the fence to give something that big more than a little pinch.

I was about as far out from the house as I could get when I thought I heard something. I stopped and cocked my head to make sure I wasn't imagining it. There it was again.

A dog! A barking dog!

To understand how exciting that was to me, you need to understand that, other than migrating birds, I hadn't heard or seen a wild animal since the hives hit. I looked to the left and right, and a moment later, I saw it, a large, sleek collie, running along the edge of the forest, barking and raising hell, back and forth, back and forth along one spot. On its third pass, a tentacle whipped out and brought it down with a yelp and whine. Happened so fast, I actually jumped back.

No sir, I thought. *Not today.*

I turned the power off at the terminal and squeezed between the lines. It wasn't any easier going in the grass beyond our fence, but I did my best. I already had my gun out even though I didn't exactly know what I was going to do with it yet. Shoot the tentacles, I suppose, but what if there were more than the one? What if this was a trap? What if there were more Macks out there, waiting in the woods. The dog yelped again and I tried to put on more speed, but my bones were throbbing and each step made it ache deep in the marrow.

By the time I got there, the poor thing was all wrapped up in a green, slimy tentacle that had popped out of the ground. It coiled around the old boy like a boa constrictor, leaving only his head and legs free. He still had some fight in him, though. As the head of the tentacle slithered out from underneath, it made the mistake of getting too close to his mouth. He growled and showed his teeth, and when it grazed his muzzle, he snapped his jaws and sank his teeth in as deep as they would go. The tentacle head tried to whip away, but the dog's jaws were rigid.

I couldn't let it go on any longer, so I clicked the safety off my gun, aimed at the base of the tentacle, and fired three times. I hit it twice and the tentacle loosened from the dog's body and whipped its head out of her jaws. The dog got to his feet but didn't run off.

"Go on, boy!" I yelled. "Get! Get outta here!"

He must have only spoke Russian because he didn't move a muscle. In fact, he looked downright angry, and even though his ears was pressed to his head and his tail curled between his legs, his teeth were still bared and his eyes dilated so wide they looked all black. The tentacle whipped at him and he snapped at it. I fired my last two bullets at the base. It must have been enough for the fool thing because it started to retract, slowly at first but gaining speed until the last of it sucked into the hole with a wet slurp.

I looked over at the dog. He was in a state, fur all dirty and tangled and so skinny that I could see his ribs. He stopped the Dirty Harry routine once the tentacle disappeared and took to wagging his tail and letting his tongue loll. I holstered my gun.

"You're welcome."

He didn't reply.

I turned my attention to the tentacle hole. Hadn't seen one come out of the ground like that without a full hive close behind. I was out of bullets, but I still had my knife on my belt. Daddy's knife. I took it out of the sheath, crept up to the hole, and leaned over, seeing if I could catch a peek inside. I don't know what I was thinking. The knife wasn't going to do no good. I guess I was just curious. I put my face right over it.

"You stay on in there, you nasty old hive."

The dog barked.

"That's right. Me and Dirty Harry here—"

A cloud of green gas spewed out and hit me square in the face. I fell back, gagging, and then everything went black.

I woke up in a room that was my room and wasn't my room. I don't know how else to explain it. There were my posters, my records, my record player, my books, but everything seemed a bit off. It was too clean, too bright. When I sat up, I saw that someone had opened the curtains so that the sun poured in through the window. I pulled the covers back and saw that I was wearing a pink chiffon nightgown that weighed about a ton. Thing was buttoned up to my neck, and I was surprised I hadn't sweat off ten pounds in the middle of the night.

I got up to look out the window and gasped. I wasn't on the farm no more. I was in the city. A woman pushed a stroller on the sidewalk in front of the house, and a man carrying a wire basket filled with milk bottles tipped his hat to her and smiled as he passed. A boy with a sling filled with newspapers rode his bike down the middle of the street, swerving to avoid a barking collie. An old car, baby blue and about the size of a whale, turned the corner and honked and waved at a man in a business suit leaving the house across the street.

"Amanda May!"

I turned around, mystified. It was a woman's voice. Kind of reminded me of—

"Amanda May? Hurry down here before your breakfast gets cold."

Momma?

I walked over to the door and opened it, and when I stepped out a little girl nearly ran me over.

"Watch it, sleepyhead!" she yelled.

She sprinted down the hall singing "Amanda's late for schoo-ol! Amanda's late for schoo-ol!"

"Ruth-Grace Jett, you stop teasing your sister and come eat your breakfast."

I walked slowly down the hall and paused at the top of the stairs. A woman was standing at the bottom. She was fully dressed, hair done, make-up on, wearing a dot-print dress covered in a frilly, peach apron.

"Amanda, why are you still in your nightgown? You're thirty minutes late. You're going to miss the bus!"

Then she bustled away.

It really was my Momma. She'd been dead for almost ten years.

"I just don't know what's gotten into her," I heard her say.

Then a man replied and I nearly jumped down the stairs. I turned the corner and went into the kitchen and stopped short.

Daddy was sitting at the table.

He was wearing a blue, short-sleeved button-up shirt and thick-rimmed spectacles. His flat-top was stiff with Crew Cut, and he was more clean-shaven than I'd ever seen him. He took a bite of white toast and a dollop of grape jelly plopped on the napkin he'd tucked into his collar.

"Amanda May! Rise and shine! How's my little peanut? Get enough sleep?"

"Daddy?"

Daddy laughed and dabbed his lips with the napkin.

"The one and only!"

"You're not . . . not . . ."

"Not what, sweetie? Not bad looking, right!"

He laughed and Momma chided him with an "Oh, Bill."

I nearly ran across the kitchen and gave him the tightest hug I could muster. I wasn't going to let him go. Not ever.

"Whoa!" Daddy laughed. "Okay. Okay. Careful, 'Manda. You're going to choke me out."

I loosened my hold on him.

"You're here."

"Of course I'm here. Not for long, though."

"Don't go."

He peeled me off and held me at arm's length.

"What's got into you?" he asked, not unkindly. "You okay?"

"Yeah. I'm just . . . I'm just real happy to see you."

"Ain't you just the sweetest pod. Er, peach."

"Daddy, why are you dressed like that?"

He looked down at his clothes.

"You don't like my outfit?"

"No, it's fine, but . . . don't you think they'll get dirty on the farm?"

"Farm?"

"Yeah, you know. With the goats, and the cows, and the chicken, and the plants, and the you-know-what."

"No, I don't know what. You feeling okay? Momma, I think she's sick."

"Let me see, dear," Momma said, and came over and put her hand on my forehead. It was cold and smooth. "She feels fine to me."

Daddy stood up and took his napkin out of his collar.

"Speaking of late. Mr. Sokolov is going to be mighty peeved if I am."

"Bill, mind your language."

"Yes, dear."

He gave her a peck on the cheek.

"Off to the bank to make our millions!" he said and kissed me on the top of the head on his way out of the kitchen.

"Amanda May, sit down and eat your breakfast," Momma said, steering me to the table. "And where is your sister? Ruth-Grace! Ruth-Grace you come eat right this instant!"

I missed the bus, so Momma had to give me a ride. Ruth-Grace was not pleased about that turn of events.

"No fair!" she whined. "I want to get a ride to school, too!"

"You stop, Ruth-Grace, and get your little self out to the bus stop."

"But Momma!"

"Do as you're told, not as you will, young lady."

Ruth-Grace crossed her arms and stomped to the front door.

"You can stomp all you want, little miss," Momma called after her.

She looked at me and put her hands on my cheeks.

"Are you okay, Amanda May?"

"Yes, Momma. Just sleepy I guess."

"Well, you run upstairs and get dressed. I put your clothes out for you last night."

"Okay."

"Likety-split. I've got to vacuum."

Momma babbled on and on the whole way over, and all I could do was stare at her. Halfway through the drive, she caught me looking and stumbled to a stop.

"Why, Amanda May, what's gotten into you?"

I blushed and smiled and looked down, trying to stifle my tears.

"Nothing Momma. I just had a bad dream last night is all."

She put her hand on the back of my head and patted my hair.

"It was just a nightmare, sweetie."

"I know."

She pulled up to the curb in front of James Monroe High School. I heard the late bell ring.

"Here's a note," Momma said, handing it to me as I got out. "Don't forget your lunch."

The secretary, a short, fat lady with a poodle cut, scolded me for being late.

"You better get to Mr. Gomez's class."

"Mr. Gomez?"

"Yes. Your History teacher."

"Teacher? Mr. Gomez?"

"I believe that's what I said, isn't it? Scoot! I understand you have a quiz in there today."

I counted the numbers on the classroom doors as I walked down the halls. I needed to find room 127. I was all the way down at 101. I'll tell you what, though: the posters on the walls freaked me out. All of them featured white boys and girls with red cheeks and crew cuts or bouffants playing sports or goose-stepping. Slogans were splashed across each one. *Confederation. Conformity. Country. Facts In,*

Facts Out. Do As You're Told, Not As You Will. One featured a girl wearing black leather pants and a black leather jacket walking her dog being assaulted by a group of cherubic boys in green uniforms. The dog was attacking one of them. One of the boys had his knee in the girl's back. The slogan read *Subversion is Sedition.*

A door slammed open in front of me, and Vlad Sokolov was dragged out by three young men wearing the same uniforms I saw on the poster. He was screaming, "This is bullshit! Bullshit!"

I held my books to my chest and pressed myself against the lockers as they dragged him down the hall to the office. Vlad saw me and his eyes went wide.

"Amanda! Get out of here! Run! Get—"

One of the boys punched him in the stomach.

"Shut up, freak!"

They dragged him down the hall, head hanging. He shot one more terrified look over his shoulder at me before they turned the corner.

"Skipping class, Miss Amanda?"

I turned around, and there stood Gomez Gomez. He was all dressed up in the same green uniform as them other boys.

"Gomez Gomez. Is that you?"

He smiled, his teeth wide, white, and straight.

"That's right. Gomez Gomez. Where are you supposed to be?"

"Um, your dad's class."

"Dad?"

"Yeah. Gomer Gomez. Your dad."

Gomez's face remained blank. He looked like he was about to kill me, like he was angry that I knew something he didn't. His eyes swept left to right over and over, and then a grin broke out on his face.

"Yes. Of course. Gomer Gomez. My father. You have a quiz in his class. This way." He clamped a hand on my arm. "Come along."

I didn't mind the Gomez family. I'd knew the twins since Kindergarten. Our families had been going to the same community events, football games and parades and the like, for years.

But it wasn't like we was best friends. To be honest, Gomez kind of bothered me. He was a little slow, and when he felt like someone was smarter than him, he always tried to intimidate them, just like he was trying to do to me right then. I wasn't going to let a twerp like him treat me like that, so I yanked my arm out of his grasp and punched him.

"Get your hands off me, Gomez."

That silly smile disappeared from his face.

"Subversion is sedition."

"Subversion? Where'd you learn a big word like that?" His face turned red. "I'll tell you what. I'll go to class. But if you lay so much as a finger on me again, I'll break it."

He seemed to struggle with several emotions all at once. Anger. Embarrassment. Fear. Disgust. Then something weird happened.

He shimmered.

A ripple of green light rolled up from under his shirt and over his face, and for just a moment I wasn't in school no more, I was lying on my back, staring up at a gray, winter sky. I was cold. Freezing actually. I gasped for breath, like something was squeezing my chest. And there was a dog barking and growling nearby. Just like that, the scene disappeared and I was back in that hallway, looking at Gomez Gomez.

"Do you need to see the nurse?" he asked.

"N-no. I'm . . . uh."

He reached out to grab my arm again, thought better of it, and stopped.

"You should come with me."

I gathered my wits. Forced myself to recover.

"I'm fine. I'm just going to go to class, Gomez, okay?"

I turned and walked away, a little unsteady. Room 127 was only a short walk down the hall.

Daddy always said he wasn't the greatest student. He was smart but hated school. He liked playing football but didn't like the coaches. He earned C's and B's. Back in the 1950's, this meant they tracked him in the vocational program, which was exactly to his taste. He knew what he wanted to do with his life: the farm.

He and Momma didn't have too many pictures from high school. I've flipped through their photo albums a hundred times, and all they had were black and whites of old family members, most of them dead. The ones I liked the most were from before me. Christmas 1965 (that's when they got hitched). Honeymoon at Niagara Falls. There were a few snapshots of Spotsylvania High School, too. Back then it was located where City Hall is now.

There was one picture in particular that I liked to look at. It was a shot of a classroom taken from the doorway. All the kids were sitting at their desks, attentive, looking at their teacher, an old man dressed up in a shirt, tie, and jacket pointing at a blackboard filled with writing.

That's the scene I walked into that morning, and it freaked me out. It freaked me out even more when all the kids looked at me at the same time. Mr. Gomez, who was dressed in a tie and a short-sleeved shirt, turned around to greet me.

"Ah. This must be our new student. Class. Say hello to our new student."

And all together, all at once, all of them said, "Hello new student."

I gave them a half-smile.

"H-hi."

"We've just had a student withdraw," Mr. Gomez said. "An unfortunate subversive. You may take his seat right there." He pointed at the only open desk in the room. It was in the back under one of the huge windows. When I didn't move, Mr. Gomez snapped his fingers at me. "Miss? Do as you're told, not as you will."

I felt the eyes of all the other students on me as I walked to the back of the room and sat down. Mr. Gomez returned to his podium.

"Now where was I? Oh yes. The Attack on Pearl Harbor. Can anybody tell me the date of the attack?"

Every last one of them kids raised their hands, eagerly, but wordlessly, waving them, desperate to be picked. Mr. Gomez pointed at the girl sitting in the desk in front of me.

"Sally?"

"December 7, 1941."

"That is correct. And can anybody tell me the United States' response? Billy?"

"President Franklin Delano Roosevelt signed Executive Order 9066 and restricted the rights of all Japanese Americans."

"Also correct. And does anybody know how the Japanese American community responded?"

The other students' faces fell. I looked around. Every last one of them was reading their notes which they'd copied word for word from the blackboard, but evidently he hadn't told them what to think yet. So I raised my hand. Mr. Gomez smiled and pointed to me.

"Yes, miss . . . ?"

"Amanda. The—"

"Yes, Miss Amanda. You may speak now."

"Thank you. The Japanese didn't respond. They were arrested. The government rounded them up and put them into internment camps."

Mr. Gomez paused and tilted his head a little. His eye twitched. There was a girl sitting next to me, prim and proper, her hands folded on the desk in front of her, a big smile plastered on her face. She whispered "Stop," out of the corner of her mouth. Mr. Gomez chuckled.

"That's certainly one way of looking at it," he said, rolling his eyes.

All of the children laughed. All except me.

"No. That's the only way to look at it."

The room fell silent, and the girl next to me whispered "stop" again.

"The Japanese," Mr. Gomez said, drawing out the end of the word. "Did what they were told, isn't that right, class?"

"Yes, Mr. Gomez!"

Oh no he did not. Not today. I didn't even think to raise my hand.

"Only because they were forced to," I said.

"Forced to? Is that what you call their voluntary relocation? These people were patriots. They did as they were told, not as they would. It is the central tenet of our belief system." He stomped over to a poster on the wall that said the same thing and pounded on it with his fist. "Do! As! You're! Told!"

The other kids repeated what he said.

"Do! As! You're! Told!"

I sat there, my mouth half open, staring at him in disbelief. A lock of Mr. Gomez's hair had fallen into his eyes. He swiped it away. Straightened his tie. Gave the class a little smile.

"Now, Miss Amanda. Wouldn't you say you agree?"

"Agree with what?"

"With what the Japanese Americans did, of course. They obeyed. It's easier to obey. It's easier to go along. That, Miss Amanda, is what this country is all about! That, Miss Amanda, is the very definition of patriotism! Wouldn't! You! Agree!"

He had, while delivering this crazy speech, made his way down the row, and by the time he finished it, his face was inches from mine. I waited a tick, just to draw the moment out a little longer. He smelled like the fields, like earth, like he'd been rolling around in the woods. His eyes were bright and green.

I thought about doing something crazy to break the tension, something like putting my finger in his ear or tweaking his nose and saying "boop!", but in the end, I just answered his question honestly.

"No."

I'd never been sent to the principal's office in my entire life. Wait, no, that's a lie. I got in a food fight during lunch in elementary school and wasn't allowed to eat in the cafeteria for a week, but even then I didn't have to talk to none of the administrators. I just got chewed out by my teacher. And Daddy. Not simultaneously, which isn't as much of a blessing as you'd think.

Every day at eleven, I marched into a little room off the main office where they stored books and extra school supplies and ate my lunch there. Seeing as I was naturally quiet and more comfortable by myself, I didn't view it as much of a punishment.

On the last day, I went up to the Vice Principal, Mrs. Marsh, and asked if I could eat there every day. She looked at me like I had a bug crawling out of my mouth.

"Amanda May, why on earth would you want to do that?"

I shrugged my shoulders. I was too young to explain myself, how I preferred low-lighting and quiet spaces to the chaos of the lunchroom. How I was much more comfortable reading a book alone than being forced to interact with a bunch of people I had very little in common with and who I didn't think were very smart anyway. Mrs. Marsh pursed her lips and shook her head.

"You can eat lunch with the rest of the children," she said. I heard her mutter ". . . just don't get it" under her breath as I walked away.

I felt just as weird and awkward sitting in the waiting room of the Main Office of that crazy school waiting to get punished for telling the truth. The office was eerily silent, and a couple of times I caught the secretary and a few of the guidance counselors staring at me. Why weren't the phones ringing? Why weren't they typing anything?

The nameplate on the principal's door read Mr. Greene, and he'd left it open a crack. I caught a glimpse of Vlad sitting in the chair across from Mr. Greene's desk. He had his arms folded across his chest, and he was glowering something fierce. I could hear Mr. Greene scolding him.

". . . don't understand what it is we're doing here, Mr. Sokolov, do you? You don't understand the importance of our mission?"

Vlad continued to glower. Mr. Greene sighed.

"Okay. I can see this is getting nowhere."

And without further word or warning, he opened his mouth wide, wider than I ever seen possible. His jaw unhinged and a nest of tentacles fell out. I jumped out of my seat, and Vlad started to scream but it was covered up by the fire alarm blaring in my ear. I spun around to run and there was Gomez standing next to me.

"Fire alarm, Miss Amanda." He stepped aside and gestured to the door.

Kids were walking in the hallway outside, gabbling excitedly as they left the building. I shot a look back at the principal's office, but the door was shut.

I ditched Gomez as soon as we got outside, losing myself in the crowd. I found a place behind a boy who looked like a linebacker and tried to make myself small.

"You're too loud."

It was the girl from class, the one who kept whispering to me.

"What?"

"Kids who make it past the first day keep to themselves. They don't talk back. They don't disagree. They just stay quiet. Kids that don't, well . . ."

She nodded at the front door of the school. Mr. Greene had just come out, followed closely by Vlad. We were standing under the trees only about ten or fifteen yards away, so I could see them plainly. Vlad had changed. Gone was the rebellious slouch, the half-angry sneer, replaced by the same disturbing blankness all the other kids wore on their faces. The girl put a folded piece of paper into my open palm.

"Come out to the bonfire at Hurkamp tonight, okay?"

She slipped away, and I unfolded the paper to read what she'd written.

"Escaping," it read. "Burn this."

I was hoping to sneak into the house unnoticed, but the door creaked when I opened it and Momma called out to me from the kitchen.

"Amanda? Can you come here?"

I pursed my lips. Damn.

"I'm just going up to my room. I have a lot of homework."

"Amanda May Jett. You come into this kitchen this very moment."

Man. The gears in this town were well greased, weren't they?

I slumped into the kitchen where she was leaning against the counter. She was still fully made-up despite working on the house all day long. Her hair was done, her clothes were pressed, and she was doing the dishes in a pair of shiny black flats. She looked like the most beautiful woman in the world. My amazement must have shown because the stern expression she wore on her face melted.

"Why are you staring like that?"

"Nothing, Momma. It's just . . ."

"It's just what?"

"You're so pretty."

She blushed, then quickly regained her composure.

"If you're trying to butter me up, young lady, it will only half-work in your favor. Do you know who I got a call from this afternoon?"

"Yes, ma'am."

"What do you have to say for yourself?"

"Momma, he was lying about the war."

"Who? Mr. Greene?"

"No. Mr. Gomez. He was saying that the Japanese—"

"I don't need to hear what he said. You disobeyed your teacher. That is not okay."

"But Momma—"

"Don't you 'but Momma' me. Wait until your father gets home. You go up to your room and do your homework until he dies. I mean does."

Her face rippled, just like Gomez's had out in the hallway in school. Her skin flipped back and forth between green and skin-colored, and I swear I heard a dog barking over and over. I got dizzy and cold again. I flipped back into the house, and Momma was there but it wasn't her. She was an IT: one of those things that Mrs. Mack had turned into. Her head was leaning back and a nest of tentacles reached out of her mouth, squiggling in the air.

". . . manda are you okay?"

The world swam back into focus. Momma was there. Her face was her face.

"Yeah. Just feeling a little sick."

She put her hand on my forehead.

"Oh honey, you're ice cold. You need to get up to bed this instant."

I didn't have the strength to fight back. I really did feel cold. And weak. And all of the sudden my ears were ringing and my clothes were soaking and I heard a splattering sound and Momma gasped. We both looked down. I'd wet myself.

After a long, hot bath, I seemed to warm up a little more, but I was still shivering. I went to bed and slept for a while, and when I woke up it was almost dark outside. My parents were talking downstairs. I drifted back to sleep, waking again when my door opened and a crack of light fell on my eyes.

"'Manda? You up?"

It was Daddy.

"Mm-hmm."

"You hungry? Momma gave me some spaghetti to bring to you."

"Not just yet, Daddy."

"Okay. I'll leave it on your dresser."

I kept my eyes closed, listening to him come into the room. I heard him set the tray down. I fell back asleep for a time, and when I woke up again, it was completely dark out.

The bonfire.

The memory shot into my head like a bullet.

I sat up, feeling a lot better, and clicked on my bedside table light. My stomach grumbled and I swung my legs over the side, suddenly starving. I couldn't remember the last time I ate. The dinner Daddy brought me sat on the dresser: a bowl of spaghetti and a glass of milk. I went over and chugged the milk, finishing it off in five big gulps, and when I looked at the bowl, I let out a scream and then covered my mouth to cut it off.

It was filled with worms.

Big, thick worms squelching around in blood.

I knocked the bowl off the dresser, and it landed on my rug and splattered all over the place. It took more than a few breaths to get a hold of myself, but when I was ready, I opened the door a crack to see if anybody was in the hallway. It was clear, so I tiptoed out. Momma and Daddy were still downstairs, arguing in hushed tones. Daddy sounded like he was trying to be reasonable, and then Momma's voice cut through his with a short, "Shut up, Bill!"

I stopped where I was. I'd never heard Daddy go quiet when someone talked to him like that. I crept to the top of the stairs to listen. I couldn't hear much at first, nothing distinct, but then their voices rose again, Momma's being the loudest.

"It's not working. We have to move on to the next stage."

"Just give it a little more time."

"More time? How stupid are you? It should already be over. She's fighting it. I don't know how, but she's fighting it."

"I think you're missing the point."

"And what point would that be?"

"That we're wasting all our resources on this one girl. Why?"

"Because of what she did. You remember what she did?"

"Yes."

"She can lead them. You know that. You've seen it before. And now she's resisting. If she's resisting, she's immune. You remember the last time that happened."

"I remember."

"If we don't get her now—"

"I know."

"Look. Did you see this? I found it in her pocket."

There was a silence, then Daddy said, "Who gave this to her?"

"I don't know. There's another one out there, Bill. If they find each other—"

"What are you doing?"

I gasped and spun around. It was Ruth-Grace, standing in the hall behind me.

"Going to the bathroom."

"No, you're not. You're eavesdropping."

"No, I—"

Ruth-Grace pushed past me, heading for the stairs, but she only made it one step down before I grabbed her by the pony-tail and yanked her back. She opened her mouth to scream, and I clapped my hand over it.

"Shut it, Ruth-Grace," I hissed.

She bit my hand. I shoved the meat of my palm harder into her mouth.

"You shut up or I'm—"

She flailed in my arms, harder and harder. She was so damn strong. I turned around, trying to force her back into her room but she was jerking so hard I had to stop. I clamped my other arm down on her throat, cutting off her wind, but that just made her thrash around more, like a cat on a leash.

"Ruth-Grace, is that you?" Momma called.

Ruth-Grace's face turned pink, then red, and in one last-ditch attempt to break free, she threw herself left and right, left and right. It was too much. I was still a little weak and I couldn't hold on. She flew out of my arms, hit her temple on the railing, and collapsed face first in a heap.

Momma poked her head around the stairs and I turned back around, trying to block Ruth-Grace's body. Her foot was sticking out between my legs, so I nudged it behind me.

"Amanda, you're up! Feeling better?"

"Yeah." She gave me a look. "Yes, ma'am."

"What was that noise? Were you and Ruth-Grace fighting again?"

"No, of course not."

"Is she up there?"

"She's . . . in the bathroom. I'm just waiting for her."

"Is she taking too long? Ruth-Grace! You get out of the bathroom right now."

"It's fine, Momma. I don't have to—"

"Nonsense, Amanda. Ruth-Grace? Do you hear me?"

"She hears you. She's just—"

Momma circled around the railing post and took a step up.

"Momma, she's fine!"

"Amanda, stop yelling at me."

"I'm not yelling!"

"Amanda May Jett, what has gotten into you?"

She was halfway up the stairs now. I took two steps down so that we met face to face in the middle.

"Momma! I'm just so upset about getting in trouble, and—"

She focused on something behind me.

"What's that?"

Our eyes met.

All of her concern, her carefully constructed concern, vanished. Her face rippled, her skin fading to a sickly green, and I felt nauseous again. Her jaw unhinged, and a tangled nest of tentacles fell out like a load of snakes. I knew what was going to happen next, and if I didn't do something, I'd be a goner for sure. So I reached out and grabbed one, squeezing as hard as I could.

Her eyes widened and the nest buzzed and twisted and squirmed. One bit me. Another one wrapped around my wrist. I grabbed another and squeezed, squeezed until I felt both burst. Green slime squirted through my fingers, burning my skin, and I grabbed two more.

Momma clawed at my eyes but I kept her at arm's length. Two tentacles reached for my face, their ends opening to reveal two rows of fangs. A little trail of green gas filtered out, polluting the air with a moldy, mildewy smell. I yanked her head to the right and slammed her temple into the wall. She weakened a little, so I threw my weight the other way and slammed her head into the other side. That did it. The snakes went limp and she slumped to the ground.

"What's going on up there?" Daddy called.

"Nothing!"

The skin on my arms was burning, so I wiped them off on the carpet. Daddy's chair scraped against the linoleum. No time to do anything but run.

I pounded down the stairs and straight out the front door. When I was half a block away, I turned and looked over my shoulder. Daddy was standing in the doorway.

It was cold out, colder than I first thought, and gravel and rocks bit into my freezing feet as they slapped on the asphalt. All of the porch lights were out, but as I ran into town, they started to flick on one by one. Doors opened. Forms appeared in the frames.

I crossed Route 1 and aimed for downtown, slipping into the rhythm of the run. I'd trained for field hockey for last three years, and I played soccer for five years before that. Exercise wasn't nothing new to me. If any of them crazy people wanted to try and run me down, they were more than welcome.

I headed up Princess Anne, cut right onto Hawke, and left onto Charles, slowing down when I reached Amelia. I could smell the bonfire by now, saw the smoke clouding the night's sky. Hurkamp came into view, the bonfire roaring and crackling, and it looked like the entire student body had come to the park.

I was only in my nightgown, but it wasn't difficult to blend in. I wandered through the crowd, looking for the girl who slipped me the note, finally spotting her over near the fire department, talking seriously with a small group of other kids. I was about to head over to her when somebody grabbed my arm and pulled me back. It was Gomez.

He was still dressed up in that ridiculous uniform, only this time he'd added a gray-green overcoat. He was wearing an officer's hat, too: black leather brim, yellow cords from temple to temple, and a death's head insignia underneath a strange looking badge, a hive encircled by squirming tentacles. His eyes ran up and down my body and he smiled.

"A little under-dressed aren't you, Miss Amanda?"

I think I've told y'all that I'm not a big girl. But that didn't mean I was weak, and it didn't mean I'd never dealt with jerks like Gomez Gomez. I smiled back at him and drew nearer.

"You like what you see, Gomez?"

He blinked, lips trembling.

"I don't know what—"

I stood on my tiptoes and tilted my head. His breath smelled like mold.

"Would you like me to . . . touch you?"

"What?"

Finally, I thought. A chance to put all them self-defense classes Daddy make me take to use. I followed the steps just like I'd been taught. I grabbed him by the back of the neck, pulled him close, and, using him as ballast, launched my knee right into his balls. Gomez grunted and whelped, his eyes crossing as he sank to the ground. He didn't let go of my arm. Got to give him credit for that.

"Fucking . . . bitch."

"Aw, Gomez," I said. "I know you don't really mean that."

Then I brought my knee up again, hitting him right in the nose with a satisfying crunch. There were so many kids around us that I expected a few to notice, but none of them did. They closed in around him as he lay there on his back.

I went over to the benches where the girl and her friends were standing before, but they weren't there anymore. I scanned the crowd and spotted them on the other side of the park, near the sidewalk on George Street. She turned around, seeming to look for something (hopefully me), and I waved but she didn't see me.

"Hey!" I cried, and then realized I didn't know her name.

Gomez stumbled out of the crowd surrounding the bonfire.

"You bitch!" he screamed. "I'll get you!"

I ducked into a group of kids to my left. They stopped talking and looked at me. I gave them a sheepish smile.

"Hi."

None of them said a word. I peeked around the boy I was hiding behind and saw Gomez stumbling toward the firehouse. Dark forms appeared on the streets surrounding the park, moving slowly.

"She's here!" one of the girls next to me said.

"Shut up," I hissed.

One by one, they all pointed, saying "She's here! She's here!"

I backed away, heart pumping, and ducked into another knot of kids standing closer to the fire. The heat was so intense that I couldn't believe they could just stand there, but they were. My feet were freezing, and I hugged my arms around my body, shivering. I stumbled around, squeezing between couples, swerving around the knottier groups, heading for the girl, not hearing anything except the sound of my own breathing, and when I emerged on the other side, she was gone. I turned around, and every kid in the park was staring at me.

They raised their arms as one and pointed.

"She's here! She's here! She's here!"

They surged forward.

"She's here! She's here! She's here!"

My throat constricted, and then I couldn't breathe. I fell to my knees, clawing at my throat. The kids continued to advance, and I crumbled to the cold earth, my eyes staring dead into space. The first of them, a girl, reached me and wrapped herself around my legs. A boy wrapped his arms around my torso. A different girl took my head. A fourth my throat. They were going to crush me to death. The dark forms closed in above, their hands shapeless shadows, and as they squeezed tighter and tighter I thought, "What a strange way to die."

Then I thought, *No sir. No sir, not today.*

I grabbed the hands that were crushing my windpipe and squeezed, pulling the thumbs back until they cracked. The faces above me, suddenly filled with hate and rage, shimmered and scratched, like watching a filmstrip go off the reel. A dog was barking in my ear. Their hands became slick and cold and slimy.

And then I wasn't in the park anymore.

I was on my back, staring up at the slate gray sky, pulling a tentacle off my neck. The collie was next to me, biting and tearing at it, shredding it with his teeth. It all became so clear to me. The gas had knocked me out, put me in their world.

I slapped around for something to use as a weapon, a branch, a rock, anything, and my hand landed on something cold and hard and my heart leaped.

Daddy's knife.

The tentacle around my neck whipped away and shot into the air above. The end opened up, revealing two rows of sharp teeth. I held up the knife as it plunged, impaling the thing. Green stuff oozed over my hand, burning my skin, but I didn't let go. I cut the head off and rolled to the side.

"Get out of the way!" somebody yelled.

I turned and looked and there was a group of people surrounding me. Some were wearing military gear, some were in jeans and hunting jackets. All of them were armed. M16's, rifles, revolvers. I gaped.

"Move!"

I did what I was told and they opened fire. The tentacle exploded in a burst of green and purple meat. When it was clear they had killed the thing, they stopped. The echoes of the gunfire receded into the morning, and I stood there, staring at them.

"Who the hell are you?"

The one in the lead was wearing an eye patch and a face mask, one of those black ones with the print of a skull on the front. It was supposed to make him look scary, but to me, it looked silly. Like he was a little boy dressed up for Halloween. He whistled and called for the dog.

"Maggie! Maggie May! C'mere girl!"

The dog bounded over to him, tongue lolling. He kneeled down and let it lick him. Laughing, he pulled off the mask and my mouth dropped open.

"Ray?"

He smiled as he pet his dog.

"The one and only."

The first deep frost hit us the next day. We all went out into the woods that morning and found a hive pushing up through the ground. The tentacles around it had all gone limp and gray. A few Macks lay nearby, about as cold and dead as they could get. I poured kerosene on it and set the whole thing on fire. We threw the Macks on top and let them burn.

For the next week, we searched the surrounding countryside. Every hive or Mack we found was in the same condition. We burned them all.

New Years came and went. We celebrated with a raid on Momma Mack's trailer. Burned it to the ground. The next morning, I went out to the edge of the property to visit Daddy's grave. Ray and Maggie May came with me. She loved running the perimeter, and I laughed as she sprinted along the fence, barking.

I found the mound of earth and the cairn I made to mark where I buried him. I couldn't find anything in Maurice that looked remotely like a headstone, and I didn't want to make no hokey-looking wooden cross. Daddy wouldn't have liked that anyway. So I let it be. Maybe one day I'd figure out a way to mark it proper.

"This your dad?" Ray asked.

"This is my dad."

The wind blew and I turned my face into it, inhaling deeply. It smelled like snow. I was standing a little behind Ray, and I could see the swelling and scars around his eye patch. The right side of his head was smooth and shiny where there should have been hair. He caught me looking.

"Pretty amazing, isn't it?" he asked. "Me finding you."

"How did you?"

"Luck, I guess. If Maggie May wasn't such a runner, and if you hadn't freed her, we might have missed your place altogether."

Maggie May came over and licked my hand. I scratched her behind the ears.

"Best dog I ever knew."

"Wait until she wakes you up in the middle of the night barking at the wind. You won't think so highly of her then."

"Ray. I thought you'd be mad at me. Why aren't you?"

It took a while before he responded, but I let him have the time.

"It wasn't your fault."

"Wasn't my fault? You cried for help. I had a machine gun."

"We shouldn't have taken you like that. Your dad was sick."

I was already shaking my head.

"I left you there to die."

"I don't hold it against you. There aren't too many of us left, you know. We're stronger together."

A few flakes fell from the sky. One lighted on my nose and I stuck out my tongue.

"You think they'll come back in the spring?" he asked.

"Maybe."

"What'll we do then?"

I stared at Daddy's grave for a while, then squinted into the distance, trying to see where Maggie May had run off to.

"I dunno," I said. "I guess we'll fight."

THE HIVE

SEASON 2

THERE'S ALWAYS TWO

For obvious reasons, Daddy did his level best to keep his illegal drug organization "solvent and secret." His words, not mine. It seemed like an unusual business strategy to me.

"I think you need to take a marketing class, Daddy."

"Marketing's for suckers. I don't need none of that fancy book learning."

"Plenty of millionaires say otherwise."

"'Manda. You know how I feel about rich people."

We both said the next thing together:

"Ain't nothing rich folk can do that I can't do better."

"Except," I added, "getting rich."

"Yeah, well, I never thought I'd get rich off of selling pot. All I want to do is make enough to keep us in hardtack and hog."

Despite his efforts to the contrary, word eventually spread about the superior quality of his weed. I remember one time a reggae band from Richmond pulled up to our house in a van that looked like someone had stolen it from a movie about a bunch of pot smoking hippies. Rainbows streaked the side, a moon-bubble poked out the top, and if that wasn't enough, someone had etched a white pot leaf on the spare tire cover on the back. Then there was the band's name: Jah Leaf. How they ever drove anywhere without getting pulled over was a mystery to me.

Daddy didn't normally do business out of the house, and for good reason, too. But he must've felt them boys was innocent enough because he greeted them like they was long lost friends. Brought them inside and smoked them out until two in the morning, sent them packing with four ounces of Spotsylvania Special and a head full of Johnny Cash.

Our visitors wasn't always so well-meaning, though.

The next time someone came calling—this was, oh, about three years after Momma died and two years before Ruth Grace Hogg broke my leg with a field hockey stick—I was watching *Star Trek* on the tube and Daddy was banging around in the kitchen trying to fix our refrigerator. That thing was always hanging on the drop edge of yonder, but he managed to keep it chugging along with a healthy application of used compressors and electrical tape. He stood up to stretch his back and, looking out the window, said, "'Manda, get up and go to your room."

"I'm watching *Star Trek*."

He was already at his gun safe.

"Dammit, 'Manda. I ain't got time to explain!"

I started to do as I was told when he yelled, "No! Stop! Get down!"

"You just told me to go to my room."

"Don't move. Get down."

"Which is it?"

"Get down!"

I'm assuming that if you're this far into the narrative, I don't have to tell you how hard-headed I could be. I blame my Daddy and my Nana, not to mention the contrary nature of rural people in general. In my mind, Daddy was acting weird, and it had to do with whatever he saw out in the yard. Was it a bear? A cougar? A puma? Hell, plenty of them had come across our property before and Daddy'd never thrown a hissy fit. Whatever it was, I'd be damned if I didn't get to take a look. Turns out it was something worse.

I went over to the front window, and there, leaning up against the fence as casual as they came, was a pothead.

He had shoulder-length hair and a big, bushy mustache, and he was wearing construction boots, blue Wranglers, a denim button-up, and a jeans jacket. He looked like an ad for cigarettes.

"Who's that guy?" I asked.

"'Manda, get away from the window!"

"Why?"

Daddy took a Magnum out of the safe and slapped a clip into it. I thought, "oh" and went over to the couch and sat down.

"Stay there."

"I ain't going nowhere."

He slammed out the front door and yelled, "Hey!" before firing off a couple of shots. I did what came natural to most people who found themselves unexpectedly in the presence of gunplay. I threw myself to the floor and covered my head.

"That's right!" Daddy cried. "Keep running! And don't come back!"

Then he stomped back into the house, through the living room, and straight out the back. Two seconds later he fired off three more rounds. "You think I'm stupid, boy! Tell whoever sent you I got plenty more bullets for them, too!"

When he came back in, he was muttering something about "young people these days." I got off the floor and watched as he popped the magazine out and un-chambered the live round.

"You get him?"

"Oh, hey 'Manda."

"'Oh, hey 'Manda?' Daddy, what the hell?"

"Don't say 'hell' babykins."

"Daddy, you just shot two men!"

"I didn't shoot nobody. I just put a scare in them, that's all."

"Oh. You sure?"

"'Manda, I think I'd know if I shot somebody."

"Well, who were they?"

"Just some boys who thought they could get the drop on me. That's the problem with this business. There's always someone out there who thinks he can take it all away."

"But there were two of them out there."

"There's always two, 'Manda. Remember that. There's always two."

I couldn't always remember every last word Daddy ever told me, but I remembered that. There's always two. It became real important to me after he was gone and I was all alone.

January was usually the second worst month for winter weather in Virginia. We didn't get straight up white-outs (that came in February), but it could get pretty snowy. Even when we had electricity and gasoline, a few feet of snow made it awfully difficult to get anything done. Basically shut the farm down now that we didn't. I was used to it. Grew up working through it. Ray and all his people had a harder time adjusting.

To make matters worse, it wasn't like Daddy and I planned for the end of the world. Sure we had a farm, but we grew just enough for the two of us and a little more to sell at the farmer's market as a cover for his pot business. If I was by myself, and if I didn't eat all that much, and if I could stretch what I canned into casseroles and chilis, and if I slaughtered a hog, and if the chickens doubled their egg output, I might have had enough to last a couple of people through March.

But it wasn't just a couple of people anymore. It was me, and Ray, and about ten others, including Timmy Carter, and Timmy Carter was one of the biggest human beings I'd ever seen. He wasn't fat, neither. It was all muscle. All two hundred and forty pounds of him. Gentle as a lamb, Timmy Carter was, but he needed three times the amount of fuel as the rest of us just to get through half a day.

That year, though, January didn't show us very much in the way of frozen precipitation.

Oh, we had us a few two-inchers here and there but nothing too devastating. Lulled us into a false sense of security. Then the twelfth hit and things got interesting.

The storm started out innocent enough with the typical Nor' Easter people in our parts was used to, but that night it ramped up to an out and out cyclone, with winds so strong that I heard trees out in the woods cracking and crashing to the ground. By the next morning, we had half a foot of snow piled up, one of the walls had blown over, and a portion of the barn roof had ripped off and flown away. The storm didn't let up neither. That afternoon half a foot grew to two feet, then three. When evening came around, it was at least three and a half.

The barn had to be fixed, wasn't no question about that, but it was too dangerous to get up on the roof. Some of the guys went in and put up a ladder and nailed some scrap plywood to the inside, and that seemed like it would work, at least until the storm stopped. The wall, though, was an entirely different problem. There was no way we could fix it, not in the middle of a snow cyclone, so we decided to post guards.

It wasn't as bad as it sounds.

Earlier that month we built a little shack for anybody to use when they were minding the wall. It was a cozy little den, complete with a double door, a window, a couch, and a chair. We even outfitted it with an old cast iron stove Daddy'd stowed away in Maurice.

I was on guard duty with Gary T the second night of the storm. It was three in the morning, and I'd just got back down from the shack's roof where I'd been sweeping off the snow for the hundredth time. I came inside to see Gary T with his ear pressed up against the window. I went over to the stove to warm up, watching him the whole time.

"Your ear stuck to the glass or something?"

"Shh."

"The only reason I ask is because—"

"Shh! I think I heard something."

I turned my back to the stove, smiling as the heat swam up my jacket. I liked to get my pants nice and hot before sitting down on one of the old chairs. Then I'd balloon a wool blanket over the stove and use it to catch the heat and get nice and toasty.

"You feeling alright, Gary T?"

"I said—"

"I know what you said, but the only thing to hear out there is the wind howling."

"There's a woman."

"A what?"

"A woman. She's out there. She was crying for help."

My bones might already have been frozen and my blood might have felt like ice cream, but that didn't mean I couldn't get any colder because I did. I knew exactly what he was talking about. Gary T had heard the Wailing Woman of Spotsylvania County.

Legends abounded about that nasty old creature. Some said it took on the form of a beautiful young girl with long red hair and wearing a shimmering, silver dress. Some said it looked like a black-toothed old hag dressed in black rags. Still more said it appeared as a headless woman, naked from the waist up and carrying a bowl filled with blood.

The myth went something like this: Once there was a young girl who got engaged to a Confederate soldier who died in the Battle of Wilderness. After she died (of a broken heart, of course) her angry soul combed the woods, looking for victims to slake her thirst for revenge. She liked to mask her appearance in storms and gales, drawing her prey out of their homes by calling for help with the most pitiable of cries. She didn't care who she beguiled: men, woman, children. Once you heard her cry, you were done for. She lured you deeper and deeper into the woods until you were hopelessly lost, then disappeared in a wave of eerie laughter, leaving you to freeze or starve to death as you searched for an escape that could never be found.

"Gary T, I think maybe you need to get away from that window," I said.

"We've got to help her."

"Gary T, I was just out on the roof, and all I heard was the wind."

"There it is again! Didn't you hear it?"

"No."

"She needs me."

And before I could stop him, he pulled away from the window and burst out the door, leaving it wide open as he ran into the storm.

You all know I wasn't very old when this happened. Hadn't even graduated high school yet, so I didn't have the experience I might have needed to judge my reaction properly. Science tells us that a teenager's brain is akin to a toddler's. They're impulsive and thoughtless, always looking for the easy way out. But even though that was probably the case with me, I'd gone through enough crazy things in the last four months to reign all that in.

I liked Gary T. He was an okay guy. He generally did what he was supposed to do, and he hadn't tried to hit on me like a few of the others, men and women included. But I barely knew him, and if I'm being honest, my first impulse was not to go screaming out into the middle of a blizzard after someone I barely knew on the off-chance that he might actually listen to reason.

Then I thought about how Daddy might react if he was there with me. A part of me wanted to say he'd tell me to access my inner Nana, close the door, and warm myself up by the stove. Then again, this was the man who, when Gomer Gomez, someone he didn't like very much and didn't know very well, got himself attacked by aliens, drove out to help without even a pause. This was the man who, when Seb Mack, the no-good son of the white trashiest woman in the history of white trash women, told him his mama was going to sacrifice his little sisters to the same aliens, drove out to a trailer in the middle of nowhere when saving a Mack (little sister or not) was the last thing anybody wanted to do. This was a man who . . . well, I guess he learned his lesson after that because he had no compunction locking Lynn and Leo and

Charlene up in the barn when they came stumbling out to our place.

Still. It didn't sit right with me. How would I explain to Ray and Timmy Carter and everybody else why I didn't do anything to help Gary T? Just thinking about looks they'd give me was enough to make me want to Rambo out into the woods.

"Where'd he go? I dunno. Said he heard a woman calling for help and sprinted out to save her. I didn't go after him because he was probably chasing a banshee, and everybody knows what happens when you . . . a banshee. You know, wails a whole bunch and lures people out into the woods to . . . okay, okay, well, just hear me out. This one's called the Wailing Women of Spotsylvania, and—"

Yeah, that wouldn't fly at all.

So I zipped up my jacket, checked my belt for my Bowie, pocketed my sidearm, and beat my arms against my chest three times.

"Okay, Amanda May," I said to myself. "Let's go save Gary T."

Turns out trying to track someone through a blizzard ain't the easiest thing to do. I don't know if you're familiar with the term "white-out conditions," but it don't concern office supplies. I first heard it in elementary school, which was the last time we had a blizzard. All I remember was a man on the TV standing in the middle of a swirling cloud of snow, his parka and mittens frosted twice over and once more for luck as it pelted and choked him, describing the storm as if nobody could look out a window and see it for themselves. He kept yelling "white-out conditions!".

"Daddy, what's that mean?" I asked.

"What, white-out conditions?"

"Yeah."

We watched the screen. A huge gust of wind nearly toppled the reporter, enveloping him in a thick blanket of snow. Daddy pointed at the TV.

"That."

That's pretty much what I ran out into. Gary T was nothing more than a gray shadow in front of me. Drifts five, six, seven feet tall had piled against the shack and the house and the wall. I called out his name, "Gary T!" but the wind swallowed my words, giving me a nice mouthful of snow for my effort.

I followed him as best I could out to our west field, the one where me and Daddy first saw Leo coming out of the woods. The wires were down and the fence post with the transformer, too. I saw Gary T, or his shadow, at least, crest a hill and drop out of sight.

Fearing the worst, I picked up my pace. I reached the downed wires and stopped, turning around to see if I could see any of the farm buildings. I couldn't.

And that's when I heard it.

Not the Wailing Women but a rumble, as if a mountain was rolling through the country, heading right for me. I couldn't tell what direction it was coming from, in front of me, behind me, on either side of me. I'd heard about thunder-snow before, but I'd never actually heard it. This was too long and drawn out to be thunder anyway. It kept coming and coming, getting louder and louder, and now, instead of worrying about saving Gary T from an ice banshee, I was worrying about whatever it was that was heading my way.

I pushed through the snow and made it to the hill, but in my panic I didn't mind my steps and suddenly I was falling, tumbling down, rolling end over end. Didn't hurt a bit, really. Probably the softest fall I ever took. When I reached the bottom, I sat up and there was Gary T, about ten yards ahead of me.

"Gary T!" I yelled. "Get back here!"

He still wasn't no more than a blob in the storm, but I saw him turn around. The rumbling sound drew nearer, taking over even the noise of the wind. Then a huge shadow rolled through the field, and Gary T was gone. I pushed forward until I reached the spot where he was. A path had been cleared in the snow at least two car lengths wide, but Gary T was nowhere to be seen. And I swear on my Nana's dead, black heart that the next thing I'm about to tell you is true.

The storm stopped.

No warning. No clues. No nothing.

One second the wind was howling and the air was filled with a solid sheet of white and the next, nothing. Took my breath away. The storm clouds were still in the sky, but nothing came out of them. I stared around me in wonder. It was simply the most confounding thing I ever saw. Then I got a feeling like someone was watching me. You know that feeling. Everybody does. A cold, iciness that started in your belly and spread into your chest, then the creepy crawlies started creeping and crawling.

If I'd been in a movie, the soundtrack would have been a full chorus of strings winding higher and higher as I turned around to see what was behind me, but this wasn't a movie, this was real, and when I made the full 180 degree rotation, there was a girl standing there, her mouth open in a soundless wail, her eyes silver and bright, her dirty hair falling in a tangled mess over her shoulders. She grabbed me by the throat and started to squeeze.

I don't remember much of what happened next. Just flashes of images. Breaking the choke hold the way I was taught. Shoving the girl away. The rumbling roar coming back towards me. The storm ramping up again. Pushing through the snow as fast as I could, heading for a grove. Branches whipping against my face.

I shot a look over my shoulder and saw a huge, round shadow raging forward. The branches cut the snow blindness some, but the storm was so thick and the wind so heavy that I still couldn't see much at all. The shadow shot closer, cracking branches and uprooting trees as it rolled through the woods. I dodged as best I could, left and right, right and left, but the snow cut my speed, and the shadow gained on me. If I didn't get out of the way, it'd roll right over me.

I came to a hill and tried to run up, but my feet kept slipping and sliding until it was pointless to continue. I slid to the bottom and pulled my gun out of my pocket, simultaneously trying to bite my mitten off my right hand. I got to kneeling position and aimed into the storm. I was just about to fire when I felt a jolt of sickening energy, and then I was sinking, sinking down into the snow, and I realized there were two hands around my waist, pulling me in. I don't think I'd ever been as terrified in my life. For someone who faced down a gorilla like Ruth Grace Hogg, that's saying something. I screamed and accidentally fired off a wild shot, and then I was pulled into the earth . . . and dropped into a cave.

It was dark but warm, with a low, flickering fire providing an orange glow. The opening of the cave was covered in roots and thick vines, and I heard the shadow thing roll past like a freight train. Dirt shook from the ceiling and some roots waved overhead, and then it was gone, replaced by the calm hush of snow falling on the other side, and then, nothing. The storm was gone again. I was shaken but okay, more amazed at what had just happened than anything else.

A figure huddled against the wall in the shadows in the back of the cave. All I could see was bare skin and one glinting eye peeking out from a tangle of black, disheveled hair. I sat up and dusted the snow and dirt off my parka.

"Hello?"

Whoever it was shifted, and I saw a flash of a breast, a single, dirty foot. Was it the Wailing Woman? Why hadn't she killed me yet? I tried again.

"My name's Amanda. Amanda May Jett. Are you . . . . Are you okay?"

The girl started whimpering and I thought, oh Lord, here it comes. First she'd start to cry, and then before I could do anything about it, she'd cut my head clean off. I didn't know what to do. I backed up as far as I could to the cave's entrance without leaving. I didn't want to leave. That thing, whatever it was, was out there looking for me. But I didn't want to stay, neither, not if whatever or whoever was sniveling in the corner was going to take my skull for an ornament.

She started crawling for me, so I pointed my gun at her and she stopped. That settled it for me. No Wailing Woman I ever heard of cared about getting shot with no .357. This was some weirdo who apparently liked to run around naked in the woods in the middle of a blizzard.

"You want to tell me who you are?" I said. "Tell me what's going on here?"

She whimpered again and crept forward another foot so that her whole body was in the light of the fire. Then she parted her hair like a curtain, revealing the face it was hiding. Even features, big eyes, and about enough dirt on her skin to plant some flowers. But that wasn't what blew me away. What blew me away was . . . well, I wasn't too sure. You ever see someone and know that you knew them but had never met them before in your life? Is that déjà vu? Reincarnation? Spiritual serendipity?

Whatever it was, I knew her. I'd seen her before. I didn't know where or how or when, but I felt like we'd been—if not close, then, then . . . . I couldn't define it. She was fully in the light of the fire now, her tangled hair out of her face but hanging down over her body. She had a lot of hair. I lowered my gun.

"Do I know you?"

The girl tried to speak, but it was like she didn't have a tongue. She made strange noises from her throat, and her mouth worked, but no actual words came out. The fire popped and sent sparks into the air, and her eyes flitted back and forth, back and forth, as if she was trying to count each one. She sobbed when they faded, and I was halfway between feeling sorry for her and wondering when she was going to unhinge her jaw and swallow me whole.

"Hey, hey. Shhh." I kind of squat-walked forward, reaching out for her. "You're going to be okay, hear? You saved my life, and I've got a gun, see? You're going to be just fine. Can I?"

I touched her hair with my fingertips and zap! Another bolt of sickening energy hit me right in the gut. I felt like the strongest girl in the world and like I was about to vomit at the same time. I said, "oh" and went to my knees and the girl shrank away. The feeling left as soon as she did, and all of the sudden I knew who she was. I sat back on my knees, astonished.

"You . . . you're . . ."

"B-bonfire," the girl said. "E-escape."

I woke up curled up next to the smoking fire, shivering on the ground. To tell you the truth, I'd barely slept all night. Too cold. And the knowledge of what was out there and who the girl in the cave was weighed heavy on my mind. I'd given her my parka to cover herself, and she wrapped herself up in it and went to sleep on the other side of the fire. She was still there in the morning, a mass of knotty hair and two pale feet sticking out of either end of my parka. Looked like a human burrito. I pushed my way out of the vines and roots and into the daylight.

The world was cool and clear, as if nothing from the night before—the blizzard, the monster, Gary T—had ever happened. I investigated the groove the shadow had made in the snow, but it wasn't nothing more than a curvy indent. I thought I saw something sticking up out of it, something black and hard. Looked like . . . oh lord no. I went over and cleared the snow away from it and jerked back, feeling sick.

It was a boot.

Gary T's boot.

I started to dig out around it, but a few scoops in and the white snow had turned red. Blood red. It was all over my hands. I dug a little more, carefully this time, trying not to go too deep. The leg ended at the knee. After that, there was just . . . I didn't know what it was. Gary T, I guess, or what was left of him. It looked like he'd been shoved into a blender.

The girl came out soon after and we stood there looking at the mess of blood and guts and bone that used to be a human being. She must have been freezing there in her bare feet. I would have given her my boots if I could. Instead, I reached out to touch her shoulder, holding up my hands when she flinched.

"It's okay. It's okay."

She frowned at me.

"You got a name?" I asked. She kept frowning. "A name? What you're called? Uh, *wie heißt du*?"

I don't know why I asked her that in German. I'd taken two years of it in school, and for some reason I thought, well, maybe she ain't American. It didn't help. Her frown just deepened. I pointed at my chest and said, "Amanda, remember?" I pointed at her. "And you are?"

She shook her head.

"You don't know who you are, or you don't want to tell me?"

She nodded.

"Which one? You don't know who you—"

She was already nodding again.

"Okay. Alright. I get it. You understand English."

She nodded.

"Good, because the only other thing I remember from German class is *Wir züchten Kühe für unseren eigenen Gebrauch*. That means 'we're raising cows for our own use'. I don't think that'd help much in this situation."

She kept staring at me.

"Okay. Well, I gotta get back to my farm. I don't think you can stay out here. You want to come back with me?"

"F-farm?"

"I have a house and food. It's safe there. You'll be okay."

She still didn't answer. Some people are just hardheaded, you know? Daddy used to accuse me of being that way, but I'll tell you something: if I found myself naked in the middle of the woods in the middle of a blizzard and somebody gave me a parka and was nice to me and didn't shoot me when she could have and then invited me back to her house, I'd accept that invitation. But you could lead a horse to water and all that. Sometimes people don't know what's best for them. I shrugged and rolled my eyes.

"Alright then."

I was about ten steps away when I heard her come up behind me, but I waited until we were out of the woods to speak again.

"You're going to like my farm. It's got a wood stove and you can have your own room. And we got a dog. You like dogs?"

"M-m-Maggie May?"

I shot her a sharp look.

"How'd you know that?"

"Th-they're c-coming. F-f-for you."

YOU BETTER BELIEVE IT

It might shock some of you to hear this, but I wasn't always the polished and refined author you've come to know and love. In fact, I was actually a bit of a tomboy in my youth. I liked to dress in sweatpants and sweatshirts, hated combing out my hair, and rarely, if ever, changed my socks. I found it difficult to clean my room or make my bed or do any of the things Daddy told me to do, and I absolutely despised bathing. Many and ferocious were the fights he and I had about that particular topic. My argument was simple: What was the point? I was just going to get dirty again the next day.

"Because you stink, 'Manda. And I have to smell you."

"Daddy, that's mean."

"No, it ain't. It's the truth. Ain't nothing worse smelling than a twelve-year-old except a twelve-year-old who's been rolling around with goats all day."

Daddy always did have a pretty way of making sense.

All of my wayward personal hygiene came to an end the day I matriculated to intermediate school and met The Sexy Seven. That actually sounds kind of weird now that I wrote it down, but that's what they called themselves. The Sexy Seven. There was only one intermediate school in the county back then, which meant I came into contact with the kids who lived in the new housing developments on the north end for the first time, and the north end was rich. Not filthy rich but a lot richer than the rest of us. That's where The Sexy Seven hailed from.

Their name was an impressive display of alliterative cleverness for a group of girls whose average GPA was in the low twos, a number that was skewed by the single B-average student among them. And even that was a bit deceptive given the fact that the girl who earned that B-average was homeschooled and had transferred from Alabama in the middle of the prior year.

What they lacked in intelligence they made up for in pure, unadulterated meanness. It ain't nothing new, middle school mean girls, that is, but until you've been on the receiving end of an all-out Mean Girl assault, you don't know what emotional pain feels like.

Unfortunately for them, there were only six official members of The Sexy Seven, an oversight that I wish I could say was uncharacteristic. Or unnoticed. It took a barb from a more powerful enemy to point it out to them. Because of their lack of mathematical prowess, The Sexy Seven were desperate for another member. It was a matter of group pride, if such a word could be used to describe the lowliest, no-good, back-stabbing, two-faced, double-crossing, lying, cheating, gossiping, petty, spiteful, hateful, vindictive, sad, nasty, vulgar, filthy pieces of trash I ever had the displeasure of coming into contact with. It couldn't be just any girl, too. They had to find one they could bully and mold into one of their own. A project. Someone they could raise up from the muck and the cow flops of Spotsylvania County and fashion into a rare and precious jewel, like a Red Beryl or a Musgravite.

That's where I came in.

"'Manda," you might say, "why didn't they just change their name to The Sexy Six?"

That's a good question. Mainly I think it was because they'd already established themselves under their current moniker, and changing marketing strategies was bound to lose them some followers.

Anyway. You know where this is going. They propped me up and got me all a-swirl with their nonsense. Within two weeks of the beginning of my seventh grade year, I went from a bath-hating, goat-smelling tomboy to a two-shower-a-day where's-my-conditioner-and-make-up girly-girl. Daddy must've thought I'd been taken over by an alien. If he was worried, he needn't have been.

It all ended in October.

I can't remember how it all went down. Maybe I got more popular than the Queen Bee. Maybe I did or said or thought something they all found offensive. Maybe a boy took an interest. Who knows. I just remember one afternoon collapsing at the kitchen table and crying my eyes out until my make-up ran down my face like a charcoal river.

Daddy was standing next to the refrigerator, drinking his afternoon cup of joe. He watched me weep for a little while, wisely waiting for it to finally peter out before saying anything.

"Don't worry, 'Manda. They'll get theirs one day."

"You think so?"

"I know so. I don't believe in God, but I believe in karma. See, karma's the universe's way of—"

"I know what karma is. I just want it to happen to them sooner than later."

"That ain't the way it works."

"I know."

"You want something to drink?"

"Yeah. I guess I do."

I heard him banging around on the wood stove for a while, and then he put a steaming mug of blueberry tea in front of me. My favorite. I took a sip and wiped a tear from my eye.

"Why did they do that, Daddy? They were so nice and then they . . . . I never did nothing to them."

"I wish made sense, 'Manda, but it don't. They're just kids, for one, and that's a big part of it. Some of them'll never grow out of it. I think they're so miserable inside that they need to control other people. Being in control makes them feel good. At least for a little while."

"It's mean is what it is."

"I think it's kind of sad."

"I guess. But if they ever try to do anything like that to me again, I'm gonna break every one of their noses."

Daddy leaned back, a little shocked.

"I don't care, Daddy. Nobody treats me like that and gets away with it. You better believe it."

He put his hand on my back and gave it a rub.

"I believe it."

And then I broke down crying again. It was just too much. Daddy rubbed my back and let me let it out.

"You'll be okay, sweet-pea."

"Don't call me sweet-pea."

"Okay."

I'm not sure why I told Timmy Carter that story. Maybe it was because the hike from the farm to the food bank was long and hard and boring and we'd made the trip over a dozen times over the course of the past couple of days, or maybe it was because I missed my daddy and wanted to bring him back to life, even just for a moment.

Timmy Carter might have had arms like a rhinoceros, but he was one of the most gentle people I'd ever knew. He was quiet and reflective and, unlike most of the men I ever met, actually listened when I spoke to him. Neither of us said nothing for a while, just focused on slogging through the snow, picking 'em up and putting 'em down. I'd trailed off into my own thoughts when Timmy Carter spoke up for the first time since we left the farm.

"What's going on with that girl you found?"

"Girl?"

"Don't try to play like you don't know, Amanda. I saw two sets of footprints in the snow the day after you went missing."

Damn. That's the thing about Timmy Carter. He might not seem like he was all there, but that don't mean he actually isn't. It's the quiet ones you got to look out for.

"How'd you know she's a she?"

"I didn't. You just told me."

Well if that don't beat the barn.

"Timmy Carter, you sly little dog, you! How'd you learn that trick?" Timmy Carter smiled and tapped his forehead. "I'll be tarred. Ray swore up and down nobody would find out."

"Ray's in on it, too?"

"Damn!"

"It wasn't like you two were being secretive. I've seen you bringing food up there. I'm surprised you let her use your daddy's room."

"Yeah, well, Daddy don't have no use for it no more."

"He was a good man, 'Manda. You were lucky to have a good man like him to take care of you."

"I know."

Timmy Carter stopped and gently touched my shoulder.

"Not everybody had a good man for a father."

He rolled up his sleeve and showed me his forearm. It was puckered with old scars, some slug-like, some long and thin, some with legs from the stitches sticking out the side.

I didn't know what to say to that. Daddy might have been a little gruff with me sometimes, and he certainly didn't mince words when he needed to get his point across, but he never raised a hand to me or momma in anger. Or anyone else for that matter. He liked dogs and kittens and babies. I couldn't imagine a life with a man who did to me what Timmy Carter had done to him.

"Damn, Timmy Carter. Now you're making me feel bad."

"Didn't mean to. You had something nice, and that's beautiful."

That made me laugh.

"It sure is a good thing he ain't around to hear that. He'd never let me forget it."

"I bet he wouldn't."

A stray snowflake fell on Timmy Carter's nose, and he squinted up into the sky. It hadn't snowed in a couple of weeks, not since the blizzard, but even though the weather had been clear and sunny, the temperature never got higher than twenty. I looked up and saw a mass of dark black clouds rolling in from the west. The air pressure changed, grew heavier, more oppressive. You know how you can smell the snow on the wind before a big storm? Clean and sweet? Yeah. We smelled that. Living in Virginia was often like living in a biosphere that was subjected to every kind of weather all in the same day, but with the relative calmness that followed the last storm, I guess we just weren't expecting another one so soon.

"Timmy Carter, you ever see a storm roll in like that before?"

"Not a snow storm, no."

Another plug of black clouds appeared, this one north of the first one. Two different storms, balled up like bears and screaming toward us. I believe I saw lightning streak across the front of the new one. Seeing as that did not look good for either of us, we started to run. Which was a pretty hopeless enterprise because have you ever tried to outrun the weather on foot? In about two feet of snow? That's about as smart as asking a goat to build a computer, which is to say we was quickly overtaken by both storms. The snow whipped around us, stinging my face, choking me, stealing my breath. Went from bright and sunny to midnight black in about five minutes.

Then it got worse.

Remember that rumbling sound that I heard right before Gary T had his guts torn out? It ramped up behind us. I reached out and grabbed Timmy Carter by the neck and pulled his head down so I could shout in his ear.

"You hear that?"

"Yeah!"

"We gotta hide!"

"What is it?"

"Same thing that got Gary T! Come on!"

I cut to the right, thinking maybe we could escape out the side of the storm, but it seemed to turn with us. We turned east; it turned east. We turned north; it turned north. That wasn't natural, not by a long shot. If we didn't get out of it pretty soon, well, I didn't want to think about that.

Fortunately for us, and unfortunately for the storm, I was a Spotsylvania girl, born and raised. Farms and fields and rural attitude ran through my veins thicker than blood. I knew where we were like I knew the layout of my own house.

We'd been tramping through an open field heading north-west when the weird storms hit, an open field that was just to the west of Ni River Reservoir, and Ni River Reservoir was *my* reservoir. I don't mean that I owned it, but I wouldn't be a good citizen of the county if I'd never been there. Ni River Reservoir was the story of every summer of my life. I fished there, boated there, swam there, camped there, hunted there. And because of that, I knew there was a stone shelter in the woods, one every kid I'd ever knew played in. It was our natural fortress, literally, because if we ever got caught in a thunderstorm, we could hide in it. The rocks had to be at least ten feet tall and stuck into the earth like giants had thrown them from the top of a mountain. If they couldn't withstand whatever the shadows threw at us, I don't know what could.

We broke out of the woods and onto the shore of the reservoir, and the storm followed us. Then a huge, rumbling ball shot out of the gloom and skidded across the ice, sending a gusher into the air. I only saw it for a second, but it was black and green and studded with horrible looking spines. It wasn't a hive, but it wasn't not a hive either. It was a new terror, that was for sure.

I watched it spin out on the slick surface, the spines chunking into the ice as it scrambled for purchase, trying to zero back in on us, but I couldn't watch too long before icicles started crashing down all around. I slipped as I ran on the frozen sand, and one of the icicles stabbed me right in the shoulder. I cried out and fell, and Timmy Carter ran up behind me and grabbed me and launched me forward. Then a second rumbling ball shot out of the woods and landed right where we'd just been, bounced once, and crashed through the ice.

"Where are you going?" Timmy Carter yelled.

I pointed my good arm at the pile of stones sticking out of the woods where the water curved back into a little harbor.

"Stone fort!"

He helped me up and we made a run for it. It was only fifty yards away, but we were exhausted. Running through snow ain't the easiest thing to do in the world. On top of that, my arm had been pierced by an ice knife, which, now that I think about it, is the first time I'd ever said something like that out loud. We made it to the rocks and clambered up the side, but it was covered in snow, and I couldn't find where we usually went in.

"Where's the opening!" Timmy Carter yelled.

"I don't know! It's covered in—"

And then something cracked and I fell through. Timmy Carter jumped in right after me. The rumbling sound shook the rocks all around us, the sand beneath us, the very air itself. The spiny ball crashed into the fort, shaking snow and ice and centuries-old dirt onto our heads, and even though my teeth rattled so hard that I thought they'd fall out, and even though I felt the concussion so deep in my bones that they ached, the shelter held firm.

There was a moment of silence when all we could hear was the whirl of the storm above us, then a second crash came, and a third, and a fourth. Over and over, the spiny balls rammed into the rocks. It seemed to go on forever. I was screaming, and Timmy Carter had curled up in a ball next to me. Felt like we were in the middle of World War II, and I think I finally understood why soldiers lost their minds.

Then suddenly, it stopped.

I waited for another ball to hit. And waited. And waited. Then one did and I screamed, but the impact was much weaker than before. After a time, the storm diminished, and the wind grew weaker and weaker until there wasn't any, and through the hole in the rocks, I saw the sky above turn blue and sunny.

I checked the icicle in my arm but it had already cracked in half, and the shard in my arm melted, leaving the wound open but numb. I was about to crack a joke about it to Timmy Carter when another voice took my place.

"Well ain't you two the most unlucky bastards to ever live?"

A light filled the stone fort, and sitting across from us was a bearded old man holding a shotgun. Timmy Carter sat up to turn his full bulk on the guy, but that didn't seem to bother the old man very much. In fact, he aimed both barrels at his chest and smiled, revealing the brown and gap-toothed palate Daddy used to refer to as "The Spotsylvania Scowl."

"So much meat on your bones, big fella. You're going to be a popular one."

Our new friend's name was Otis. At least that's what he told us as he marched us along.

"Name's Otis if you were wondering," he said.

Timmy Carter didn't respond, but I sure did.

"Mister. I don't care two shakes what your name is. Why're you doing this? We don't mean you no harm."

Otis rewarded me with a hit between the shoulder blades with the butt of his shotgun.

"Keep it zipped, little girl. Hangnail don't like his meat spicy."

He marched us along the reservoir's edge for a mile or so, then banked north and pointed us into the woods. Even though I'd grew up in the rural hinterlands of deep Spotsylvania County, VA (the northern-most southern county in the Old Dominion), I was consistently amazed at the number of trees that grew in our area. Or anywhere, for that matter. I had friends who lived in the city, and every summer, Daddy let me spend a week or two at their houses. It was surprising how fast I got used to the streets and concrete, the short walk to any store or theater or restaurant I had a mind to patronize, the clusters of people, the access to public services like the library (where, truth be told, I tended to spend most of my time on those visits).

And Fredericksburg was not that big of a city. I could walk from one end to another in less than an hour. But when the visit was over and Daddy came to pick me up, I was always astounded on the drive back by the quickness with which the city gave way to the wide open spaces and untamed forest that comprised the rest of the world. We took trips out west a few times where I saw the real landscape of the United States, and I realized just how much of the country belonged to nature, how we were just visitors, vacation renters borrowing time on our little patch of earth.

That's exactly what we tramped through on the way to whatever fate lay in store for us. Woods, woods, and more woods.

Y'all know I'm not a whiner, but the worst part of the whole ordeal wasn't the snow or the cold or the fact that some backcountry hillbilly got the drop on us. No, the worst part was that he made us keep our hands up the whole way. I took it upon myself to let him know exactly how I felt about it.

"Otis, you mind if we put our hands down? You got all our weapons. Ain't like we—"

Without a word, Otis took two steps forward and kicked me square in the patootie, sent me flailing face first into the snow. I guess Timmy Carter didn't take kindly to it because as I was pushing myself back up, Otis was already saying, ". . . wouldn't do that if I was you."

I got to my knees and wiped the snow off my face and shook it out of my hair. Sure enough, Timmy Carter'd turned to confront Otis, who had leveled that shotgun right at his ample chest again.

"You ever seen what a shotgun can do to a man?" Otis asked. He started cackling. "I have! I have!"

I got to my feet and touched Timmy Carter's arm to let him know I was okay.

"Otis, you dumb hillbilly," I said. "All you had to do was say no."

The old coot's black eyes fell on me, and the crazy smile faded from his face.

"Don't call me that."

"What? Hillbilly? You don't like that? Hillbilly?"

Otis' face went from angry to apoplectic in the space of three seconds. Even Timmy Carter seemed concerned about it.

"Name's Otis! Otis Enoch Abernathy the third! Wait, no, the fourth!"

"That's a great name, Otis. But I still like Hillbilly better. How's Hillbilly Hank sound to you?"

He started to take a step toward me but Timmy Carter got in his way.

"It's okay, Timmy Carter," I said. "I can handle myself just fine."

He hesitated before moving aside.

Otis's eyes flitted back and forth between the two of us like a fart in a fan factory. He looked like he was trying to figure out what to do next, whether he was going to shoot us or just say something nasty. In the end, he didn't do either. He spat on the ground.

"Keep moving. Hangnail's waiting. And keep your goddamn hands up! This ain't no nature hike."

After a few minutes, Timmy Carter glanced over at me.

"That was stupid."

"Yeah. Got to him, though."

"Shut up, you two!"

We didn't talk for the rest of the hike. He steered us through the woods, taking us farther and farther north. About an hour later, he drove us up an embankment and down the other side where we was met with a solid wall of thick brush. Trees and thorny bushes and vines all intertwined to form a barrier twelve feet high, like someone or something had built it to keep the outside world out, which was exactly what someone had done because Otis set us to one side, reached into a spot in the thicket and felt around, his eyes rolling up like he was trying to solve a physics problem. Then he gave us a brown smile.

"Y'all want to see some stuff?"

He yanked down hard, and the wall of branches and thorns shuddered, and there was the squeal of metal on metal, and then the whole thing rolled inward, revealing a wondrous sight.

It was a farm.

Not that a farm should have been wondrous to me, for obvious reasons. It wasn't the farm itself that was incredible but two things about it that knocked my socks off: the sheer size of the main house and the three huge hot-houses next to it.

This wasn't no mere farm. This was a survivalist compound.

Otis motioned for us to go inside, pushing on something to close the gate behind him. A gravel driveway led up to the main house, which was lit by a warm, glowing light. Something on the roof glinted in the sun. I Solar panels. A figure on a horse came galloping around from behind the house, reaching us in less than a minute. It was a woman all cartooned up in western wear, denim this and denim that and steel-toed boots and a fifty-gallon hat. Even had herself a pair of six-shooters in holsters.

Looked kind of ridiculous to me. The get-up I could understand. Plenty of people dressed that way in Spotsy, though I'd hazard a guess that we were more inclined towards camouflage pants and sweatshirts than Crazy Horse Montana gear. But the guns were silly. Gave me a good chuckle, though. Revolvers? Seriously? She could've gotten herself ten semi-automatics that were a hundred times better. She circled around us and nodded at the old man.

"Otis."

"Annie O."

"What you got here?"

"What, this? Fresh meat for Hangnail."

"Hangnail's sick."

"Ain't that always the case."

She looked at us some more, doubt showing in her eyes.

"Are they sick?"

"Not from what I can tell. Found 'em out at the reservoir running from them damn balls. Jumped right into my lap, the dumb bastards."

Annie O circled around us a few more times.

"Girl's a little scrawny, but I like the big fella."

"I knew you would! Didn't I say that? Didn't I?"

I ain't sure if he was expecting us to respond or not, but even if he did, there wasn't no way I was going to give him the satisfaction.

"Talkative pair," Annie O said.

"I taught 'em right."

"Alright, then. He's eager to start, so come on."

She spurred her horse and galloped off toward the big house.

Oh man.

Timmy Carter and I shared another look. He didn't look scared, but I was downright terrified. Strangely enough, though, I also felt angry. Too much had happened for me to let this bunch take me out. Hives trying to kill me. Macks trying to kill me. No way I was going to let a kooky old man and some middle-aged cosplayer get away with it.

Otis shoved Timmy Carter in the back and said, "Get moving, big boy. Hangnail's waiting."

Timmy Carter stumbled forward, and I saw something in his expression shift. He'd had enough. He stood erect and rolled his shoulders back.

"You ever heard of this Hangnail, Amanda?" he asked.

"I had me plenty of hangnails in my time, Timmy Carter," I said.

"Oh yeah?"

"Oh yeah. I always think I can pull them out but then they just keep going and going."

"Those are the worst."

Otis shoved him.

"Move it, meat!"

"You know what I think, Amanda?"

"What's that, Timmy Carter?"

"I think there ain't no bullets in that old scatter-barrel."

Otis pumped his shotgun.

"You want to test that theory, boy?"

He shoved him again, and Timmy Carter began to sing.

"Whooo-eee!"

Another shove.

"I'm warning you!"

They got into a rhythm.

"Hangnail, hangnail, ingrown hair!"

Otis shoved him on the word 'hair'.

"Prickly peach or a por-cu—"

Shove.

"Do you want the vodka? Do you want some—"

Shove.

"Do you want salvation for the worst of your—"

This time, Timmy Carter timed it perfect. Right when he was supposed to say the last word, he ducked to the left, and Otis, already in mid-shove, flew forward and landed flat on his face. The shotgun exploded underneath him. He shook and went still.

"Damn, Timmy Carter! You killed Otis!"

I went over and kicked the old man in the ribs. He whelped and rolled onto his back. His eyes were wide open and he was hugging the shotgun to his chest, but I couldn't see no blood nowhere.

"Please don't hurt me."

I yanked the gun out of his grasp.

"What's the matter with you?"

"Nothing. Nothing's the matter with me. I'm just a crazy old fool."

"You got that right."

I heard a couple of cracks like fireworks going off, and up by the big house came Annie O herself, thundering down the drive. She had the reins between her teeth and was firing both six shooters at us like she was Clint Eastwood. A few hit the dirt at our feet, but that was about it because here's the thing about riding a horse and shooting: it don't work. The shooting part, that is.

Trying to shoot a gun while you're riding a horse is about as accurate as a cat balancing a checkbook. Still didn't hurt to move around, make it harder. There were snow-covered hay bales humped like dead rhinos in the fields beside us, each one at least ten feet high and just as round. We took cover behind the nearest one.

"They've got my gun! They've got my gun!" Otis yelled.

I peeked around the bale and saw him streaking up the drive, waving his arms. Annie O rode right by him, sending up rocks and snow in her wake. She fired again, and I ducked behind the bale.

"How many you hear?" Timmy Carter asked.

"Seven." Another shot cracked in the air. "Eight."

He pumped the shotgun and a single casing popped out.

"How many are left, do you think?"

He tried to crack it open to see, but it was clear he'd never handled a gun like that in his life.

"Give that to me, Timmy Carter. You're like to blow your own head off." He handed it over and at the same time, Annie O shot off two more rounds. "That's ten," I said. I cracked the shotgun open. There wasn't any shells left. "Timmy Carter, squat down and let me get on your shoulders."

"What?"

"Just do it."

I clambered up and tried to balance myself, holding onto his bald head with one hand and the shotgun with the other.

"No! Don't stand up all the way. Just enough to let me peek over the top."

He did and Annie O squeezed off another round and I ducked, hissing.

"Eleven. She's right there. Scoot forward." I cocked that shotgun back over my shoulder just like it was a bat and I thought to myself, "here's to three years of softball."

Annie O's horse galloped closer and closer. I took a deep breath. Had to time it just right.

Riding a horse to the food bank cut our trip in half. We quadrupled our load, too, filling up our empty packs and a full tarp we found with enough canned food and other non-perishables to last at least a month. Timmy and I let the bigger animal plow a path in the snow as we walked home. About halfway there, I stopped to make sure the tarp was strapped on tight. Didn't want to lose no beefaroni or cheese ravioli in white sauce.

Timmy Carter watched as he was uncertain about any animals larger than Maggie May.

"You want to explain to me why we didn't use your horse to do this in the first place?"

"Who, Lucky? Lucky might be big, but she's the laziest princess I ever did meet."

"She's a horse, isn't she?"

"Only in the strictest definition."

"How so?"

"Daddy treated that old girl better than me. Pampered her like she was king's consort."

"Gross."

"Not like that, idiot."

I finished my work, and we walked her the rest of the way home.

It was dark out by the time we got back to the farm, and the temperature had dropped significantly. I was ready for the day to be over. Just wanted to stand in front of the wood stove and let the heat bring my fingers and toes back to life. Ray was waiting at the new section of the wall, Maggie May barking behind him. He opened the gate with a squeal and she bounded for us, nipping at our fingers and hopping around in the snow. I squatted down and pet her, scratching behind the ears.

"How you guys doing?" Ray asked me.

"Don't ask."

"Okay. That's not Lucky, is it? I thought—"

"No, it ain't Lucky. We took her off someone."

"Who?"

"Let's get all this put away first. I need to get warmed up by the stove, get a mug of tea in me."

"Okay."

Later on, we told him everything. About the storms, how Otis caught us, Hangnail's farm.

"I think they were going to eat us," I said.

Timmy Carter laughed.

"Think? They kept calling us 'meat'."

Ray was quiet for a time, thinking.

"You think they're something to worry about?" he asked.

"Uh, yeah."

"But there's only two of them, right?"

"Two of them and Hangnail, whoever that is."

"Okay, so three. We got at least ten people here, and plenty of guns."

"I don't think that matters one bit, Ray. They're sick. And desperate. Ain't no telling what they'll do."

"It's kind of sad, isn't it?"

"Sad?"

"Just the fact that the world's come to this is all."

Timmy Carter and I shared a look.

"We can get all philosophical some other time," I said. "Right now, we gotta watch out for that crew. They come for us again, we have to take them out."

Ray sat back and looked at me, a little shocked. Made me laugh.

"What's that look for, Ray? You know who I am. Ain't nobody does something like that to me and gets away with it."

"Yeah, I believe that."

"You better believe it."

LUCK AIN'T PLANNING

I don't think I've ever told y'all this, but Daddy loved birds. Ravens, specifically. As an adult, he didn't like to keep them as pets, staying true to his feelings on caring for animals after a full day of caring for animals, but when he was a kid, he actually domesticated one.

"I wanted to name him Edgar for obvious reasons, but your Uncle Zeus said that was stupid.

'We live forty minutes north of Richmond,' he said. 'You might as well just name him 'Raven' if you're going to name him that'.

'Fine. What would you name him?'

Zeus didn't even hesitate.

'Bertram'.

'Bertram? What's Bertram mean?'

'It's German for raven'."

"I'm not sure what I liked about that thread of logic the most, the obvious contradiction or the confidence with which it was stated. Either way, Bertram sounded better than Edgar, so that's what I named him."

Daddy always was a bit of a weirdo. I think he liked the name as much as watching the expression on people's faces when they asked.

"Hey, what's your raven's name?"

"Bertram."

"Bertram? What's that mean?"

"Raven."

"You named your raven, Raven."

"Yeah. Makes it easier for me to remember what he is."

Daddy trained Bertram to talk, fetch, and deliver messages. Even took it to competitions up and down the east coast, won a few badges. He kept them in a display frame that he hung in Maurice. Best Elocution. Fastest Delivery Time. Highest Soarer.

"Bertram was a grade A raven," Daddy used to say.

"You ever miss him, Daddy?"

"God no. Damn bird lived five years longer than he was supposed to. We only competed for three years when he was younger. Then he got kind of mean. Wouldn't stay in a cage, so I kept him in the barn. Used to swoop down at me and peck at my head. I wanted to shoot him, but Nana wouldn't let me. Probably the best decision I ever made."

One day, Zeus drank some bad well water and took to vomiting. He was dangling on the drop-edge of yonder. But the world still revolved and the family had to eat, so Nana sent Daddy out to draw some water from the stream that ran behind the house.

Daddy loved to play in that stream. Caught crawdads and frogs, splashed through its shallow depths, jumped from rock to rock. It was there where he came to understand the inner workings of the natural world, how the water flowed, how the creatures ate.

It was something he passed down to me, and when it was my turn to play there, I used to lie on the sandy banks and imagine him as a boy doing the same thing, staring up at the sun-dappled canopy, listening to the hushing wind and the buzzing insects and the tweeting birds.

He had to be, oh, maybe ten when it happened. Usually he and Zeus played together, Zeus being only two years younger and a boy. (Daddy's sisters were in their teens and had no interest in fishing for crawdads and rolling around in the mud.) But of course Zeus was busily plying his illness in his room, working Nana half to death changing sheets and emptying basins, so that left Daddy to do the job on his own, taking Bertram along for company. The stream never wandered and never winnowed, so you can imagine his surprise when he ambled out there, Bertram on his shoulder and bucket in hand, to find only a dry bed littered with dead mudbugs and flopping fish.

"I was as near to a state of shock as I'd ever been," he said. "That stream was as regular as the sun. There was a little pool, and I picked up a couple of fish and put them in it. Not that it would help, but I did what I could."

He and Bertram followed the bed upstream, him by foot and Bertram by air. All sorts of treasures littered the bed. Rusty coins and arrowheads. Bike frames and hubcaps. At one turn he saw what looked like white bones sticking out of the mud; around another, he found a clutch of nudie magazines.

He followed the bed for at least a half mile before he found out what happened. A tree had fallen across the stream and was blocking the water. It wasn't no regular tree, neither. The woods surrounding our farm was filled with huge oaks, and this was one of the biggest. He hopped up on the bank to see the damage and hadn't taken but two steps before he froze in his tracks.

"I'd walked into the middle of a nest of snakes. Copperheads. They didn't see me at first, but I knew enough about them not to even think about making any sudden movements. I was about to back away when one sensed my presence and uncoiled, hissing. I had just enough time to think *good lord* when it struck.

"I swear to God, 'Manda, everything I'm about to tell you is the truth. Out of nowhere, Bertram came screaming down through the air and snapped that snake up in its beak before it could bite me. Nabbed it by the head and just flew off."

That just about knocked my socks off.

"That's planning and effort, right there, Daddy," I said. "You trained that bird good!"

Daddy laughed.

"Planning and effort had nothing to do with it, 'Manda. I got lucky. And luck ain't planning."

You know who wasn't lucky?

Ray.

I know I haven't talked about him so far, but to be honest, after a couple of weeks in his company, I found that I did not like Ray very much at all. He seemed like an alright guy at first, but he had a tendency to ignore me, and I think it was because I was a girl. He took to ordering me around like the farm was his, and I took to avoiding him as much as I could. The man might have been military, but he didn't have no country training.

Let me explain.

March came in like a lamb, which was truly a surprise after all that grousing old man winter did a few weeks earlier. He was a tenacious old coot, though, and held on to the land with them hardscrabble nails, trying to keep Mother Earth from tilting back toward the sun by sheer force. But Mother Earth liked to indulge her children, and eventually she had enough of his attitude and sent him packing. Then, as if to make up for it, she let the sun warm the land, melting the snow and filling the streams. It felt as though the world could breathe again, and with those first, tentative breaths, the wildlife returned.

We couldn't believe it.

It was our common belief that the Hive had destroyed nearly everything it could get its slimy tentacles on the fall before, insect and reptile and bird and beast alike, from the great black bear to the lowliest worm. Wiped them out faster than any disaster in history, manmade or natural.

But we were wrong. First came the birds, whole flocks of them. Geese and ducks and sparrows and hawks and ruffs and eagles and cardinals! Then we saw deer. Whole families.

Bucks and does and fawns. Maggie May just about lost her mind, and it took all we could take trying to keep her from running off all tail and tongue, half-catawumpus after every last living thing that dared set foot on or near our property.

Of course, with the warmer weather came the fear of The Hives coming back to life, but I thought we might have a few more weeks.

"How do you know this?" Ray asked.

I tell you what. I never had a brother to irritate the hell out of me just by breathing, but Ray had become about as close to one as I'd ever get.

"I dunno," I said. "Just a feeling."

"Just a feeling. Feelings aren't going to save us when those things wake up. And with those blizzard balls crashing around all over the place—"

"Fine, it's more than a feeling. The Hives froze up with the frost, right?"

"So? It's nearly sixty outside."

"If you ain't the most hardheaded . . . yeah, it's sixty degrees in the air. But the fields are still frozen. Go on out and try to dig you a hole, see how long it takes to break off the handle."

Timmy Carter stifled a snicker and Ray shot a one-eyed glare at him. He couldn't really argue about that, but instead of admitting he was wrong, he sputtered something about "we'll see" and walked off, his shoulders all knotted up and a black cloud hanging over his scarred head.

"What's got into him?" I asked Timmy Carter.

"He's angry."

"What about?"

"I dunno. Something."

I didn't dwell on it. I was too busy hunting deer to care. I would have thought I was a bonafide angel the way everybody carried on when I brought the first one back. It was a three-point buck, not too big, but not too small neither. I cleaned and butchered it myself out back, and when I cooked the first steaks, well . . . . after three weeks of pasta and red sauce, I guess I understand the rapture they all felt.

In all the excitement about the deer, I forgot to warn everybody about the well. I'm not saying I'm taking responsibility for what happen, but I don't necessarily feel good about it, neither.

Those of you who have well-water know the struggle. Yeah, you don't have to pay the county for something that should come for free, but you also have to be extra careful about your source of hydration. Back in the Civil War days, people dug their wells shallow, forty feet shallow, and that wasn't good for nobody. Shallow wells go dry easier for one, but they're also susceptible to collapse and poisoning. I don't think I ever knew anybody who purposefully poisoned a well or anybody who'd had their well poisoned on purpose, but I knew plenty whose wells ended up that way. Floods can do it. So can letting your cows flop too close to it or digging an outhouse in the path of the source.

As long as I could remember, we used a well that Daddy dug himself. The thing was over 180 feet deep, tasted clean and clear, best water I ever had. But even that one turned weird on occasion, and every now and then the stuff that came out of the pipe was red-brown and smelled like sulfur. We didn't drink the water then; had to boil some from the stream. But there was two other wells on the property, one that'd been dug over a hundred and fifty years before and had since collapsed, and another that'd been dug in the early 1950's and was as corrupt as a senator.

It sat at the bottom of a hill behind our house, and for some reason, Daddy never filled it in. I think maybe he liked the way it looked down there, with the crumbling stone housing topped by an antique roof. It looked homey, gave the property an old-timey feel that he appreciated. Any time someone suggested he tear it down, he'd say "people look at that well and the barns and the old whitewashed house and they don't think 'Marijuana'. They think Thanksgiving and apple pie, the 2nd Amendment and Old Glory." Whether or not that's true, he never got busted. Gotta give him that.

As for me, he didn't worry one bit about that old well. I might have been a hard-headed tomboy, but I wasn't stupid. That well was a catch-all for all kinds of snakes and birds and other unfortunates, and I'd even seen Daddy dump stuff in it on occasion, so the last thing I wanted to do was accidentally fall forty feet into a polluted pit of trash, reptiles, and animal carcasses.

But Ray didn't know this. And neither did anybody else who'd come to live on the farm.

It was March fifth, and we were gathered in the kitchen, five us, including Timmy Carter, Ray, and me. It was a typical Virginia late winter. Some days the temperature rose to the low 50's; some days, it stuck hard to near freezing. Maggie May lay at my feet enjoying the heat of the open wood stove. Timmy Carter and I had just come back from a week of ranging the countryside, checking for Hives or any stray Macks.

By all accounts, the range was a successful one. The burned husks of Hives we found from the fall before had decayed over the winter. The pyres of Mack corpses were nothing but black spots. Sure it was muddy and cold, but Timmy Carter and I returned much heartened.

Ray filled our cups with water from a pitcher.

"Tastes a little funny," he said, taking a deep gulp.

"The water?" I asked. "Is it coming out orange?"

"It did. Then it shut down all the way. We've been using the other well."

I put my cup down on the table with a thock.

"What other well?"

"The one at the bottom of the hill."

Ray started to take another drink, and I knocked the cup out of his hands, splattering everybody at the table.

"Amanda, what the hell!"

"Everybody put your cups down." They all looked at me like I was crazy. "Do it! Now!"

Ray put his hand on my shoulder.

"Amanda, can you explain what's going on."

"I should have told you. Damn! Of course you didn't know."

"Didn't know what?"

"How long have you been drinking this?"

"Since last night. Why?"

"I'm surprised you're not sick yet."

"Amand—"

"That well's bad. Always has been. Hell, Ray, Daddy used to dump stuff in there."

His face went just about as pale as the rain.

"Oh sh—"

"Yeah, no kidding."

I started to gather up my backpack. Maggie May hopped to her feet, tongue lolling.

"You give this to her?"

Ray was staring at the table, shocked.

"What? No. I'm trying to think who's been drinking this."

"You'll know pretty fast. First comes the fever, then the vomiting."

"Where are you going?"

"We're going to need water."

"I thought you said—"

"We use the stream when the well stops working. Boil it."

"We need medicine. Penicillin. Antibiotics."

"First things first. Timmy Carter?"

Timmy Carter was already on his feet.

"I'll get people to help."

I knew what he was really thinking about. There was a new girl he'd taken a shine to. Francis or Francine or something. I hadn't seen much of her or gotten to know her very well. She was a cute little thing. Timmy Carter had been away for a whole week, so I guess he had him some catching up to do. He bounced away from the table like his legs were on springs. Ray, on the other hand, looked like he was going to hyperventilate.

"This is my fault. I made everyone sick."

"Maybe so, but sitting around feeling bad about it ain't going to solve the problem."

"What do I do?"

I was already halfway out the door, Maggie May on my heels. She thought we were going for a hike.

"I dunno. Help."

And I left.

The stream ran through the woods at the bottom of a hill about quarter a mile from the house. Maggie May and I banked around the gate and walked along the wall, setting a fast clip, eager to leave the chaos that was about to set in behind. To be honest, I kind of enjoyed getting away from the farm, emergency or not. Don't get me wrong; I loved the place. It was and always will be my home. But I'd lived there forever, and I was getting to the time in my life when I needed to not be there anymore. On top of that, it reminded me too much of Daddy. Everywhere I looked, he'd put his stamp on something. Maurice. His guns. The couch where I found him.

I was about a foot away from the woods when Maggie May started barking and baring her teeth. I felt dizzy all the sudden, like something in my inner ear went haywire and showed me off-balance. At the same time, I felt an electric current run through my body, starting around my pelvis and running up my spine, shooting out my arms and into my fingertips. Maggie May kept barking and barking, and I had to struggle to focus, to not concentrate on the sensation because as strange and scary as it felt . . . I can't lie, it felt good. Felt real good. It reminded me of the first time I kissed a boy, a sexy zing that hummed through all of my nerves.

I managed to draw my sidearm, and whoever or whatever it was stepped around from behind the tree, and I let out a sigh of relief. It was the girl. The banshee. She stood there, plain-faced and quiet, like she wanted to say something but couldn't. Maggie May, when she realized who it was, wagged her tail and trotted up to lick her hand. That weird zing slowly disappeared, and I lowered my gun.

"Holy moly, girl. You can't just scare people like that."

"W-want to come."

"You want to come with me?"

She nodded.

"I'm just getting some water."

"W-want to come."

"It'll do you some good. About time you got out of the house."

I meant that. She'd been holed up in Daddy's room ever since we rescued each other out in that blizzard two months before, and that kind of isolation don't do nobody no good.

I will say this. The girl was beautiful. Some people just have it. Evenly proportioned features, thick hair, full lips. That was her. In the late winter sun, she looked hale and hearty, even if she was still a little pale. On anybody else it would have looked spooky, but it suited her.

We didn't speak as we walked, which I liked. It's why me and Timmy Carter got along so well. He shut up and I let him shut up. We had just about reached the stream when I noticed something was wrong. I couldn't put my finger on it exactly. Something about the woods was different. I didn't figure it out until we reached the water. Or where the water was supposed to be.

Because there wasn't any water anymore. The stream was dry.

Maggie May was jumping around in the bed, chomping on the flopping fish and tossing them up in the air, snorkeling and snuffling and having herself a grand old time. She barked when she seen us.

"Yeah, Maggie May," I murmured. "You're having yourself a grand old time."

"W-water?" the girl asked.

I hopped into the bed, squatted down, and put my hand on the bottom. The sand was still wet.

"Must have just happened."

"T-trees."

"Yeah. Daddy said this happened before. Tree fell and—"

"No. Trees."

I looked and she was pointing upstream. Sure enough, it was blocked, this time not by a single tree but by several. And rocks and dirt and leaves, like the world's most industrious beavers had scoped the place out, took a meeting, and decided 'Yep. This is spot'.

I started over toward it to see what was going on when the girl said, "N-no."

"Why not?"

"Don't. Not. Safe."

After everything I'd been through, you would have thought that maybe I'd listen to someone for once. Maybe I should have. Maybe for once in my life, I should have considered the fact that my first impulse might not always be the best. But unfortunately for me, well, remember that conversation we had a few months back about frontal lobe development and teenagers? Yeah. That. Add to that the chip on my shoulder I had for anybody who tried to tell me what to do (thanks, Daddy), and there was no way I was going to not investigate that damn dam. What did she know, anyway? She'd been holed up and invalid for over a month.

I got about halfway up the side when Maggie May started barking. It startled me and I slid back a few feet, uncovering something slick and white. I peered at it for a closer look, flicked some dirt off it, dug around the edges a little. Maggie May stopped barking and I thought, "Good." The old girl was driving me crazy.

"Hey, girl," I said. "Come check this out."

I turned around, but the girl was gone. And Maggie May. Just up and vanished.

"Hey? Maggie May?"

I looked around all over, but they'd totally disappeared.

"You playing tricks on me, girl?" I waited a tic, but she didn't reply, and nary a bark was heard. "Where'd they go?" I muttered.

"Runned off."

I recognized that voice. Old and scraggly, reminded me of long hair and black gapped teeth. I turned back around, and there he was on top of the dam, smiling that ugly smile at me. Otis.

"Hi there. Amanda, right?"

I started to draw my sidearm, but he pulled out a rifle so big it might as well have been a cannon.

"What's that, a punt gun?"

"You want to find out?"

"You think that's supposed to scare me?"

"Yeah."

He aimed it to my right and fired, blowing a hole in a tree along the bank. My pale face must have been all the words he needed. He looked over my shoulder and nodded.

"You might remember my friend?"

Somebody spun me around and there stood Annie O. Her face was still swole from when I knocked her off her horse with Otis' shotgun. One eye was all bunged up, too, and her lip healed cockeyed.

"Hi there," she said, and then she clocked me in the face.

Didn't black out, but it hurt like hell. Like about to knock me crosseyed. My ears was ringing and my eyes teared up. I fired off a few rounds before she hit me again, and maybe I hit her or maybe I didn't, but when I'd exhausted my clip, there was a pause and a chuckle, and then she ripped my gun out of my hand. And then she kicked me in the ribs. And then she kicked me in the ribs again. I'm pretty sure she broke at least one.

"That's enough, Annie O," Otis said. "Hangnail wants her alive."

"Oh, she'll be alive," she said, and kicked me in the kidneys this time. "Enough."

Here's the thing about riding in the payload of a pickup truck with broken ribs: it don't feel good. I'm pretty sure Annie O was driving because that truck hit as many hard turns and potholes as possible. I rolled around in the back like a ping pong ball. At least at first. After the third time slamming into the wheel well, I braced myself against the cab and a wooden toolbox that had been bolted into the steel.

For those of you who're thinking 'Now why didn't she open that toolbox up and get her a weapon? Even a screwdriver would have done the job!' Well, that toolbox was locked up with a fat old padlock the size of a softball, and between the ribs and the careening around, it wasn't really like I was thinking straight.

I did, however, find myself a nice, sharp shard of wood about the size of a penknife and jammed it down the back of my jeans. Maybe I shouldn't have brought a shiv to a gunfight, but it was better than nothing. After a while, I the pickup slowed down and stopped and one of them got out of the cab, and then I heard the sound of a gate opening. The truck moved forward, and the tires crunched on gravel, and I knew we'd made it to Hangnail's farm.

I'll spare you the details of how they got me out of the truck. You can trust me when I say that as much as breaking my ribs hurt, the process of clambering out of that payload and walking into the house was worse. You'll probably not be surprised to know that Annie O and Otis were none too kind about it, neither.

They dragged me through the house and into a hallway with stuffed heads mounted on the wood paneled walls. Deer, bears, antelope, moose. Antique guns were hanging farther down where the hallway turned into a set of stairs. They carried me down by my armpits, my toes barely scraping each step, finally stopping at a set of double doors.

"You knock," Otis said.

Annie O grunted and shook her head.

"You scared?"

"No. But it's your turn."

"Fine."

She was about to do it when the lock clicked and the doors swung slowly open, revealing a long, deep room with a thick, oak table in the middle of it. A fire crackled in the fireplace in the back despite the warm weather, and a figure in black sat with his back to it. I couldn't see anything but greasy hair on a hung head. Must have been Hangnail.

"Mr. Hangnail, sir?" Annie O said.

Hangnail didn't move, and she and Otis shared a nervous look.

"Let's bring her in," Annie O said.

Otis nodded.

I kept my eyes on Hangnail as they dragged me over to a chair to his right and shoved me down in it. If any of you ever had broken ribs and were forced to sit, you know how much that must have hurt. I sucked in a gasp and tried to blink away the stars. Then they hovered there behind me, nervous as two polecats.

Now that I was closer, I could see Hangnail's mouth and nose underneath all that hair. He was smiling. Or grimacing. I couldn't tell which. And he was sweaty and sneering and all hunched over with his hands resting palms down on the table. Sure enough, he looked like he was suffering his namesake.

I squinted at him, trying to see the eyes behind that hair, and then I knew. I knew who he was.

"Gomez Gomez?" I said.

That's right. Gomez Gomez. Gomer's son. The last time I saw him, he was crumpled over on the ground after I kicked him in the gonads, his face red, the tendons in his neck sticking out. Or maybe that was hive-reality Gomez. Did it really matter? I was there. He was there. Everything I felt, my momma's hand on my forehead, the pain of the rocks biting into my feet as I ran across town, was real. If it was real for me, then it was real for him. Well, good. Gomez was a jerk before he died and joined the Hive. Now he was a jerk *and* a traitor to humankind.

And a weirdo, too. Because did he say anything when he saw me? Did he make an effort to recognize me? Did he smile or snarl or do anything more than hang his head like a whipped puppy, gritting his teeth, lips pulled back so I could see his gums? Well. I'll let you figure that one out. Otis cleared his throat.

"Sir? Mr. Hangnail, sir?"

Gomez's eyes snapped on him.

"Here she is, sir. We brought her to you like you asked. All in one piece."

Gomez continued to stare at him without saying a thing. I craned my neck back to look at Otis, trying to gauge his reaction. Strangely enough, he looked like he was listening to something. Then I felt it again. The dizziness. Just like before with the girl. Only this time, I heard a crackling static, like a radio signal was trying to punch through my brain, a winding feedback whine that shot into my ear and made my head hurt. This wasn't some throbbing ache from getting knocked in the head, this was like someone was pushing a guitar string into my ear. Then through it all came a voice, distant and thin at first, then gradually fuller and fuller. I finally caught the edge of a word right in the middle of a sentence.

". . . id I not tell you to bring her to me undamaged?"

Gomez's mouth hadn't twitched an inch. Otis cleared his throat again.

"Uh, yes, sir. Yes, sir, you did, but, see, Annie O—"

"Don't blame it on me!" Annie O yelled.

"I told you not to touch her. I told you to leave her al—"

Gomez blinked hard and a gash appeared in Otis's face, stretching across from his cheekbone to his chin, a jagged, ugly gulch.

"Please, Otis. Do not lie to me. Do not play games. Take responsibility for your behavior."

"But—"

Gomez blinked again and another gash formed on Otis's other cheek.

"Annie O?" Gomez asked. "Do you care to say anything?"

"No. No, sir."

"There will be repercussions for this insolence. I will attend to you both later. Leave us for now."

"Sir, if I may—"

Gomez blinked and the two were sent backward out of the room, their feet dragging on the hardwood, flying one by one out the door, which slammed shut behind them. He turned his eyes on me, and I tried to sit up straighter. I might have had my ribs cracked, but there wasn't no way I was going to let a little weasel like Gomez Gomez get the best of me.

"Hangnail, huh? Sounds about right."

"Mock me if you must, Amanda May Jett, but—"

"Oh, I will. What's the deal with your hair? I know we're low on food and such, but there's still plenty of shampoo and conditioner to be looted."

He blinked hard and this time the gash hit my lips. Felt like getting cut with a cinderblock. It took me a few minutes to recover, but when I did, I said, "Neat trick, Gomez. That all you got?"

"Better than what you have."

I would have smiled but even the short sentence I'd just managed to get out made me sick with pain. I swallowed it back along with my pride. And some blood.

"What's the matter, Amanda? Can't think of something sharp to say to me?"

The dizziness crept up inside again, tickling the back of my throat, warming my belly and below. Just a hint and then it was gone. I spit blood on the table.

"Why?" I asked.

"Why what?"

The little snake was going to make me say it, wasn't he? Make this as painful as possible. And hard, too. Turns out that lip cuts are just as bad as scalp cuts. They bleed and bleed and bleed. Difficult to make any sense when you're sputtering blood.

"What do you want, Gomez?"

"Do you mean what do I want from you? Your life, of course."

"You really think so?"

"Yes. Not before I torture you first, but it's going to happen."

Here's the thing about people: we're all the main characters in our own stories, and the main character don't die. If we get in a predicament, we fight or fox our way out of it. If we need saving, we get saved. But that ain't the way the world really works. In the real world, everybody dies.

Sitting there across from Gomez Gomez after he threatened to kill me, I should have been freaking out for that very reason. I believed him. I believed he was going to do it. I wasn't in any position to deny him his intentions, neither. But somehow, I felt cool. Calm. Collected. I don't know why. I wasn't trying to be conceited or nothing.

Next thing I knew, that weird dizziness hit me. Hit me full-on all over my body, and I thought, "she's here." The girl. She'd come to save me.

Gomez Gomez must have felt it, too, because his eyes went spastic, bouncing around in his skull. Then the door exploded inward, sending shards of wood flying through the air. One of them stuck Gomez right in the shoulder so hard that he fell backward. Then she was there, the girl, standing in the broken door frame. She stepped into the room like a short, pale, scraggly-haired superhero, followed close behind by a barking Maggie May.

Gomez rose up from the ground, stiff as a board like he was being pulled by wires. He blinked and all of the shards shot back at the girl, sticking her in the arms and legs and torso. Maggie May attacked him, biting his leg and whipping her head back and forth. Gomez blinked and she flew off, hitting the wall with a whelp.

The girl was suddenly next to me, bleeding from all her wounds and a little unsteady on her feet. She reached her hand out and I took it, and a surge of energy welled up inside my body. Never felt nothing like it in my life. It filled me top to toe, heating me up like a reactor. But it didn't hurt. It felt good, like virtue, like righteousness, and it surrounded my cracked ribs and soothed them, and it filled my aching head and soothed it, too.

And once that was done, I felt the energy build and build until I couldn't control it no more. It poured out of my eyes and my mouth, shooting green beams of power that hit Gomez Gomez in the chest and stomach and head. He turned white hot as it consumed him, and his arms and legs stiffened, and he formed an X as the power lifted him off the ground, head flung back, hair burning, mouth wide open. The energy burned in from his fingers and toes to the core of his being, and he disappeared into the light and crumbled into dust. Then he was gone, nothing more than a pile of ashes on the floor.

We found Otis and Annie O lying in a pool of blood by the front door.

"Did you do that?" I asked the girl.

The girl stared at them but didn't respond. I had to shoo Maggie May away from the blood. She was a little stiff as we walked out of the house, limping a little on her front right leg, but otherwise she seemed okay.

Otis's pickup truck was sitting in the driveway. I had to fish his keys out of his pocket. We drove back to the farm in silence, Maggie May sitting between me and the girl as a buffer. I don't know what happened between us back there, but as awesome as it was, it scared the hell out of me. There was a lot to unpack, but at the moment, I was too tired to even think about anything other than getting home.

It was dark by the time we pulled up to the gate, and that's when I remembered how that whole thing started in the first place.

"Crap," I said. "The water."

"W-water?"

"Yeah, for Ray. And anybody else who gets sick. Damn."

I was about to get out and open the gate when it rolled aside. The new girl, Francine? Frannie? Whatever her name was, she opened it. I drove in, giving her a wave as we passed. She didn't wave back.

"We're going to have to go out and tote a whole bunch back from the stream and—"

I stopped talking.

Timmy Carter was in the headlights, standing over two mounds of dirt in the front yard. He was holding a shovel.

"F-for what?" the girl asked.

I cut the engine and turned off the lights. Then I leaned back, staring out the windshield, seeing everything and nothing at the same time.

"Nothing," I said. "Never mind."

THE STUPIDEST THING I EVER HEARD

I never was one to watch horror movies. They always seemed a mite bit silly to me. Man-wolves running around the wilderness. River people with gills in their necks. Serial killers with chainsaws. I get that lots of people loved that kind of stuff, but all I ever saw was rubber masks and plot holes.

To me, there were plenty of real-life things to be worried about. Would we sell enough crop to make it through the winter? Would the pregnant cow breach? Would Daddy ever get busted by the feds? That was more frightening than some crazy fool trying to chop my head off with a machete. Daddy had about a bazillion guns, anyway. Anything like that ever tried to come at us . . . well, talk about bringing a knife to a gun fight.

But there was one movie that freaked me way out.

Salem's Lot.

Daddy took me to The Virginians Dollar Theater to see it, against his better judgment, he claimed.

"It's kind of cheesy, 'Manda. You really want to go?"

I was ten, and all my friends at school saw it when it first came out, so I was bound and determined not to be the only one who hadn't.

"Cheesy? Britany Grayson said she was like about to soil herself it was that scary."

"Yeah, well, that don't surprise me none. Her daddy's the same way."

"So can we go?"

"Sure, I guess."

And that was that.

To understand how special this was to me, you have to understand how often Daddy actually took me to the movies, which is to say never. It wasn't the money but the distance that seemed to bother him the most. And he liked movies to a degree, but he wasn't all the much into them. If we did get to go, it was usually a second run show. I didn't see *Close Encounters* until nearly ten years after it came out. Same with *ET* and *Back to the Future.* So for us to see *Salem's Lot* less than a year after its original run, well, that was more than a treat.

I dressed to the nines for the event. (My experience with The Sexy Seven did have some kind of positive effect.) Came downstairs in a summer dress and flats, had my hair all curled up, even put lipstick on. I had a disposable camera left over from some birthday party or another that still had five pictures left, and I let it dangle from one wrist and held a little black purse in the other.

Daddy took one look at me and one look at what he was wearing (which was what he always wore: an old pair of jeans with a rip in the knee, a faded green flannel, and a baseball cap), and said, "Oh."

"That's okay, Daddy," I said. "It ain't like we ever go out together or nothing."

He was already heading back up to his room.

"I ever tell you how much you remind me of your mother?"

"No."

"Well, you certainly got her sharp tongue."

He spiffed up the best he could. He was still wearing his baseball cap when he came back down, but at least he'd put on a white, collarless button up that he tucked into a pair of khakis. Daddy wasn't a fat man but he wasn't an athlete, neither, and his belly pushed out over his belt.

"These pants got tighter over the past year," he said.

"Or you got fatter."

"That's the tucked-in shirt doing that. False advertising."

"Did you say 'fat-vertising'?"

"I'm sorry, did you say you actually wanted to see this movie, little girl?"

I zipped it after that. Daddy had a good sense of humor, but he could be touchy about his weight.

I remember everything about that night so clearly. The Virginian's wasn't exactly known for its luxurious trappings. (It was a second run theater after all.) I guess you could say that the freshest thing about it was the popcorn. The floors were sticky and the seats squeaked and the cushions poked my butt, but that didn't bother me one bit. Once the lights went down and the projector clicked to life, I was totally entranced.

It was a hum-dinger of a flick.

Now that I think about it, Daddy was probably right. The movie was a bit cheesy, but I was ten and I'd never seen nothing like it. Really melted my glue. There was one scene in particular, the one when Danny Glick came floating up to his best friend Mark Petrie's window and demanded to be let in? Damn near gave me a heart attack. Couldn't sleep with the window open for a month afterward. Daddy tried to comfort me about it in his way. That's to say he teased me.

"First of all, 'Manda, you got to make friends to worry about something like that happening to you."

"Haha, Daddy."

"Seriously, though. Do you really think a silly little cross would be able to get rid of a monster? That's just a whole bunch of flapdoodle if you ask me."

"But vampires are evil and the cross is from heaven."

"Nah. Best way to stop a vampire is to throw a poppy seed bagel at it."

"Excuse me?"

"Vampires ain't supposed to be sexy immortals in stylish capes. That's Hollywood hogwash. They're supposed to be disgusting monsters. Long fingernails and bucktoothed fangs."

"Oh."

"Wasn't no religious symbol that got rid of them, neither. Nope. Anybody who wanted to kill a vampire had to lop off its head or stake it through the heart."

"Were those stakes made out of bagels?"

"No, smart aleck, they weren't. See, legend has it that if you threw a whole bunch of poppy seeds at a vampire, it'd get distracted by counting them all and you could slip away."

I didn't know what a pregnant pause was at that time of my life, but that's exactly what I did.

"That's the stupidest thing I ever heard in my life."

"Stupider than two pieces of wood scaring off a monster just by holding them up?"

I had to think about that for a second, but in the end, I decided I was right.

"Yeah," I said. "Stupider than that."

I guess you're wondering why I remembered that particular detail. One morning in early April, me and Timmy Carter went out to where the tree had blocked the stream. We were going to chop it up and use the wood for the stove and such. When we got out there, we saw that the stream had flooded the surrounding woods, but the bed was still dry. I thought to myself, "Huh. This is how lakes is started." Then I hopped up on the trunk and said, "We need to start at either end, Timmy Carter. Start in the middle and—"

"What's that noise?" he asked.

"What noise?"

"Listen."

I cocked my head and sure enough, I heard it. Gurgling and glurping. Sounded like the water was draining or moving or something. I felt a thrumming in my feet, and then a hole opened up in the middle of the trunk and water shot out of it, blasting Timmy Carter full-on in the chest. It knocked him about two feet back and flat on his behind. He rolled out of the bed, spitting and sputtering, and crawled up the bank like a half-drowned horse. When I got done laughing, I said, "Damn, Timmy Carter. You okay?"

He nodded and burped. We watched the water shoot out of the hole.

"You know what?" I said. "I bet we could use this."

"The water? I know."

"No. I mean, yeah, for drinking and such, but . . . this might be a long shot, Timmy Carter, but do you know anything about hydro-electricity?"

"I was a bouncer at a nightclub."

I studied the water jetting downstream. It had formed a nice flow by this point.

"We need us an engineer," I said. "Worst case scenario, we could build us a water wheel. You up for a something like that?"

"You mean other than all the planting? Didn't you say we should clear a new field?"

"Yeah. I did say that. Maybe this could be a side project."

Timmy Carter sighed. I knew what he was thinking. Working a farm ain't no joke. The planting alone is enough to bust a back or two even with gas-powered tractors and harvesters and other equipment. We had to do it primitive: by hand. Food Bank (that's what we named Annie O's horse) helped. A lot. Lucky tried, but she was too much of a princess to be much good for anything, so we could only use her for little projects and chicken stuff before she balked and outright refused to do anything anymore. I often found myself wishing for mule or an ox, and believe me, we searched all our neighbor's barns, but the Macks and the Hives had emptied most of them of their precious cargo, and other than a few chickens and wily cats and one ornery sow, we didn't find much in the way of useful farm animals.

I stared at that stream for a good, long, look. *There has to be a way*, I thought.

And that's how I found myself in Maurice holding a wide-mouth mason jar of BB's and crying my eyes out. It was just a little thing, but it was enough to stoke the engine of grief that always seemed to be chugging along in my chest, sometimes slow and sluggish, and sometimes, like right then, redlining hot and hard. I looked at the label on the jar. Peaches. Daddy used to say they were my favorite when I was a baby. That just made me cry harder.

The BB's were just one jar among many that Daddy had carefully organized on his workbench, each one containing a specific size of nail or screw or bolt or washer. It was positively German in its precision, and after I got over being impressed by his thoroughness, and after I wiped the tears away, I began to wonder about the many hours he stood out there planning and separating and plinking little pieces of metal into little glass jars, one after the other. I'd like to be driven crazy by it, but I could see how he took himself a measure of calm from the activity.

I was thinking about all that when I heard a shout outside followed by cries of dismay, and I jammed the jar into the front pocket of my jeans and hurried out the sliding door to see what was going on.

A group had surrounded someone sitting on the front porch of the house. Timmy Carter was kneeling next to whoever it was, and when I finally cleared my way through, I saw it was Frankie, the cute little girl who had just joined our steadily growing group a few weeks before.

I already mentioned how Timmy Carter had taken a shine to her, and judging by the way he was holding her hand and by the way she was gazing at him, I believe that shine was reciprocated, which was both disconcerting and comical at the same time. Disconcerting because I'd never thought about Timmy Carter that way; comical because they were a study in physical juxtaposition. Timmy Carter stood himself over six feet tall and was built like a tank. Frankie stood maybe five foot three and weighed a hundred pounds soaking wet. I heard the tail end of what she was saying as I pushed through the group.

". . . came up from behind and bit me!"

She was covering her neck with her hand, and I could see the blood running through her fingers. Most of us were still slogging around in the same jeans and long sleeve shirts we'd been wearing the previous fall. Frankie, however, wasn't having none of that nonsense. She was a cute little thing, that much I'll admit, and I could see why someone would be attracted to her. When she showed up at the farm, she was wearing designer jeans that hugged her hips and thighs and a shirt that did the same to her top half. Had nearly every man on the farm drooling over her from that moment on. Since then, the weather got even warmer, unusually warm for that time of year if you ask me. And humid. Felt more like late summer than late spring, like August was tired of being a Leo and picked up stakes to live as a Taurus.

Frankie adjusted her wardrobe accordingly, wearing shorts that seemed to have no other purpose than to barely cover her panties and a tight tank top that hugged pretty much every curve she had like it was grafted on to her skin. Sitting there surrounded by all the testosterone she could possibly want, she looked like she'd been waiting for this moment her whole life.

Timmy Carter said, "Let me see it."

"Okay, but be careful."

The way she said that, all tremulous and timid, made me want to scoop out the inside of my skull. She caught me rolling my eyes and narrowed hers. Timmy Carter pulled her fingers aside and she sucked in her breath, but other than a mess of smeared blood, there wasn't much wound to speak of.

"You sure it bit you?" I asked.

"Yes."

"Doesn't look like much of a bite."

"Didn't feel like one, to be honest. Felt more like two bee stings."

"Bee stings?" I leaned in closer to get a look. Frankie was none too pleased about it because when I leaned in, she leaned back. "Stop moving. Let me see it."

The blood had already dried, so I pulled my canteen off my belt, unscrewed the cap, and poured some on her neck. She hissed as I scrubbed it clean, and then I could see them. Two pin-prick punctures in her neck.

She pushed me away.

"Okay, you're done."

"Who did this?"

"Wasn't no 'who' in the equation, sweetie. It was an 'it'."

"Don't call me sweetie."

"Whatever."

"You talking about a Mack? That what bit you?"

"Is that what you call them? Macks?"

"Yeah."

"Okay, well, yeah, it was a Mack. But it was worse than I'd ever seen one before. Skinny and drawn. Emaciated. Emaciated means—"

"I know what emaciated means. Where'd this happen?"

"I don't know. Out in the field."

"Which field? Where?"

She waved her hand all around.

"Pick one."

"It's important." She stared at me. "Was it up on a hill? Over there past the stream?"

"Yeah, actually—"

"How far? A mile? Two?"

"About, yeah."

"What were you doing out there by yourself?"

"I don't know. I needed some air. Just wanted to take a walk. What do you care, anyway?"

I must have looked stricken because Timmy Carter said, "what is it, Amanda?"

"Frankie, you sure about this?" I asked.

"Pretty sure."

"Pretty sure or certain."

"I'm certain, okay. Why? What's the big deal?"

"Was there an old building there? Burned down?"

"Yeah. Now that you mention it, there was an—"

I finished her sentence for her.

"—old iron gate out in the middle of nowhere."

Most of the guys had dispersed by that point, having been bored to tears by any situation that didn't include Frankie needing help. I looked over my shoulder in the direction of the stream, thinking. Then, out of nowhere, another voice, thin and hesitant, broke the silence.

"Ch-church."

We looked at the front door where it came from and there stood the Girl. She looked better than before, fuller, less pale, but her hair was still long and stringy, and she still had that haunted, hollow-eyed stare.

"Church?" Frankie said. "What's that supposed to mean?"

"She's talking about the burned down building," I said. "It used to be a church. First Country Baptist. Got firebombed by the KKK in the 60's."

Frankie suddenly understood what I was getting at. Maybe she wasn't so dumb after all.

"So the field I was in? With the gate? That was a—"

"G-graveyard," the Girl said. "Graveyard."

The old First Country Baptist Church site was about two miles west of the house. If there weren't any hills to climb or woods to navigate, and if there weren't creeks to cross or bogs to avoid, it would have taken us maybe forty minutes to get there. But creeks and bogs and woods abounded in the

Spotsylvania wilderness, and it took us the better part of an hour to finally make it to the site. Timmy Carter came along, of course, and so did Frankie. I tried to talk her out of it, citing her delicate condition, but the girl was tougher than I gave her credit for.

"What are you, sixteen? Seventeen?"

"Seventeen."

"I'm not going to let a teenager tell me what I can and can't do."

"What are you, twenty-three? Twenty four? You're not that much older than me."

Timmy Carter snorted, and Frankie gave me a crooked smile, saying "oh sweetie. You ever hear of a backhanded compliment?"

The Girl followed us, too, keeping a careful distance. Frankie kept looking back over her shoulder at her, and whenever she did, the Girl stopped where she was and wouldn't make eye-contact.

"What's with the Crypt Keeper back there?" Frankie asked.

"She's been through a trauma."

"No kidding."

She tromped off ahead of us through the woods and Timmy Carter came up next to me.

"Am I missing something, Timmy Carter?"

"She's nice to me," he said. "You bring out her bad side."

"Well, that's not my fault."

"G-gene competition."

It was the Girl. Now that Frankie was gone, she seemed more relaxed.

"What's that?" Timmy Carter asked.

She frowned at him like he should have understood and walked away.

"You thinking what I'm thinking?" he asked.

"About what?"

"About them bites in Frankie's neck."

"I hope not."

"Be serious. What did it?"

"It was a Mack."

"No. I think it was something worse."

"You trying to tell me it was a vampire?"

"You saw the bite. It drew blood didn't it?"

I looked up at the sun steadily rising in the sky.

"Yeah," Timmy Carter said. "Sun's out, I know."

"Timmy Carter, it wouldn't surprise me one bit if vampires started showing up out of nowhere. We got aliens, zombies, and now," I gestured at the back of the Girl as she picked her way through the woods in front of us, "banshees."

"That what she is?"

"Who knows."

We walked in silence for the next half hour, finally emerging from the woods at the base of the hill where the old First Country Baptist Church used to stand. Frankie was waiting for us there, and the Girl was wandering around and sniffing the air with her eyes closed. Even though it was spring, the hill seemed dead and dormant. A cloud covered the sun, casting our shadows on the dead grass.

I'd seen pictures of the church before and after the KKK burned it down, and both of them didn't do nothing but make the place feel creepy and creepier. Picture one: an old black and white, faded with time, depicting the congregation standing on the lawn. This was not a sprightly bunch. Their faces were flat and serious, and they all stared at the camera as if they would push the weight of history through the lens and onto our shoulders. Picture two: taken at night. The church is burning brightly behind two white-sheeted forms. Between them was the lower half of a naked, black body hanging from a makeshift scaffold.

Every time I came across the hill in my many wanderings around the Spotsylvania countryside, I thought of the second picture. Sometimes I imagined what it was like before it happened, whether I could sit at the bottom of the hill and see the top of the cross on the steeple jutting into the sky, whether I would hear the choir singing or the soaring voice of the minister, the shouts of children playing after the service, the bell pealing in the promise of a new chance to worship.

"What's she doing?" Frankie asked. She was looking at the Girl who was still sniffing the air. Her eyes were open now, and they batted back and forth just like they'd done when I first spoke to her in that cave a few months before.

"Beats me," I said.

I trudged up the hill, drawing my gun. We were low on ammunition, and a recent trip out to Blue's proved fruitless. Place was gutted. To be honest, I wouldn't have been surprised if Blue had done it himself, cleared out all his guns and ammo and lit off for some underground bunker he'd been preparing for just such an occasion as what The Hive afforded the world.

But then I found what looked like a smear of blood on the floor in his office in the back, and there were dark footprints in the dust on the floor, and something told me that these signs and symbols portended a grimmer fate for Daddy's old friend. Because of that, I only had three bullets left.

The old church sat like an empty shell atop the hill. A stiff wind blew over the trees, and the rusty graveyard gate squeaked in the distance. The grass in the front had grown tall from years of neglect, but I found the depression where Frankie had been attacked easy enough. The stalks were pressed down in two directions, one leading away from the church, one toward it.

"Anybody bring their garlic and holy water?" I joked.

I turned around to smile at Timmy Carter, and when I did, I saw a dark form pushing through the tall grass to his right. I started to shout his name, but it was too late. Whatever it was jumped into the air and took him out. I ran to the spot where he'd been but he was gone. Frankie was spinning in place, saying "No no no no no," then the black form shot out and took her down, too. I did the only thing I could think of.

I ran.

There's an old military corpse Daddy used to exhume pretty much every time the thought it applied. Let's see if I can remember it. Hmm . . . Oh yeah!

"Moor your craft higher than the enemy."

That's what it was. *The Art of War*, I think. I never read it, but Daddy repeated it so many times that it stuck in my brain. As we climbed yet another tree to sit in a blind for a thousand hours: "Moor your craft higher than the enemy." As we fixed the bird feeder with squirrel-proof domes: "Moor your craft higher than the enemy." As we stored sacks of flour and nuts and other edibles on the highest shelf of the pantry: "Moor your craft higher than the enemy." Probably said it to me while he was changing my diapers, though I'm not sure how that would have helped.

So did I hightail it for the homestead? Try to outrun my clearly superior-powered enemy on foot? Course not. I ran for the bombed out shell of the First Country Baptist Church. Had to be something I could climb in there to gain the advantage. Maybe there was a chair or a table still left. Maybe there was a, uh, a . . . I actually don't know what might have been left in a church because I'd never been to church. Just wasn't in the family.

Not that I was actually thinking all of that. People in stressful situations don't think. They react. I had just about reached the threshold of the church when that feeling I got before, the one when me and the Girl took out Hangnail, filled my body. Something in my gut urged me to stop, and I planted my front leg and dragged my back leg and skidded to a halt. A blur shot in front of me, crashed into what remained of the door frame, and tumbled a dozen feet into the old building where it lay in a heap, still and quiet.

I guess I didn't need the higher ground after all.

I raised my gun and moved forward carefully, well aware that it could be a trap, crunching over old glass, kicking moldy beer cans out of the way. And then I was standing over it. Or him. Because it was a boy. He was lying on his stomach, naked, his long blond hair, tangled and dreadlocked, spilling over his back and shoulders. I nudged one dirty calf with the toe of my boot, but he didn't move.

"Hey! Get up!"

He didn't.

I heard something scrape behind me and I whirled around, gun out, but it was just a crow skittering around the debris.

"Get out of here, old man!" I snapped.

When I turned back around, the blonde boy was on his feet, already lunging for me, arms out. I fired off two shots and hit me, and my gun went flying, and both of us went down. My foot got caught under some of the old subfloor, and I felt a pinch in my leg, the one

Ruth Grace Hogg broke with her field hockey stick. *Oh no,* I thought, and then my head hit the ground and a piercing whine filled my head.

I tried to sit up, but the boy was slung over my body, and even though he looked like he only weighed a buck ten, it was distributed across my legs and chest, so I had to scoot out from under him all while minding my leg because I was fifty percent sure I'd done something bad to it again.

Blood stained my clothes. I hoped it wasn't mine. I had a feeling it wasn't. I managed to get to my feet and try out my leg. It hurt to put weight on it, but it didn't feel broken. At least it didn't feel like the first time I broke it.

"N-no!"

It was the Girl.

She was standing a few feet away, staring at the boy lying face down in the rubble. Her eyes were filled with dread and heartbreak.

"Mmm-mmm," she said. She looked at me, and I felt a powerful hatred vibrating from her body. I held out my hands, saying "Hey, hey" as I backed up. Shadows shuffled out of the corners of the church, and then I saw them.

More kids, my age or a little older. Naked, with long, matted hair obscuring their faces and covering their bodies. At least a half-dozen. I drew Daddy's knife as they fanned out in a circle, and I felt the heat of a dozen plus eyes zooming in on me. That strange, icy feeling filled my belly again, and the power thrummed between us. I wasn't no dummy. I saw what happened to Hangnail. I knew what was going to happen next.

"Don't," I said.

They cinched the noose. I hopped around in a circle, lunging at them with the knife. They all reached for me as one, and the first burst of power seized my frame and my arms and legs shot out, paralyzed. It was like metal rods had been inserted into my bones. My teeth clenched together and my eyes clamped shut. I'd never experienced such a combination of fear, pain, and exhilaration in my life.

Another jolt shot through me, and my arms flew down to my sides, ramming into my thighs, and something popped in my front pocket followed by a metallic ticking sound, and I thought, *Daddy's BB's.* Then I thought, *That's a stupid last thought to have.*

I waited for the end. For the energy to swell inside of me and burn me to a crisp.

And I waited.

And waited.

And waited.

Slowly, I realized that the metal rods were no longer in my arms and that the power, the pain, and the adrenaline were gone.

I thought, *Wait a minute. Why aren't I dead yet?*

I opened my eyes.

I was standing on the ground, safe and sound. And when I looked around me . . . Remember when I told you about the stupidest thing I ever heard? This was even stupider.

All them Macks, because that's what they were, I knew it now, Macks straight from the belly of the Hive itself—maybe not evil Macks, maybe not the kind that we hunted down and killed and piled up and burned last fall, but Macks of a kind. They were all of them staring at Daddy's BB's that had spilled out of my pant leg and spread all over the ground. They were whispering to themselves. I cocked my head, straining to hear what it was they were saying.

"Forty-five, forty-eight, fifty-one, fifty-four."

Holy moly.

They were counting.

Counting the BBs.

Something wet dripped down my leg, and I realized that when the mason jar popped, the glass must have cut my leg. Nothing I could do about it right then. I pressed through the circle and limped a few steps beyond, stopping to cast one more look over my shoulder. They were all still there, whispering away. There were thousands of BBs in that jar. At the rate they were going, it'd take forever to count them all.

~

I found Frankie crumpled up in a ball on the slope of the hill. Timmy Carter was all the way down at the bottom. They were both out cold, but only Timmy Carter came around when I tried to wake him up.

"You okay, Timmy Carter?"

He sat up and checked his arms and legs and torso.

"Head hurts."

"I bet. That little devil kicked a field goal with you."

"Frankie. Is she—"

"She's fine. She's right over there. She's still knocked out, but she's okay."

"You're bleeding," he said, pointing at my leg.

"Yeah. I'm fine, though."

Timmy Carter insisted on picking Frankie up and getting her off the hill. In fact, I think he intended to carry her all the way back to the house by himself, but his knees buckled when he reached the bottom of the slope and I said, "Whoa there, Timmy Carter. You better put her down."

"She's hurt."

"She's going to be a lot more hurt if you drop her."

He set her gently down in the grass and brushed her hair out of her eyes.

"You kill it?"

"Them."

"You kill them?"

"No."

"Why not?"

"Didn't need to."

Timmy Carter had this way of substituting silence for talking. It was a special talent, at least for someone like me. Chances were he didn't mean anything by it half the time; he was just a quiet person. But I could tell he was irritated with me. Probably felt like I was being coy. A breeze kicked up, stirring the tall grass, and I heard a bang in the distance from the direction of the church.

"Let's get Frankie back to the house. I'll tell you all about it on the way back. I'll take the bottom, you take the top."

Took twice as long to get home as it did to get out there. Turns out carrying a 110-pound woman between the two of us wasn't as easy as I thought. I'm a thousand percent sure that Frankie's legs weighed fifty times more than her upper body. It's all about weight distribution, and Frankie had herself some powerful kickers. My leg ached with each step, and the last thing I wanted to do was carry someone through the woods, up and down hills, and across creeks for two miles. Still, I couldn't make Timmy Carter do it alone. He looked as pale as the reaper, and we had to stop several times to give him a rest. Looked like he caught himself a case of the concussions.

I went back out to First Country Baptist later that evening. The Girl and all her friends were gone. To tell you truth, I was a little disappointed. No, it wasn't that. I didn't want to kill any of them. A few hours before, when they were circled around me, blasting my body full of that tendon tearing energy, I actually felt kind of connected to them all. I know that sounds strange given the fact that they actually were trying to kill me, but it's true.

I searched every corner of the dead church but couldn't find any evidence that they were ever there. The only thing I found was Daddy's BBs. They were lying on the ground exactly where they'd fallen. I stared at them for a tick, wondering if I should even bother picking them up. After a while, I did, making sure to count every last one, whispering under my breath as I did so.

". . . three, six, nine, twelve, fifteen, eighteen, twenty-one . . ."

NEVER GIVE UP ON FAMILY

Daddy's brother, my Uncle Zeus, was about as ne'er do well as ne'er do wells get. That boy had problems that ran deeper than the ocean, which was funny because he was about as profound as a puddle. My Nana always knew he was going to be trouble, too.

"Papa Jett was on a bender when he was conceived, and the second he grew feet, he started kicking me like about to lacerate my organs. He was a breech birth, came out all jaundiced, and we had to leave him in the hospital for a week just to get his skin the right color. Damn near cost us the house."

That pretty much defined the rest of Uncle Zeus's life. He refused to walk until he was two, not because he couldn't (he could), but he just liked making life hard for his family. He loved to use his vocal cords, though. Screamed to wake the devil for months after they brought him home, and when he learned how to talk, his first word wasn't "Momma" or "Daddy" but "Hell." (Come to think of it, maybe that was why Daddy always had a hard time with me using that word. I get it because anything associated with Zeus was bound to dredge up bad memories, but he didn't have to take all that out on me.)

Zeus tore a holy terror through Spotsylvania County for twenty years, from elementary school all the way up to the day he robbed a bank and got himself thrown in the federal pen. He was in and out of jail ever since. And every single time he got out, Daddy let him come home and stay in his old room.

It wasn't like Zeus wasn't likable because he was. Charmed the pants off of every woman he met, even the ones he didn't want to sleep with. I wasn't no hussy, but I wasn't no prude neither, and I could understand why women liked him. He wasn't the handsomest but he was funny and merry, always ready with a joke or a great story, and he was always willing to shuck responsibility when something more appealing presented itself. He won me over and broke my heart dozens of times, and I was his own niece.

The last time I saw him was when I was in sixth grade. He'd been staying at our place for about a year, his longest stint going straight since he was in elementary school. Got him a construction job and a bank account, even got himself a girlfriend. I never met her, but Daddy said she was nice.

It all fell apart the morning of my twelfth birthday, when I awoke to quite the gift. Uncle Zeus had stolen my mint condition Mr. Wrinkles do collection, one of Daddy's antique Colt revolvers, and about ten thousand dollars in cash. The Mr. Wrinkles theft was insulting enough, but Daddy was going to use his money to fix up the house. Replace the roof. Get a new hot water heater. Not no more. Uncle Zeus bought him a whole bunch of cocaine, got drunk, and boosted a Cadillac which he promptly ran into Lake Anna.

The look on Daddy's face when he found his safe door wrenched open that morning was a strange mixture of anger, disgust, and sadness, and I didn't know which one would win out until I told him my Mr. Wrinkles collection was gone.

"The collector's edition?"

"Uh-huh."

All the sadness drained out of him, leaving the other two to battle it out. He pressed his lips together, his eyes searching for something, anything, to focus on. I thought his head was going to explode. Then he stomped straight out of the house.

I knew better than to badger him about it, but I was only twelve, and I had a ton of questions, so I waited a full five minutes to follow him. He was in Maurice, going to town on a punching bag hanging from one of the beams. He beat that thing until his face was red as a fire hydrant. When he'd had enough, he went over to his worktable and took a tug from a bottle of whiskey.

"You okay, Daddy?" I asked.

"No. Not yet."

"You mind if I ask you a question?"

"Don't suppose I can stop you."

"What's wrong with him?"

He studied long and hard on it. Between pulls on the bottle.

"Well, Amanda," he said. "I don't rightly know."

"But I'm just a kid. And his niece. Why would he do something like that to me?"

Daddy shrugged.

"There's some people who want to get along in the world and not make no fuss. They're content to follow the rules and live the way they're supposed to because it makes them happy. Then there's some who see the world as the enemy, and they'll bark and rail and rage against it to their dying days for the same reason. Your Uncle Zeus is one of the latters."

Now it was my turn to study on it.

"Will I end up like him?"

I'd never seen Daddy cry, but he came damn close then. His face softened, and he gave me a smile the likes I'd remember for the rest of my life, full of sadness and warmth.

"'Manda May Jett, you're the most caring, loving, beautiful person I ever knew, other'n your mother, of course. You're nothing like your Uncle Zeus, and you never will be. Your Uncle Zeus is a plague upon everyone he ever met. You're the cure."

"Then why do you let him come home whenever he wants?"

"Because he's family. And you never give up on family."

That's why, seven years after the last time I saw him, and less than a year after the end of the world, when Zeus showed up at the farm, I let him stay.

Let me back up a little bit and set the scene.

Early one morning a month after the events at the First Country Baptist church, I sat up in bed in a cold sweat. I'd had the worst nightmare I could remember. Daddy was in it, and he was trying to kill me. I don't remember all the details, just that wherever I ran, that's where he was. The last thing that happened before I woke up was his face in mine as he strangled me to death, and he was saying, "family's family, 'Manda. You belong with me."

I went down to the kitchen and boiled some water on the stove. My water wheel project was cancelled due to lack of interest. The stream had burst through the dam anyway. At least it was running again, which was good for us because since the good well never came back up, and since I didn't know a lick about digging another one, it was the stream or nothing.

The sun had barely peeked out over the tops of the trees when I went out onto the front porch with a cup of tea. I'd just sat down in Daddy's rocker when I saw a figure slip over the east wall and drop into our compound. Rather than panic and start shooting up the place, I decided to watch the events unfold as they would. You might be thinking to yourself, "Now why in the hell'd you want to do that?" No reason, specifically. Except that I only had one bullet left, and I didn't want to waste it.

Then you might think, "Why didn't the wall guard catch what was going on?" and you'd be right to ask yourself that question. The answer is simple: we didn't have enough people to guard the wall anymore. Not 24-7. Three people died from the well-poisoning, and after that, three more figured they'd try their fortunes elsewhere. We took turns minding it at various points during the day, keeping a rotating schedule so that if we were being watched the watchers couldn't ever be sure of when our watch was on watch. What that meant was that sometimes we had people up in the middle of the night and sometimes we didn't. Sometimes the wall was guarded. Sometimes it wasn't.

Don't get me wrong. If I'd seen more forms than one slipping over, I'd have raised the alarm and got to work, but it was clearly just the one, and whoever it was kind of fell over the side all awkward and cussed when he landed because of the thorny bushes we'd planted around the base. That made him scream and cuss some more, using a word that I don't think my Nana would have liked to hear too much, which is saying something considering how much she enjoyed using colorful language. After a minute of watching him flail around, I realized that I didn't have to worry about a thing because if this was a raider or a marauder or a murderer or a Mack or worse, well, first I don't think he would have quite acted that way, and if he was one of them things, he was like to be pretty bad at it.

No. He wasn't nobody I had to worry about coming to rape us and kill us.

He was worse.

I had my suspicions, but it wasn't until I saw him saunter up the driveway, picking prickers and sticky leaves out of his hair and arms and clothes that I understood how much worse. He was muttering to himself, using that style of subsonic critique specific to rural folk the country wide, a kind of running monologue simultaneously describing and complaining about everything around him. He crossed the yard and stepped onto the gravel drive, and I saw who it was.

I thought, "Uh-huh."

Uncle Zeus.

He plucked the last pricker out of his shoulder and gazed at the house with his hands on his hips. He looked like he was thinking "home sweet home," though knowing Zeus, he'd probably put a cuss word between the noun and the adjective. After a second, he started for the front door like he owned the place, like he hadn't been in jail for the last five years. I'd pulled the rocker back in the shadows, and he couldn't really see me, which was probably why, when he reached the front step, he jumped when I said, "That's far enough."

He didn't stop, though. He kind of half-squatted/half-walked a few steps forward, squinting in my direction.

"Who's there? This ain't your house. This here's private property. You'd best be—"

I already had my gun sitting on my thigh, so I checked my clip and snapped it back in. Only had the one bullet, but Uncle Zeus was a Jett and a Spotsylvania boy born and raised. He knew what the sound meant. He stopped and stood straight up.

"You move one more step and that'll be it for you," I said.

"No, it won't."

"Is that a risk you're willing to take?"

He sauntered forward.

"Little girl. If you wanted to shoot me, you already—"

I palmed the slide and chambered the bullet, and Uncle Zeus cowered in place.

"Okay, okay. You take it easy now."

"Call me 'girl' again."

"Well, that's what you are, ain't you?"

"Mister. I could be an old woman or a teenage transvestite and it wouldn't matter one lick. I'm still the one with the gun."

"Transvestite? Look. Where's Bill Jett? He's the rightful owner of this place."

"Not no more."

"What'd you do to him? He had a daughter, too. I swear if you hurt them . . ."

"Daddy's dead, Zeus."

There was a beat you could run a bear through.

"'Manda, that you?"

"Would it matter if I said I wasn't?"

"Ho-ly crow! 'Manda May Jett! Well, hell, g — Well, hell! What's the matter with you? I 'bout near stormed the house. I would've taken you out."

"Who's this?"

That was Timmy Carter. He must have heard the voices. I've already told you how big Timmy Carter was. Man had biceps like a bus, shoulders like mountains, and legs like, well, I don't know. I'm all out of metaphor. Let's just say his legs were huge. It was all gym muscle, true, but gym muscle's still muscle. We didn't have a gym, so he made due. Once I seen him hook up two heavy chains to one of the wall posts and spend the morning shaking them, left right, left right, causing ripples to run up the muscles of his back and shoulders. This was in the middle of February, mind, and Timmy Carter worked up such heat that it plumed off his body in great gouts. It was a marvel to watch.

"Oh, hey Timmy Carter," I said. "This here's my Uncle Zeus. Don't loan him anything valuable."

Zeus said, "Come on, 'Manda. That ain't fair."

"Where's my Mr. Wrinkles?"

That made him think.

"The doll?"

"The collection."

"I—"

"It was a collector's item. I could have used it to go to college."

"'Manda, that was five years ago."

"A cat never does lose its stripes."

"That don't make no sense."

I aimed the gun at him again and stood up. Timmy Carter came up behind me, saying, "Whoa, whoa, whoa."

"Don't worry, Tim," Zeus said. "She's not going to shoot me. Ain't that right, 'Manda."

I studied on it, holding the gun on him. He smiled and I shook my head. Then I put it back in its holster. Timmy Carter let out the breath he was holding and the air lightened considerable. Then Frankie showed up at the door.

"What the hell's all this noise? It's five thirty in the morning."

I turned around and pushed past her and into the house.

"Sorry, Frankie."

"That mean I can come in?" Uncle Zeus called.

"No!" I yelled.

"You can't leave me out here."

"Just watch me."

I retreated a few steps into the hall, far enough so he couldn't see me, and watched to see what would happen next. Uncle Zeus started to walk forward like he was going to come in anyhow, but Timmy Carter stepped in front of him and he backed off, hands up. That made me smile.

Frankie came into the kitchen while I was getting the stove hot for breakfast. Eggs. Again.

That's the thing people don't tell you about owning chickens. You'll never want for eggs. Our coop produced so many that we couldn't eat them fast enough. Not even Timmy Carter. It was our sole source of protein all winter long, and we were all getting mighty sick of them. I couldn't wait for the spring fruits and vegetables to bloom, and not the hothouse hydroponics we grew in the basement all winter, but the real deal. Salt of the earth type stuff. There's a difference in taste. Trust me. I'd already seen some asparagus and strawberries come up. My mouth started watering just thinking about it.

"You can't leave him out there," Frankie said.

"Oh, yes I can. You don't know my Uncle Zeus. He's a liar and a criminal. He'll bring this place down."

Timmy Carter came in.

"You're just going to leave him out there?"

"Aw, hell! You, too, Timmy Carter?"

"Amanda, we're down six people. We're going to need help with this place. You said it yourself."

I pretended to tend to the little flames licking at the kindling. He was right. Daddy used to hire day laborers to help with the fields. We needed at least twelve people to make the farm work during the year. I closed the stove grate with a whine and a clank and clapped my hands on my jeans.

"Fine. But I'll need help keeping an eye on him. He's up to something, I swear. And if he ain't now, he will be."

I didn't have to worry about keeping an eye on him for too long. We found out exactly what he was scheming a few minutes later.

Uncle Zeus sauntered into the house looking like the cat that ate the goldfish. It took all I could take to not punch him in the face. He seen me standing in the kitchen and headed my way. Timmy Carter followed him and threw a .22 and a screwdriver that'd been sharpened to a point onto the counter.

"This is all he had."

"Well, well, well," Zeus said. "Looks like brother Billy did alright for hisself after all. Fixed this place up nice."

The smile on his face as he looked around reminded me of a fox.

"Don't touch anything," I said.

"'Manda, is that any way to talk to family? You been right ornery since I snuck over your little wall."

"You're surrounded by a bunch of people with guns, Zeus. They might not know you, but I do, and they like me, and I don't like you. So I'll let you do the figuring on that one."

He shot a look at Timmy Carter.

"You mean Hercules over here? I faced down bigger meat than him in Petersburg."

"I'm sure you have."

"Big guys always fall the hardest."

"See, Zeus. That's the thing you don't understand here. In prison, maybe you got to fight one on one. Maybe you had that shiv or some other weapon. And maybe you could beat Timmy Carter up. I doubt it, but let's just pretend you could. But out here, in my house, if that happened, I'd just use it as an excuse to shoot you in the back of the head."

Zeus whistled and laughed.

"Well damn, 'Manda! If you ain't the sweetest little peach."

"Don't call me that."

"You used to like it when I called you that. I'm beginning to think Billy never taught you no manners."

"Manners? You mean like the ones you learned in prison?" He gave me a tight smile. "What do you want, Zeus? Food? Water? Take some eggs and a jug and get the hell out."

"That ain't what I want."

I followed his eyes as he cased the kitchen.

"You looking for Daddy's stash? Golly gumdrops if you ain't the stupidest man alive."

"Well, where is it?"

"Gone, Zeus!"

"All of it? The whole crop? When?"

"When do you think? Before all this happened."

"Well, that's a mite disappointing, but fortunately for you, that ain't why I'm here."

"You mind telling me why, then?"

Then Zeus did the strangest thing. He hunched forward a little and cocked his head like he was listening for something.

I'd just about had enough.

"What are you d—"

"Shh!"

I looked at Timmy Carter, who shrugged.

"Seriously, Uncle Zeus."

"Just give it a minute."

Then we heard it. First the sound of a revved up engine, then the sound of a massive crash, then men yelling, then gunfire. The window shattered and I hit the deck. Timmy Carter said, "Frankie," and ran off. Uncle Zeus took the opportunity to snatch his knife and .22 off the counter, and by the time I was on my feet, he was already aiming it at me.

"You gonna regret talking to me the way you done."

Zeus marched me across the property to the gate. Or what was left of it. Men I ain't never seen before were running all over the place.

Fully armed men. A couple of our guys were running out of the house, firing at the attackers. One was shot to bits a few feet from me. Another managed to hit one of the intruders before he got lit up from all sides.

My good-for-nothing uncle walked me through it all, not even ducking, his long hair breathing behind him in the new morning sun. Storm clouds were rolling in from the west. I could see them dark and dangerous in the pink and orange sky. Timmy Carter and Frankie were already kneeled up against the wall, their hands clasped over their heads, and Zeus pushed me up against it next to them.

"Mother Absalom!" he yelled. "I got me some fresh meat." He turned to us. "You're going to like Mother Absalom. She's a right funky animal."

One of our people, a woman named Betty, ran out of the gate, heading for the woods, half-dressed. She shot a panicked look over her shoulder, and Uncle Zeus fired off a wild shot and missed.

"Come on, Zeus!" someone yelled.

And then she appeared. Mother Absalom. The tallest, baddest, ugliest beast I ever seen. If Ruth Grace Hogg had an older sister, she would have looked just like Mother Absalom, gorilla arms, monobrow, beard and all. She wore her hair in a mullet mohawk (it's a thing, trust me), had a wallet on a chain clipped to her Dickies, and preferred her flannel jeans jacket sleeveless.

I didn't blame her for that last one. Gorilla arms is gorilla arms, and hers was particularly impressive. The snake tattoo she had rolling in and out of the muscular lumps of her biceps and triceps only made it that much cooler looking. And did she carry a gun? Of course not. If you're going to adopt the fashion choices of a lumberjack, you better be prepared to arm yourself like one, which was why she was carrying two axes.

Throwing axes, that is.

Mother Absalom.

She took three steps and hurled one of them at Betty, caught her right in the back. Betty went down hard, bounced in the gravel, and lay there, arms out, body twitching.

"If you're going to use that thing, better make the bullets count," Mother Absalom said to Zeus.

She tromped over to Betty's body and ripped the axe out of her back. Then she stomped back our way, wiping the blade off on her pants.

"That your niece?" she asked Zeus.

"Yeah. 'Manda May Jett, meet Mother Absalom."

"I'm sure she don't care one bit, Zeus."

"Manners is manners."

"You learn that in the pen?"

"That's funny. 'Manda said the same thing."

"I guess we're just two peas in a pod." She stopped in front of me and scowled. "Well, it looks like you picked the wrong man for an uncle."

"Funny how I already knew that."

"Ha! You're right, Zeus. I do like her."

"She's got her daddy's sharp tongue alright," Zeus said. "She don't watch it, I'm like to cut it out."

"Oh come on now. I'm sure that won't be necessary."

A few fat drops of rain splattered in the dirt. Timmy Carter and Frankie were looking west at the clouds. They were closer now, and darker. I'd never seen a storm move in so fast.

"Looks like we gonna have us a goat-drowner," Zeus said.

Mother Absalom laughed.

"Goat-drowner! I like that."

I said to Timmy Carter, "get ready."

"Shut up, girl!" Mother Absalom yelled. She backhanded me so hard my teeth clacked.

If you didn't know it already, I was getting awfully sick of everybody calling me that. But my feelings about the matter were trumped by the sight of the last one of our people, a man named Vernon, dashing out of the gate. He took a pot shot at Zeus and Mother Absalom, and it went wide. As he back-peddled, Mother Absalom whipped her axe at him fast as a snake strike, and it thudded right into his chest. He fell dead on the spot. Mother Absalom tsked as if she didn't relish the task

"Shame. That there was a strong one. Could've used him." She looked down at my face with an expression that was almost regretful. "You know, usually I try to say something smart in situations like this. Take my time. Draw out the suspense. But I don't feel like that today."

She took out her second axe and twirled it in her hands. For the first time in my life, I seen a mote of doubt ripple across Uncle Zeus's face.

"Hold on, Mother Absalom."

"What do you want, Zeus?"

"This wasn't part of the deal."

"Yeah, well. I changed my mind."

It happened so quick that I didn't even have time to react. Mother Absalom stepped toward me and raised her axe over her head. I closed my eyes. Uncle Zeus said, "Wait! No!" And then a sonic boom sounded from the west, hit so hard that it shook the ground. The mulleted crazy-woman standing over me stopped.

"What the hell was that?"

We all craned our necks toward the sound. A black line of rain was rushing toward us, a wall, really, advancing like nature's storm troopers. Lightning flashed inside its core, and the rumble grew louder and louder. Trees cracked as the wall ripped forward, and I was brought back to two months before when I first met the girl out in the middle of that blizzard.

I knew what was about to happen next, and the worst thing was that I couldn't do anything about it. We were already backed against Daddy's wall. Frankie had the right idea. She hopped up to her feet and ran. Mother Absalom spun around and launched the axe at her, but Timmy Carter rammed her knee with his shoulder and the axe flew strange. He didn't have to do that, though, because the wind picked it up like it was a toy and blew it up and up and up until we couldn't see it anymore.

He was on Mother Absalom fast as a fox. He head-butted her and she grunted, and then he popped up and put one knee on her chest and one in her neck. Mother Absalom wasn't one to be easily subdued, though. She punched him right in the balls and he keeled over to the side.

Then the storm was on us, and with it, the two black balls roared across the landscape, tearing up the earth. Lightning zapped the wall in three spots, and it exploded with shards of wood and metal. A group of Uncle Zeus's men was impaled. Mother Absalom, who was on her feet now, standing over the prone figure of Timmy Carter, was sucked into the sky, followed close behind by Uncle Zeus, then Timmy Carter, then me.

I don't know if any of y'all ever been sucked into the sky by a super-mega-death-ball-storm, but it feels a whole lot like being an ant in a clothes drier. I was whipped around in all directions, this way and that, and my neck felt like it was going to break clean in two. Those of you who think it was anything like being Dorothy in *The Wizard of Oz* have another think coming. First of all, she was in a house, and second of all, that was a book, dummy, and a fantasy book written for kids. Ain't no way it mimicked reality in the slightest.

Mother Absalom whipped by, screaming and spinning like a top. Timmy Carter passed me next, twisting and tumbling. I might have seen Uncle Zeus but couldn't be sure. Chunks of rocks and dirt and trees zipped all around us. A hunk of earth struck me in my bad leg and it felt like the old fault line cracked. Then Uncle Zeus really did fly by me, screaming all kinds of filth he probably learned in prison, at least until a tree branch hit him in the head and knocked him cold.

Gradually, though, the winds started to die down. Happened abruptly, like we'd hit a wall. We dropped in stages, a hundred fast feet at a time. Stole the breath from my lungs. If that wasn't scary enough, the rain and clouds started clearing up, and I saw what was going to happen to us.

There was a Hive sitting in an open field, it's pink and green flap pulsing in the dying storm. And we were heading right for it.

The wind turned from feral to focused, and I found myself shooting along a tube funneling me directly into it. I thought about the prior fall when I blew up my first Hive with a stuffed dog crammed with explosives. I thought about the first time I killed a Mack, Seb Mack, that little runt. And I thought about poor, pregnant Lynn and Charlene and

Dez and Gomez Gomez. Maybe this was finally payback for all the wrong I done to them, even if they were the enemy. Even if they were trying to kill me first. Oh well. There was nothing to do about it now.

I shot into the hive's opening with a wet slurp.

At first it was dark. And warm. And smelly. "Smells like roasted goat shit," Daddy had said at one time. He was not inaccurate. Little by little, the smell grew worse, or better, I couldn't tell. Was I just getting used to it and then my brain, realizing how bad it was, reset.

I was on my knees, and my hands and feet were bound by something soft, slick, and slithery. I heard a sniff and some movement and realized that there were other people in there with me.

"Hello?" I said.

"'Manda, that you?"

Great. Uncle Zeus.

"I'd just about hoped you were dead, Uncle Zeus."

"Now that's just hurtful."

"Well, it's true."

"I can't say I feel the same about you. You shouldn't take this personal, you know."

I laughed.

"Which part? The sneaking onto my farm and being a lying jerk part? Or the killing my friends and trying to kill me part?"

"You always were a smart little princess, you know that? I never knew why Billy didn't take a whip to you."

"Probably because I'd take that whip away and beat him with it."

Now it was his turn to laugh.

"That's what I'm talking about right there. If you were my daugh—"

"You can stop right there, Zeus. I ain't your daughter, and I never will be."

"You as cold as a witch's titty, girl."

"And you're as stupid as stupid comes."

He snorted, and that's where we let it lie for a time.

Gradually, the darkness gave way to a sickly, green light, and I saw that we weren't the only ones in there. We'd been stored in some kind of circular chamber, the walls of which breathed and pulsed, breathed and pulsed like the lungs of an animal, which, I guess, it was. The green was warmed by pink all of the sudden, creating a color combination that I'm sure only the homeless or drunk people was familiar with. I could see a lot better though. All around the chamber were other people, all of them on their knees, just like me. Some of them were alive. Some were so decomposed that they was little more than skeletons. And there were some weird skeletons in there, too. Bodies and shapes I'd never seen before.

Zeus was opposite of me, Timmy Carter between us to the right, his head hanging on his chest. Mother Absalom was between us on the left, and she was coming around. If I was at six and Zeus was at twelve, Timmy Carter was three and Mother Absalom nine. I wondered if this had been done for a reason.

"What the holy horseshit is all this?" Mother Absalom muttered. She read the room, saw the dead and the living, and the weird skeletons, too, and a sneer formed on her lips. "Zeus, you got to—"

"Working on it."

"Well, work faster."

The pink and green lights pulsed on and off in a clear rhythm, accompanied by an electric hum that rose and fell. Then an opening formed at my one, first a line with folds, then lips, then a hood, then the opening itself. The smell grew worse, stronger, accompanied by a squelching sound and, even worse than that, scrabbling and chittering, like a horde of insectile crabs was stampeding our way.

And wouldn't you know it?

That's exactly what poured out of that slit: dozens of insectile crabs. Crabs by themselves is insectile enough with them eyes on stalks, but these ones scrambled about not just on crazy crab legs but also on what looked like dozens of little feelers on the bottom of their bodies.

I didn't pay too much attention in Biology, but I knew enough to know that that wasn't right. Didn't help that they was covered in white fur, neither, like polar bears. All in all it was, by definition, the creepiest thing I ever seen.

Then they started eating everybody.

Swarmed the first body they seen and picked it clean like, well, like crab-things swarming a body, I guess. Fortunately it was a dead body, but that don't mean it wasn't the most godawful sound I never wanted to hear.

There's a condition called 'Misophonia'. I learned about it in psychology. Have you ever been driven crazy by sounds? Maybe like the sound of people eating makes you want to stab them in the ear? You got yourself a bad case of Misophonia. People eating don't bother me, probably because I'm pretty bad about smacking and slurping and chewing and gulping myself. But hearing them crab-things smack and slurp and chew and gulp down all them dead bodies make me study hard on developing myself a case of the Misophonia.

Then they hit the first live person and it got exponentially worse. I don't think I have to explain how adding screams and cries and moans and pleading to all the other stuff would create an untenable listening situation. They made their way around the circle counterclockwise, and it looked like Mother Absalom would be the first of our little foursome to be eaten.

"Zeus!" she yelled.

"I said I'm working on it!"

They finished the dead man lying next to her and scrabbled over.

"Zeus!"

"Almost there!"

It was too late. They were on her. Zoomed over that gross, breathing floor and started on her feet. She was screaming and cussing (Daddy would *not* have approved), then Zeus popped free, wielding that shiv in his hand. He waded into the melee, stomping and kicking and sweeping them things off her. They scattered, unaccustomed, I assumed, to any sort of resistance. Zeus reached behind Mother Absalom and cut her loose, and she fell flat on her face. Based on the way her legs looked, the missing chunks and the associated bleeding and such, falling on her face was probably the most appropriate reaction. It shouldn't have bothered me one bit, not after what she done to me and mine, but it did. That's the difference between a person like me and a person like her: I feel empathy.

The crabs regrouped and moved on to the next easiest target, that being a dead woman lying next to where Mother Absalom just was. Meanwhile, Zeus dragged her to the center of the chamber. Then he came over to me and started cutting away at my tentacle binds. When he was done, I got shakily to my feet and rubbed my wrists, trying to get the blood flowing into them again.

"Give me that," I said, looking at his shiv.

"Why, so you can—"

I punched him in the nose. I wasn't a super strong girl, and I sure wasn't no pugilist, but between Daddy and them self-defense classes, I knew how to break a nose.

"Ow! Goddammit, 'Manda!"

Zeus's hands flew up to his face, and as the blood poured down his chin and between his fingers, I pried the shiv out of his grip and set over to Timmy Carter, who was still passed out.

"You broke my nose!" Zeus yelled.

I cut the tentacles off Timmy Carter and tried to catch him as he fell, but that man was too much muscle for me.

"That was the plan."

"I just saved your life!"

"Gimmie a break, Zeus. Help me with him."

Between the two of us, we managed to drag him over to the middle of the chamber next to Mother Absalom. Then I set to stabbing and ripping apart the wall. Zeus joined me. The crabs picked up speed, moving from body to body faster and faster. Before long, they'd be on us again. I cut a fist-sized hole in the side and punched all the way through, and fresh air filled the Hive and oh, I never thought I'd smelled something as clean and clear and wonderful as that.

I was about to start ripping more hunks out when the crab-things all stopped, perking up their eye-stalks as if they'd heard a silent alarm. Then they filed as one toward the slit in the wall they'd come out of and disappeared into it. Zeus and I stood there watching it, amazed, then shared a glance.

"That don't seem good to me," he said.

"Uh-uh."

The green and pink lights warmed up again, and down through the top of the chamber, a form appeared, feet first, then legs, then torso, floating down to us with his arms spread out, palms up.

It was Daddy.

He looked at me and Zeus when he landed, a beatific expression on his face. Then he held his arms out to me and said, "'Manda."

"'Manda, don't you move," Zeus said.

"I ain't going nowhere."

Because that wasn't Daddy. I knew that. It might have been a thing that looked like him, just like the thing that looked like my momma, but it wasn't him. If I went over, he'd unhinge his jaw and send another nest of tentacles out at me, and I'll tell you what, I'd had enough of people with nests of tentacles in their mouths sending them out at me.

Daddy's smile twitched. He looked down at Timmy Carter and Mother Absalom lying unconscious on the pulsing floor, and with a twitch of his hand, he flung them to either side of the chamber. Their eyes flew open and their bodies went rigid, and I could tell they were trying to scream, but no sound came out.

Daddy turned that smile on me.

"I just want to talk, 'Manda."

You probably know that I didn't care a lick about Mother Absalom, but Timmy Carter'd become a good friend to me over the course of the past year. He was as kind and capable a person as anybody would ever want to meet, and seeing him suffer like that at the hands of a monster that not only killed my Daddy but had the gumption to take on his skin, boiled my blood if you know what I mean. I palmed the shiv against my forearm, feeling the point of it press into my skin.

"Okay," I said. "But put them down, first."

Daddy smiled even wider.

"Okay, 'Manda. Anything for my little sweet pea."

He dropped his hands, and Mother Absalom and Timmy Carter dropped.

"'Manda, don't," Uncle Zeus said.

"Shut up, Uncle Zeus."

And I started walking across the floor, trying to ignore the squelching my shoes made. Daddy held his arms out to me now, a soft expression on his face that, if I didn't know any better, I might have mistook for love. But it wasn't love. It was greed.

"That's right, girl. Come to me. It will all be over soon."

I closed my eyes when I reached him, let his arms drape around me. But before he could complete his embrace, I brought the shiv up behind him and jammed it through the back of his head.

He squealed and twisted, and a blast of power shot out of his hands, sending me flying backward. I hit the wall and fell, but it didn't knock me out. That was the Hive's one serious design flaw. Everything was soft and giving. I got up on my hands and knees.

Daddy was twirling around the chamber. He grabbed the shiv and yanked it out of his head, and green, slimy fluid spewed out of it in a torrent, and then it was his turn to fall to his knees. He stayed there, staring at us. He burped up some green stuff that stained his mouth and ran down his chin.

"You're going to die. All of you. You think you can—"

Uncle Zeus stomped up to him and kicked him in the face. Daddy fell back, and Zeus stomped on his head until green jelly came out.

Then the crabs came back. They poured in from two slits this time, more and more of them. They swarmed over Daddy's body, swarmed over the other bodies, swarmed over everything that was between us and them.

Me and Zeus ran to the part of the wall we'd already tore open and started digging away with our hands. Purple and green fluid ran out over my arms, burning my skin. We ripped and tore and ripped tore until I felt certain I could get a body through. Zeus jumped back and started dragging Mother Absalom by the arms, and we pushed and bullied her through, then we went for Timmy Carter and did the same to him.

A crab scuttled for Zeus' leg and he jumped up and stomped on it. Another one chomped on his foot and he screamed and reached down to pull it off, and that was his fatal mistake. Three more leaped onto his arms and shoulders. Then another and another. I knocked one off but it didn't do much good. Zeus turned to me, a look of profound surprise and regret on his face, and said, "'Manda. Go."

"But—"

"Dammit, girl! Go!"

He turned around to face the throng of monsters flowing like an ocean toward him and threw himself in the middle of it all. They swarmed.

Mother Absalom was dead. Bled out from her wounds, I guess. Timmy Carter, thank goodness, was not. He was shook up, light-headed, and sick, but he had nary an injury on him.

The storm had brought us clear into Caroline County, a few miles south of Lake

Caroline herself. I knew exactly how to get back, but with Timmy Carter being injured again, it took us more than half the remainder of the day to walk home.

Not that it mattered.

The walls were completely destroyed, and the barn, and Maurice, and the house, too. Mother Absalom's men and our people lay dead all over the torn up fields. Timmy Carter searched and searched for Frankie, calling her name until he went hoarse, but she never showed up. We never found her body, neither.

I fell to my knees in front of what used to be my front porch and looked around the destruction, dazed. I had no idea what to do next.

THE HIVE

SEASON 3

unDEFEATED

Daddy, like most men of his generation, loved football. In the fall, he went to every Spotsy home game on Friday, watched a few college games on Saturday, and settled in every Sunday for a few hours to curse and fume at the Redskins. He loved it so much that he even played it in high school, a fact he liked to remind me of. Frequently. He really liked to bring it up whenever he watched my soccer or field hockey games, which was pretty much every time I had a soccer or field hockey game.

"It's like Coach used to tell me all the time. 'Jett! You need to be more aggressive!'."

"Is this the time you made that one interception or the time you blew your coverage during the playoffs?"

"You can be as smart-alecky as you want, little girl, but I know what I'm talking about. I was the—"

I joined in to finish the sentence with him.

"—starting linebacker for the Spotsylvania Knights three years running."

"Haha, 'Manda. You can make fun of me all you want, but we—"

"Won states two years running."

He usually fell silent after that, and I'd have to spend the rest of the day being extra nice to him. Sometimes it worked, but Daddy could be prickly, so if it didn't, the best course of action was complete avoidance. You might call that cowardly, but I call it smart. Time heals everything, from fist fights to murder, and hurt feelings ain't no different. And I definitely was not a coward. I wasn't weak or shy out on the field. I played my position, I did my job, and I never got angry, even if we were losing bad, even if the other team played dirty.

The one time I expressed something close to poor sportsmanship (we lost a soccer game to a team that liked to cheat and get physical for no reason, then complain about it, and I refused to shake their hands afterward), Daddy chewed me out when we got back in the truck.

"But Daddy, they were throwing elbows and kicking our knees."

"I don't care 'Manda. Learn from it and figure out how to beat them next time."

"That ain't right. Why should I take the high road when they obviously can't?"

"Because it's not what we do. They want to act like jerks, let 'em. But I'll be a monkey if I'm going to let my own daughter do the same."

When it came to that particular subject, it didn't get any better between us the next season. That was the year I turned thirteen and started eighth grade. The trials and tribulations of The Sexy Seven were two years behind me, and I, along with the rest of the school, had moved well past them sorry little witches. Oh, there were still cliques and cabals. Our school was firmly stratified into a dozen different categories. Of course, there were the conventional striations. Jocks. Goths. Nerds. Losers. Pretty People. But as we grew up and took on more interests, even those time-tested groups began to cleave. Some of the Jocks were also smart. Some of the Pretty People were also Goths. It was downright confusing to most of the adults in our world, but the kids knew what was going on.

As for me, I staked my flag firmly with the Soccer Girls. We were a lively bunch. Maybe we weren't the most academic, and maybe we weren't the best looking, but we stuck to each other as tight as ticks, from the sleekest striker to the brawniest back. Nobody messed with us, not even the remnants of The Sexy Seven (now pared down to the Sexy Three).

It was all because of our coach, Wendy Wulfang. (We all called her Windy behind her back, not because she liked to talk or even because she was out of shape (she wasn't) but because we were kids and we couldn't come up with nothing better.) Windy Wulfang was the exact opposite of my Daddy in every way possible. Actually, that's not completely true. They were both about six feet tall and weighed somewhere between two twenty and two thirty-five. After that, the similarities stopped. Where Daddy was quiet and reserved, Coach Wulfang was loud and brash. Where Daddy avoided conflict like the plague, Coach Wulfang didn't just invite it, she created it. And where Daddy's view on competition was "play fair, play good, and respect your opponent," Coach Wulfang's was "win at all costs." It was a dichotomy that led to some pretty tense situations, and not just between Daddy and Coach Wulfang.

To Daddy's credit, after one particularly heated discussion in which he finally had enough and confronted her on the wiseness of her decision to have me take out their lead defender, an action that got me red-carded, he dropped the whole thing. I remember the conversation well. He was driving me back from the game, one hand on the wheel, the other picking at his lip. He wouldn't talk to me or look at me, and when I turned the radio on, he reached over and turned it off.

"Daddy, are you mad at me?" I asked.

I actually saw him decide to pull himself together. He took a breath and let it go. Then he cleared his throat.

"No, 'Manda. I ain't mad at you. I don't like what happened out there on that field, though."

"I get that."

"Are you okay with it?"

It took me a bit of figuring, but eventually I said, "Yeah. Yeah, I am."

"You don't think that was the least bit uncalled-for?"

"It's a part of the game. That's what you've always told me. Someone tries to take me out, tough. Shut up and do your job, right?"

That quieted him down. We came to a stop sign, and he sat there for a while. The turn signal ticked and tocked.

"'Manda, you might've wrecked that girl's knee."

"I know, Daddy. I don't feel good about that part."

"Do you feel good about any of this stuff?"

"What stuff?"

"Soccer. This year. Your coach."

I didn't even hesitate.

"We're undefeated."

Undefeated was the exact opposite of the way I felt the month after them hive balls destroyed my house, my farm, and everything and everybody I had left in the world. Barring Timmy Carter, of course. To be honest, I don't know exactly how I felt other than angry. And that anger boiled up inside me day in and day out, hotter than the summer sun, and that year was one of the hottest I'd ever experienced.

"It's not healthy to hold on to all that hate, Amanda," Timmy Carter said.

"I don't care."

"I don't think you know what you're talking about."

"Maybe I don't, Timmy Carter. But maybe you don't, neither."

"Okay."

"Do me a favor, huh?" Timmy Carter looked at me, waiting for what I was going to say. Almost made me feel bad. "Keep your mouth shut, okay?"

"What?"

"Unless you want to talk about killing Macks or burning Hives, there ain't nothing for us to say to each other."

I shouldn't have been so nasty to him. He'd stuck by me through nearly everything so far. It wasn't like he hadn't suffered a loss. We never did find Frankie. But I was still a teenager, and I was immature, and I felt like my pain was the only thing that mattered. Worse thing was that I knew I was acting selfish, knew I was wrong, and I wasn't particularly proud of that, so I tried to overcome it the only way I knew how. Revenge. I was going to kill The Girl, and I was going to make sure it hurt.

The one miraculous thing about the destruction of my family house was the fact that the gun safe didn't fly away. Daddy'd anchored it into one of the metal support beams which itself was anchored into the concrete foundation. Sure it bent backward, but it remained intact. That's good old American construction values right there.

All of Daddy's guns were in perfect condition, too. Timmy Carter and I had a devil of a time taking the bolts out and moving the safe into the hole that used to be the cellar, but we managed. That's where we camped out. Put a tarp up to keep out the weather, gathered what cans we could find, and made due. At night, we hugged our guns and hoped for the best. During the day, we did us some hive hunting. Would've made Daddy proud, dedicated, as he was, to recycling and hunting and all.

I've talked about Virginia weather before, how we could see all four seasons (with all their subtleties and quirks) in a day, usually in spring and fall. But summer in the state that kills tyrants could be downright oppressive. I know, I know. My lone star brothers and sisters might have a bone to pick about that particular complaint (not to mention my creole, dixie, and sooner relatives), but that's like making fun of Californians for freaking out during a cyclone. Weather is relative. We're used to what we're used to.

The morning we set out to kill The Girl and all them was one of the hottest, most humid mornings I could ever remember. The night hadn't been all that much better, but at least the sun wasn't out. Once the old girl peeked over the tops of the trees and spread herself over the earth, our tarp caught the brunt of it, and sleep, as elusive as it was before, was more than an impossibility.

We set about the makeshift camp, quietly getting ready for the mission. I boiled some water from the stream for our coffee, and Timmy Carter broke out the fancy stuff for breakfast: SPAM and peaches in syrup, both of them straight from the can. We ate and pondered. I started to feel bad about how I'd treated Timmy Carter the day before, so I said, "Timmy Carter?"

"Yeah."

"I'm sorry about what I said."

"What'd you say?"

"About not talking to me unless we were talking about killing." He did his silent thing, as he was wont. "You're right. I'm angry. But it feels good right now. I think I need to use it."

"I get it."

"I knew you would."

He up-ended his can of peaches and drank the syrup, and when he was done, he put the can in the crate we were filling up with the empties. Then he said, "You mind if I give you some advice?"

"As long as it's good advice."

"Hate's a powerful engine, 'Manda. You let it burn too long, it'll blow you out."

I didn't have anything to say to that. I wasn't ready.

We geared up, strapping as many weapons as we could to our arms and legs. I took my

Magnum and Daddy's Bowie knife, of course, as well as one of his hunting rifles. Timmy Carter took a shotgun, a Glock, and a machete. I watched him strapping all of that firepower to his body, wondering how it'd turn out if we actually ran into something that needed that many bullets to put it down. Not that it mattered. We were low on ammo. Gun's useless without it. Maybe that's why he took the machete. He climbed out of the foundation pit and reached down to pull me up.

"You sure you want to do this?" he asked.

"Yeah, Timmy Carter. I think I told you enough times."

"You didn't exactly have a positive experience there."

"Listen, I appreciate you being concerned for my well-being, but there ain't no need for you to protect me. You're not my daddy, you're not my husband, and even if you was, I'd still tell you to back off."

"That's not what I meant."

"Would you have asked me that if I was a man?"

"Amanda, you need to back off."

"Then don't—"

"There's no reason to do this. Why can't you just let it alone?"

"It ain't only about her. You remember what we ate for breakfast this morning right? And for dinner last night?"

"Yeah, but—"

"We're out of food. The Food Bank is empty. This is the only place I know that might have something."

"How can you be sure?"

"I ain't, but you saw the place. It's got plenty of land, and solar power, and greenhouses. There's bound to be something there we can use."

"Okay."

"Okay? That it? No more arguing? No more lecturing. No more asking me if I'm sure I want to do this?"

"Okay is okay."

"Well, okay, then."

We filled our canteens from the boiled water left over from breakfast, then headed south, following the creek that paralleled Brock Road. After about two miles, we turned east. It was going to be a long hike. And hot. I'd sweated through my clothes by mid-morning.

The woods were thick and lush already, reminding me of mid-summer even though it wasn't even close to mid-summer yet. And things were crashing around in the brush that were bigger than what I normally heard crashing around in there. I wasn't no expert on nature, but I seen me an episode of National Geographic or two, and I swear at one point I heard a heavy huffing, like the sound a gorilla made, and if you don't know anything about gorillas and Spotsylvania County, Virginia, the Piedmont area is not their native habitat. Seconds later, I caught a glimpse of the rear end of a kangaroo bouncing away, leaping through the bush like a, well, like a kangaroo, which was a bit of a shock as kangaroos were also not native to this place.

"Timmy Carter. Did you—"

"Yeah, I saw it."

He slapped the back of his neck, grimacing, and when he pulled his hand away, it was covered in green gook and his own red blood, and the insect, or whatever it was that bit him, was crushed in his palm. Timmy Carter had himself a lot of palm, too, and that bug was squished all over it.

"That don't look like no mosquito I ever seen," I said.

"No kidding."

"Is that fur?"

"I think so."

He wiped his hand off on a tree.

"Let's get out of the woods, huh?"

We double-timed it as best we could, but it was pretty hard to march and keep an ear out for weird creatures at the same time. Timmy Carter took the lead, using his machete to cut away the creepers and the palms that seemed to belong more in a jungle than they did here. We reached a clearing about halfway to the reservoir, and I stopped to take a drink.

"You ever feel it this hot this early?" I asked.

Timmy Carter had paused right in front of me, seeming to listen to something out in the woods. Then he fell into a squat and yanked me down with him.

"Shh!" he hissed.

"What is it?"

"Listen."

I did, and I heard what he was talking about. A clicking sound followed by the noise of millions of little things moving through the underbrush. Fast. And I knew exactly what was heading our way.

"Timmy Carter, we've got to get out of here."

I spun around, looking for an escape. Maybe we could find a cave or a rock fort, something we could hide in, but there wasn't too much in the way of caves or forts of any kind in that part of the Spotsylvania wilderness. But we did have trees. I pointed at a nearby oak.

"There!"

"The branches look dead."

"Not the lowest one."

"How do you know?"

"It's that or nothing."

The lowest branch was a doozy, plenty thick and plenty strong, but it hung a foot higher than I could jump. After the third, futile leap, Timmy Carter said, "Let me try."

He jumped and jumped, even took a running start and used the trunk to kick off, but he still couldn't quite grab the branch.

"I'll hoist you up," he said, and he linked his hands for me to step into them.

"And then what? You think I can pull you up myself?"

"You're right. Got any rope?"

"No I don't got—you know I don't have any!"

The clicking and chittering grew nearer, reminding me of a wave of cicadas, rising and falling, rising and falling.

"We're out of time," I said. "You get on my shoulders and grab the limb."

"You can't hold my weight."

"It's all I got, Timmy Carter."

He paused, doubtful, and a polar crab scrabbled out of the brush, one of them gnarly leg-eaters that killed Uncle Zeus. It stopped when it saw us and raised up on its hind legs, front claws waving in the air. It might have been cute if I didn't know what it was capable of. When it was done with its little dance, it shot forward, aiming for Timmy Carter's feet. Timmy Carter backed up, shocked, and I lunged forward and crushed the nasty critter under my boot, stomped it three times, four times, ten times more just to make sure it was dead. Timmy Carter looked like he'd swallowed a bug—maybe that furry one that he smashed against his neck.

"Is that—?"

"Yeah, Timmy Carter. I told you about them. Now are you going to get on my shoulders or what?"

He nodded, still looking at the mess of white fur and gray and green guts that used to be the polar crab, but he didn't move.

"Hey!" I snapped. I clapped in his face and his eyes clicked on mine. "Let's go!"

I didn't have to squat down too far for him to get on my back, but he was right about the weight. I couldn't stand up straight. First I fell into the trunk with my face, then I reeled back and started to stumble the wrong direction.

"Wrong way! Wrong way!" Timmy Carter yelled.

"I'm trying!"

The first big wave of polar crabs scuttled through the dead leaves to my left. They weren't heading directly at us, not at first, but when their eye stalks seen us, the whole swarm turned as one.

Timmy Carter leaned back toward the trunk, and once our momentum started, we couldn't stop. I stumble-ran, tripped and fell, and then the weight was off my shoulders, and I was face down in the dirt. The first polar-crab bit into my boot and I pushed myself off the ground.

"Amanda, here!"

I reached up blindly, and Timmy Carter grabbed my wrist yanked me off the ground. The polar-crab kept gnawing away, its teeth piercing my leather boot, and then I was on the branch, hanging like a sack over either side. That dang polar-crab didn't seem to be bothered one bit. It finally chewed through the leather and its teeth bit into my toes and I screamed like I never screamed before.

I been plenty injured. Already told you about most of them. But there was something about getting eaten by that weird space crustacean that freaked me out. I guess it was because I'd seen what it did to Mother Absalom and Uncle Zeus. I'm not sure how to explain it, but I think it must have tapped into one of my deepest, darkest, most primal fears.

If pulling yourself up on a branch and turning around to sit on it is a delicate maneuver on its own, try doing it with a space crab eating your foot. When I was finally in position, I whipped out my Bowie and sliced off its stalk-eyes. Timmy Carter tried to pull it off, but it just sank its teeth into my meat and I *screamed.*

"Ahh! Jeez! Knock it off, Timmy Carter!"

He put up his hands in surrender. That polar-crab was latched on tight, I'll tell you that much, but I knew what to do. See, every summer, Daddy liked to have himself a crab feast. Invited all his army buddies and a couple of our neighbors over to the farm, set up a whole bunch of picnic tables, and spent the afternoon drinking beer and eating crabs.

My point is that I wasn't a stranger to crab anatomy, and if these was in any way similar to the things I'd ate for as long as I could remember, then getting it off was only a matter of cracking it open. Hurt like a bitch turning my foot to get to its underside, but pain's a mighty good motivator (as well as the threat of having my toes eaten while I was still alive). I jammed my knife into its apron and yanked up, pulling its shell in two, and it sprayed Timmy Carter in the face with a squirt of black bile. Then I gutted it with six quick swipes, scraped the bottom half off and dropped the top after it. Both pieces landed in the herd rushing beneath us below.

I'm not sure which I liked better—the relief of getting that damn thing's teeth out of my foot or the look on Timmy Carter's face.

"You okay, 'Manda?"

"I'll be fine, I—"

Then the whole tree shook so hard that I thought it'd been rammed by an elephant, or maybe that kangape thing I'd seen earlier. I nearly fell off. We waited, holding onto the branch as tight as we could. I even wrapped my good leg around it. Then another blast came, and another, and another. The trees to my left shook and cracked and fell, sending birds scattering into the air, and out of the brush a huge bug, a bug the likes of which I'd never seen, marched into the clearing.

The polar-crabs were weird enough, but at least they was built on a scale I understood. This new thing was big *and* weird *and* scary. It had a fat, clunky body and clear wings, and its face looked like a mess of strawberries with tumors growing out of them. Its head had a single stalk sticking out the top with what looked like hairy helicopter blades that ended in ugly, pock-marked balls. It lumbered along amongst the much small polar-crabs like a tank, scanning the path in front of it. Soon another one followed, and one more after that. Three in all. One at the font, one in the middle, and one towards the back.

Two squirrels, frightened by the alien march, leaped from tree to tree, trying to escape, but squirrels being squirrels, one freaked out and jumped the wrong way and right into one of the larger creature's open mouth. Damn thing didn't even seem to notice. The other squirrel zoomed a little too close to the one in the back and got impaled on the creepy horns sticking out of its head.

For some reason, that made me mad. Poor little critter was probably just waking up from its winter hibernation and lo and behold, a stupid alien bug-thing scares the hell out of it and spikes it dead on its stupid space-horns. It would have been one thing if the squirrel had gotten eaten by a hawk or an owl or a fox or a snake. That was natural. But them damn aliens certainly was not, and those squirrels were our squirrels.

I said, "I don't know about you, Timmy Carter, but I'm sick of this."

Timmy Carter was farther out on the branch than I was. He didn't seem too concerned about what I was saying. I shifted my weight again and the branch creaked.

"Wait. Stop. Don't move," Timmy Carter said.

I scanned the parade below us. Bug after bug after bug was marching through the forest. Gnarliest creatures I ever did see. When the last wave of them trundled under, a mass of polar-crabs, one of them tank-bugs, and another mass of polar-crabs taking up the rear, I don't know, I guess I just got angry. I guess I felt like they were getting away with something. I took out my anger by stabbing the trunk with my knife.

"Stupid aliens."

Chock. Chock. Chock.

"Think they can come here and do this to me."

Chock. Chock. Chock.

"Amanda. Stop moving so much."

"Took out everybody I ever loved."

Chock. Chock. Chock.

"Amanda. Calm down."

"Killed my daddy."

Chock.

"My farm."

Chock.

"My dog."

Chock.

"Amanda!"

"Ain't you mad about Frankie?"

"Yes. But right now all I'm concerned wi—"

The branch creaked and cracked and Timmy Carter held out his arms like he was trying to stay balanced. We looked each other right in the eyes.

"Amanda," Timmy Carter began, and then there was a squeal like a rusty steel beam breaking in half, and the branch snapped, and down he went.

At the last second, he managed to grab onto the end, his legs dangling in the air. The final tank-bug lumbered underneath him, and his feet were inches from its hairy bladed stalks. I grabbed onto his forearms and tried to pull him up, but he was just too big.

"Can you reach the trunk with your legs?" I asked.

But before he could do anything, the creature below stopped and looked up. All of the little polar-crabs behind it stopped, too, and they started to swarm like ants. The monster's tongue zipped out of its mouth and snapped around Timmy Carter's leg like a lasso, and the rage and anger boiled up in me, washed over me like a wave. I thought, "Uh-uh. Not today."

Without a second thought, I jumped down onto the thing's head. My foot screamed when I landed, but that wasn't going to stop me. The thing tried to shake me off, and I latched onto its spiky horns. The polar-crabs behind it crawled up its legs and onto its back, heading for me. I only had a minute. Two at the most. The monster's tongue was pulled tight, yanking on Timmy Carter's leg, but he didn't let go, and I knew exactly what I needed to do. I crawled out onto that disgusting thing's warty face, flipped my knife in my hand, and started sawing away at the base of its tongue.

"Hurry up, Amanda!" Timmy Carter yelled.

"I'm trying!"

I told you before how Daddy kept his knife in tip-top shape, and since he died, I did the same, so you can believe me when I tell you that that blade could have sliced a truck in half. But that monster's tongue must've been made out of space metal or something because no matter how hard I sawed and hacked and gouged, the damn thing wouldn't give.

"Hold on tight, Timmy Carter!" I yelled.

I took out my .357, placed it up against the slimy surface, and fired. That did it. A chunk of its tongue blew off and black stuff poured out of the wound. I went back to hacking away at the rest, ignoring my burning skin, and cut all the way through. The monster screamed and squealed, rearing up on its hind legs, sending all the polar-crabs heading my way falling off this way and that. I flew back and hit my temple on its head-stalk. Stars dotted my vision, but I managed to wrap my legs around . . . I don't rightly know. Something that was sticking out of its body.

Wasn't nothing left for me to do but stab and stab and stab, and that's what I did, making my way back up to the front of its head and going for its eyes.

"Stupid bug!" I screamed. "That's what you get! That's what you get!"

It was squealing and squealing, but it couldn't do nothing more than fall down, and that's when I jumped off and shoved my rifle in its mouth. I had seven rounds. Six in my pocket and one in the chamber. I fired and reloaded, fired and reloaded, fired and reloaded, kept at it until I didn't have any more left, and the thing had stopped squealing. But I wasn't done. I tore a chunk out of its face with my knife. I beat the side of its head with the butt of my rifle. Any time one of them stupid crabs came scrabbling up,

I kicked it, or stomped it, or mashed it, or stabbed it.

I guess you could say that I was in my first bonafide frenzy. Hadn't ever felt anything like it in my life. I'm not going to lie. I liked it. I liked it more than staving Seb Mac's head in with the grip of my gun. I liked it better than hitting Annie O's face like it was a baseball. I liked it more than the time me and that banshee girl took out Hangnail. When I was done, I was breathless and spent and covered in bug gook, but that tank-bug was D E D, and there were at least thirty of them polar-crabs lying smashed on the ground around me.

"How about that, Timmy Carter!" I yelled.

But when I looked up, he was gone.

Coach Wulfang had us so pumped up with aggression by the end of the soccer season that I had turned into a bully. I was shouldering kids in the hallway, laughing at kids who looked different, and I even stole a little sixth-grader's hot bun at lunch one day just because I could. When a few of my teachers told Coach Wulfang what was going on, she paid lip service to them about disciplining me, but the only thing that happened was that I had to run a few extra laps after practice one day.

"I hear you've been making some noise," she said to me when I was done.

"I guess."

"Your grades up?"

"Yes, ma'am."

"Okay, then."

And she gave me a wink.

Daddy didn't like my behavior at all, and he did what he could as far as it pertained to his house and his rules, but when it came to soccer, ever since he told Coach Wulfang off, he'd adhered to a strict diet of I'm-going-to-let-Amanda-deal-with-this-one.

It all came crashing down during the last game of the season. I won't go into all the nitty-gritty, but all you need to know was that we were finally playing a team that was equal to, if not better than, us. Even worse, they played clean. I was like about to lose my marbles.

Second half. One to one. Five minutes on the clock. Coach Wulfang was apoplectic. She had gone from smugly watching on the sideline (arms folded over her chest, wrap-around sunglasses hugging her temples) to screaming and hollering and pacing back and forth. None of us knew what to do. Our brand of smash-mouth soccer wasn't working. Rather than coach us, Coach Wulfang mocked us.

"Stop plodding around like slugs!"

"My grandma's faster than that!"

And my favorite, "You're passing like a bunch of left-footed lepers."

I got so heated that on one play, a girl from the other team beat me and was about to score, and I just took her out. Slide tackled her from behind, making sure to hit the back of her calf with my cleats. She screamed and went down, her leg all wonky. They carted her off the field on a stretcher. The refs red-carded me, of course, and my teammates had to hold some of the other girls back as I left the field. They beat us anyway. Took us down three to one, and they didn't need to break nobody's leg, neither.

Daddy was not happy, and he punished me accordingly. It wasn't the double chores that bothered me so much as the silence. It felt like something had broken between us, like he didn't really want to be around me all that much. I could take him being mad. I could even take him yelling at me. But the notion that he'd lost respect for me was too much to bear. It was two weeks before I scrounged up enough courage to talk to him.

It was a Saturday, and we were eating breakfast, and he was about to get up and start loading the truck for the Farmer's Market.

"Daddy?" He didn't say anything, but he stopped. "You mad at me?"

"No 'Manda. I ain't mad."

"You're disappointed, I know."

"No. It ain't that, neither."

"Then why won't you talk to me? I'm about to die over here."

"I think you know the answer to that."

"I don't."

"Then you really need to start asking yourself some hard questions."

"What questions? Can you give me a hint?"

He sighed.

"All that anger, all that aggression . . . sure, you played hard, but are you proud of yourself?"

I trailed the line of monsters as they roamed their way across the county. At first, I thought the direction they were heading was a coincidence until I realized it wasn't. They were aiming for Hangnail's farm. I hid in the woods once we made it to the front gate. It was wide open, and sure enough, standing there ushering all the monsters in, was one of the boys who attacked me at The First Country Baptist Church.

So The Girl called those stupid monsters, huh? Probably had the whole thing planned out since last winter. And now Timmy Carter . . .

I let the idea roll around in my head. Timmy Carter was gone. It was just like all the rest. People I loved, people I barely knew, people I hated. Charlotte. Lynn. Daddy. Toni. Ray. Gary T. Mother Absalom. Uncle Zeus. Frankie. Maggie May. And now, Timmy Carter. He was the only person left in the world who gave a damn about me and who I gave a damn about.

I turned back into the woods, numb. I was angry, yeah, angrier than I'd ever been in my life, but all I could think about was what Daddy said to me so many years before. Once again, I let my anger get the best of me, and once again someone got hurt.

No, Daddy. I wasn't proud of myself back then, and I wasn't proud of myself when it happened again.

DR. HUNTINGTON & THE MELONHEAD CHILDREN

One of my all-time favorite things to do was have myself a sit-down in the screened-in back deck and sip a drink and enjoy the view. Summer, fall, winter, spring, any chance I got to get out there, I took it. I know that might not sound all that scintillating, but trust me, there wasn't nothing more relaxing. Nothing more relaxing. After dinner was usually the best time. Finish the dishes and, depending on the weather, pour a big old glass of sweet tea or lemonade or hot chocolate or apple cider or, if Daddy was feeling magnanimous, Irish coffee, and go on out there and have myself a nice long set.

Much like everything else in the house, the back deck wasn't nothing to sneeze at. Daddy built it himself with a little help from Blue, and, well, Daddy was a pot farmer and Blue owned a gun shop, and the deck reflected that lack of expertise. It might not have been the prettiest piece of architecture in the world, but it did what it was supposed to do, and that's all I needed.

Summer was the best time for sitting. My favorite part was watching the sun fall behind the trees and listening as the swell of the cicadas merged with the sounds of the birds. Sometimes the moon might peek out from between some clouds, and sometimes dogs might bark way off in the distance, and sitting there sipping on a drink with my legs tucked under me, everything seemed right with the world. And if it started to rain, watch out! Nothing was better for the soul than listening to a storm in my favorite chair.

As soothing it could be, my back-deck-setting-sabbaticals wasn't without their spooky qualities. This was Spotsylvania County, after all. Many a gloaming I heard and saw things that I'm not sure were real or not. I'm not saying I'm crazy, I'm not, and I'm not some tinfoil-hat wearing nutter railing against fluoride in the water or screaming about Civil War ghosts or nothing, but in my short seventeen years, it had been my experience that not everything in the world played by the rules. If the Hive and the Macks and all them bugs that killed Timmy Carter were anything, they was proof of that statement. Hard proof. Hard as rock.

I remember one time I was sitting out on the porch in the middle of August. I was splitting my time between working on the farm and summer swim team, both as a coach and a competitor. The Hive and Ruth Grace Hogg and her bone-cracking field hockey stick were still a year away. A heat wave had just been broken up by a late afternoon thunderstorm that rolled through the countryside with a fury that rattled our windows and blew a couple of shingles off our roof, but now the heat and humidity had been replaced by a sweet, summer breeze and temperatures that were relatively bearable, and by that I mean it was only ninety-four degrees instead of ninety-nine with a heat index of a hundred and ten. The sun had nearly set, and I closed my eyes to see if I could catch the beginning of the night sounds. The swoosh of wind. The tweet of birds. The . . . what was that?

I opened my eyes and leaned forward, certain I'd heard kids playing out in the woods. That by itself wasn't so weird. Kids played out in the woods all the time. Just not in our woods because there weren't no kids around where we lived. Hell, the edge of the nearest farm was two miles away, and it belonged to Mr. Boone, and Mr. Boone's house was two miles from that. Not to mention the fact that he was eighty-three years old and a permanent bachelor. There hadn't been children on his property in close to a hundred years.

The rusty screen made it difficult to see into the darkening forest, which itself sat about a barn's length away, so I got up and opened the door, hoping the sproing of the spring wouldn't frighten away whoever (or whatever) was out there. Then I stood on the back step, peering into the evening light. I didn't see nothing for a while, just the regular sprinkling of fireflies and the same old green canopy I'd been looking at all my life. But I knew there was something out there, so I focused my attention and focused my attention, and everything seemed to go dim, the sounds of the bugs, the wind, until . . .

There!

I caught a glimpse of something bright yellow followed by a high-pitched laugh. Seconds later I heard someone running around in the leaves, cracking branches, and another splash of color, this time neon blue. I hopped down the stairs.

"Who's out there!"

I scanned the tree line, cocking my head like that would help me hear better. It was surprising how fast the evening turned to dusk, and all of the sudden the peepers threw up their song and cicadas swelled even louder. Then I heard it again. Footsteps crunching in the underbrush. The snap of a branch. A child giggling.

"I heard that!"

I ran into the woods for about half a football field until I stopped because it got dark really quick. Dark dark. All I could see were the trees and brush right in front of me and some fireflies hovering a few feet away. Only they weren't hovering natural; that's to say chaotic like. Usually, fireflies chose their path in the same way a toddler destroys a clean room. Ain't no rhyme or reason to it, they went this way and that. But these was different. They were actually creating a pattern, circling around in the dark, making a figure-eight, like one of them infinity symbols I saw in a textbook once when we were learning about world religions. I leaned forward.

"Hello?"

A rush of wind swooshed through the trees overhead, blowing the fireflies away, then I heard nothing but cricket song. But there was something there. I could see it. A dark outline in the night. I held my breath and took another step.

"Hello?"

Two, bright orbs flashed to life right in front of me.

I screamed and jumped back, catching my foot on something and falling square on my behind. You might be laughing, but I swear, if you had been there, you would have done the same thing. I half-expected the eyes to be gone when I got up, but they weren't. They were hovering in the dark, and I noticed how big they were.

"Who are you?" I asked.

The eyes blinked, and then a voice floated out of the bushes, high-pitched but coarse, like whoever it was got a sore throat by sucking on a helium balloon. Might have been a boy, might have been a girl. Couldn't really tell, but for the sake of making it easier, I assumed she was a she.

"I am a harbinger, Missus. I'm a waif, a wanderer, a witch."

See? A she.

"Huh. That's a lot to take on."

"Missus must not be here. Missus must not ever be here."

"Where? In the woods? These is my woods. That's my house right back—"

I turned to point it out, but all I could see was the dark outlines of the trees. Knocked me speechless. How far in had I gone? The eyes stayed put, staring at me, unblinking. Then whoever or whatever it was whimpered. I looked down and saw a tiny foot caught in a badger trap.

If you don't know what a badger trap is, good for you. Nobody in this world should have to experience them things. Daddy didn't have no problem with hunting. Of course he didn't. He was as avid an outdoorsman as anybody else in Spotsylvania County. But he hated traps. Called people who used them cowards.

"But Daddy, sometimes them badgers and coons got to be got rid of, don't you think?"

"Not like that. Traps are nasty things. I'm all for controlling the animal population, 'Manda, but if you want to kill a creature, do it fast, and do it yourself. Ain't no reason to make 'em suffer."

I could see his point. Badger traps were like miniature bear traps, all metal and sharp teeth. This one had more teeth than most, too, like it'd been custom made for maximum pain. And it was rusty. Whenever Daddy found something caught in a trap, he let it go. Showed me how to do it. Just had to pull it open and reset the pin. And that's what I set out to do right then and there. I was down on one knee, inspecting it when the girl spoke.

"It hurts, Missus."

"I know it hurts. That's some long, sharp teeth you got stuck in your foot."

I reached out for it and the girl tried to pull away, hissing.

"Don't," I said. "You'll just make it worse." I reached for it again and she flinched. "You going to let me free you or what?"

More rustling sounds came from behind her, and she started to panic.

"Hurry, Missus!"

"Well, maybe if you stopped moving."

"Hurry! He's coming!"

She shot a look behind her, and I took the opportunity to grab the trap. Once she felt that tug, she near about lost her mind. She got to jerking and pulling so hard that it reminded me of a cat I found once tangled up in a laundry line. Traps like that were set on at least ninety pounds of pressure, so it wasn't no easy task to pry it loose. But that's what I had to do. Grab them teeth and pull them apart, so that's what I did. That girl screamed and screamed, a high pitched wail that sounded like a demon from hell, and then I got those teeth wide enough apart so she could pull her foot out, and she jerked away and fell on her backside.

And did she thank me? Did even she take a second to look at her wounded foot? Nope. She stood up, hopping on her good leg, and said, "He's here, Missus! Flee! Flee! Flee and never come back!"

Then she skittered away, loping all lopsided off into the brush, followed by the sound of more children laughing, like there was a whole group of them out there. I waited a tic, wondering what had just happened, before I remembered what she said and decided to get out of there.

But here's the thing: even though I walked and walked, I never got any closer to the edge of the forest. In fact, it felt like I was going in the opposite direction. I even stopped a few times and looked around, worried that I'd gotten my head screwed on wrong, but I knew I hadn't. The Jett family had an inner compass as reliable as the tides, and not one of us had ever gotten lost at any point in history, ever. (At least that's what Daddy said.)

Because of this, I really wasn't all that scared at first, but I definitely kept an even march forward, and I definitely didn't feel like looking behind me. I felt like I was running out of a dark basement in the middle of the night. It got worse the longer I went and I realized that I still couldn't see my house, but then its outline slowly emerged from the gloom, the lights of the upstairs bedrooms glowing warm and yellow in the dark, and I picked up my pace until I was running, and I didn't stop after I burst out of the tree line, neither. I'd almost reached the back deck when Daddy's disembodied voice floated out of the dark, saying, "Kinda weird, ain't it?"

I'd never had a heart attack before, but two scares in a row like that felt pretty much as close to one that a teenaged girl could get. I shrieked and hit the deck, which, of course, caused my daddy to start laughing. I stood up, and now that my eyes had adjusted, I could see him better. He was sitting in the middle of the backyard on the portable glider he'd built himself, the little red coal of a spliff hanging in between his fingers.

"Damn, Daddy! You scared the bejesus out of me!"

"Don't say damn, 'Manda."

"Why the hell not?"

"Because it's—" he slapped a mosquito biting at his neck. "Damn skeeters are eating me alive."

"What're you doing out here?"

"Just setting. Having a smoke and a beer."

I went over and sat down next to him, the cooler he used to pack his beer sitting between us on the slats.

"Can I have a drink?"

He thought for a second, then handed over his beer. I nearly fell off the glider. He'd give me a shot of bourbon in my coffee on cold nights, but ask him for a beer and the answer was always no. Was this some kind of initiation I didn't know about? First I had to rescue a weird kid from a beaver trap in the forest, and then I got to drink a beer? Whatever. Beggars and choosers and all. I took a sip, grimaced, and spit it out.

"Ugh. How do you drink that stuff?"

"You get a taste for it."

"It's gross."

"Yeah, well."

"Can I have a smoke, instead?"

"Don't push your luck, little girl."

I decided not to, choosing instead to just be with him and enjoy the company. The night sounds swelled around us. Every now and then the tip of his joint glowed in the dark.

"Daddy?"

"Yeah?"

"What are those things?"

"What, them kids?"

"Uh, yeah."

"I don't rightly know what they are. They been here as long as I have. Longer, I think. At least, that's what your Nana told me."

"Really?"

"Really."

"And you never chased them or caught them?"

"Oh, I chased them plenty. Me and your Uncle Zeus. Never caught them, though. Got close but never caught them. Uncle Zeus said he talked to one once, though."

"Of course he did."

"Actually, I kind of believe him on this one."

"Oh. Did he talk to the one with the yellow shirt? Because I did."

He shot me a look like he was impressed.

"How about that. Well, he said he saw one once but only for a little bit. Said it was too dark to see it all the way. All he could see was a big, round head and glowing eyes."

"Did he see the infinity symbol?"

"The what?"

"Never mind. What'd they talk about?"

"Zeus asked him, or she, or it—whatever—where it lived. It said it lived with its brothers and sisters with a man in the woods. Doctor Huntington."

He pronounced it 'Hunt 'em down'.

"That's it?"

"Well, Zeus said he asked if he could see it—where it lived—and it laughed and hissed at him. Told him to never try to find them or he'd be sorry."

"Huh."

"'Huh' is right."

Every time I walked through the woods behind my house, I thought of that story, those glowing eyes, the crazy laughter. I never did see or hear them again after, no matter how many times I stood on the edge of the woods wishing they'd show up, no matter how many times I called out to them. I never was brave enough to set foot inside, though, at least not any time after four in the afternoon, and definitely not during the month of August. Or September. Or even early October for that matter.

I waited a whole month before I set out to see if I could find Timmy Carter's body. You might be asking yourself, 'why a month?' Well, because I was scared, that's why. I ain't afraid to admit it. I was scared of what was out there, scared of my reaction to it. In hindsight, I think that I'd had so much taken away from me that I couldn't believe that Timmy Carter was gone, too. Because if he was dead, it was my fault. My fault entirely. I lost my cool. I blew my biscuits.

Eventually, my need to find out what happened, to know for sure that he was dead, overrode the fear and the guilt, and I purged my ya-yas, screwed my dome tight, and decided to make it as right as I could.

It didn't go well.

The world had gotten strange and gotten stranger. For one, it'd grown hotter, more humid. August in Virginia was already a riot of steamy mornings and stormy afternoons. I learned early on in life that if I wanted to go swimming or have a nice picnic by the stream, it was morning or nothing, and sometimes even that didn't work out.

But now it seemed like everything had turned positively sub-tropical, like the equator had widened. Significantly. Plants and bugs I'd never seen before (and not just the alien kind, neither) cropped up all over the place. It rained hot and heavy seemingly out of the blue and then cut off like someone had tweaked the spigot closed. Creepers snaked up the sides of abandoned houses, snakes slithered through the undergrowth, and I'll be goddamned if I didn't see a mosquito the size of a fist impale a rabbit one fine summer morning.

And that's not even accounting for the sounds that percolated from the newfound brush. Hoots and hisses, caws and calls, all kinds of creepy music the likes of which I never wanted to hear, not live, at least. There were weird things out there, let me tell you. New weird things. Newer, weirder things than the previous newer weird things.

Even though I'd lived my entire life in that area, and even though I'd traipsed through them woods a zillion times, it soon became apparent that I was lost. I blamed it on the climate. All my usual landmarks were difficult to pick out of the exotic foliage, or covered, or missing altogether.

For example, my original plan was to march north for a mile before cutting over to Todd's Tavern, using Mill Pond as a guide, where I'd take a break and a bite before the next part of the journey. I left the property a little after sunrise, and I figured I'd be there before mid-morning, but Mill Pond had been washed out in some areas, and in others, it was overgrown with weeds and vines, and in other areas, it was completely missing. I figured I must've walked for three hours, heading north and north and north, before I realized that I was lost completely. I went through all the stages, denial, bargaining, etc . . . . When the last stage hit, rather than freak out, I took me a seat on a log near a little creek and dug into my backpack for a can of ravioli. I was sitting there, munching and thinking, when I heard them for the second time in my life.

First the sound of footsteps in the underbrush. Then wild laughter.

It was them crazy kids again.

I guess they'd stepped up their game since the last time I saw them because one of them threw a rock the size of a fist at me. Missed by a mile, crashed into the creek and sent up a nice sized splash, but there wasn't no doubt about the meaning. The next one thudded at my feet. I put my can of ravioli down.

"You think that's funny?"

Skittering through the leaves. More laughter. They were all around me. I picked up a rock of my own, a nice brainer, and got to my feet.

"I swear to god, if one of you hits me—"

A rock slammed into my shoulder. Wasn't a huge one, but it was pointy, and whoever threw it had an arm like a piston because it hurt like a sonofabitch.

"Ow! Damn!"

Another rock hit me in the thigh, this one coming from the other direction. I saw one of them peeking out of the brush about twenty feet away, a big, round, fleshy head and a pair of yellow eyes. I wound up and fired, and it cut through the air like a meteor, hitting that fat head fair and square between them ugly, yellow eyes. I played softball every summer for five years, first string center field and back up pitcher (a weird combination, I know, but this was Spotsylvania County after all, and sometimes we just didn't have the numbers). I didn't spend fifteen hours a week practicing underhand lobs, you bet. More like twenty hours a week shooting bullets. That old melon-headed kid dropped on the spot with a shriek. Then he started crying something fierce, the baby.

His brothers and sisters didn't take too kindly to that. Rocks rained down on me from all directions, hitting me in the back, the head, the face, the legs. I covered up the best I could but there wasn't nothing else to do but snatch up my bag and my gun and run.

Wait a minute, you're thinking. *You had a gun and you didn't use it? What on earth . . . ?*

Well, of course I had a gun. I had more than one gun, actually. I had two hunting rifles and three handguns. But I wasn't going to use them on a bunch of creepy kids. They might have been weirdos and jerks, but they were still kids. And it wasn't like I had ammo to spare. If I was going to attack The Girl, I'd need all the firepower I had.

So I ran.

Branches whipped me in the face, and I barked my shin on a fallen branch so hard that I could feel the bruise swelling as I limped along. Running with all them guns strapped to my back, not to mention what I had loaded in my backpack, didn't make it any easier. Neither did the melonheads. They shadowed me, laughing, giggling, growling, throwing rocks every now and then, but never showing themselves, the cowards.

Until they did.

One of them leaped out of the brush to my right, claws out, growling, and jumped up and latched onto my shoulder. I felt a searing pain as it bit into the muscle, and I screamed and rammed it into the trunk of an oak tree to my right. It whelped and fell to the ground, dazed. I only saw it for a second, but man it was an ugly little thing. Its head was at least two-thirds of its body, and it was covered in pink and purple veins and patches of weedy hair. Its eyes were wide-set and red, and its mouth, while tiny, was filled with pearly teeth that had been sharpened to points. Where it got that K-mart t-shirt from, I have no idea, but it was dyed the brightest shade of red, redder than its eyes. It growled at me and gnashed its teeth, but when I drew my foot back to punt it, it dropped its tough-guy act and skittered away into the bushes.

"You better run you melon-headed freak!" I screamed.

Then I felt a prick on the back of my arm like I'd been stung by a bee, and when I wheeled around, a man was standing there. He was tall and thin, with perfectly combed, salt and pepper hair and thick glasses perched on his face. He was wearing pressed, black pants and shiny black shoes, and I could see a perfectly knotted black tie under his white lab coat. There was a name stitched on his left breast pocket, but I couldn't read it. My vision had gone blurry.

"Who're you?" I managed to say.

And then I was lying on an operating table. A bright light gleamed overhead, and I heard the beep and whirr of machines all around. I tried to move, but my arms and legs were strapped to the rails. My head was free, though, and when I looked down, I saw I was wearing a gown and slippers and nothing else.

"Hey!" I yelled.

I instantly regretted that decision. I'd only had a hangover once in my life. It happened the June before the Hive landed. I'd gone out to an end-of-the-year party and drank my fill, which isn't too much if I'm being honest. I spent the rest of the night puking up my guts in the woods and woke up the next day at home in bed. Daddy took one look at my rat's nest hair and pale face and bloodshot eyes and puke stained shirt and laughed.

"That'll teach you," he said.

"It ain't funny."

"No, it ain't. Not for you at least."

I shuffled off to the bathroom to get cleaned up.

"You're grounded, of course," he called after me.

As terrible as I felt all that day (and a little into the next), it paled in comparison to the way I felt waking up on that operating table. Joined to that was the fear of not knowing where I was or what'd happened to me.

In a moment, the swinging doors to the operating room pushed open, and two people backed in: the man from the woods and one of them melonheads. They turned around, and I saw they were dressed for surgery. Masks and head-coverings, smocks and latex. The melonhead was holding a tray with scary looking instruments on it. It set it down on a stand to my left and the doctor leaned over me.

"Hello, my dear."

His mask puffed out when he spoke.

"You're Dr. Hunt 'em down, aren't you."

"My my my. Is that what they call me?" He tsked. "Such provincial nonsense."

The melonhead bumped into one of the IV stands and spun around, panicked, knocking the tray of utensils over. They hit the floor with a metallic clatter.

"Confound your clumsiness, Bertholdt! Pick those up immediately!"

The melonhead scrambled around, his pudgy fingers struggling to grasp the sleek, gleaming instruments. He dropped them over and over, cut his fingers on the blades. He kind of reminded me of a little baby.

"Now look at what you've done, you idiot," Dr. Huntington said. "Put them on the tray and take them back to be re-sanitized."

Bertholdt did as he was told, flashing a red look at me on the way out, like it was my fault he was a klutz.

"You must forgive poor Bertholdt, my dear. He is a clumsy git sometimes, but I absolutely depend on him."

My eyes rolled around, looking for a possible way out, all while my mind was screaming: What was going on? What was going to happen to me? The doctor picked a syringe off the tray behind him. It was filled with a thick-looking, green liquid.

"We tested your blood earlier. You have such interesting cells."

He flicked the plastic to pop the air bubbles.

"Mister," I said. "I don't know who you are or what you want, but it'd be in your best interests to let me go."

"Oh, I doubt that very much."

Then he jammed that needle into my arm and pushed the plunger down all the way, and that's all I knew again for a time.

The next time I came around, I was dizzy and sick, and I could feel the stuff the doctor pumped into me running through my veins like sludge. I turned my head to the side and vomited. It was brown and green.

Bertholdt was standing at the foot of the operating table. His red eyes fixed on mine.

"Go away, Bertholdt," I said. "I don't have time to deal with your mess right now."

I saw the edges of a smile creep up on his lips. Then he held a scalpel up and twirled it in his fingers. He leaped onto the bed with an agility that I didn't expect from such a tiny, oblong thing, his feet straddling me on either side, and squatted down, that evil smile plastered across his face. I did the only thing I could think of. I hawked up a loogie and spit it at him. I'm not going to tell you what he did with it out of fear you might puke, but I will say this: it didn't seem to bother him one bit. He liked it so much that he pointed the tip of the scalpel at my eye and slowly edged it forward.

I turned my head and he hit me, and you might not think something so small could be so powerful, but he was. I saw stars. And when I turned my head the other way to avoid the knife, he hit me again. And again. And again until I couldn't do nothing more than moan and spit blood. Then he put his hard little hand on my forehead and held it tight.

Things were not looking good for this little girl, I can tell you that much. I never in a million years thought that this was the way I was going to die, getting my eyeball carved out by a nasty little thing like Bertholdt.

The scalpel snuck closer and closer, and Bertholdt's smile grew wider and wider. I closed my eyes, wondering if I'd feel any pain. The metal edge of the scalpel kissed my lid, and then there was a noise from the hall, a whoosh of air as the door swung open, and the weight of that evil little midget was suddenly off me. I opened my eyes and saw pudgy fingers fumbling with the straps on my right.

"Bertholdt's a vile little stump, Missus. A wicked creature, yes."

I recognized that voice. It was the first one of them things I'd ever seen, the one that told me to steer clear of this place.

"You got that right," I said.

"Missus didn't heed my warning, did she? Missus maked a bad mistake. But I doesn't forget. Missus free me, me free she."

She undid the cuff of my right foot then my left while I worked on my left hand. When I was free, I swung my legs off the operating table and, still feeling a little unsteady, hopped down and almost landed on Bertholdt, who was passed out on the floor.

"Your clothes, Missus."

The melonhead girl was handing them to me, my jeans and shirt, my socks and boots.

"You know where my bag is?"

A noise came from the hallway, and she said, "He's here! He's here! Missus must flee! She must flee and never return!"

"What? Where?"

"Now!"

And she shoved me at the double doors and I burst out the other side . . . and into the field behind what used to be my house.

It was night, and the insects were singing their song. The moon was out, full and bright, and the air was hot and heavy. I didn't even turn around to see where I'd come from. I walked straight to where I was camping in the foundation, sat down in the corner and drew my knees up to my chest and rocked back and forth, back and forth.

I can't tell you how long I sat there. Could have been an hour. Could have been a few days. The sun was out and then it wasn't. I got hot and I got cold. It rained. Not once did I think to eat. I seen things. I heard things. I don't know if they was real or not. Sometimes I thought they might be, but then . . . the sounds were unlike anything I knew. Strange animals sniffed around the foundation. I saw a hawk with a dog's head snatch a rabbit with a snake's tail sitting in the grass on the edge of the woods.

And those things? Those melonheads? I heard them running out there. I saw their eyes in the night. When they came too near, I screamed at them, holding the only weapon I had left, an old butter knife, out in front of me like it was some kind of sword, my eyes wide and terrified, and they scattered, giggling, and ran back to the woods.

And I saw all the people I loved or knew who had died. I saw Timmy Carter. I saw Ray.

I saw Maggie May. I saw Zeus. And last of all, I saw Daddy. He was standing at the other end of the foundation, looking at me.

Daddy, is that you?

Amanda, honey, you need to get out of here.

I don't want to. I want to go with you.

You can't come with me, baby. I'm gone.

I miss you, Daddy.

I know.

Don't you love me?

You know I do.

Then why can't I come with you?

Because you're needed here. You need to help.

Help who?

Everybody else.

I can't do it.

Yes, you can.

I can't do it! That crazy doctor shot me full of something evil. I think I'm dying.

You're not dying, 'Manda.

But it hurts, Daddy. It hurts so bad.

I know. But people need you. You need to wake up, 'Manda. 'Manda—

"Wake up!"

My head rocked back and my cheek stung like someone had slapped me. Everything was blurry at first, but then I saw the tarp me and Timmy Carter put up over the foundation, blue and tattered just like we left it. There was the little stone grill we made to heat our food. I sat up, wondering who'd slapped me awake, and lord almighty was I surprised. Not exactly happy, I gotta admit, but surprised and, well, maybe a little relieved.

HELP IS HELP

I almost failed ninth-grade Algebra when I was in tenth-grade. I'm not proud of it. I take full responsibility for it. It might please you to know that the failing wasn't necessarily a result of my substandard mathematical skills, although that had a lot to do with it. I was supposed to be in Geometry in tenth-grade, but I'd failed eighth-grade math and had to retake it in ninth-grade, which meant there I was in Algebra I as a sophomore.

I don't know why I resisted math so much. I think it had to do with my lack of respect for math people in general. They always seemed liked humorless stick-in-the-muds to me. If I'm being honest, my brush with mathematical inadequacy had more to do with a serious case of the "I know betters" mixed with a sudden manifestation of "who gives a crapitis" than any real learning deficiency. Add to that my natural inclinations and a hormonally charged tendency towards magical thinking, and I had myself a serious situation by the time April rolled around.

What can I say? I was a stupid teenager.

I complained about it to Daddy, but he didn't have anything useful to say.

"Why don't you study more?"

"I do, Daddy. I'm trying as hard as I can. See?"

He looked at the open math book on my lap and the half-blank sheet of paper in my binder, and then he looked at the episode of *Star Trek* I was watching on the tv. It was the one where the crew ended up in the bizarro world of The Enterprise, where everybody was evil. One of my favorites.

"All I see is a little girl watching that brain-melter and ignoring her homework."

"I got some problems done."

"Uh-huh."

"Watching tv helps calm me down."

"Uh-huh."

"It does!"

"Amanda, you either turn that thing off, or I'm going to throw it out the back door."

"No, you won't. You won't be able to watch your stories."

"*Generations* don't air no more, 'Manda, so the joke's on you."

"What about football?"

"You really want to test me on this?"

I knew better than to push it any further.

"Sorry, Daddy."

"Yeah, you will be. Now turn that thing off."

"Yes, Daddy."

As you might have guessed, my magical thinking did not work out in my favor, and come May, Daddy made me stay after school for tutoring. By eighth-graders.

"Seriously, Daddy. You might as well stick a gun in my mouth. I'm not going to let some diaper-wearing middle-schooler teach me nothing."

"It ain't like you have a lot of options here, 'Manda. Why are you so busted up about it, anyway?"

"Because they're twelve years old, Daddy. It's embarrassing."

"Well, you know what's going to be more embarrassing? When you have to repeat Algebra I as a senior."

"But—"

"Help is help, 'Manda. Don't matter what size package it comes in."

Help is help. Easy concept to understand. Not an easy concept to embrace. People, especially Americans, and especially Americans who lived in Spotsylvania County, Virginia, liked to think they can get through life on their own accord without help from nothing or no one based on no evidence whatsoever. For some reason, when one of us managed to do something all by our lonesome, we all thought "that's the way to do it." Don't matter what it is. Build a house. Win a game. Pass a class. But that was a lie. Because ain't nobody ever truly done something alone. Not when you really drill down on it. The truth is that everybody in the whole world needs each other. Every last one of us. Plain as day.

There ain't no other way of saying it: August was the armpit of the summer. Hot, steamy, wet, and terrible. That year wasn't no different. If anything, it was worse. Late summer has a smell to it, you know? Musty and moldy and dank, the culmination of five months of heat and thunderstorms sitting around in stillwater puddles and drainage ditches and holes filled with rotting leaves. Multiply it by one half, and you got what I was dealing with.

The bugs had upped their ante, too, I'll tell you what. I was used to the flies and the cicadas, but now there were clumps of gnats buzzing all over the place, swarms of them the size of beach balls. Except for by the canal path or in the still pockets of the river, we'd never had that much of an issue with them down here. Not no more.

One morning, in the middle of the month, I walked out of the front doors of Courtland High School and right into a fat patch of them. I should have known better; I'd been walking out that door for almost a month and it was like to be the hundredth time I walked straight into a patch of bugs. I started to sweat as soon as I left the building, and based on the thermometer hanging on the brick wall of the overhang, it was going to be a barn burner. It was already eighty-eight degrees out, and the humidity made it feel at least ten degrees hotter.

Now that the cooler weather was supposed to be coming, I'd volunteered to prep the beds out by the rear building and plant garlic out where the beans and broccoli and Brussels sprouts was near close to picking. I paused there in the shade, enjoying the morning as best as I could. A warm breeze blew in from the stadium, bringing with it the smell of the hay drying on the old football field. I heard children squealing from the practice field to my left. Marquan was out there watching them, armed to the hilt. He had a rifle slung over one shoulder and a pair of handguns on his hips and a knife and a baton on his belt and a bandolier strapped across his chest half-filled with bullets. I'm glad he was the one who volunteered for that. Babysitting wasn't my thing even when I wasn't armed. I wouldn't trust myself around all them irritating kids if I was.

The door opened behind me and out came Frankie. My savior. That's how she wanted me to see it. It was her that found me huddled out in the corner of my old basement, shaking and hallucinating and crying, and it was her that drove me the nine or so miles from the farm to Courtland High School, and it was her that reminded me of her heroics on a daily basis, if not out loud then with subtle jabs and a generally condescending attitude. I swear there wasn't enough antacid in the world for me when it came to dealing with her.

"How's our little trooper doing today?" she half-sang, finishing with a nervous laugh.

"I'm better, Frankie, thank you."

I didn't even look at her when I said it. I couldn't. It was all I could do to keep from gritting my teeth. Frankie strolled out into the drive, holding her hands to the sun and swishing her hips.

"You must be awfully happy I found you out there with a day like today greeting you. So sunny and beautiful."

"I'm thinking I'm going to sweat off at least ten pounds out there in the garden."

"Nope. Not today."

"Uh, yeah today."

"You're coming with me. Ailani's orders."

Ailani.

Ailani was the de facto leader of whatever this place had become. Village? Town? Fortification? I'd knew people like her before. Ailani was a Serious Person. Serious People Got Things Done. Serious People Didn't Take No Guff. Serious People Had No Time For Foolishness. She reminded me of a school administrator, which was fitting, I guess.

"What for?" I asked. "I gotta get the garlic in the ground."

"You said you knew a guy who owned a gun shop, right?"

"Blue. Yeah. He's dead. Shop's cleaned out. Don't you think I already looked?"

"Ailani wants you to do it again. Says if he was as much of a survivalist as you say he was, then you might have missed something the first time around."

"Like what?"

"I don't know. That's what we're going to find out."

As critical of Ailani as I could be, she was the one who relieved the National Guard Recruiting Center of all their APCs and supplies, and she was the one who knew them APCs could run on diesel, and she was the one who went around from gas station to gas station, filling up tank after tank and gas can after gas can, and she was the one who drove all them back and formed a ring around the campus and went out and got car after car after car and did the same until there was a wall two cars deep circling the school and its fields and parking lots, so it ain't like she's entirely stupid. Blue was a survivalist. She was right about that. Maybe I did miss something.

So that's how I ended up heading back out to the darkest depths of Spotsylvania on a scavenging mission with a girl I could barely stand. (That would be Frankie, for all of you who weren't paying attention.) I'm sure you can understand why I was conflicted about that arrangement. At least she didn't drive like an idiot. The roads that wove through the woods back to Blue's shop twisted and turned in places, and the switchbacks could be unnerving.

Given my daddy's penchant for weapons and such, it might surprise some of you to hear that I'd never rode in a military vehicle before. Here's my review: it was hot and uncomfortable. I guess the price of armored plating was sweat and a sore butt. I watched the woods blur by the barred window, thinking.

"You never did tell me why you came back to the farm," I said. Or rather, yelled. Them trucks was loud and cranky.

Frankie said, "What?"

I raised my voice.

"That day you found me. What were you doing back there?"

"Same thing we're doing today, scavenging."

"You was looking for my gun safe, weren't you?"

Frankie slowed down as she took a tight turn and didn't speak again until we were straightened out.

"We didn't think you'd need it anymore."

That's all either of us said for a long minute. Plenty of questions crossed my mind, though, not the least of which being, "Kind of like you didn't need Timmy Carter, huh?" I knew better than to bring it up again. I done it before, about a week after I was rescued, I asked her if she missed him, and all she said was, "Oh, honey. He was sweet and all, but . . ." and left it hanging there. Damn. I guess love is a fickle beast, ain't she?

But you can be damn sure I hadn't forgotten him yet. Soon as I could, I was going to hit Hangnail's farm myself. The Girl was about to f-f-find out exactly what it meant to p-p-piss-off a Jett. I've said it before: Daddy didn't raise no bleater.

We got to the intersection at Route 1 and boy howdy was it a mess. Shells of cars, bodies on the shoulder. We had to go around a blockade of tanks that were blocking the sign for the new high school, ended up off-roading it through the bush. Crossed the Ni River and made it all the way to the Mattaponi before we decided to try and get back on the pavement again. There was a bridge there, an old one, with wide, stone pillars sinking into the water, and an old, crumbling concrete wall. It was covered in weeds, and it looked like it would fall over if anybody so much as blew on it.

"The people in your county sure don't like to take care of their infrastructure," Frankie said.

"It's just an old walking bridge. Plus, if you didn't know it, we got ourselves an end-of-the-world situation going on."

"Sweetie, that bridge was falling apart long before any of the hives landed."

"Don't call me 'sweetie'."

"That's what you're worried about?"

I swallowed my acid.

"How about we keep driving? I'd like to get to Blue's and back before the sun goes down."

"Over that thing? No way."

I hated to agree with her, but I had to. It'd be one thing to die during a fight with an alien invader. That seemed noble and valiant. Getting crushed to death because Spotsylvania County didn't want to raise its taxes didn't. But like I said, it was a walking bridge and way too narrow, so the only way across was to go down into the bed and climb the embankment on the other side. I opened my mouth to say something, but Frankie already popped the APC in gear.

"I got it," she said, and she steered the car forward.

The water was low and easy to cross, but getting up the other side was a bit of a challenge, mainly because the embankment was covered with leaves and lined with trees, and even though the APC was made for that kind of thing, it felt like it would flip backwards with every foot we climbed.

I don't know exactly why I did what I did next. I got a feeling that we were being watched, I guess, or maybe I just wanted to see if the wheels were going to get caught on a mud slick and spin us into a wipeout. Whatever the reason, I rolled the window down, pushed the bars open, and stuck my head out to see what was going on behind us. Sure enough, the wheels were kicking up dirt and weeds and mud, all of which splashed in the water behind, but that's not what caught my attention. What caught my attention was a slash of bright colors from the woods on the other side. Blues and reds and yellows. I knew exactly who it was.

Uh-uh, I thought. *Not today.*

I yanked on the handle and popped out of the door, dropping about five feet farther than I estimated and landing on my heels on the edge of the water. The old break in my leg flared up again. I don't mean it broke, but I felt the pressure on the line. Even worse was when I tried to hop onto my other leg to compensate, my foot slipped on a rock and I rolled my ankle.

"Amanda!" Frankie yelled. "Get back in here!"

I looked all around me, biting back the pain, looking for them little blobs of primary colors, but I didn't see nothing but green. I splashed across the water and up onto the other bank, stomping around and kicking up leaves.

"I know you're out there, you little hobgoblins!"

I pulled out my gun and stomped farther in. It was a loaner from Ailani, a little .22. Tiny, yeah, but enough to stop one of them creepy melonheads. Frankie revved the engine behind me and honked the horn.

"Amanda, you coming or what?"

I waved my arm and squatted forward. Something rattled in a bush a few feet away. Or someone, I should say. The weeds were thick and tall, almost reaching my chest. I wasn't going to be nice this time. I was going to throttle whoever it was, wrap my hands around its neck until it told me what that crazy doctor shot into me. One more step. I was reaching for a knot of weeds and bushes, about to pull them aside, when I heard something that froze my bowels. It was a hiss and a clicking sound, like a snake. Then I thought, "Hold on."

"You trying to scare me?" I said. "Well, how's this for a scare?"

I pushed the weeds aside and jumped forward, gun out, and a big green scaly thing leaped for me, all teeth and fang and claws. I screamed and fired off my .22, and then it struck me, and I tumbled to the side. It scrambled up to me on its spindly legs, mouth wide open, and I near about soiled myself. It looked like a combination of a snake and a spider, with the snake's body ending in a pulsing, spider's thorax. It reared back on its hind legs, exposing its underbelly and I fired all the bullets I had into it and blood and gook splashed all over me and it squealed and fell, and I got up and ran.

Frankie had backed down into the water and gotten out, and she was already running toward me when I came limping out of the woods.

"Run!" I yelled, and we both sprinted for the APC. I lurched for the passenger door (which was still open), hopped in and yanked it shut. Frankie jumped in on the other side. She slammed it into gear and stomped on the gas, but the tires only spun in the water, and before we could move another inch, a roar sounded out from above us.

"Go!" I yelled.

Frankie put it in reverse, backed up a few feet, and put it back in first. The APC finally caught some traction and we hit that slope hard, but before we made it halfway up, something flew down from above and crashed onto the hood.

Frankie screamed and I yelled "Jesus!"

It was a monster, of course, the same one I seen a few months before, the thing with legs like a kangaroo. Only now I saw the whole thing, and it wasn't just a kangaroo. It had an ape's torso with goat horns growing out its skull. It bared its chest to the sky, loosed another roar, and then started pounding the bejesus out of the windshield, smashing right through it and reaching for Frankie. She fell to the side and right into my lap, and the thing roared again and swiped its massive paw around the cab, tearing ruts into her leg and shoulder. Then it grabbed her by the waist and ripped her out threw her away. I saw her body hit the bridge and fall onto the rocks below.

I fell out the passenger side, narrowly avoiding another swipe of its claws, and splashed into the water. The monster continued to tear the vehicle apart, ripping off the hood and digging into the engine like it was play dough. It smashed the roof and the windows popped and that's all I needed to see. I got up, turned, and ran.

And the thing followed me.

I don't think I'd ever ran faster.

I dodged pricker vines and branches and saplings the best I could, but the dang things seemed to be reaching for me, catching at my clothes, my boots, my arms. The creature didn't have the same problem. It muscled through the undergrowth and the woods the same way it muscled through the armored car, knocking down trees, shattering trunks, leaving a few with sharp hunks of wood jutting up into the air like swords. It got close enough to swing at me, and it would have walloped my head into pulp if I hadn't tripped on a root. I hit the ground hard, falling flat on my face and knocking the air out of my lungs.

I rolled to my right gasping for breath, and the monster's fist smashed the ground where I'd just been, and then it was over me. It smelled rank, too, like wet fur and feral animal, and it roared and carried on, beating its chest, bragging about how strong and tough it was. Then it cocked its arm, preparing to punch my skull into the ground, and I closed my eyes and held out my arms and then a flurry of shots rang out. Machine gun fire. The thing whelped and kicked me aside and I hit a tree trunk so hard that I thought I'd broke my back.

The first thing I thought was that Ailani had sent someone to tail us. Then I thought maybe there was some other group out there and they'd come to our rescue. Neither one of those was true. Because when my vision finally cleared, I saw who it was who'd saved me. Standing among the destroyed tree trunks and shattered logs was Frankie. She was battered and bloody, and her shoulder hung strange, and she looked about to keel over, but she bit back the pain and eyeballed that kanga-goat-ape thing with a hateful glare I didn't think she had in her.

"Missus!"

The whisper hit my ear so sharp that I hissed. The melonhead girl from Dr. Huntington's surgery from hell, was beside me, blue eyes sparkling.

"We're here, Missus!"

Frankie screamed and fired another burst of bullets at the kangape (that's how I started thinking of it), striking it in the chest and legs, but all that seemed to do was make it even angrier. It charged her and she fired until the clip was empty, dodging at the last second.

"Watch this, Missus!" the melonhead said.

She put her hand to her mouth and made a weird ululation, and out of the woods charged dozens of blobs of primary colors. Melonheads. All of them. She joined them as they swarmed up the kangape and started beating it and stabbing it with all kinds of weapons. Some had scalpels they must have stolen from the doctor, some had kitchen knives, some had spears they'd carved out of branches. The gape roared and flailed, but the melonheads dug in with their claws and hung on for dear life. It reached back and flung a few off, but for every one it got rid of, two more took its place. They gouged out its eyes. They sliced the backs of its legs. They stabbed it in the neck. It grew weaker and weaker, finally falling face first and impaling itself on one of the shattered tree trunks it had created with its own fists.

The melonhead girl trotted back to me, blue eyes sparkling, shirt clotted with gore and fur.

"See, Missus! See what we can do?"

Then she put her hand to her mouth again and made the ululation, and the other melonheads scattered back into the woods and were gone.

"Wait!" I called as she turned.

"We can't be late, Missus. He will be angry."

"But I don't even know your name."

She smiled at me with her pointy, blood-stained teeth.

"Berenice, Missus." And she ducked into the brush and sprinted away to join her friends.

"We misses the Missus! Missus comes and sees us!"

To say Frankie was messed up was an understatement. Broken ribs, broken foot, broken leg. The back of her head looked like, well, it looked like she'd fallen twelve feet onto a rock, which was exactly what happened to her. For all her girly-girly-ness, Frankie was a tough old girl, wasn't she? Tougher than I thought. Should've known. She survived the invasion. Survived Mother Absalom and my no-good Uncle Zeus.

I draped her arm over my shoulder and we gimped back to what remained of the APC. There was a first aid kit in one of the side compartments, and even though the vehicle was mostly crushed and the compartment door bent and hard to open, the kit was still pretty much intact. I cleaned out her head wound and packed it and wrapped a bandage around it. I wrapped her foot, too, just to put some pressure on it, but there wasn't much I could do about them ribs or the leg. Wasn't first-rate hospital care, but it'd have to do.

"You're going to have to stay here," I said.

"Okay."

"I'll put you in the cab and head back to Courtland."

"It's crushed."

"The back's still good. Door's broke, but I think I can get it open."

I did. Found a pry-bar in a different compartment and wedged it in and hung and yanked and pulled until it finally gave. If it wasn't for the fact that the kangape had already compromised the shell, I don't think I'd have been able to do it, but there you go.

Getting her in took some doing. And some screaming. Mostly on her end. When I got her as comfortable as I could, I put our canteens in on the floor and clapped my hands.

"I better get going. It'll take a couple of hours to get back to the high school. I'll rustle up a crew."

"Get back before dark, okay?"

"Okay."

"Don't leave me here."

"I won't."

I turned to leave and she said, "Amanda?"

"Yeah?"

"I really did like him, you know."

"Timmy Carter?"

"Do you think he's alive?"

"No."

I started off again.

"Amanda?"

I sighed.

"Yeah?"

"Those things. What were they?"

"Which ones?"

"Those kids."

"I don't rightly know. Daddy said they'd been around since before he and Zeus were little."

"Their heads were so . . ."

"I know. I kind of think of them as melonheads."

"Melonheads?" She laughed a little and started coughing and holding her ribs. "Oh my, that hurts."

"Broken ribs do that."

"They seemed to know you."

"It's a long story. I'm just glad Bertholdt wasn't with them."

"Bertholdt?"

"Never mind. Anyway, they helped us."

"I know, but they were so small, though. And strange."

"Help is help, Frankie. Help is help."

DESTINY

My tale of revenge ain't one for a Hollywood movie. There wasn't no good girl, no bad girl, no pristine heroine, no bullying nemesis. And there certainly wasn't no love story involved. It came down to a couple of tweenagers at summer camp, and it was petty and mean and something that I regretted for the rest of my life.

Don't worry. I'm not bringing Daddy into this story. Not too much, at least. As bad as what I did, he wasn't in no place to act like an expert on morality. The man never set foot in a church (not that church-stepping was the apotheosis of ethos), blaming Nana's wholesale refusal to adhere to any social or political standard as the reason for his heresy. Maybe that's why he decided to make a living selling drugs.

Here's the story.

When I was twelve, Daddy sent me to a sleep-away camp for two weeks. We had a pool we could swim at, and a lake, and I took sailing classes and archery classes and pottery classes and played soccer and basketball and we got to eat in a big cafeteria and get snacks at a commissary every night. It was one of the best times I ever had in my life.

Except for The Beast.

That wasn't her real name, but that's what everybody called her. Her real name was Destiny. I got along fine with The Beast for about the first minute or so, but after that, she was all insults and "accidents."

"Get out my way you skinny little redneck."

"I didn't mean to elbow her in the face. It was an accident."

"You play basketball like a white girl."

"Her stomach jumped in front of my foot."

I could handle The Beast fine on my own. For every punch, kick, scratch, and hair-pull, I gave back ten times worse. Had to. The girl was five inches taller'n me and weighed about thirty tons. If she wasn't Ruth Grace Hogg's sister, she had to be at least a distant relative.

So The Beast learned to leave me alone pretty quick, which was good for me, but not so good for some of the other kids. One of them was my friend Daniel Dickerson. Daniel Dickerson was a small fry, a cute little thing with a blonde bowl cut and a button nose. Everybody liked Daniel Dickerson. His personality was infectious. But all of the qualities that drew people like me to him because we wanted to be friends also drew people like The Beast to him because they wanted to hit him. Wasn't nothing new. Kids like Daniel Dickerson been attracting kids like The Beast since there's been kids like Daniel Dickerson and kids like The Beast. That's to say forever and a day. The weirdest thing was that initially that attraction was Shakespearian. The Beast was a big, black girl from Baltimore, MD. Daniel Dickerson was a tiny asian boy from Reston, VA. They had about as much in common as a snake and Van Gough.

But oh my lord did she love that boy. The first time she saw him eating fruit loops at breakfast she was like about to choke on her bacon. Watching her try to woo him was about as painful as a pulled tooth, but once she realized that Daniel Dickerson didn't just not return her affections but actively spurned them, well, you ever see that movie, *Alien*? That's when the real Beast truly came out.

I don't think I need to go into all the details of the hurting she put on poor Daniel Dickerson, and we were proud of him for putting up as much of a fight as he could. For such a little squirt, he could really take a punch! And I'd like to say somebody did something about it, but they was all happy that The Beast had decided to sharpen her fangs on a different victim's bones, and I'm ashamed to say it, but that included me.

(For those of you wondering where the camp counselors were during all this, you have to understand that a certain amount of rough-housing and bullying was always bound to fly under their radar. The Beast was slick and devious, and she didn't always broadcast her assaults on national TV.)

So Daniel Dickerson was as brave and as strong as he could be for as long as he could be, but even the toughest cowboy on the ranch cried in his whiskey at some point, and even though Daniel Dickerson was more akin to a junior ranch hand and more likely to cry into his chocolate milk, he, just like everyone else, was not immune from his emotions.

One morning, my tent counselor, Veronica, asked me to go down to the dock shed and pick up a paddle for an activity she had planned for after ice cream night at the mess hall, and boy howdy was I happy to do so. The dock shed was at least a mile and half from the tents where we all slept, and her asking me to go all that way by myself meant she knew that I'd do what she asked and not make no fuss or screw it up, and that meant a lot to me.

"There's a key hidden in a fake rock behind the shed," Veronica said. "Don't forget to put it back, and don't let anybody see you do it."

I nodded solemnly. This was a sacred task, and I could be trusted to achieve my objective. I took my time walking, though, enjoying my freedom. I stopped at the commissary and bought a candy bar and a soda. I took a couple shots with some kids playing HORSE on the basketball courts. It was about an hour by the time I finally made it to the dock. I knew I was running late, so I ran around to the back and there was Daniel Dickerson sitting on a stump. I must have startled him as much as he startled me because he jumped up and spun around.

"Holy moly! You scared the life out of me, Daniel Dickerson!"

He didn't say anything, and at first I thought he was monkeying around, but then I saw his shoulders shaking and I knew he was crying.

"You alright, Daniel Dickerson?"

"I'm fine."

"What're you doing back here all by yourself? You know it's ice cream night, right, and—"

"Leave me alone!"

"Daniel—"

"I said leave me alone!"

Then he let out a sob to shake the rain out of the clouds. I let him do it for a while, let him get the worst of it out. Then I said, "Did The Beast do something to you? She hurt you again?"

"I don't know what her problem is. She's always picking on me and hitting me and pinching me and nobody will help. Not even you!"

"I'm sorry, Daniel."

"What did I ever do to her, anyway?"

"Nothing, Daniel. You didn't do nothing. Some people is mean like that, I guess."

"She better leave me alone. I might be little, but I can take care of myself."

"That's the spirit! Like my daddy always says, moor your craft higher . . ."

I stumbled to a stop, not because I'd forgotten Daddy's catchphrase, but because Daniel's left hand had dropped to his side, and in that hand, he was holding a steak knife.

"What you got that steak knife for, Daniel?"

"Nothing."

"Really? Nothing?" He didn't respond. "You fixing to use that on her?" He still didn't respond. "Well, let me make you a deal. You let me have first crack at her, okay? If I can't get her to leave you alone by the end of the day, you can do all the damage to her you want. Deal?"

"How?"

"Never mind that."

"How will I know?"

"Oh, you'll know." He fell silent again. "What do you say? We got a deal?"

He finally turned around, and his eyes were red and puffy.

"Tonight?"

"Yep."

"Okay. But if you don't get her . . ."

"Can I hold onto that knife until I do?" He took a step back. "Just for safe keeping. I'll give it back if I don't hold up my end of the bargain."

"Promise?"

"Promise."

"Okay."

There wasn't no way in hell was I going to give that knife back to him, but I sure meant what I said. I was going to get The Beast. Daniel Dickerson was a friend to everyone. He was one of the nicest, smartest, funniest kids I'd ever knew. Hurting him was like hurting a puppy.

I left him there and went back to the main campus, paddle in hand and anger in my heart. I was angrier than I'd ever been. I stopped at the commissary again for another candy bar and a bottle of eye drops "for my allergies," and that night during dinner, I spiked The Beast's orange juice with it. I'd heard about it from an older kid, an eighth-grader who said his big brother did it to a teacher he didn't like. Said the teacher threw up in the middle of class and had to go home sick, so I thought that's what'd happen to The Beast. She'd get sick for a bit, throw up, you know, maybe get some diarrhea. As it turns out, spiking someone's drink with eye drops is a lot worse than I'd been led to believe.

That night, she got up to puke and got lost along the way to the bathroom. Then she fell down, broke her wrist, and had a seizure. They had to call an ambulance and everything.

When the dust settled and we got word that she was okay, the guilt sank into my bones and started eating away at me like a cancer. I waited a day before I went to Veronica and fessed up. Telling her about it was terrible. The look of horror on her face was worse. She brought me to the camp director, who listened to my story, and when I got to the part where I spiked her drink, she stopped me.

"What did you say you put in her drink?"

"Eye drops."

"From the commissary?"

"Yes, ma'am."

She exchanged a look with Veronica.

"Amanda, do you know what epilepsy is?"

"Yes, ma'am. A kid in my second-grade class had it. It gives you seizures."

"That's right. That's what Destiny has. That's why she had a seizure."

"But . . . the eyedrops . . . I—"

"Sweetie, we don't sell the commercial brand here. Our eyedrops are homeopathic."

"Homeopath—"

"It means—"

"I know what homeopathic means. So, I didn't spike her drink?"

"Oh, yes you did. Just not with anything that would hurt her."

"Oh."

I got sent home that very day. Daddy had to drive all the way up to get me. Didn't say a word the whole ride back. Two and a half hours of pure silence. That hurt worse than thinking I'd almost killed someone.

If August was the armpit of summer, September was the armpit of August. Not hot enough to be summer and not near to cool enough to be fall. That's the way it was supposed to be around here. Not that year, though. The world was changing. Getting hotter. If we didn't know it before, we sure did now.

I was standing on the roof of the school one morning, looking out over the weed-choked parking lot and the woods beyond, when a funny-looking mosquito the size of a basketball buzzed up the side of the building, caught in the updraft of a humid, moldy smelling breeze. I near about jumped out of my skin.

"Holy cow!" I cried.

It hovered over me as I fell flat on my butt, its wings buzzing like a chainsaw. Dang thing had claws and paws and a funny tail and a needle or a blood-sucker or whatever those things were that was longer than its body. I drew my gun, a .357 I got out of the armory (the old equipment room in the main gym) and trained it on the thing. It buzzed and buzzed and cocked its head at me like a dog. Made me laugh out loud.

"You go ahead and try it, you nasty thing. See how good you fly without a head."

Either it understood English, or it decided I wasn't worth the effort, because it stroked the air with its paws and them papery wings ramped up and it buzzed off into the morning.

"Unnerving, isn't it?"

I turned around and Ailani was standing there with her hands in her pockets, following the bug as it flew away. I'd never noticed how beautiful she was. She had the most stunning green eyes I'd ever saw, and I remembered Frankie telling me her dad was from Chicago but her mom was Hawaiian. She also said Ailani was a lesbian, but I didn't care about any of that. Frankie seemed to think it was important, though.

"She's from New York City," she said.

"So?"

"I'm just saying."

Frankie said a lot of things like that. I tried not to think about it too much.

Back on the roof, I holstered my gun and stood up and dusted myself off.

"It sure was ugly, but it ain't the scariest thing I seen. Not yet, at least."

"That's right. The, uh, what did you call it? The Kangaroo-Ape?"

"Kangape."

"Kangape. Right."

I squinted one eye closed, wondering if she was making fun of me.

"What's going on, Ailani? I thought you were leading that scavenging party."

"I am. We're leaving soon."

"Good. Pick me up a candy bar, will you?"

"Anything else?"

"Probably need some tampons soon."

"I'll see what I can do."

"You do that."

"Amanda, we need to talk."

"What about? I've been doing my share. I finished my work on the patch out back. And I did some extra work out on the football field. Is that what you wanted to hear?"

"Not necessarily, but thank you for doing all that. You've really been a credit here, Amanda. We couldn't—"

"Alright, then. I'll be on my way."

"Amanda, wait."

"What?"

"Rumor has it you're thinking of going on a little mission of your own."

Damn that Frankie. I knew I shouldn't have even hinted about it to her. But I thought . . . it had to do with Timmy Carter, and I thought she might want to come along.

"Where'd you hear something crazy like that?"

"I think you know."

"Wish I did."

I pulled out a pair of binoculars and pretended to scan for something on the horizon. It was a strategy I learned from Daddy.

"If you're ever guilty of something, clam up tight. Nobody can't arrest nobody for not talking."

Daddy's shaky understanding of our legal system aside, I did find it useful in social situations. People got uncomfortable in silence, like they couldn't abide a single moment to gather their wits in thoughtful contemplation. If it did get quiet, they usually started yapping it up in order to, I don't know, pollute the air, I guess. But not Ailani. She was a sharp one, she was. She let me be quiet, let that gap build between us, and all the sudden, I was the one who was uncomfortable.

"Okay," she said. "We can play that game if you want. But listen. I can't tell you what you can and can't do—"

"You're damn right you can't."

"—but I can tell you that whatever it is you're thinking of doing, it sounds dangerous. I'd hate to lose someone like you, Amanda. So before you go off and do whatever it is you need to do, I'd like you to think about it first."

"I ain't saying I'm thinking of doing nothing, but let's pretend I was. You think I wouldn't have a plan?"

That gap between us became a yawning canyon.

"Better be a good one, then."

"Uh-huh."

She started to leave but stopped and half-turned back.

"One more thing, Amanda. You're on your own with this one. I can't let you take any of my people."

That really boiled my butter. Not just what she said, but the way she said it, like I was some kind of impulsive kid. The Nana Jett in me wanted to give her an earful. Who did she think she was talking to? I didn't care if she came from New York City or Washington D.C. I'd been through too much to let anyone think they could talk to me that way.

But then Daddy spoke in my ear, and I didn't say anything.

Here's what he said: forget that old girl. She don't matter. Don't matter at all.

The truth is that the thought never crossed my mind to enlist any of her people, other than Frankie, of course. If I was going to kill The Girl for what she did to Timmy Carter, I was always going to do it myself.

If The Girl was any good at setting up a perimeter or guards or trying to protect Hangnail's farm, somebody, anybody, would have seen me slip over the front fence and drop onto the gravel driveway that split the two cornfields right down the middle. I'd meant to jog straight up that driveway and right up to The Girl herself, put my gun against her head and pull the trigger, that's how angry I felt, but, land's sake, I had to stop a tic and take in what she'd managed to do to the place before I killed her. The transformation was dramatic. Them hay bales were long gone, replaced by rows and rows of yellow corn that stretched up to the house, with its solar panels gleaming and the greenhouses still standing in the back.

My first thought was that The Girl might have been able to plant that corn, but if she didn't harvest it soon, it was going to rot on the stalks. As soon as that thought finished forming in my mind, it was followed by the reason why she hadn't done anything with it yet. Lumbering through the fields were at least a dozen of the monsters that ate Timmy Carter, those fat, weird things with the clear wings and tumors growing out of their faces, and they were eating . . . the corn?

Which led to my second thought, which was that The Girl must have fortified the fields with fresh bodies because why else would those things be grazing out there? Where did she find the bodies? Were they Macks? Or was she going around killing people?

As if to settle the matter, the ground shook beneath my feet and the breath of a snort warmed my back. I turned around, and one of them monsters was right behind me.

There wasn't nothing I could do. The gun I had wasn't no match for it. The thing had the drop on me anyway. I stumble-stepped back and fell flat on my butt, bending a corn stalk, and gaped up at the pure, alien strangeness of its face: the rainbow of colors striping rubbery skin, the strawberry-like growths all over its face, that bone-stalk sticking out of its head. It leaned forward, opening its mouth, and I saw a pink tongue and flat teeth and it chomped down at me and I scrambled back as fast as I could, and the corn I'd set on popped up and went right into dang thing's mouth. It tore it up out of the ground with a satisfied grunt and started to chew away, then it snorted again, pulled its head back, and thundered off toward another part of the field.

I barely had time to stand up and dust the dirt off my jeans when that old feeling, that sexy zing, hit me right in the head. It was a mite weaker than I remembered, but I hadn't felt it so long that it still made me dizzy. Then a form rattled out of the corn and smacked me in the face, knocking me flat, and I thought, "Great."

I got up again, jaw aching, and spread my legs a little, holding out my hands like I was getting ready to field a grounder. I'd played this game before. My gun wouldn't be no use here. The only way I'd get out of this alive was by luck and timing, so the next time I felt that zing and heard that rattle, I braced myself and took a swing, but the form zipped by and slugged me in the kidney, and I went down with a grunt.

Okay. Last one.

I closed my eyes and concentrated. It was just like the batting cages. Anticipate the pitch. Put the bat where you know the ball will be.

Wait for it.

Wait for it.

Zing! Rattle!

I stepped to the side and stuck out my foot, waiting for the pain as whoever it was hit it full force . . . but it never came. And suddenly, he was there. A boy with brown hair and bright green eyes. He didn't do anything. He just looked at me. Then Zing! Rattle! Zing! Rattle! Zing! Rattle! and they surrounded me. Another boy and two girls. Brown skin. Olive skin. Pale skin. The only thing they had in common was the color of their eyes. Wasn't nothing I could do about it, and I didn't want to do anything about it. These kids wasn't on my list. Just her. I put my hands up, palms out.

"Okay. I get it. Ya'll got the drop on me." I smiled when I realized what I was going to say next. "Take me to your leader."

I tried to provoke them as they marched me up the gravel drive to the house, but none of them seemed to be in the mood to talk.

"You guys sure are fast. The Hive got some sort of cardiovascular training program in there?"

Nothing.

"Since you guys are spineless cowards, how do you walk at all. You should be mounds of jelly on the ground!"

Nothing.

"Ya'll remember the time you tried to kill me and it backfired and I killed one of ya'll instead and then escaped because of a jar full of—"

The brunette shoved me so hard that I stumbled to my knees, which was exactly what I was waiting for. I grabbed two handfuls of dirt and gravel and threw it into his face and he froze and they all froze and I swear I saw them following the little grains and pebbles, their mouths working (three, six, nine, twelve) and then I hauled off and socked that brown-haired kid in the jaw, sent him sprawling. My gun was jammed down the front of his pants, but when I leaped for it, I felt that zing and the air around me curdled, and it was like trying to move through a solid wall of heavy water.

And then I just stopped. Hung there in the air, suspended like a fly in amber. There were four pulses latching onto me from behind, like invisible lines, and I had no doubt who each belonged to. Rather than fight, I tried to feel them out, see what I could do or how I could use them to my advantage. I reached out with my mind and grabbed the first one. It was silky and soft, like a water-filled tentacle, and it thrummed with power as it waved in the air. I pulled on it, used it to turn myself around, felt its grip loosen, felt all of them loosen, and then I was facing them, the green-eyed Macks, the Girl's nasty old friends.

The pulses looked like tubes reaching out from their chests. Judging by the scared looks on their faces, they hadn't expected me to turn around. I pulled the girl on the left toward me, and she tried to resist, but it wasn't no use. I was stronger, and I was more determined, and I was angrier. When she planted her heels in the gravel, it just made me even madder, so I yanked as hard as I could and she jerked forward. I didn't know what I was going to do once I had her because I still couldn't move my arms and legs, but that didn't bother me none. The important thing was that I had that power, too. I yanked on the line and the girl flew through the air, and I clothes-lined her as she passed. Then I yanked on another one, but instead of hitting him or anything, I let him fly by.

"Not so tough when somebody else is stronger, huh?" I said.

Then the brown-haired boy got off the ground and I felt his link wrap around my neck and squeeze.

The Girl was in one of the greenhouses. She was feeding meat from a bloody bucket to a teeming mass of polar crabs swarming in a pit they'd dug. Steam rose from it in clouds, and water dripped from the glass above.

Living on a farm, I've heard a lot of gross sounds. I've helped birth all kinds of animals, from piglets to calves to foals, and I've butchered fish and chickens and sows, and the noises that accompanied all that were some terrible noises in their own rights. But knowing what I knew about the polar-crabs and their eating habits made the sound coming from the pit probably one of the worst things I ever heard. They clicked and clacked and smacked and cracked with a ferocity to match the worst demons in hell.

Didn't bother The Girl none. Or the green-eyed devil minions she called friends. She didn't look up as they dragged me toward her, choosing instead to reach into the bucket and calmly toss bloody hunk after bloody hunk into the pit with the placid expression of a nun at prayer.

The pulse around my neck squeezed tight when we got within five feet of her, and did she stop what she was doing? Take a tic to acknowledge the presence of the person who took her in from the cold, gave her a place to live, food to eat, a reason to live? I might not have been the most cultured critter on the planet, but Daddy certainly taught me my manners. The Girl wasn't cool, she wasn't tough, and she wasn't impressing nobody. She was rude. My Nana would have smacked my head silly if I ever pulled something like that.

"Hey, G—" I started, but the brown-haired boy tightened his noose and cut off my wind. Didn't hold it long. Just enough to make a point.

Alright, Brownie. Alright.

Eventually, The Girl saw fit to address me. First she wiped her bloody hands off on a white towel she'd draped over her shoulder. You know, to make me wait. Then, without looking at me, she said, "You didn't have to kill him."

"Kill who? I've killed a lot of hims."

"You know who."

I had to think for a minute before I remembered who she was talking about. The blonde boy. The one with the dreads.

"You mean old Dreadlocks? He tried to kill me first! You were there!"

Brownie tightened his pulse again, but this time it was more irritating than painful.

"You mind telling Brownie to back off?" My voice was harsh and raspy. "Choking me out's making it hard to think."

She gave him the curtest of nods, and the tentacle around my neck loosened.

"We were seven. Now we are six."

"So?"

"We needed him."

"For what? You putting together a basketball team? That's two too many if you are."

"You don't understand. He—"

"No, you don't understand! What is all this? The polar crabs? Your flunkies? If you're going to kill me, kill me. Don't stand there acting like some stupid James Bond villain. You going to explain your plans for world domination t—"

Brownie tightened his grip for the third time, but this time he didn't stop. I fell to my knees, choking, clawing at that slick, invisible pulse, but that was about as useful as boobs on a bull. I did it anyway. What else could I do?

I didn't start to panic until my vision went black. I thought, *It's now or never Amanda May*, and sent out my mind to loosen the pulse, and it did. Only a little at first, testing it, seeing if I could get it to work as well as the first time, and it did. The pressure released enough for me to breathe again, and I took in a whopper of a gulp. My vision cleared, and I felt the zing as The Girl joined in, and another and another, but they didn't know what I knew, that I was—well, if not one of them—just like them. The Girl did, though, and when she realized what was going on, she yelled, "Stop!" but none of her friends listened.

Brownie doubled down and so did the others, but it was too late. The more they fed their pulses, the stronger I got. No more bluffing. I harnessed all that energy like I did before, right in that very house four months before, I drew it into myself, felt it working around my bones and tendons, warming my muscles, healing my injuries, and when I was ready, I sent it blasting back out at all of them, and they flew backwards into the air, one, two, three, four, all but The Girl, but even she stumbled a little. One crashed through the glass, another hit her head on a beam, and the other one slammed onto the concrete. Brownie still had my gun jammed into his pants, and I stalked over and snatched it out, making sure to clip him in the temple with the grip when he tried to stop me with a feeble grab. Then I set out to finish what I'd come there to do.

"You really think I'd be that easy to get rid of, Girl? You're not paying attention, are you?"

She backed up, looking around, panicked. This was not a part of her plan. She flattened herself against the greenhouse glass and I pushed the barrel of my gun into her temple. She closed her eyes.

"What now?"

"Please. You don't want to do this."

"How'd you lose your st-st-stutter, huh? You get yourself a post-apocalyptic speech therapist?"

"It took time. To be myself again."

"Whatever."

"Amanda. Please. You don't know what you're doing."

"Yeah, I do." Then I turned around and shot one of her friends. Brownie stood up and I shot him, too.

"That look like I don't know what I'm doing!"

"Please! Stop!"

I turned the gun back to her.

"This is for what you did to Timmy Carter."

"But—"

I pulled the trigger, but she sent out a pulse that caught the bullet as it left the barrel. It swerved and she pulled to the side and it cut a rivulet in her skull.

"That's okay," I said. "I have a few more."

"Amanda! Stop!"

Holy. Moly.

That voice. Like an elephant with a head cold. Then the man himself was there, standing at the greenhouse door, two buckets in each hand.

"Timmy Carter?"

He dropped the buckets and ran over, and I braced myself for his hug . . . but he ran past me and right over to The Girl and engulfed her in his arms. Then he pulled back laid a kiss on her that would've made a pimp blush.

Oh.

Oh my.

"You okay?" he asked.

She nodded up at him, smiling.

"She wouldn't have been able to do anything I didn't want her to do."

"I know, but—"

"You don't have to worry about me, Timothy."

Timothy?

Timmy Carter brushed her hair off her forehead and turned around to look at the bodies bleeding out onto the greenhouse floor. Then he finally looked at me.

"What did you do?"

Remember the time I poisoned a little girl and she had a seizure and Daddy picked me up from summer camp and didn't say a word to me for the entire two-hour drive? As bad as that was, the long walk back to the high school through the heat and humidity was a zillion times worse.

When I finally slunk back onto campus, Frankie happened to be on door watch. Her leg was splinted and wrapped from ankle to thigh, and she was wearing a neck brace, and her face was all swole and bruised, and she had the temerity to say, "Jesus, you look like hell."

"Timmy Carter's alive," I told her as I strode past.

Then I went straight back to my bed in the commons and sat there and stared out at nothing and said nothing and stayed that way for a long, long time.

THE RETURN OF THE HIVE

When I was sixteen, an alien hive fell on my neighbor's lawn and killed his entire family. When I was sixteen, me and my Daddy blew that hive up with a dead dog stuffed with explosives. When I was sixteen, I killed a little boy. When I was sixteen, I killed a pregnant lady that'd turned into a monster. When I was sixteen, I watched my Daddy die. When I was sixteen, when I was sixteen, when I was sixteen.

There ain't no cure for the bad things you done. Even if you thought you did them for the right reasons. If you done it, you done it. No take-backs. The blood of everybody who'd died over the last year was on my hands. Daddy. Maggie May. Ray. Gary T. Gomez Gomez. Otis Enoch Abernathy. Annie O. Mother Absalom. Uncle Zeus. Everybody else at the farm. All of them. It was all my fault. All my fault.

I didn't know how long I lay on my cot in the commons letting that mess rattle around in my head, and I didn't care. A day? A week?

I slept. I stared at the ceiling. I slept. Repeat. Repeat. Repeat.

One day, Frankie limped by, took one look at me curled up in a ball on my cot and said, "Amanda, you've got to get up."

When I didn't move or say anything, she poked me in the back with her cane.

"Come on. Get up."

"No."

"You've got to eat."

"Not hungry."

"So you're just going to lie in bed until you die?"

"Go away."

"Amanda—"

"Go away!"

Lying in bed was exactly what I had in mind. All day. All week. All month. Forever. Frankie knew that. Why'd she even bother to ask? Why did she care so much? That girl hated me from the day I let her onto my farm. She sighed as she stood there, and I could practically feel her eyes rolling.

"You better not soil that bed, little girl."

"Get the FUCK away from me!"

The din of the commons dimmed, and even though I had my eyes closed, I knew everybody was looking at me. It was all

Frankie's fault. If she'd of left me alone, I wouldn't have had to yell at her.

"Fine," she said. "You piss yourself, you're on your own. We don't have any more cots, and I'm not going clean up after you."

I willed myself to sleep after she left. Even that brief interaction left me weary through and through. My soul. My bones. My everything. So I slept. It was easiest. I didn't have to think about what I'd done.

I dreamed about Daddy. I was sitting out on the lawn on the glider and he was right next to me, drinking a beer and smoking a spliff and I couldn't help it, I started to weep. He wasn't impressed.

"You can cry all you want, sweetness. But when you're done, the problem's still going to be there. Might as well skip right to solving it."

"That's fine for you to say, Daddy, but I killed people!"

"You did what you had to do."

"Did I have to kill Seb Mac? Or Lynn? Or Charlene?"

"Yeah. You did."

"I had to watch you die! And I had to bury you! You left. You left me here all by myself, and I have tried, Daddy, I tried to do everything you'd do. I tried to save people. I tried to save the farm. I tried to save the world, but it didn't work. They took it from me. They were too strong, and I'm too weak. I let you down. I'm nothing. I'm nothing. I'm nothing."

He put his hand on my shoulder, and that's how I woke up.

"Amanda?"

It was Ailani.

"I don't need to eat, and I don't need to pee."

"I'm not asking you to."

"Then go away."

"I can't do that."

I ain't proud of what I did next. If I've said it once, I've said it a hundred times: Daddy didn't raise no bleater. The Jetts were tough. Fighters. Nana Jett was meaner than a copperhead. When life got difficult, we didn't retreat, we met it head on and damn the consequences. One thing we certainly didn't do was cry.

But that's what happened.

I cried.

It came up from the depths of my body and shook me. Literally. I tried to hold it back, tamp it down, swallow it like I knew Daddy would have done, like he would have told me to do, but I couldn't.

Ailani patted my shoulder and it the rest of it came pouring out in one snotty, lung-stretching, tear-filled sob, and if everybody wasn't already looking at me or fleeing the commons, they certainly were now. Even though it seemed to last forever, I know it didn't. When it was all out, I lay still, stunned at how much better I felt and how nothing felt better at all.

"You done?" Ailani asked.

I nodded and wiped my nose with the back of my hand.

"Sorry."

"Sorry for what?"

"For bawling like that. I feel so stupid."

"You don't have anything to feel stupid about. You're human, Amanda. Humans have emotions."

"Yeah, but—"

"There aren't any 'yeah-buts' about it. It is what it is."

I sat up, and to my surprise, the commons hadn't emptied out at all. And nobody was looking at me. There were a few half-glances here and there, but none of them looked mean or pitying or judgmental. In fact, a few even seemed, I don't know, nice? Like they wanted to help?

"Okay," I said. "What day is it?"

Ailani let out a little chuckle.

"You mean what month."

"What?"

"It's October, Amanda."

"Oh." Then, realizing how long it was since I last knew the date, "Oh!"

Ailani stood up and held out her hand.

"You feel good enough to rejoin the world?"

I gave the offer a nice long think. Did I? I still felt low and weak and empty, but that hole was gone, at least for now.

"I'm not sure."

"Listen to me, Amanda. All that stuff you got running around in your head? It's not real. Understand?"

I nodded even though I didn't.

"You're the strongest person I've ever met. You've borne more than some of these big men we got here. So when you start thinking to yourself otherwise, when you start selling yourself whatever nonsense that makes you feel bad . . . ."

She could see I'd kind of tuned out. I couldn't help it. All I could think of were the faces of all the people I'd let down.

"Hey," she said. "Hey. Look at me."

I did.

"I want you to see something."

The noise of the kids playing in the auxiliary gym echoed off the walls as we walked down the back hall, the open doors at either end allowing enough to let us see where we were going. I cringed at it, both because I wasn't in no place to hear something like that and because I was worried about how much attention it'd attract. I had to remind myself that the Courtland Colony wasn't like what I had at my house. The school was one hundred percent American made, with iron bones and cinderblock skin. We had numbers, too, and Ailani posted guards all over the roof and had them patrolling the parking lots, not to mention the wall of cars we plugged every hole with, and all the APCs and other military vehicles we'd stole. Any Macks or Hives wanted to try and get at us, they'd have themselves a gory time of it.

She led me out the door to a little courtyard that used to be some kind of patio where the students could eat lunch. The last time I looked, the concrete was dug up and the ground tilled, but that's about as far as they'd got. Not a pretty picture if you catch my drift.

Now, though . . .

"Good goodness," I said.

Gone were the rocks and chunks of concrete, the pieces of the benches, the shards of wood, the big stump of a tree, all replaced by stalk after stalk of beautiful, yellow corn. They were tall, too, too tall for me to even reach without getting on someone's shoulders.

"Good goodness is right," Ailani said. I could hear the smile in her voice. "You want to see something even more amazing?"

She pulled a machete out of the loop in her belt and cut a stalk down.

"Go ahead. Look."

I didn't need to be told twice. I picked an ear off the fallen stalk and my oh my was it big. It was hands down the biggest ear of corn I'd ever held in my life. I shucked the husk to get a better look and blinked hard. Ailani laughed as she put her machete back.

"The kernels are so big," I said. "Are all of them like this?"

"That's one of the biggest ones, but yeah. They're pretty huge."

I looked in the direction of the stadium.

"So that means—"

"Yep. Best view's from up high."

There was a hatch on the second level that we used to access the roof. When we popped out of the hole, one of the guards posted on the north end gave us a nod and a wave, and we headed to the front. The walkie-talkie Ailani clipped to her belt squawked twice and she pushed a button to silence it.

"Needs fresh batteries," she said.

"We out again?"

"These things get used up faster than you think when we're using them all the time. I'll send someone out."

A guard named Wendell was keeping watch there. He gave us a curt smile and went to the south-east corner to crib a cigarette from another guard. The sun was setting to our right, shining its dying light on the field in the middle of the stadium. If I was knocked out by what they'd grown in the back, I was downright comatose by what they pulled off in front.

They'd planted more corn, of course. From one end zone to the twenty-yard line, the field was thick with it. But the rest of it was chock-filled with all kinds of other food. Green beans, peppers, cucumbers, tomatoes, melons, pumpkins, beets, squash, sweet potatoes.

"How about another 'good goodness'?" Ailani asked.

I obliged her.

"Golly day, Ailani. You did it."

"*We* did it. Thanks to you."

I gave her a bit of the stink-eye.

"Maybe a little, yeah, but this," I gestured at the football field, "I didn't have nothing to do with this."

"Oh, yes you did. Nobody knew how to farm before you got here. Best we could do was dig up the ground and put a seed in it and hope for the best."

"That's pretty much it."

She slapped my shoulder.

"You stop that now. You see all that food out there? That's—" Her walkie-talkie squawked again and she turned it down. "That's because of you. We're going to make it through the winter."

A trickle of sweat rolled down my back.

"What winter?"

"You know what I mean."

Wendell trotted over, flicking the cigarette he was smoking over the edge of the roof.

"Ailani!"

"What?"

"We got a situation at the road."

She started to respond when someone started firing a machine gun in the near-distance. All three of us ran to the roof's edge. Several of our people were running toward the chainlink that separated the school from the neighborhood on the other side. I looked at Ailani, and I looked at Wendell.

"What are we going to do about that?" I asked.

Because standing there on the other side of that chainlink face was an army.

An army of Macks.

Hundreds of them.

My belly froze, and I forgot to breathe. How many more were in the woods to the east? On the other side of the Vo-Tech Center? Out on the road?

"Ailani," Wendell said.

She was swiveling around, seeing what I was seeing, thinking what I was thinking. The guards on the roof were running for the hatch and that seemed to shake her out of her stupor.

"No! Stop!" They couldn't hear her, so she grabbed her walkie-talkie and cranked it up. "Roof guards! Get back to your posts!" They stopped and looked at her, and when they didn't move, she yelled, "Now!"

"What do you want us to do?" Wendell asked.

"Stay here. Do your job."

She started to run for the hatch. After a few steps, she turned her head and yelled back to me.

"You coming?"

We'd just reached the tennis courts when it felt like all the oxygen was sucked from the air. Ailani and I went to our knees, trying to breathe, but it wouldn't come. Then that pressure, that horrible pressure I felt nearly a year before, built up all around us and pressed down. The ground blurred and shook and hummed, and Ailani's mouth was open wide like she was screaming, but I couldn't hear anything, and then the pressure exploded with a sonic eruption, and the ground shook and leaped even more, and we fell on our sides, and then it was silent. Ailani was first to get up, gasping and terrified.

"What was that?"

"You never felt it before?"

"No. Have you?"

"Oh, yeah." I turned and looked toward the road, and I could see it. The rounded, green-brown top poking into the sky. "They're here."

More Macks thronged Smith Station Road, thousands of them, packed in hip to hip, standing on the other side of the buses we'd jammed back to back to form a wall that stretched all the way down to the stadium fence and around the parking lot and across the front of the Vo-Tech building. An entire company of men and women stood on our side, armed with all manner of weapons, from police batons to little .22s to the .50 caliber Brownings bolted into the top of one of the APVs facing the front gate, which was two more school buses parked nose to nose at the intersection. Nobody was shooting, though, and the Macks didn't move an inch. Frankie, who was manning the gate, hustled up to us as best she could, hopping like a pole-vaulter on her cane.

"What's going on?" Ailani asked.

"Nothing, yet."

"Where did they come from?"

"Nobody knows. They just appeared, and then that thing came up from under the ground."

"*Under* the ground?"

"Yep."

"It didn't fall from the sky?"

"Nope. Shot up straight up through the road."

"I've seen that before," I said. "Last fall. Boiled right up."

Ailani jawed into her walkie-talkie.

"Hold your positions, people. Do not fire until I give the order. I repeat. Do NOT fire until I give the order."

Then we walked, Ailani, Frankie, and me, up to the gates. And as we did, the buses started to move aside. Ailani shouted into her radio.

"Who's doing that? Close the gate! Close the gate, goddammit!"

But there wasn't anybody to stop the buses from moving because there wasn't anybody in them. The buses were moving on their own. An inch or two first, then a foot, then six feet, before finally stopping wide enough to let an army through.

The Hive sat on the other side, pulsing and green and pink and brown. And boy did it ever stink. Oh my goodness did it stink. Some of the company closed in, guns raised, while others backed away, almost involuntarily, their hands on their weapons but too shocked to do anything with them. We pushed through the crowd, Ailani yelling, "Move! Move!".

The Hive split open when we reached the front, exposing its oozing center, and a fresh wave of stench hit us like a wall, and little creatures flittered out, filling the air with a high-pitched buzzing sound. Then the Hive pulsed and hummed, and out of the opening slipped a creature the likes of which I'd never seen.

It looked like a man, or maybe it just had a man's body. Two legs. Two arms. A head (I think). But its limbs were gnarly and knobby, and its twisted spine ended with a burbling hunch where its neck met its body. The only thing visible on its face was its mouth, which was wide and large and filled with brown teeth. The rest of it, its nose, its eyes, its forehead, was covered in a rubbery patchwork of scarred skin. Polar-crabs swarmed out of the opening, surrounding it as it limped toward Ailani and me, clicking their claws as if anticipating their next meal. When they all got within a few feet, Ailani pulled out her gun and said, "That's far enough."

The creature turned its blind face to the sky, mouth working as if tasting the air. Then it stopped and leveled its head in her direction.

"I am the Voice of the Hive."

None of us said a word. What were we supposed to say to something that looked like that? Our silence seemed to unnerve it a little. It tried to engage us again.

"I send greetings from the Hive. We are most happy to meet with you this fine day."

"Good for you," Ailani said. "What do you want?"

"I come of offer terms of your surrender."

Ailani snorted.

"*Our* surrender?" She looked to her left. She looked to her right. "I think you might need to use a different pronoun."

"We have no desire to do battle—"

"I bet you don't."

The polar crabs clicked angrily around the monster's clawed feet, and it smiled with its teeth.

"Such arrogance. Your colony is surrounded. You are low on food and ammunition. We need not attack. We need only lay siege. You will die. Or you can come to terms."

"We'll take our chances."

"No," Frankie said. "Let it speak."

"Frankie—"

"No, Ailani. I want to hear this. What could we possibly have that it wants?"

Ailani gave me a look, and I shrugged. Didn't hurt to hear their offer, I guess.

"Alright," she said. "What's the deal?"

"The Hive will leave your colony alone. The Hive will withdraw as far as the water to the south. The Hive will allow your colony to forage as far as the village to the north."

"In exchange for what?"

The monster pointed a clawed talon directly at me.

"Her."

Ailani laughed out loud.

"You must be joking."

"The Hive does not quip. The Hive consumes."

"You arrogant—"

"I have no ego. I am but the humble voice of the Hive."

It bowed its head and spread its green arms in mock supplication, and I saw my chance. I pulled Ailani's machete out of the loop on her belt, took one step forward, and stabbed it in the neck. The monster fell to its knees, hands trying to cover the wound. Green fluid sprayed my feet, burning the skin. Then it collapsed, shaking, on the asphalt, as the life ran out of it.

The polar crabs went nuts. Two of them scuttled up my leg, biting and tearing at my flesh. I sliced them off easy enough, but they left great big gashes. Frankie turned and half-ran, half-limped away.

"Frankie!" I screamed, but she kept going.

The Hive shuddered to life, and tentacles whipped out, aiming for our people. One grabbed Ailani by the ankle and upended her, but I cut it off with an angry slash of the machete. I reached out my hand and she took it and let me help her up. The company unloaded on the Hive and the tentacles reeled, even as polar crabs and other monsters poured out of the pulsing, pink opening.

"Sorry about that," I said as we backed up.

"Sorry about what?"

"I . . . I might be a little down in the dumps right now, but I ain't suicidal. I'll be damned if I was going to let that thing take me."

"That thought never crossed my mind, Amanda." Ailani picked her walkie-talkie off her belt. "John! Zeda! Get your butts in the buses and close the gates!"

A polar crab clicked across the road for us, and Ailani raised her gun and fired, hitting it in three shots. Then she handed me her spare firearm.

"Time to show up, Amanda."

If I didn't know any better, I'd have thought the aliens brought a bunch of dead meat to a gun fight. Sure the Macks overran the fences in about as much time it took to say the word "fences," and sure they were able to jump over the cars and APVs like they were toys, but they weren't no match for our firepower. They surged toward us, wave after wave, and we cut them down, head shots, leg shots, body shots, tore that pack to ribbons and tore the ribbons to bits.

The Hive was a different story. It whipped its tentacles out at us with a fury unrestrained, ripping people from the tops of the buses and smashing them on the road, dragging them screaming into its mouth. The polar crabs overwhelmed our lines, and though we stomped them and shot them, and though their shells burst and their black guts exploded, they swarmed us and took us out two or three at a time. It was a horrible thing to watch a someone's legs be eaten out from under her, to watch her body shake as they ripped through her stomach, her chest, her head, leaving nothing but shards and bone.

But the Macks didn't relent. No matter how many we cut down, they kept coming. The tentacles tore our buses apart piece by piece and flung them back at us. We were losing. And that's when someone came tearing up the road in an APV. Whoever it was barreled through the first two lines of cars, slamming them aside, and came to screeching stop. Then hatch popped open, and Frankie clambered out.

"I'll be," I said.

She manned the Browning bolted to the top, pulled the slide handle, and unleashed hell. Machine guns and sidearms were all very well and good when attacking an enemy, and I don't mean to disrespect them at all, but a .50 caliber Browning is a different magnitude of power on its own. If a Browning could shatter concrete, fracture steel train rails, and punch through tank armor like they was blocks of cheese, you can imagine the damage it did to a biological organism like the Hive. And we had two of them, too! After Frankie emptied her ammo into the mass of meat, leaving the road and the fields black with guts, a second APV drove up to take her place.

In a last-ditch effort, the tentacles shot out toward the armored cars, aiming for the Brownings, the tires, whatever it could wrap around and squeeze, but that was its final mistake. Ailani shouted into the walkie-talkie.

"Everybody focus on The Hive! Now! Now! Now!"

And we did. We tore through each tentacle, chopping away with bullet, ax, and machete, leaving them squirming and gushing green on the black road. Then we marched forward, hitting it with everything we had. Disarmed (or should I say "de-tentacled?"), the Hive fell onto its side, and the second .50 cal tore it to bits. When we were done, there wasn't nothing left a pile of pulpy ooze. Kind of reminded me of a deflated pumpkin.

"Hold your fire! Hold your fire!" Ailani yelled, and one by one, the assault stopped, leaving the day silent and still. Only the moans and cries of the wounded and dying bled into the air.

We looked at the carnage, the squashed polar crabs, the flopping tentacle meat, the rotting Macks, and couldn't believe it. We'd won. Handily. Little by little the cheers rose up all around. We won! We won!

"Damn," Frankie began. "Can you belie—"

And then the second Hive erupted in the middle of the parking lot.

Here's all ya'll need to know about what happened next: bullets and brains and squeals and screams and running and chaos and blah blah blah. You've seen it before, probably produced by people better at depicting it than me. I don't mean to diminish what happened. It broke my heart. So many good people died. So many brave men and women bashed to pulp by them damn tentacles or ripped to shreds by Macks or gobbled to the marrow by the polar crabs or . . . now see what you done? Almost drew me back into that nonsense. I already told you what a polar-crab-gobbling looks like, anyway, and trust me, it ain't a pretty thing to watch. Probably even worse for the gobble-ee.

You'll be happy to know that some of us survived, I guess. Me, for one (of course), but so did Ailani (thankfully) and Frankie (no comment), and about a baker's dozen of the rest of us.

That was it.

Out of the two hundred and fifty some odd people who woke up that morning with no way of knowing how horrible it would end, we were down to a mere platoon. And the squad of guards on the roof. And the fifty or so kids sniveling in the Aux Gym.

Oh, we were a sorry lot, too, as we hunkered down in the back of the library, licking our wounds and trying to formulate a plan. Some of us were worse for the wear. Frankie was already busted up from before, but now her arm hung at a weird angle, at least until one of the others jammed it back into place. And Ailani's left eye looked about to swell bigger than a basketball. I guess everybody sported some kind of injury, some worse than others. Broken fingers, charred skin, holes and bruises, gashes and gouges and half-chewed limbs. One lady'd even been shot, caught in the gut with a bullet in the chaos that followed that second Hive bursting out of the ground.

I was surprised more of us hadn't been done the same. Ours was not a crack paramilitary troop, you know. We hadn't exactly spent our lives training for a world-ending alien invasion. Sure, Wendell was a former cop and Ailani seemed like she had some kind of Army in her, and I'm sure there were more than a few that had soldiering experience in one way or another, but most of us wasn't battle-trained at all. We were accountants and teachers, food-service workers and lawyers, musicians, carnies, salesman, nannies, marketing reps, personal trainers, mechanics, stay-at-home-moms, comptrollers, and in one case, a lion trainer. On the whole, had about as much military experience as an alligator.

The weirdest thing that happened after we made it to the relative safety of the school (given the situation) was that other than a few bursts of gunfire from the roof and the occasional sound of the Hive slugging away (uselessly, I might add) at the nearly impenetrable shell of bricks and steel and concrete the comprised the outer walls of the indomitable Courtland High School, the enemy didn't try to breach the lower level at all. As far as we knew, Macks and polar crabs were stewing around in the parking lot like, well, like a bunch of mindless Macks and polar crabs, weathering the occasional pot shot from the roof, but otherwise unoccupied, unaware, and unconcerned.

"What are we going to do?" Frankie asked. In addition to all her other injuries and her wonky shoulder, it looked like half her face was burned black. I couldn't tell if it was skin or soot. "Anybody have a plan? Anybody?" When nobody answered, she looked at Ailani. "Ailani?"

Ailani was in shock. She didn't look up. It appeared as though she was only capable of sitting and staring. Frankie snorted, disgusted.

"So much for our great leader."

"Hey," I said. "Knock it off, Frankie."

"You knock it off. Unless you didn't notice, those damn things just wiped us all out."

"Yeah, I noticed. But you ain't helping nothing."

She smiled at me, but it wasn't a nice smile. It reminded me of middle school.

"I'm not listening to some pimply-faced little girl."

"Don't call me little girl."

"Oooh! What are you going to do? Fight me?"

I got to my feet, testing my leg. The old break had twinged in the run back to the school, and my other leg had been raked and shredded, and I might have been tired and angry, but I wasn't going to let her talk to me like that.

"No, Frankie. I ain't going to fight you. But I am going to talk. You all know me. You know what I done—"

"Yeah. You sat in the Commons for a month crying."

"Yeah. Yeah, I did. But that don't confront me none. And it shouldn't confront none of you, neither. I dare any of you to raise your hand if you ain't been in the same state within the last twelve months. Go on, do it."

Nobody but Frankie raised their hand. She looked around at them, shaking her head.

"Alright then," I said. "So this is what we're going to do. I've been in worse spots than this, and I've lived, so there ain't no reason why we can't get through this, too. We're going to get out of this. We're going to live. We're going to—"

"How?" Frankie said.

I looked around at them, and they was all looking back at me. And I . . . well, I didn't know what to say. I didn't really have anything in mind. At a loss for what to do next, I limped over to Ailani and knelt down in front of her.

"Hey. Hey, Ailani. You okay?"

She looked at me with her one good eye but didn't say nothing.

"We're in a bit of pickle here, Ailani." Frankie snorted again. "We're going to need your help, okay? Can you do that?"

"Help?" she whispered. "Yeah. Yeah. Help."

She seemed to notice her surroundings all of the sudden, her eye wandering all around the room, looking at the faces of the people waiting for her to stand up and tell them what to do.

"How many?"

"Dead?" Frankie said. "Hundreds."

"How many left?"

"You're looking at it."

Gunfire popped above us.

"Wendell still up there with his guards?"

"Yeah," I said.

"All of them?" I nodded. "So that's thirty."

Frankie said, "You're going to fight those things with thirty people?"

"Thirty-ish," I said.

"Are you serious?"

"No," Ailani said. "Not fight."

"So what? Do you have some magic plan that—"

"Shut up, Frankie!" I snapped.

"No, I won't shut up! I'll—"

It only took three steps for me to span the distance between the two of us and crack her in the jaw. Hurt like a sonofabitch, too, but the satisfaction of watching her ass hitting the ground was worth it. Then that old familiar feeling zinged through my body, so strong and pure that I saw stars for a moment, like I was the one who'd just had her clock cleaned. I reeled and reached out, hoping somebody would catch me, but nobody did, and then it was my ass's turn to hit the ground.

"You little skank!" Frankie yelled. "None of us needed to die."

I was too busy trying to fight off the effects of the zing to respond.

"Shut it, Frankie."

That was Ailani.

"Don't try to protect her. I heard what that thing wanted. We all did."

"I said shut it!"

"Just her, it said. Just give us her and we'll leave you alone."

"Who?" someone asked.

"Frankie, no."

"Who do you think?"

I raised my hand.

"Me," I said. "It wanted me."

"Amanda."

"No, Ailani. She's right. None of this had to happen. All I had to do was go with them."

"Amanda, they would have killed us anyway."

My head finally cleared enough for me to be able to stand up.

"Maybe," I said. "Maybe not. There's only one way to find out."

And that's how I found myself walking out the front doors of a perfectly safe shelter and directly into the swarming tentacles of the enemy.

It wasn't as bad as you might think, you know. I mean, the Macks were, but only because they stank and were rotting and I could see their bones beneath their sloughed-off skin. And the polar crabs, too, but only because they all stood on their rear legs when I came out the front door and raised their claws in the air and started clicking and clacking all at once. And the Hive was, well, it was the Hive. Even though it sat calm and still in the middle of the parking lot, it didn't set an exactly welcoming table.

I knew everybody was watching from the library window and from the roof. Ailani made like she was going to walk out there with me, but I told her not to bother. When she started to argue, I said, "what do you think will happen to you if you step outside?"

"Same thing that's going to happen to you," Ailani said.

"No."

"No?"

"This is my choice, mine and mine alone. I can take responsibility for what happens to me, but I'd never forgive myself if something happens to you."

"You say that like you're going to live."

"Who says I'm not?"

I'll be the first to admit that down there surrounded by all that stinking flesh and all them horrible monsters, I was beginning to doubt the wisdom of my decision. The only thing I had in my favor was that zinging feeling and a hunch. Until I saw something else. Just a momentary blur, but I saw it. Primary colors. Yellow, red, blue, and green, dashing along the forest line that separated the school grounds from the neighborhood behind it.

The Macks and polar crabs cleared a path for me as I made my way toward the Hive, but they filled in behind me, blocking off all hope of escape. I stopped at the edge of the sidewalk and stared up at the alien thing waiting for me.

"Well," I said. "I'm here. What do you w—"

A tentacle plunged at me, snatched me up, and held me in the air. I could barely breathe, it was squeezing me so tight. Then I heard the voice, the voice of the Hive, buzzing in my head. It filled my skull so loud it felt like about to split wide open, and the voice was terrible and huge, like it was made up of all of the species and all of the beings of all of the planets it had conquered, all of them speaking their own language in a poisonous babel that wormed its way around my brain. I'm telling you, I could feel it. And through it all shot the voices of Earth, the human voices.

"She is the one."

It swelled in waves and waves of sound, spiking my eardrums.

"Such a puny little thing, after all. So frail and insignificant. Did she really think she'd be able to win?"

Once the echoes of the voice dissipated into nothing, I gathered my strength and cleared my head. When I spoke, it was with a strangled rasp.

"Killed more of your kind on my own for such a puny, insignificant thing, didn't I? Just like I'm going to kill you."

The tentacle squeezed tighter and I felt something in my elbow crack. I couldn't breathe. My eyes felt like they were about to pop straight out of my head. I thought . . . nothing. Nothing but fear, but I tried to tamp that down. Fear was just an emotion, chemicals in the brain. Maybe I was dying, maybe it'd be painful, but it wasn't no different than taking a swim or watching TV. It was just something that was happening. Then the tentacles loosened a little, enough for me to breathe, and that I did. I took myself a great, whopping breath.

"Were all of our pets so arrogant?" the Hive asked. "Were all of our pets so stupid?"

"She's so brittle. Her bones so easy to crack." It gave another squeeze.

The zing came back, stronger than before. It pulsed through my body, feeding me, fortifying my muscles, my tendons. It was like my skin had turned to iron, and the tentacle, though it kept the pressure on my neck, didn't hurt me anymore. I took another great, sucking intake of breath. The dizziness left. My arms flexed, my legs flexed, and I knew what was coming.

The guards on the roof began to shout, and the Hive's grip loosened. I heard a massive crunching sound, cracking and whining, like something huge was pushing through the woods that lined the back of the school. I found myself spinning around to face the source. The tops of the trees were shaking. The Macks surged toward them, and the polar crabs flooded in, flowing toward the most beautiful and most horrible thing I'd ever seen.

Five of the beasts from Hangnail's farm lumbered out of the woods, each driven by a figure perched on top of those strange, chitinous horns. Behind them, beneath them, and in front of them scuttled thousands of the polar crabs.

The Girl and her Children. And Timmy Carter, to boot.

The two lines crashed, blue polar-crab on red polar-crab. And Macks. And tentacles. The Macks were torn to shreds, chewed to the nub, and, lurching to the side, set upon by the crabs, even those belonging to the Hive. It was chaos. Absolute chaos. Then Wendell and all the roof guards opened fire, adding more to the mix. Through it all stomped the monsters, kicking through the Hive's forces like elephants to ants.

The Hive was not to be discounted. No, sir. It roared to beat the god of thunder himself. The ground shook and the school shook and the air shook and the asphalt cracked and popped and exploded in great big chunks.

Then the Hive ripped itself out of the ground, using its tentacles as legs. It waded into the fight, holding me out like a shield and aiming for the nearest monster tank. It crashed into it, tentacles pummeling and ripping. The beast roared and reared back, and I saw the rider, the brown-haired boy I shot, pull back on the massive chains he was using as a bridle. The beast stomped on the Hive with its hooves, and I started to scream, and then I was airborne, flying across the parking lot. I landed on the grassy slope next to the tennis courts, the heavy weeds and jungle growth softening the blow. A little. Knocked the wind out of me, and I think I felt another rib crack, too, but I wasn't broke, I wasn't bleeding, and I wasn't dead.

Before I could figure out what I was going to do next, blurs of primary colors zipped out from behind the pine trees lining the drive to the school, and the melonhead kids were suddenly standing around me.

"Missus! We are here for you!"

"Berenice?"

"Yes! Yes! Berenice is here! And Marco and Gorga and Raquel and Bertholdt too! We are here! Here for you!"

She pulled on my arms, clucking and cooing over me, and my gosh did her strength surprise me. For a second I thought she'd haul me all the way to my feet, but she stopped when I was sitting up. I coughed and my side flared with pain. Yep. That was a cracked rib.

"Golly gumdrops, Berenice. You're strong."

She blushed so hard I thought steam would come out of her ears.

"Missus is too kind," she said.

I looked around at all her friends, and I'd be lying if I said their encephalitis heads didn't freak me out. And their red eyes. And their sharp teeth. Crazy old Bertholdt was staring at me with an intensity that bordered on . . . well, no, actually, really was . . . hunger. Berenice started to hop in place.

"Come, Missus! Come with me!"

"What? Where—"

"We will clear a path! You will follow!"

And that's what happened. Getting to my feet made my ribs scream, but I did it, and the melonheads formed a circle around me, Berenice in the front and Bertholdt in the back.

"Where are we going?"

"You must find her, Missus! You must find her and join hands!"

"Who?"

She pointed at the battle raging in front of the school.

"Her!"

If you've never cut through a swath of meat and bone and shell and claw while being protected by a bubble of seven little murder midgets like Berenice and Bertholdt, you ain't seen the most disgusting thing in the world ever. They were like termites to a rotten fence. They were like puppies to a new couch. It was quite the experience. Bertholdt was the absolute worst of the bunch. Went out of his way to cause the maximum possible damage. It wasn't enough for him to stomp a crab or trip up a Mack. He had to pulverize and decapitate, disembowel and eviscerate. He took tongues and slashed scalps, gouged eyes and smashed claws. He was too much.

But it worked. They tore a path straight through everything, and one by one, The Girl and all her friends jumped down off their creatures and followed us until we were standing right in front of the Hive. The melonheads widened their circle to include all five of us. The Girl looked at me and said, "Hold my hand."

I did, and Brownie took the other side, and we formed a ring inside the melonhead bubble. The moment the last two linked their fingers, power surged up inside me, filling my body, my bones, and my blood. My muscles seized, and my head flew back. The surge peaked, and, right when I thought it would blow my skull into fragments, all of the oxygen was sucked out of the air inside the bubble and blasted out in a green sonic ring of pulsating fire, cutting through our enemies: the Macks, the polar crabs, and the Hive.

Everything stopped. The silence in the wake of the battle was absolute. Then the Macks all slid in half, tops separated from the bottoms, and their guts spilled out in sick, wet piles. The polar crabs cracked and black stuff squelched out. Then it was the Hive's turn.

Nothing happened at first. Then it started to hum with some kind of glowing energy that highlighted the red veins that knotted its hide. The thrumming grew more and more powerful, and thick, green goo blasted out of the hole before the whole thing exploded in a hail of fluid and shell and innards that splattered against the side of the school and all over us and the dead Macks and polar-crabs littering the ground all around us.

The power that coursed through us slowly petered out, and we let our hands drop. Like the last time it happened, when The Girl and I killed Hangnail, I was left both exhausted and energized by it all, but the amazement at what we'd revealed inside the Hive trumped how tired I suddenly felt.

Timmy Carter jumped down off his creature and joined us as we waded through the offal, heading over to see what remained of the Hive, and I almost laughed out loud at the way he looked at the melonhead kids when he saw them for the first time, kind of a mingled expression of curiosity, amusement, and disgust. Then he looked at me for an explanation, and I did laugh. I pointed at Berenice.

"Timmy Carter, meet Berenice. She's my friend." Berenice beamed up at me. Bertholdt scowled. "Oh, and this is Bertholdt. Watch out for him."

Timmy Carter gave them both an uncertain nod.

"So, Timmy Carter. I'm a little surprised to see you lot here. Last time we met, you was none too pleased with me."

"Yeah. It wasn't easy, but I eventually won them over."

Ailani and all colony crowd filed out the front of the school and stared around at the carnage in wonder. When Timmy Carter saw Frankie walking among them, he brightened up considerable. He looked like he was about to go over to her, but then she saw him, too, and . . . well, let's just say I could tell by the expression on her face that the happiness was not returned. Timmy Carter saw it, too. I don't think I've ever seen someone so relieved and regretful at the same time.

Berenice tugged on my hand, pulling me toward the remains of the Hive.

"Missus! Missus! What is that, Missus?"

She was pointing to the dead, black muscle suspended in the middle of the gooey wreckage of the Hive's innards. I circled the thing, tripping over a severed tentacle that twitched and sent me near to swallowing my own heart. The bottom was already turning black, and I could see the fibrous outlines of what used to be its various chambers. I wish I could say I'd never been inside a hive but I can't. I will say this, though: the damn thing was huge. Cavernous.

The black thing hanging in the middle beat one time, a weak, heavy thud—boom BOOM—paused, then beat one more time. And that's when I knew. That's when we all knew. I was just about to tell her what it was when Bertholdt burst through from the other side, screaming "Eeeeahhhh!" as we were showered with more black and green glop.

Berenice wiped a clean place on her face so she could see.

"Bad, Bertholdt! Wicked boy!"

Bertholdt squealed with joy and stomped around inside the dead Hive.

"It's a heart, Missus!" he cried. "A heart! A heart! A heart!"

Daddy was a perpetual motion machine. From the moment he woke up to the moment he went to bed, he was busy getting things done. And if he wasn't working on something (the farm, the animals, the pot), he was crashed out pretty much wherever he could lie down. All he needed was a flat space. One time I found him snoring away on the kitchen floor, usually in the middle of the afternoon, half a sandwich in his hand, as if he thought, "I'm hungry, but I'm too tired to make it over to the couch."

"Daddy, we should just build you a cot in there," I often said.

"Nah. That'd take away from the fun."

His naps weren't long. Twenty minutes here. Ten minutes there. Just enough to provide him with energy for the next project he decided to take on.

I couldn't imagine him going on a vacation of any type, likening it in his mind, as someone of his disposition would, to the apocalypse. That's why I was shocked when, one summer, he said, "'Manda, pack your bags. We're going to the beach."

I suppose I had something to do with it. Toward the end of that school year, a whole bunch of my friends was talking about their summer plans. I didn't join in because my summer plans were basically what I did all the time: help out on the farm. But they kept on talking about some beach they were going to. It was all I heard about for the last month of school. the beach this and the beach that. I played along like I knew what they was talking about. One of them even showed me a sticker she got the year before, a big white thing with the name of the place printed on it. OBX. I even told some of them I'd been there before.

"OBX?" I said. (I pronounced it like it was a word. 'Ohbix'). "Oh yeah. Of course. Uh-huh. Sand dunes. Seafood. Kite shop."

They laughed at me, of course.

That night while we were eating dinner, burgers and salad again, I said, "Daddy? Where's Ohbix?"

"What?"

"The beach. Danni Tyler and Emma Jarvis said their families go there every summer."

"I think you mean O.B.X."

"Oh."

Now I knew why my friends laughed at me.

"It's in North Carolina. It stands for Outer Banks. O.B.X is an acro—"

"I know what an acronym is."

He took a bite of his burger and chewed thoughtfully. I picked at my bun.

"'Manda, is there something wrong?"

"How come we never go on vacation?"

"Is that what this is about?"

"Danni and Emma go to the beach every summer. They're always talking about how fun it is."

"I bet."

"Can we go?"

Daddy didn't say anything for a long time, and I knew better than to push him. He didn't speak until he was almost done eating, then he said, "I'll think about it."

"Really?"

"It don't mean we can go, but I'll think about it."

He didn't have to think long. As it turned out, Daddy knew a guy who knew a guy who had a trailer on the sound. It was musty and the beds smelled funny and the stove didn't work and there were weird stains on the carpet, but I didn't care about any of that. We spent our days sunning on the beach and playing in the water. I don't think I'd ever seen Daddy so relaxed and happy before in my life.

He actually slept in all week! (Although for him, sleeping in meant getting up at seven in the morning instead of five). One day he bought a football and we went out and tossed it around until my arm was numb. We ate fruit we bought at a stand on the way down, made turkey sandwiches for lunch, and at night, we cooked shrimp fresh from the ocean on a Webber grill Daddy brought with us. It was the best time I'd ever had in my entire life.

My favorite thing about it was the outdoor shower. It didn't come with the house. Daddy fixed one up himself with a bucket and some rope and a ring of shower curtains. It might've been as country as country came, but boy was that the greatest feeling in the world.

That's how I got the idea for the outdoor showers we built behind the Aux Gym. We might have gotten power from the windmill the Vo-Tech kids built before the end of the world (and the solar panels we looted from some of the richer houses in the neighborhoods around us), and even though the toilets still flushed, without a well for miles around, water for cooking and bathing was a different story, so we relied on the natural humidity and whatever rain came our way, which is to say a LOT of rain.

After I washed all the gook and blood and gross stuff off, and after I washed my hair, I went back to the commons where everyone else was sitting. I was wondering why nobody else was using the other showers (we made a bank of eight) when I saw they'd gathered around a figure in a white lab coat. He turned around, that icy smile plastered on his face, and I lost my mind.

One second I was squeezing the water out of my hair, the next I was rushing straight for him. Because that was Dr. Huntington, the crazy man who injected me with that poison for no reason at all. Before I could hit him, a little red blur sped in from the right and then I was flat on my face. I pushed off the ground and a kick to my middle sent me spinning onto my back, and then he was on me, Bertholdt, the little freak, punching me in the face, breathing his rotten breath all over me. He was babbling in some weird language that sounded half like some kind of German mixed with hysterical laughter. I covered my head with my arms, but he still managed to get in some shots to my temples.

When he slowed down and got tired, I found an opening in all the punching and pushed him off, shoving so hard that he flew a few feet into the air before hitting one of the brick pillars. The good doctor hadn't moved an inch. In fact, he was staring at me, shocked. I got to my knees, grimacing, and prepared to launch myself at him, but Berenice jumped in my way.

"No, Missus!"

"Get out of the way, Berenice."

"But he's a friend, not a foe! Look! See!"

Everybody else was staring at me, just as horrified as Doctor Huntington. Ailani. Frankie. Timmy Carter. The Girl. Brownie. To say I was confused would be an understatement. Timmy Carter, always the sly one, said, "He's on our side, Amanda."

"On our side hell." I stood up, fists clenched, hoping the doctor would say something stupid so I could have an excuse to punch him. "He shot me full of green goo. Probably trying to turn me into one of his little frea—" I glanced at Berenice. "Trying to experiment on me."

"No, Missus! No!" Berenice said. "Dr. Huntington wants to help her."

"You should listen to your new friend, my dear," Dr. Huntington said. "She may be small, but she's wiser than you know."

"First of all, don't call me 'dear.' Second of all, if you're such a friend, then why'd you shoot me up with that stuff?"

The doctor looked at me like I had a cockroach sneak out of my eye.

"Why, to help you, my dear."

"I told you not to call me that. And help me do what?"

"Kill the Hive, of course."

THE HIVE

SEASON 4

DR. HUNTINGTON'S MIRACULOUS HIVE JUICE EXTRACTOR

I think I've already told ya'll about my various failures over the year that the Hive ruled the Earth. I failed to save my Daddy. I failed to save my friends. I failed to save my farm. I failed and failed and failed again. That's a lot of failure for a teenager to handle, and it wasn't the kind of failure that didn't mean anything, neither. These was the kinds that brought grown women to their knees. I can't say it didn't affect me because it did, but one of the reasons I was able to get over it wasn't just because of Ailani and the return of the Hive and such, but because, well, even though I made my own decisions (I don't think nobody could have stopped me from doing what I set out to do once I set out to doing it), I never felt like I was responsible for anything other than myself. There's a comfort in that, but it's a kid's comfort, and if there's one thing kids don't never understand too good it's responsibility. It might not affect nobody in the short run, but it resounds like a whisper in an empty well, ringing out and out and out, and those rings might take a while to reach the bottom, but when they do, they bounce back—maybe not as hard and maybe not as strong, but they do bounce back, and they roll over a body in ways nobody could never see coming.

I never was and never will be a girly girl. I blame it on Daddy. He didn't exactly raise me like one, but he didn't raise me like the other, neither. He raised me like he needed to raise me, for the person I was and the person I had to become. The farm didn't run itself, and without Momma around and no other siblings to speak of, I took on pretty much every other role he needed filled. Need help fixing that cultivator? Sure, Daddy. I know a socket wrench from a riveter. Need to shoe that horse or deliver that calve? Sure, Daddy. I know a horse nipper from a calving chain. Need to sweeten up the Sheriff, make him turn a blind nose to the heady scent of them weeds you got growing out in the east fields? Sure, Daddy. I'll rustle up Nana's old apple pie recipe sure as starch.

I guess we were alone together for so long that I got some strange ideas in my head about men and women and fathers and daughters. No, it wasn't like that. This ain't that kind of story. I'm talking about Daddy and Daddy alone. I guess I always supposed it was going to be him and me and no one else. I was fine with the way things was, so why shouldn't he be? But people get lonely, and even though Daddy had me and Blue and his pot buddies, it ain't the same thing as having a partner, someone who you don't just share physical affection with, but someone to talk to, keep you company, share a cup of coffee by the fire on cold winter nights, go for a walk, lean on in bad times and share victories in good times. Me and Daddy, we was close, but sitting with your daughter on the porch on a rainy Saturday morning is one thing, and sitting on that same porch on that same rainy Saturday morning with your wife or girlfriend or significant what-have-you is another.

All this is a roundabout way of saying one day Daddy came home with a woman, and that woman was not my momma. That's not to say that I didn't think it was her at first, my momma that is. I came downstairs one rare Saturday morning between practices (softball or basketball or soccer or field hockey) and nearly peed all over myself when I seen her standing in the kitchen. My momma was tall and skinny with long hair and skin bronzed from years of working out in the sun, and there she was again, years after she died, her hip cocked against the counter and her back to me, a cup of coffee held in one hand and her other arm wrapped around her waist. I was about to say "Momma?" when the woman turned around and the words got caught in my throat.

"Well, hello," she said. "You must be Amanda."

So, yeah, Daddy had a type.

Ya'll met my momma before, even if technically that wasn't her. It was a reasonable facsimile. Whoever this was was even closer to the real thing. She was as tall as Momma and as skinny as Momma, and, yeah, she had Momma's long brown hair, but after that, all the comparisons stopped. This lady's voice was coarse like she smoked (which she did), and she had a softer face than momma's, too, and she wore too much makeup, and she liked to wear cowboy boots and dresses, and she had Daddy's favorite flannel on over her clothes like it was hers and I took an immediate dislike to her and I didn't know why.

"Who are you?" I said.

Her cheeks reddened and her smile strained, and I could tell she didn't like to be talked to that way, but she held onto her composure as best she could.

"My name's Elizabeth," she said. "But you can call me Lizzie."

I didn't know what was going on. Daddy'd never brought a woman home before in his life. All I knew was I wanted to eat breakfast and settle down in front of the TV for a full morning of cartoons and stories and there was some strange woman standing in the way.

I walked past her and over to the cupboard to get out my bowl and spoon, and Daddy came down the stairs and said, "Amanda May. I raised you better'n that. Ain't you got something to say to Lizzie?"

Raised me better? I had no idea what he was talking about. *Star Trek* was about to come on. I turned around from the fridge, the jug of milk in my hand.

"You want some cereal?"

Lizzie laughed.

"No thank you. I better be going, anyway." She put her coffee cup down on the counter and walked over to Daddy and planted a big old kiss right on his lips! My eyes were like about to pop out. "I'll call you?"

Daddy's face was redder'n a tomato, but he was smiling big and wide.

"Sure."

"I had fun."

"Me, too."

She patted him on the chest and rolled her shoulders straight and looked at me.

"Nice to meet you, Amanda. Maybe I'll take you up on that cereal next weekend?"

Not if I can help it, I thought, watching her sashay out of the kitchen. I wish I could say I was relieved when the door clicked behind her, but then I realized that she was still wearing Daddy's shirt.

"Daddy!" I said, but he was already heading back up to his room. And he was *whistling.* "Where you going?"

"I think I'll go back to bed for a bit."

"Back to bed? But ain't there work to do?"

"It can wait."

"But that lady stole your shirt."

"Her name's Lizzie, 'Manda. I'll get it back. Maybe next weekend."

Lizzie certainly did come back the next weekend. And the weekend after that, and the weekend after that. Pretty soon, she showed up during the week, too. More people followed, her friends, I guess, men and women her age or a little younger, which is to say younger than Daddy. They came over at all hours of the day, and they stayed up late drinking and laughing and playing loud music. It was very un-Daddy like of him, and I don't mean that he wasn't acting like a good father. He was and always would be. I mean that, well, I'd never seen him that way before. Sure, he grew and sold marijuana, but he didn't take advantage of it. And I never seen him drink more than a few beers, at least not around me. But now he was partying nearly every night of the week.

That wasn't so bad, but I wasn't sleeping very good because of it, and I guess my teachers noticed it because one of them, my AP Human Geo teacher, Mr. X (seriously, his last name was Xander, but we all called him Mr. X because it sounded cooler), asked me to stay after class one day.

"Everything okay, Amanda?"

"Yeah."

"You've been falling asleep in class."

"I know. I'm just tired is all."

"You look more than tired. You look exhausted."

"I'll be okay, Mr. X. Thanks for asking."

I turned to leave, but he said, "Amanda?"

"Yeah?"

"Do you know what your grade is in my class?"

I didn't know, but that wasn't unusual. I always got A's and B's on my interims and report cards. I didn't see why it'd be any different now. But the way Mr. X said it, I guess I wasn't doing so hot.

"I got a C or something?"

"Worse than that, Amanda."

"I got a D?"

He shook his head. My stomach felt like someone had dropped a barrel of ice in it. He picked a crumpled up piece of paper up off his desk and walked over to me, adjusting his glasses so he could read it better. The noise of the kids out in the hall was getting softer as they all filtered into their classes.

"Mr. X, the bell—"

"That can wait. Did you see what you got on your last test?"

"Yeah. I mean, no."

"I believe it."

He handed me the crumpled up paper. It was my test. He'd written a big, fat F on it in red ink, and under that 'Come talk to me.'

"I found this on the floor," he said, nodding at the direction of my desk. "Where you sit."

I looked at the test. It was on Language and Culture. Easy stuff. Mr. X's notes were really clear, I did all the reading, but even though I knew when the test was and I tried to study, I didn't. Why? Because Lizzie and Daddy and all her friends kept me up all night laughing and playing music and smoking and drinking and I got so mad that I couldn't think so I put my headphones on and listened to my CDs all night until I fell asleep and I woke up late for school and Daddy was passed out in his room and Lizzie was there too and I had to walk to school and . . .

"Amanda?"

"I know. I know, Mr. X. I'm sorry I failed this test. I understand if you fail me. I'll try to do better next time."

"I don't care about the test. I'm worried about you. This isn't like you. Is something going on?"

I looked at that dumb test and saw my stupid answers and the blank spaces where I should have answered.

"I'm just tired is all."

"You said that."

The bell rang.

"Mr. X—"

"It's not just my class, Amanda. It's everyone. Well, except for P.E, but . . ."

"I get it."

"Amanda—"

"I said I get it, Mr. X."

I crumpled up the test again, angry all of the sudden. I thought I was mad at Mr. X. Who did he think he was? My name was Amanda May Jett. I knew how to study. I knew how to get good grades. I was one of the best student-athletes in Spotsylvania High School. I stomped out of his room and down the hall to my next class, throwing the test on the floor on the way.

That night after field hockey practice, I went home to find the house empty. I fixed myself a turkey sandwich, hauled my backpack full of books up to my room, put my headphones on and got to studying. I had a test in Environmental Science the next day and I'd be bound and tied if I'd let myself fail that one.

I'm not sure what time I fell asleep, but it was gone midnight when I sat straight up in my desk with a gasp. My CD was over and my headphones sat askew on my head and I'd drooled all over my notes.

Music was blaring downstairs and somebody screeched and laughed.

That did it. I'd had enough. I ripped off my headphones, slammed open the door, stomped down the stairs, around the corner, and into the kitchen.

"Daddy! I've had it with all this—"

I stopped short.

The most beautiful creature I'd ever seen in my life was leaning against the counter next to the sink. He was tall and thin, and he had long hair and the barest hint of stubble on his chin, and even though he was wearing a flannel shirt, he didn't wear it like any of the other boys I knew. He didn't tuck it into his blocky, farmer's jeans; he tied it around his waist, let it hang down over an old pair of torn up black Levis that ended in some severely distressed combat boots.

Lizzie was there, too, darn it, and she guffawed when she saw my reaction to the boy standing next to her and shot a sideways glance at Daddy, who tucked his chin and wouldn't meet my eyes.

"Hey, Amanda," she said. "Meet my son, Steve."

Steve gave me a chin-nod.

"'Sup."

Of course.

Of course he was her son.

Now that I looked harder, all the features were there. He had her hair and her build, and even though their noses and mouths were different, they shared the same sharp blue eyes.

"H-hi," I said. "I . . . um—"

"Flustered, Amanda?" Lizzie asked.

Daddy said, "Stop, Lizzie."

"Aw. Her cheeks are blooming!"

Ain't nothing like a healthy scoop of hate and irritation to smack someone back into the world.

"You all need to stop bothering me. Staying up into the middle of the night drinking and smoking. I got tests to pass and you're waking me up with this mess. It's gone midnight!"

"Sorry, 'Manda," Daddy said. "We'll be more mindful of that from now on."

"Mindful, hell! Ya'll need to stop."

Lizzie looked over at Daddy and said, "Should we tell her about it?"

"Tell me about what?"

Daddy cleared his throat.

"'Manda, Steve's father lives out in Seattle, and he got himself into some trouble."

"So?"

"So, well, he's got primary custody of Steve, and . . ."

I tapped my foot and crossed my arms over my chest, waiting for him to finish, but after a few sheepish looks shared between him and Lizzie, I got the gist.

"He's staying here with us?"

"It's just for a little while. We got plenty of room."

"Why can't he stay with her?"

"Her name's Lizzie, 'Manda."

"Why can't he stay with Elizabeth?"

"That's the other thing I wanted to talk to you about."

Oh. My. God. That witch was moving in with us.

"Seriously? I live here, too. Anybody ever think about asking how I felt about it?"

"'Manda—"

"'Manda nothing," I snapped, and then I stomped back up the stairs.

My head might have been aswirl with anger, and I definitely was peeved, but the presence of an exotic beauty from far away cut it down. Way down. To be honest, I was half-titillated, half-concerned. Steve might have been a sexy thing, but the Spotsylvania boys were going to have the time of their lives with him. He was a jaguar in a field of apes. *Well, good*, I thought. I didn't need him rattling around in my brain, not if I wanted to play field hockey and pass my classes. A boy would just get in the way.

Like I had a choice in the matter. The truth of it all was that the damage had been done. Steve was in my head. As if to remind me of that fact, his voice floated up after me as I marched into my room.

"Nice to meet you, Amanda."

I needn't have worried about him. Steve might have been built like a snake on stilts, but he could sure enough handle his own. Proved that the first day of school. Suffice to say, his grunge chic didn't fit in with camouflage and dungarees, and it took all of about ten minutes after Lizzie registered him for him to get in a fight. Two football players thought they'd be smart and said something to him he didn't like as he passed them in the hallway, and Steve didn't even blink. He spun and punched one of them so hard it knocked him out on the spot, and when the second one tackled him, he got him in a wrestling hold and looked like he was about to choke him out before one of the APs got him in his own choke hold and pulled him off.

I was standing there when it happened, walking to English with Molly Brown.

"Who's that?" she asked as we watched them drag Steve away.

"No clue."

"He's cute, don't you think?"

I didn't answer.

Daddy wasn't home after practice, but Steve was. He'd already got his punishment: ten days automatic suspension. I walked down the drive from the bus stop to see him sitting outside Maurice surrounded by a whole bunch of junk he'd pulled out. I was tempted. In a variety of ways. But my first instinct was to run up to my room and make sure I was out of the way when Daddy came home and saw some dumb kid messing around with his Maurice like that. Steve actually waved at me as I frog-stepped myself into the house. I think I might have given him half an elbow in return.

For those of you hoping for some kind of love story between me and him, you're reading the wrong book. Steve might have blown my fifteen-year-old mind with his rock-n-roll hair and clothes and attitude, but anybody familiar with Daddy would know that he didn't care much about that at all. The stunt with Maurice was only the beginning. That night when Lizzie got home from work, Daddy had already encountered Steve's project, and while I was a little disappointed at the lack of quality yelling, he did make up for it with one of the quietest nights in over two months.

As it turned out, Steve wanted to live with his mother out on that farm about as much as I wanted to live in Seattle with his dad. He was a master in the art of screwing up, too. One thing after another. During his two weeks off, he managed to break the tractor (twice), run Daddy's truck into a pond (twice), get caught shoplifting a pack of gum and a bag of chips from the 7-11 on Lafayette (after hitchhiking into the city), get picked up by the police after passing out from drinking Mad Dog 20/20 under the train bridge with a homeless woman (after hitchhiking into the city again), and finally, the coup de grace, steal a pound of one of Daddy's choicest batches of weed, viciously denying it only to have Daddy rip through his room and find it tucked up under his bed.

The late night talks between Daddy and Lizzie transitioned from quiet hobnobs to out right roof-raisers. The pot thievery turned out to be the final straw as Lizzie could not believe her precious little baby would do something like that, even in the face of all the other dumb crap he was pulling, and even though Daddy himself told her what the little delinquent had done. I didn't have to wait until the next morning for her to exit the premises. She stormed out that very night, slinky Stevie in tow, and burned two ruts in our front lawn on her way off our property and out of my life forever.

I waited a good hour before venturing out of the safety of my room to look for Daddy. I was sure he'd be mad at me for some reason, even if, for the first time in a while, I hadn't done nothing wrong. I found him sitting out on the lawn, rocking on the glider, a customary joint burning between his fingers, and a can of his favorite beer in the other hand.

"Hey, 'Manda," he said as I approached. "You wanna have a sit?"

I did. I knew him well enough not to press. He'd just shut me down. I had to let him get used to my being there, let him get his head on right, maybe take a few tokes and a couple of swigs. He kicked the glider and the metal creaked and the springs chimed. When I was close to sure he was ready, I said, "You okay, Daddy?"

He sighed.

"Yeah. I'm good."

"I'm sorry it ended like that."

"Thanks, 'Manda."

"You're welcome." The night sounds swelled up around us. The moon came out.

"He was a slick little thing, wasn't he?" Daddy asked.

"Slicker'n snot."

"That's gross, 'Manda. Plus, snot ain't slick. It's sticky."

"Still."

"You hated Lizzie from the moment I introduced you, ain't that right?"

"Daddy, that's—"

"It's okay. I never expected us to end up like the Brady Bunch."

"Okay. I didn't like her much, but I didn't like the late hours and the keeping me up more, to be honest."

"Fair enough."

"And it ain't like I don't want you to be happy."

"I know. But I bet you're happier now, ain't you."

"I ain't gonna lie."

"Interesting how things work out sometimes, ain't it?"

"How so?"

"You wanted her out. Now she's out."

"Slick Stevie took care of that. Not me. You just said it."

"And yet the result's still the same."

"Well, that ain't fair."

"All I'm saying is if Stevie hadn't come along, you would have took matters into your own hands, wouldn't you?"

My silence was all the response he needed.

"Thought so."

"Is that what you think of me?"

"It ain't what I think. It's what I know."

Suddenly I was mad. Daddy brought home some skanky piece, nearly had me failing all my classes with all their partying, and when her delinquent son ruined the whole thing, I was the one to blame for it? Uh-uh. Not today. I stood up off that glider and spun around.

"I got news for you, Daddy. I wasn't planning nothing. You're just bitter and mean and you're taking it out on me!"

He pointed at me with his lit joint.

"Now, look, Amanda May—"

I smacked that joint out of his hand.

"No, you look. I didn't do nothing but lose sleep the whole time Lizzie was here. You've been so high for the last month that you didn't even realize it. You haven't even gone to one of my games yet. Did you know I scored two goals last week?"

His anger softened.

"Two goals?"

"Yeah. I'm on track to set a school record."

"Oh. That's good."

"Uh-huh. Because unlike you, that's all I been doing. What I should have been doing. I'm sorry your girlfriend left, but you're right, I ain't sorry she's gone."

I turned around and stomped off to the house before he could say anything else.

Later on, he tapped on my door. I was sitting at my desk, reading *To Kill A Mockingbird* for English. I'd just finished the part when Scout and Jem got attacked by that no-good piece-of-garbage Bob Ewell and Scout realized that Boo Radley had saved her life. I ain't a bawler, but that part had me weeping.

"What?" I said as I wiped the tears away.

"Can I come in?"

"No."

"Please? I got something I need to say to you."

I made him wait. Felt good to do it.

"It's unlocked."

Daddy turned the knob and opened the door. He didn't come all the way in but leaned against the frame.

"I owe you an apology, 'Manda."

"Okay."

"You were right. I ain't exactly been the best father these last couple weeks."

"It's okay."

"Do you forgive me?"

"Of course I do, Daddy."

"I love you, 'Manda May."

"I love you, too."

The tension between us evaporated, and I could breathe again.

"I'm going to grill some burgers," he said "You want one?"

"I want two."

"Two it is. You want this door shut again?"

"No. You can leave it open. Daddy?"

"Yeah."

"Did you love her?"

"I think I could have."

"I guess sometimes things don't work out no matter how much you want them to."

"Seems that way, don't it?"

That wasn't the way me and Ailani and Dr. H and Timmy Carter and everybody else was going to let things happen, though. Yeah, it took all I could take not to beat Dr. H's head in when I saw him standing in the commons like he earned it, and I can't say I didn't regret the decision not to beat his head in every minute for the next five months, and I didn't know whether or not he was serious or if I should trust him, but everybody seemed to, so I guess I had to go along with it.

I'd met people like Dr. H plenty of times in my life, usually in school. My fifth-grade SCOPE teacher. My ninth grade science teacher. My tenth-grade History teacher. My eleventh-grade English teacher. Pious and condescending, he was the type of person who could never be wrong, and when he was, he found some way to gaslight or distract or digress or change the subject or do whatever he needed to do to make himself seem smarter.

But he told us outright he wanted to get rid of the Hive. Told us it was an "affront to his principals." When a pious, condescending jerk talked like that, usually he meant it.

"I am a scientist," he said. "And as such, I believe in the natural order of the universe. Not just the Earth but the Universe. It all operates on the same principals and laws, of physics, of biology, of gravity, of meteorology. The Hive is Judas. Lucifer. It seeks to bend the Universe to its will and by so doing it will unravel us all."

See what I'm talking about? That's how he spoke to us. We were all of us sitting around a lunch table (with him at the head, of course), all of us adults except me, and he carried on like he was explaining the alphabet to a classroom filled with toddlers.

"Dr. Huntington," Ailani said. "We understand that the Hive is . . . bad. But you said you could help us kill it. Isn't that what we just did?"

"Certainly, however—"

"Without your help."

He pressed his lips together.

"You mean to embarrass me? At a time such as this, with our world in grave danger, you take offense to my knowledge? This. This is the problem with our species."

"Nobody's taking offense to nothing, Dr. H," I said.

"Don't call me that, child."

"Don't call me 'child'."

Frankie sighed and said, just loud enough for everyone to hear, "this is going great."

"Shut up, Frankie."

"You shut up, Amanda. This whole thing could have been avoided if it wasn't for you."

I couldn't help it. My mouth dropped open a little bit. A stunned silence followed. Everybody except Dr. H knew what she meant.

"What is this?" he asked. Nobody responded. "To what does this young lady refer?"

"She wants me dead."

"Amanda, don't," Ailani said.

"You heard her, Ailani. All this is my fault, right Frankie? You just said it."

"I'm just saying . . . "

"I know you're just saying. Everybody in here knows it. Why don't you 'just say it' out loud?"

"Amanda."

Frankie rolled her eyes.

"Whatever."

That uncomfortable silence fell again, and it took Dr. H's exasperated sigh to break it.

"The world hangs in balance. Monsters threaten our very existence. And we are held hostage by the whingeing of women."

"Dr. Huntington, that's enough," Ailani said. "You're a guest here, but you can't talk to my friends that way. You want to act like the president, go ahead, but you're not in charge. We're willing to listen to what you have to say, but unless you say it, you need to get out."

"My dear, what exactly do you think it is that I am trying to do?"

She stared at him, her jaw clenching and unclenching.

"Say what you need to say."

"Thank you. Simply put, the world is getting warmer, and it's because of the invaders. They are releasing carbon monoxide into the atmosphere. The carbon monoxide gets trapped, and the sunlight, reflecting off the glaciers is unable to escape, thus creating an endless feedback loop."

"I've heard this before," I said. "Isn't this about the ozone layer?"

Dr. H smirked.

"No, my ch . . . no. It is not about the ozone layer. It is about climate change. The Hive is recreating the Earth to suit itself and all of the creatures it employs. If we do not stop it, the invaders won't have to kill us off. All it will have to do is merely wait until what few of us are left go extinct."

I let that information sink in. The sound of the children playing in the auxiliary gym echoed faintly in the commons.

"How long?"

"How long what?"

"How long do we have to stop it?"

"If my projections are reliable, less than a year. Six months, if we're lucky."

"Okay," I said. "If that's true—"

"*If* it is true!"

"*If* it is true, then how do we stop it? We've been killing hives and cutting down Macks for over a year and they keep coming back. And if there are hives all over the world and Macks all over the world, there's no way we can get them all. Not in time to stop it."

"It's the age's old tale, Ms. Jett, yes? May I call you Ms. Jett?"

"Actually, yeah. You can call me that."

"Very good, Ms. Jett."

"So what do we do?"

"We destroy the source, Ms. Jett. Kill the head and the body will follow."

"And how do we do that?"

"With me," the Girl said. She must have read the doubt in my expression because she said "you know it's true, Amanda. Between me and you and the others, we have power. But we need all seven of us to have enough to do what he wants us to do."

"And I've killed two of them."

Dr. H, in what I assume was an effort to break the tension, said, "but worry not! You are not the only one of your ilk!" He gestured at the Girl. "Madam?"

"There are more of us. People like me. And you, Amanda. People who can stop the Hive. But they're not here."

"Fine. Where are they? Let's go get them."

"We have to go back. Back there."

I knew what she meant. She meant the Hive world. The place where I killed my sister and my momma. Or what the aliens passed off as my sister and my Momma.

"Okay. How? That tentacle gassed me the first time. Tried to choke me to death. I don't think I want to do that again for obvious reasons."

"We create a controlled situation," Dr. H said.

"How?"

"The gas only converts when it reacts with the oxygen in the atmosphere. It originates as a liquid deep inside the marrow of the tentacles."

"Oh, I get it," I said. "We got to collect the juice."

"Precisely, Ms. Jett."

"How do we do that?"

"That's exactly the question I was hoping you would ask. Bertholdt! Come!"

We heard a bang and a squeal out in the chorus hall followed by squeaking sounds, and then Bertholdt pushed a cart into the commons. Sitting on top of it was a gigantic, metal syringe.

"May I introduce you to—" Bertholdt lost control of the cart and it ran into one of the concrete pillars. "Damn you, Bertholdt! Fix it! Fix it! No, don't do that. Just . . . never mind. Shoo. Go back to . . . oh, now don't cry. Please, you embarrass yourself. What? No, I'm not angry. Just disappointed. Yes, of course you can still have cocoa tonight. There, there." Then to us. "Please excuse Bertholdt. This whole year has been very difficult for him."

Yeah, I bet. The little demon had nestled himself under Dr. H's arm, and his red eyes glared out at us, me in particular. He smiled with them pointy teeth.

"Now run along, Berthold," Dr. H said. "I'll be done here in a little while."

Bertholdt scurried away, nattering in his strange language.

"So what is it?" I asked, nodding at the syringe on the cart.

"Ah, yes. This. I call this Dr. Huntington's Miraculous Hive Juice Extractor."

"What does it do?"

"Why, Ms. Jett. It extracts the hive juice."

That's how one gray November morning, Timmy Carter and I found ourselves squatting in the bushes on the edge of a clearing, watching a tentacle wiggle out of a hive hole. Dr. Huntington didn't just supply us with his Miraculous Hive Juice Extractor, he also provided specialty masks, something we could use to make sure we weren't overcome by the hive gas. He called them Dr. Huntington's Superlative Hive Mist Multi-Valve Vapor Respirators, but to me, they looked like something he looted from a hardware store.

Timmy Carter hoisted the Hive Juice Extractor under his arm and gathered his feet beneath him. When we'd strapped the masks on tight, he nodded at me and I nodded at him and was about to make the go-head signal but before I could, a screechy battle cry came from the other side of the clearing, and Berenice and Bertholdt and all their creepy little melonhead brothers and sisters burst out of the bushes and attacked.

"So much for the plan," I muttered.

There are a lot of things I never thought I'd experience in my life. I never thought I'd see an alien. Or a polar crab. Or a kangape. As strange as all of them sound by themselves, none of them rank anywhere near the sight of a half-dozen melonhead children swarming over an alien tentacle growing out of the ground.

That tentacle was plenty angry, too. It whipped and swung and bashed with the strength of an ox. But them melonheads was tougher than pine knots, and every time that tentacle slung one off or smashed one into the dirt, she or he or it or whatever got up, shook it off, and jumped back into the fight. They did them some damage too, tearing into the rubbery skin with their teeth, bashing it with rocks and sticks. Bertholdt even brought himself one of the good doctor's scalpels and took to slicing the dang thing up like he was carving a pumpkin.

While they were distracting it and making it weaker, Timmy Carter and I snuck up with the Extractor. Timmy Carter might have been able to carry around on his shoulders by himself, but it took the two of us to operate it, which we achieved with the skill and smoothness of an old married couple trying to move a heavy piece of furniture.

"Pick your end up higher!"

"This is as high as my arms go!"

"Slow down!"

"Speed up!"

"Watch that stump."

"What st . . . ouch!"

It was a miracle we even moved that thing the thirty or so feet from the edge of the clearing to the base of the tentacle let alone positioned it to hit the right spot. That was my job. Had to angle the needle just right or we wouldn't hit the main vein. If I nicked it or stuck the meat, the whole tentacle exploded for some reason, coating us in green and purple goo. I'd already botched it two times out of four, and even though the melonheads thought it was funny (every. single. time), I could tell Timmy Carter was getting mighty irritated. I didn't blame him. Nobody liked to get covered in green and purple goo, even if the green and purple goo was mostly plant matter.

"Bring it closer!" I yelled.

"You're aiming it wrong!"

"Bring it closer!"

"Duck!"

The tentacle swung around with three of the melonhead children latched onto its side, screaming and laughing. I was already kneeling, so it was wasn't difficult to hit the deck, but Timmy Carter was standing up, holding the other end of the extractor. He had just enough time to drop it before the tentacle hit him square in the chest and sent him flying. He hit a dead oak tree and slumped to the ground. The tree cracked and creaked, and then it fell forward.

"Aw man," I said.

It was going to fall on me if I didn't move. The melonheads sprang off like ticks in a fire, and I rolled to the side and the tree came crashing down, crushing the tentacle, which exploded in a shower of green and purple goo.

"Dang it!" I yelled, pounding the earth. "Timmy Carter, you okay?"

He didn't answer.

"Timmy Carter!"

Still nothing.

"Timmy—"

"I'm okay. Alive, at least. Busted a rib. Or two."

Berenice came running up.

"Missus! Missus! That was the best one yet! Did you see me ride? Did you? Did you?"

I got to my knees and tried to wipe the goo off my sleeves, but it was pointless.

"Yes, I saw—the Extractor!"

I whipped around, certain I'd find it crushed under the trunk, but it wasn't. The fallen tree had narrowly missed it. It lay next to the base of the tentacle underneath some dead branches. I scrambled over on my hands and knees and broke the branches off, then slouched back.

"Oh, no, Missus! Oh, no!"

"What is it?" Timmy Carter asked. He'd gotten to his feet and was limping over, one hand covering his ribs.

"The tentacle juice," I said. "What little we got. The tree broke the container."

"What?"

I unscrewed the glass receptacle from its socket, what was left of it, and held it up to him.

"It's all gone."

Timmy Carter shook his head ruefully.

"Well, if it's any consolation," he said. "It wasn't even a quarter full." He sat down on the dead trunk with a groan.

I rummaged around in my backpack.

"We've got another container. We just need to find the right vein is all."

"Maybe. Or maybe they're all drying up. It's too late in the fall."

"I don't know what to tell you, Timmy Carter. The man wants his hive juice." I screwed the new container in. "The man gets his hive juice."

We tromped around the Spotsylvania woods for three more hours, looking for another tentacle. Timmy Carter's ribs slowed him down something terrible, and I tried to carry the Extractor for him, but it was way too heavy.

"Maybe we could hold it between us," I said.

"I'm fine."

"No, you're not. You're wheezing like an old man."

"I am an old man."

"Not so old. Seriously, let me hold the lighter end, at least."

"It'll just slow us down."

"No, it won't."

"Yes, it will."

"Why're you being so contrary?"

"I'm not."

We walked in silence, and I could tell something was bothering him.

"This about her? Because if it is, I gotta tell you, I don't get it."

"It's not about her."

"You know she tried to kill me, right?"

"She wasn't . . . "

"Wasn't what? Trying to kill me? You were there. You saw it."

"You don't understand."

"I guess not."

"She's not what you think."

"Okay."

"Besides. That's not what's bothering me."

Now I knew what he was talking about. Heck, it was bothering me, too. How could it not? That morning we awoke to a couple of people missing. Even though our ranks had been a little replenished after the massacre, we still didn't have the numbers that we used to have. That might have made it easier to feed everyone, but it didn't make nobody comfortable on the defense front. Maybe they'd abandoned the place. Maybe it was more sinister. Not knowing which only made it worse.

"You think they just left?"

"Maybe. It's weird, isn't it?"

"I think it'll be fine. People came and left the farm all the time, remember?"

"I think this is different. I think we'll find them strung up somewhere."

"Jeez, Timmy Carter."

"Just being honest."

"Don't talk that way to Ailani. She might think you had something to do with it."

I didn't think that was true, and I didn't think Timmy Carter had anything to do with anything except protecting people and being my friend. But his dark mood was justified, I think. Death and dying was pretty much the norm these days, and people got depressed pretty easy. I ain't judging. It happened to me. It's harsh to say, but nature don't care about feelings. Nature don't care about your plans for the future, your dreams and aspirations, who you love, who you hate, nothing. Nature is what it always was, a playground for the Grim Reaper. If you couldn't handle it, you became his toy.

"Ailani'll deal with it," I said.

"Maybe."

"C'mon, Timmy Carter."

"Is she a cop? She have FBI training? I like her, Amanda, but that doesn't mean she can handle a murder investigation."

"*If* it's a murder investigation."

"How many of these people did you know before the Hive came? There's bound to be a few bad actors in there somewhere. Who's to say one of them isn't a killer."

"Could be, I guess." Then, after a few seconds of silence. "Dang, Timmy Carter. Now you got me all worried."

"Didn't mean to."

Berenice burst out of the brush, a dead squirrel spiked on her sharpened claws.

"Look, Missus! Look!"

"That's . . . great, Berenice."

She skipped over, holding the squirrel like she was presenting me a trophy.

"I brings breakfast for she!"

"Oh. Thank you."

She pulled it off with a soft sucking sound, tossed it at my feet, and scurried back into the bushes, giggling. Timmy Carter took one look at me and shook his head, laughing.

By noon we were footsore and tired and we hadn't found a goldarn thing. Timmy Carter was at least half-right about the pointlessness of our efforts. The latest round of frost had sent a lot of the tentacles back into the warm core of the earth, and many of those we found outside had blackened and rotted where they were, sometimes burrowed halfway into the ground like they realized at the last moment what was about to happen but were too late to do anything about it.

At least Berenice made the most of the day. She burst around the underbrush like a puppy, hunting for "gifts" that she brought to me every so often. She graduated from squirrels to birds to coons to skunks and finally whatever else hadn't been snatched up by the Macks or the hives themselves. A couple of times, she brought me parts of them weird creatures I seen before, the snakes with spider legs, the eels with scorpion tales. At the eighth sceel stinger, I told her I couldn't eat anymore. I wasn't really eating them, of course, I was just stowing them away in my backpack, but I thought that's what she wanted me to do.

"Oh, Missus shouldn't eat the stingers! They venom your veins!"

"Right, I meant—"

"I must get a potion for she!"

"No, Berenice. That's not—"

"Wait heres!"

We ate lunch while sitting on a dead branch next to a little creek: Berenice and Bertholdt and all their friends gnawing on the bones of something they caught in the woods, Timmy Carter and I chowing down on apples and corn on the cob with beans and chickpea paste. Timmy Carter wolfed down enough food for ten men but it obviously wasn't enough. He looked mournfully at the empty newspaper we'd wrapped it all in when he was done eating.

"How many beans do you think equals a chicken?"

"A whole chicken?"

"Yeah."

"I dunno. A lot?"

"You used to farm, didn't you?"

"Yeah, but we didn't have any chicken to bean conversion charts."

"Why not?"

"Nobody ever asked before."

He opened his mouth to say something but paused.

Then the noise came. It sounded like a gorilla boxing a whale. Timmy Carter looked up and said, "you hear that?"

"Yeah. It's over there."

"Where?"

I pointed into the brush.

"There."

There was a pause in the noise, an eerie pause that set my nerves tingling, and then a roar that wound up into a high-pitched squeal burst through the silence, louder than loud, and we both slid off the log into a three-point squat. If our instinct was to take cover and prepare for the worst, the melonhead kids' was to run headlong into the scrum, which they did lickety-split, the sound of her feet pitter-pattering in the dead leaves.

"Guys!" I hissed. "No!"

"A hives, Missus!" Berenice called. "A hives!"

The next thing I heard was all their high-pitched squeals mixing in with the roars and the punching sounds. Sounded like someone put a jaguar in a wood chipper. Then the brush rustled in front of us and Berenice scrambled out covered in scratches and dirt and dragging two baby kangapes by their horns.

"I saves them, Missus!" she cried.

"Jeez Louise, Berenice!

"We go backs for more! They needs our help!"

And she dumped the things at my feet and dashed back into the fight.

Even though they was just babies, they were still about the size of a fully grown German Shepherd. They'd been beat to holy hell, I'll tell you what. Fur ripped off in patches, horns chipped and cracked. One of them was out cold, but the other looked like it wanted to get up. Its hind paws were broken but it kept twitching its legs. I was caught between wanting to comfort the poor thing and putting it out of its misery.

"Missus!" Berenice called.

Another roar.

"Help us!"

"I think we should," Timmy Carter said.

Half a tree trunk exploded up into the air and flew over our heads. I watched it crack through the branches and thud a few feet away.

"I think they'll do just fine on their own."

"Amanda."

"Have you seen one of them grown kangapes close up? Because I have."

"Missus! Help us!"

Timmy Carter stood up, wincing.

"Stop fooling around and help me with the Extractor."

I attended exactly one beer bash when I was in high school. Of course, I never made it to my senior year (thanks Hive), but that's beside the point. The one beer bash I was able to attend was thrown by the son of one of Daddy's regulars, some rich kid who lived in town in one of them mansions on Washington Avenue. This was one of the nicer places on the street, a stone-faced

Victorian that his mom and her husband bought and renovated after a fire gutted it a few years before, but he and his friends treated it like their own personal alcoholic proving grounds.

I could hear the music thrumming as I walked up to the house, and when I went to knock, the front door swung open on its own accord. What greeted me was a scene from an 80's movie. There were kids jumping on the expensive furniture, kids crashing up and down the hardwood stairs, kids throwing beer at each other. I'd only took one step into the foyer when a football player hanging from the chandelier jerked a little too hard in an effort to get it swinging and the whole thing came crashing down in front of me.

That's a little bit like it was walking into the clearing with all the roaring and the screaming and Berenice crying for help, only with less blood and guts and body parts.

Berenice was holding onto a thick tentacle as it whipped her through in the air while a full-grown kangape bounced around the perimeter, beating its chest and roaring and every now and then thundering through the middle to grapple or head-butt something. Berenice had latched on tight, her nails digging into the tentacle's rubbery skin, and she used her pointy teeth rip chunks of it out and spit them into the air. The tentacle finally got enough force to whip her back and forth like a carnival ride, but that didn't bother Berenice much. She just dug her nails in harder and whooped and hollered.

"Look, Missus! Look at mes!"

She could only hold on but so long before it finally snapped hard enough to throw her off, though. She hit Timmy Carter right in the chest and knocked him straight to the ground. The kangape took her place, whuffing as the tentacle thudded into its stomach. But it was stronger and bigger than a melonhead kid, and instead of flying through the air, it dug in its heels and ground them to a halt. It beat back the other tentacles swirling around in the air like snakes and pounded on the main line with its fists. That must have tripped an emergency plunger or something because green vapor seeped out of the ground around the base, covering the kangape in an envelope, and when the vapor evaporated, the kangape was on the ground, motionless.

"That's it!" Timmy Carter yelled.

He struggled to his feet, wincing, and tightened his mask to his face, and while the tentacle reared back to plunge into the fallen kangape's chest, he waded in with his machete and took a sizable chunk out of its side. The tentacle lurched and listed, sending the smaller ones into a buzzing tizzy. Then it was my turn. I ran in and started slicing and dicing like I was making a salad, and between the two of us, when we were done, there wasn't nothing left of that dang thing but green juice and rubbery skin. Timmy Carter stood up, breathing heavy.

"Think that's enough juice for—"

The tip of the tentacle shot off the ground, aiming to knock his machete away, but Timmy Carter jumped back and cut it in two with one powerful swipe. It must have hurt as much as it looked impressive because he went down to one knee.

Berenice sat up, looking dazed herself, and Bertholdt and the rest of his friends wandered in from the woods in various states of bruises. The weird thing was how much different they didn't look even with all them new cuts and contusions. They actually kind of looked a little better than usual.

"Missus! Missus!" Berenice said as she waddled over to the passed out kangape. "Is it going to be okay?"

"I'm sure it's fine, Berenice."

"Can we takes it with us? Please?"

I opened my mouth to say no, but then I had an idea. Timmy Carter must have read my mind, because he said, "No way, Amanda."

"Might be useful."

"You're crazy if you think either one of us can carry it back. It must weigh four hundred pounds."

He got up and started for it, machete still out, when another kangape burst out of the trees, roaring. It jumped at him, legs out. and hit him square in the chest (again), and he flew back and it landed in the middle of the clearing where the gas was still floating in the air and it sputtered and crashed around, finally stumbling out of the clearing toward where we were hiding before. I trotted after it, keeping a safe distance, and watched it collapse a few feet away, coming to a rest next to the two babies Berenice saved. It lay still a tic, eyes fluttering. That's when I saw the scar on its face, a long, shiny one that ran one ear to the corner of its mouth. When it saw the babies, it tried to reach out but its arms were too weak. I crouched forward, keeping my hands out in front of me.

"Hey, hey," I said.

The kangape grunted and growled, but it didn't have enough energy to do much more.

"It's okay. You want your baby? He yours? Here. You can touch him."

The monster let out a pathetic attempt at an angry sound, and I saw its back legs twitching like it wanted to take a leap at me but couldn't. Heck, it couldn't even pick its head off the ground. I pulled the baby kangape closer as gently as I could, leaving it so the bigger one could brush its head with the back of its knuckles. The big one made eye-contact with me and then it went still and quiet, slipping off into that green-drug coma.

Dr. Huntington wasn't none too pleased when we came back with one broken container and the other one not even an eighth full. We put them on the table where he sat, but all he did was temple his fingers and stare at them. I let Timmy Carter explain what happened. Dr. H listened to every word, tapping his fingers on his chin. When Timmy Carter was done, the doctor heaved a sigh and looked at us like we were in Kindergarten.

"Explain to me, exactly, how you were not able to mine the juice? Did the Extractor malfunction?"

"No," I said.

"Then how—"

"Didn't you listen to a word Timmy Carter just said?"

"Amanda," Timmy Carter said. "It's okay."

"No, it ain't. First of all, Dr. H, don't talk to us like we work for you."

"Oh, Ms. Jett. Make no mistake—"

"Mistake what?"

"Who has the knowledge? Who has the technology? Do you want to defeat the invaders or not?"

"Who has the muscle? Who has the legs? Do *you* want to defeat the invaders or not?"

He laughed.

"Tricks of rhetoric won't solve the problem."

Timmy Carter put his hand on my shoulder.

"Amanda."

"What?"

He tilted his head and mouthed the word "stop."

My natural inclination in an argument, if you didn't know it already, was to stand my ground and double down. If somebody wanted to jaw at me, wasn't no reason for me not to jaw back. Timmy Carter was quiet himself, but he didn't usually try to enforce it on me. So if he wanted me to be quiet, it must have meant something. I bit my tongue, took a breath, and sat down. Dr. Huntington put his fingers to his lips and wouldn't look me in the eye. He picked up one of the containers and turned it in his hands.

"It would seem as though this idea is not going to work after all."

"It would seem that way."

He paused in thought, still turning the container, looking but not seeing. He started muttering to himself.

"No, that's not certain but . . . of course, I don't believe . . . no. No. Absolutely not."

Timmy Carter and I shared a look.

"Fine," Dr. Huntington said. "I agree. It could be fun. But . . . ." He popped out of whatever world he was in and put the container back down on the table. "Despite my most strenuous misgivings, I believe there might be another way."

"Okay," I said. "What is it?"

He fixed both of us with a mischievous glint in his eyes.

"Do you believe in ghosts?"

THE GHOSTS OF ST. GEORGE'S

Did I believe in ghosts? Did I believe in ghosts. A body can't live in Spotsylvania County, VA her entire life and not believe in ghosts. Heck, Fredericksburg was only ten miles away, and between the spirits of the soldiers who fell during the Battle of Spotsylvania Courthouse and the Lady in White, Fall Hill Fannie, the Sioux Indian Princess, and all them poltergeists playing the piano in the Chimneys and tugging on dresses in the Rising Sun Tavern or milling around the foggy lanes of Sunken Road, the area where I grew up was one of the most haunted places this side of the Rappahannock.

That's not to say that everybody who lived in Spotsy and Fred had been haunted. Some people don't believe in the supernatural, believe it or not, and even if they did, ghosts didn't exactly care about marketing or exposure. I kind of felt like spirits was like cats in a lot of ways. If you tried too hard to find one, they did their best to stay out of your way. But ignore them and boy howdy did they love to rub up against your pant leg, or purr in your ear, or claw at your flesh.

I'm one of the latters. I never believed in ghosts or demons or monsters (not until the Hive landed), but for someone who held such strong convictions to the contrary, I sure was haunted a lot.

I was nine years old the first time I seen a spook. Daddy took me and my girl scout troop out to Spotsylvania Courthouse to earn our Eco Camper badges. Camping wasn't new to me. Daddy took me hunting every fall, and if we wasn't hunched down behind some deer blind, we was hunched over some fire or hunched over some tracks or hunched over a dead deer. He taught me everything, how to skin them, gut them, cut them. We did a lot of fishing out there, too ("nothing tastes better than freshly caught fish," Daddy often said), and he taught me how to clean and cook them, too. I should have been able to earn a badge on all that alone, but for some reason, the GSA only awarded credit if I pulled it off with a bunch of tenderfoot suburban Barbies.

"It ain't fair," I told Daddy. "I've camped out in them woods enough times to earn a thousand of them badges."

"Life ain't fair, 'Manda."

"I hate it when you say that."

"I hate it when you whine at me all the time. Weren't you the one who wanted to join the Girl Scouts?"

"Yeah."

"Then suck it up."

I mouthed the words after he said it. 'Suck it up' was Daddy's response to everything I didn't want to do.

Of course, I forgot how opposed I was to the whole thing the moment we got out there. I loved camping. Still do. Everything about it. Setting up the tents. The smokey smell of the fire. The crunch of the leaves and the snapping sticks as we hiked through the woods. Heck, I even loved it whenever I lost my footing crossing a creek and plunked into the icy cold water.

Them other girls weren't too keen on it, though, and they whined and wheedled the whole time. All except my best friend at the time, Brianna Moses. Brianna was a transplant from New York City, and she was as tough as any county girl I'd ever met. Tougher, if I'm being honest. The stories she told me about what she and her friends did in the city made all my adventures feel downright uneventful.

We had ourselves a time, Brianna and me, but soon it was time to bed down for the night. On the way back to our campsite, we seen dozens of white bivouacs popped up on the old battlefields.

"What're they?" Bri asked me.

"Reenactors."

"What?"

"Civil War people. They come down here all the time."

"What do they do?"

"They play fight like they was in the Civil War."

"Why?"

"I dunno. Why does anybody do anything? It's kind of fun to watch."

That night we ate chicken roasted over the fire, and Daddy gave us chocolate and marshmallows and graham crackers for s'mores, and he even told us a silly ghost story about some lady with a yellow handkerchief around her neck. When it was time for bed, Bri and I shared a tent, and after we giggled and tried to scare each other even more, the activity of the day caught us up and we conked out.

I don't know what time it was when I woke up, but it had to be round about three or four in the morning. I'd been having a nightmare about creatures oozing up from the mud on the banks of the Rapphannock, chasing me, reaching for me with their black claws, and then something was leaning over me, a form in the dark, breathing in my face.

I shrank back, a little squeak escaping my lips. That made me mad. I hated that feeling, and I'm not talking about fear. Fear don't confront me none. Fear's just anxiety on steroids; all you have to do is act and it goes away. No, the feeling I hated was helplessness.

"Amanda," the form whispered.

I sighed in relief.

"Dang, Bri. You near about gave me a heart attack."

"I have to go to the bathroom."

"So go to the bathroom."

"I have to do it away from camp."

Oh. She was talking about the other kind of bathroom. Peeing close to the campsite was fine. In fact, it tended to drive some of the sneakier critters away. But going number two anywhere near to where we slept and ate was a big no-no. Which meant Bri had to go out into the woods by herself. In the dark.

"I get it. Hold on."

Bri was a blob of white in the pitch dark as we trotted through the woods. I made sure we went at least a hundred yards in before I told her we were far enough, and I guess Bri couldn't wait because as soon as I said to stop she dropped her drawers and got to it. I wandered another ten or so yards away to give her some privacy and found myself standing on the edge of the woods overlooking the Bloody Angle. Daddy'd told me about it about a hundred times, but I tended to tune out almost as soon as he started. All I remembered was that the name was appropriate.

A fog had settled over the battlefield, thick and silvery in the light of the full moon. The night sounds swelled. I wondered if the reenactors' bivouacs were still set up in the fog, and that's when I heard the first groan. Sounded like someone was in a lot of pain.

"Hello?" I said. "Who's there?"

Another groan followed, and another, and another. Bri came up beside me.

"What is that?"

"I think it's the reenactors having fun with us. It's not funny, you bunch of dumb rednecks!"

There was a pause in the noises and I expected to hear them laughing at us, but instead, they doubled down and started whispering.

"My arm, my arm, my arm. My leg, my leg, my leg."

Bri tugged on my pajama sleeve.

"Amanda, let's go. This is freaking me out."

"Uh-uh. They're not supposed to act that way." I put my hands to my mouth and yelled, "you think it's funny trying to scare a couple of kids?"

"You have two, two, two."

"Yeah, I got two! Two fists!"

The fog at the edge of the field shifted and swirled, and I heard a thump followed by a drag. Bri tugged again.

"Amanda, come on."

I pulled free and marched out of the woods and onto the field.

"Where you at, you jerks?"

And that's when I saw that the fog was acting weird. It had formed a wall about four feet high but wouldn't spread out, as if it had hit some kind of invisible barrier at the edge of the battlefield and couldn't get past it. The thump and drag came again, louder this time, and the whispers sounded like they were coming from all around me.

"Arm, arm, arm. Two, two, two. Leg, leg, leg. Two, two, two."

I spun around in circles, disoriented by the noise, and then I stopped. Everything had gone dead silent. No more breeze in the branches. No more insects in the woods. No more eerie whispering. All I could hear was my own, shaking breath.

Then I turned around, and a corpse was standing right behind me. Its clothing hung off it in rags, blue strips of an old wool uniform, and its skin, mottled and dry, clung to what remained of a cracked and dented skull. It reached out with one tattered arm, groaning, and grabbed my shoulder with a skeletal hand.

"Your arm!"

I screamed and pulled free, but in my panic, I spun directly into the fog. More hands reached for me as I ran, shadows loomed up at me in the fog. They tore my clothes and sliced my skin. I screamed and screamed, pushing forward. If I ran into anything, I shoved it away. If something grabbed me, I pulled free. Bones cracked and shattered, and I ran and ran and ran until I found myself in the middle of a cleared out patch of ground in the middle of the field screaming all by myself in the middle of the night.

Nothing was there. No corpses. No skeleton arms. Nothing reaching for me. Nothing. Just the wall of fog surrounding me in a perfect circle.

Then I saw them, the people they used to be, soldiers—boys, really, not much older than me—wearing blue and gray, running towards each other, shooting, getting shot, dying. The battle raged until the ground was covered in bodies, one foot, two feet, three feet deep, and the battlefield was surrounded by a wall of limbs just as high, legs and arms, feet and hands, and then something touched me on the shoulder and I screamed and whirled around and shoved at whatever it was and it brought me into itself and held me there no matter how hard I tried to get away and I punched and kicked and bit and then it said, "'Manda, calm down!"

I stopped struggling.

"Daddy?"

"What's got into you? What're you doing out here?"

"I—I—Bri—"

"Bri came and woke me up. Said you'd gone bonkers out in the woods. What'd you do to your clothes? Are you bleeding?"

"She had to go to the bathroom and . . ." I peeked out from within his grasp. The fog remained but was only hovering around our feet. Gone were the monsters, the dead soldiers, the wall of arms and legs. "I guess . . . I got . . . scared is all."

"It's okay. Never mind. Come on. Let's get back to camp."

We didn't talk about what happened the rest of the trip, but on the way home, after we dropped everybody off, I said, "Daddy, I saw something out there in that field."

He didn't reply. Just kept driving.

"You hear me? There were these . . . things. Dead things. Dead people. They wanted—they tried to—"

"They tried to take your arms?"

"How'd you know?"

"The Bloody Angle isn't named the Bloody Angle for nothing, sugar pie."

"Don't call me sugar pie."

"Okay."

"So were those things real?"

"Real enough. Scratched you up, didn't they?"

"They sure did."

"I know you're scared, but to be honest, you should be kind of proud of yourself."

"Proud of myself?"

"Oh yeah. The ghosts of the Bloody Angle don't just haunt anybody. They must have seen something special in you."

"My arms, I guess."

"Mark it, 'Manda. It's a sign."

I stared out the window for a while, watching the trees blur as we drove by.

"That's the kind of sign I could do without," I muttered to myself.

Dr. Huntington's brilliant plan consisted of hiking all the way to St. George's Episcopal Church in the middle of the night to stir up some protoplasm.

"We will use my specially calibrated machines to harness the preternatural energy of the spirits trapped there and create a wormhole through which you and your friends will travel into the world of the Hive," he said.

His eyes lit up like roman candles when he talked about it, and I would have been charmed if he wasn't such a jerk all the other moments of his life.

"Specially calibrated machines?" I said. "How specially calibrated are they?"

He gave me a withering look.

"You can be assured of their accuracy, Ms. Jett. I promise you."

"Does that mean that we'll end up in St. George's when we get to the other side? Because I gotta tell you, setting us down in the middle of the capital of the Hive don't sound like a good idea to me."

Dr. H looked stricken, and right then I knew he hadn't thought of that.

"Looks like you might have to un-calibrate your special machines."

He smiled. Then, unsmiling, turned his back to me, muttering in math.

For those of you who don't know, St. George's is the most haunted place in Fredericksburg. More haunted than Sunken Road, more haunted than the Rising Sun Tavern, more haunted than the Chimneys, and yeah, more haunted than the Bloody Angle. When I tried to explain this to him, (well, his back as he walked away), all he said was, "I know, Ms. Jett. That's entirely the point."

I been around a few frustrating men in my life. Daddy. Uncle Zeus. But Dr. Huntington wasn't just frustrating, he was infuriating. He didn't just plan the mission for the dead of night, he made sure to load us all up with as much gear as possible. Floodlights, speakers, a generator, gasoline, machines, scaffolds, stands, ladders, all on top of our own backpacks, guns, knives, clothes, and anything else we thought we'd need on the other side. The melonhead kids actually shouldered more of the load than I thought possible, and Dr. H said he could only spare a few of them, Berenice and Bertholdt and two others, saying he needed the rest to stay behind and guard his laboratory. (He pronounced it "laBORatory"). He made Berenice and all them wear backpacks so stuffed with gear that they looked like hunchbacked ticks.

And that's how we found ourselves slogging down 208 overloaded with tents and packs and all manner of junk, startling at every sound, wondering when a Mack or a tentacle or some creepy monster was going to jump out at us from the woods or a bend or an abandoned car.

It was distressingly uneventful.

I'm a firm believer in jinxes, so at the time I didn't want to say anything, but when you're a survivor of an alien invasion that took over the world and changed the climate in less than a year, things don't never go right. And when they do, watch out because they was about to go terribly wrong. That kind of thinking amped me up as much as I'd ever been.

Timmy Carter's ribs were still tender but he came with us anyway, not that he was good company. He never was one for conversating, and I didn't get a chance to talk to him because all he did was hover around the Girl. He wasn't ignoring me so much as he wanted to be around her, but it still didn't feel good. On top of that, we had another two people go missing earlier that week, so Ailani stayed behind to sort that mess out, which meant that for the entire walk, I didn't have nobody I could distract myself with.

At one point, Timmy Carter said something to the Girl and peeled off to discuss something with Dr. H, leaving her to walk by herself, and even though I knew she probably didn't want to talk to me, I also knew that in order for the mission to come correct, I'd need to set myself straight with her, so I increased my pace and caught her up. A couple of her friends, Brownie and a cute little blonde girl, saw it and tried to cut me off, but the Girl shook her head at them and they backed off.

"Hey," I said. She kept staring straight ahead. "Nice night, ain't it?"

"What do you want?"

"Just making small talk."

"Small talk?"

"Yeah, you know. 'How's the weather? How you been?' That kind of thing."

"Oh."

A river raged between us, and it was up to me to build the bridge. I took a deep breath and let it out.

"I need to apologize to you. For doing you the way I done."

"You didn't do anything to me."

"Well, I mean—"

"What about Alex?"

"Is that Brownie's name? Or Dreadlocks?"

She stared at me. Hard.

Oh. So, Dreadlocks.

"You didn't have to do it."

"Yeah, I did. He was trying to kill me, remember?"

That seemed to throw her.

"No, that's . . ."

"That's what? He came at me. You all came at me. Held me up in the air like about to choke me out until . . ." I looked over my shoulder at Brownie. "Why didn't you heal him up like you done to them others? It ain't like you—"

I stopped talking. The Girl looked like she was about to cry.

"We don't have to be friends," I said.

"We're not."

"Fine. But we have to work together. I can do that if you can."

Our footsteps scuffed the pavement.

"I can do that."

"Good. So, can you tell me who we're looking for over there?"

"You don't need to know."

"Did you listen to a word I just said?"

She didn't literally grit her teeth, but I could tell her jaw was clenched tighter than a crabapple.

"Waldo."

"What?"

"His name. It's Waldo."

"Okay. Waldo and who else?"

"First things first."

She picked up her pace and joined her friends.

"Where do we find him?" I called after her. "Where are we going to stay? How's this going to work?"

I didn't expect her to answer. She lived up to that expectation.

I could have made the walk in three hours (two and a half if I was really trying) but trekking in a group wasn't nearly the same as going solo, and we had all that gear to carry, so what should have been a four-hour pace turned to five pretty quick. Made me think about the Civil War for some reason, how them generals drove thousands of men thousands of miles fast and faster, how much discipline that must have took. I'd say it was close to three in the morning by the time we made it to the corner of College Avenue and William Street. Every last one of us was pooped, even Berenice and Berholdt and all them, and even though we were less than a mile away, we all decided to stop for a tic. I sat on the curb and rubbed my feet, and the melonheads unloaded their gear in the middle of the street. Thunder rumbled in the distance as clouds rolled in from the southwest, huge and black and streaked with lightning.

Speaking of Berenice, she was oddly quiet the whole trip, and other than a few quick glances here and there, she didn't spit or say boo to me or anybody else who wasn't a melonhead. Dr. Huntington didn't necessarily treat her and her people with any kind of kindness, so maybe that was it. He snapped and snarled and called them all sorts of rude names. A burst of lightning startled Bertholdt and he dropped a light stand and broke a bulb, Dr. Huntington beat him upside the head and pushed him to the ground.

"Careful, you encephalitic idiot!" he screamed.

I'd never seen Bertholdt so cowed. I never thought I'd say this, but the look on his face after the doctor did that to him was downright tragic. I glared at Dr. H as he stomped away, muttering to himself.

"That ain't right, Dr. H," I said. "Beating one of them is like beating a puppy."

Berenice shot me a panicked look as the doctor raged around the gear she and her brothers and sisters had set aside, but when I gave her a little wave, she looked away. Then the doctor marched over to me.

"Why are we stopping? The church is less than a mile away!" He gestured at the coming storm. "We're running out of time."

"We won't have no time at all if we're too tired to do anything when we get there," I said.

"Yes, and how will you feel when you're stuck out in that storm?"

"It's just a few minutes."

The doctor simmered. He looked like he wanted to rage at me or maybe even take a swing.

"Ms. Jett, what you don't know about this will kill you."

Daddy used to say "nothing good ever happens after midnight," which was arguable. Time is a human construct. I don't think evil cared much when it struck just as long as the striking was hot. But I understood what he meant. Dark is scary. In the dark, anybody or anything wanted to do something terrible, it was easier to find a hiding place. Walking down William Street and into Downtown

Fredericksburg proper, with the close streets blocking the light of the moon, the dozens of half-opened doors and broken windows, the nine billion places something or someone could be waiting for a bunch of fools like us, tripled my anxiety. We turned right on Princess Anne, and then it was only a block to the church. The tall windows of St. George's were dark, even with the celestial fires burning bright. The melonhead crew spread out on the sidewalk as Timmy Carter tried to pry the front door open, but it was locked tight. As he went from turning the knob to pulling on it to yanking, I walked around the side to take a look at the basement entrances.

The church might have been built in the late nineteenth century, but that don't mean that was the end of the construction. They put an addition on the other side of the property (including another addition that linked the main part to it) so that the whole campus formed a U shape around the old cemetery in the middle, and they renovated the basement to make it accessible from George Street. There was an iron gate on that side, and I peered through the railings at the twin set of doors, wondering if they'd been left unlocked. I felt a tug on my jeans, and then Berenice said, "what is it, Missus?"

"Jeez, Berenice! Don't sneak up on me like that."

Her face went slack, and she looked like she was about to cry.

"I'm sorry, Missus. Yes, Missus. Berenice has been a terrible."

"Stop that. You're not terrible, no matter what Doctor H says. You just startled me is all."

"Okay, Missus." She wiped away the beginnings of a tear. "What is she doing? Do we have secrets?"

"Nah. No secrets. I was just seeing if the basement door was open."

"Is it?"

Timmy Carter had stopped yanking and pounding long enough for Dr. H to say "what in the devil do you think you're doing? Open the door," to which Timmy Carter replied a terse "it's locked." Then, in the silence that followed, I heard the rusty creak of a slow-moving hinge, and when I looked back through iron rungs, one of the basement doors was wide open. Me and Berenice looked at it with wide eyes.

"I guess so," I said.

It was blacker than black down there, so black that I couldn't see but a foot in front of me, and that was only because of the starlight and the moonlight that shined in from outside. I thought it would be easier to navigate because I'd been down there before. The church used the basement for parties and socials and the like, funeral and wedding receptions, Bible study and youth groups. And AA meetings, so many AA meetings. Even though we wasn't religious, we knew people who was. I don't remember exactly whose funeral I went to because I was six at the time, but I remember going into the basement afterward and eating cold cuts on white rolls and drinking sweet tea while Daddy walked around and glad-handed a whole bunch of people I'd never seen before. The place had a low ceiling, and it wasn't the biggest space in the world, but it worked.

One thing I didn't remember was where the door to the upper floor was. I assumed it was to the left, but it could have been anywhere for all I knew. I told Berenice to hold my back pocket so she wouldn't get lost and stepped inside.

"Missus! Missus! It is dark and it is scary!"

"I know Berenice."

"Where are you going, Missus?"

"Trying to find the door, Berenice."

I kicked something, a glass I think, and it rang along the tile and smashed in the darkness. Berenice squeaked.

"Hush, Berenice!"

"I'm sorry, Missus."

White lightning flashed outside, illuminating the empty room in front of us for a split second. Thunder rolled again two seconds later.

"Getting closer," I said.

I strode ahead, confident that nothing was in my way, but Berenice held back, pulling on my pocket.

"Too fast, Missus! Too fast!"

"Hurry up, Berenice. We got to let them in."

She squeaked again, and the weight of her hand fell off my back pocket.

"Berenice!"

Another flash of lightning exploded overhead and the room lit up like a fireball, and in those brief seconds, I saw them appear.

Dead people.

At least a dozen.

Gathered in a knot at the other end of the basement.

I stumbled back and tripped over something and fell on my rear. A third bolt of lightning blasted outside to my left. I saw it strike the street, saw the asphalt explode and hail down in the strobe light of the blast. Then a fourth hit, and a fifth, and more and more, seven, eight, nine. Somewhere in the back of my mind, I registered the impossibility of what I was seeing, but it wasn't the thing I was most worried about because each time the lightning struck, the room lit up, and each time the room lit up, the dead things at the other end grew closer and closer, surrounded by a green fog. The smell of rot filled the air.

And I knew them. I *knew* them. Years ago they were lying in the misty grass of the Bloody Angle, and they chased me into the middle of the battlefield, circled around and cinched the noose. Their voices filled my head, calling out to me from the past.

"Arm, arm, arm. Two, two, two. Leg, leg, leg. Two, two, two."

I tried to think, tried to act, but the only thing that ran through my mind was "nononononono." It was the pause before the accident, the blip in the brain, a hiccup in the hippocampus. Wasn't nothing odd. Humans froze up in the face of danger all the time. It's biology. The first thing to go in high-stress situations is your fine motor skills and your intelligence.

But then I thought of Berenice, how scared and alone she must have felt. She might have been a strange little thing, but she was innocent, and she had feelings, and for some reason she liked me. She needed me. That's when I realized what it meant to care more about someone else than I did about myself. It wasn't the kind of love a mother felt for her kids, but it was close. The poor little thing. I couldn't let her down.

"Berenice!" I screamed.

If she replied, it was lost in the thunder.

I couldn't see the monsters, but I could feel them, smell them. It felt like if I reached out, my fingertips could graze the fringes of their tattered clothes.

"Berenice!"

Another lightning strike.

A rotten face inches from mine. An anger rose up inside me, not to mention the shock of seeing something like that so close, and I struck out with the palm of my hand, aiming for the nose just like I learned in self-defense. I felt a crunch, and my hand went through its skull, but it kept coming for me, so I kicked it in the chest, sending it reeling back. The others closed in and grabbed my shoulders, my hair, my sides.

"Arm, arm, arm. Two, two, two. Leg, leg, leg. Two, two, two."

Nope, I thought. *Not tonight.*

I hopped into a squat and swept my leg around, felt it connect, heard them drop. Then a feral, high-pitched screech filled the room, followed by thuds and ripping and tearing sounds, and then a little hand was in mine, and Berenice said, "Missus! We must flee!" and she pulled me up and led me away, strangely confident in the darkness. I heard a door creak open in front of me and we passed through a threshold and then I knew that she'd found the way out. The door slammed shut once we were through, and Berenice said, "we go up, Missus! Up!"

So up we went. And up. And up. We hit a landing and turned and continued. Then again and again, which wasn't right. Wasn't right at all. The basement was only half a flight down from the main level of the church. The stairs should have ended in the sanctuary. I should have been pulling them front doors open and laughing at the look on Timmy Carter's face as I cried, "Surprise, suckers!"

I wanted to stop and figure out what the hell was going on, but Berenice was a full flight higher than me, her quick, short breaths echoing in the well.

"Berenice!"

"Flee, Missus! Flee!"

I gritted my teeth and pushed on, legs burning, taking the steps two at a time, and I caught up with her just in time to see her run through the front door and out into the blazing sun, skidding to a stop at the edge of the curb where she almost got hit by a speeding antique car. The driver laid on the horn as it sped by, followed by so many classic cars that I thought we'd stumbled into a parade. All I could see for a full minute was white-walled tires and two-tone paint jobs: seafoam and pearl and ivory and opal and taupe. And there were canvas convertible tops, and gleaming chrome grills, and gun-sight tail lights, and tail fins. A Buick trolled by slower than the rest of the others, and the old lady in the passenger seat stared at Berenice. I stepped around and put her behind me.

"Stop it, Missus! I want to see!"

"Hush, Berenice."

She fussed behind me, squirming and squiggling as I took in my surroundings. We were still in downtown Fredericksburg as far as I could tell. St. George's behind us, and across the street, The National Bank of . . . whoa. Wait a minute. The National Bank of Fredericksburg wasn't on Princess Anne Street anymore. And why was the antique car parade going on so long? A banner was strung up on the iron gates of the cemetery with the words *Do what you're told, not as you will* written across it. Another one over the front door of the bank read *Obedience is Freedom.* And yet another one strung up across the street said *Confederation. Conformity. Country.*

A group of people had gathered on the corner of George Street, and they were all talking to each other and pointing at us. At first, I thought they were looking at Berenice, but then I saw the poster glued to the telephone pole in front of me, the one with my face blown up in excruciating detail.

The word WANTED was written above my picture, and underneath it: FOR MURDER.

"Oh man, Berenice," I said.

Two men dressed in field green suits and hats turned the corner of Hanover Street and marched straight for us. I turned the other way and there were two more.

"Oh man, oh man, oh man."

AMANDA'S FINAL STAND

When I was in high school, a whole bunch of football players got beat by a group D&D nerds. You read that right. Old Gridiron Gary and his neanderthal knuckleheads got themselves bested by Dungeon Master Mike and his merry band of adventurers: Dark Elf Derrick and Amanda the Witch Queen.

I don't mean to make light of the situation because it wasn't funny, but you have to understand how singular an occurrence something like that was. In 1993, the social striations established by *The Breakfast Club, Pretty in Pink,* and *Some Kind of Wonderful* had yet to earthquake into one another, so for a bunch of sword and sorcerers to one-up the Commandants of Cool was a monumental occurrence.

There were actually four of us in our little dweeb klatch: the aforementioned Mike and Derrick and me. And then there was Rodney (Rodney the Ranger, that is). It's him that this part of the tale is about. Mike and Derrick and Roger and me had all been friends since fifth grade. We met at an after-school book club put on by our favorite librarian, Mrs. Dawson, to discuss *The Dark Cauldron* series. You know, the kingdom of Pyrain, home to Taran the pig herder and all that. To say we was obsessed would be an understatement. All of us had read *The Hobbit* and *The Lord of the Rings,* of course, but I can say with confidence that nobody else in our grade had also read *Howl's Moving Castle, The Gunslinger, Watership Down,* and countless editions of *Weird Tales Magazine* as well. Mrs. Dawson expanded our reading horizons into Science Fiction, and within a year we'd devoured *Dune* and *Foundation* and *Ender's Game* and *Starship Troopers* and *Fahrenheit 451* and *A Wrinkle in Time* and *The War of the Worlds* and *The Hitchhiker's Guide to the Galaxy.*

Making the leap from hanging out after school arguing over whether or not Fiver and Hazel qualified as true fantasy heroes or who could beat who in a battle: Gandalf or Roland Deschain (Gandalf, of course), to building our own worlds, characters, and stories was as natural as red tape to a Vogon.

This particular adventure started when Rodney decided to level up and try out for the football team. It wasn't so unusual for one of our clan to ditch the fellowship for a few months at a time in order to play sports (me and Rodney) or focus on violin (Mike) or help out with the literary magazine (Derrick). Out of all of us, Rodney was the most athletic, even more than me, but he played lacrosse and soccer—two pursuits that seemed to fit into our vision of ourselves as counterculture warriors. Heck, me being a female athlete alone was enough to elevate me to exotic status, and Rodney's two sports of choice were associated with Europeans and socialism and mass-transit systems and abstract art. When he decided to join the football team, it was, well, to use one of Daddy's favorite phrases, like "Dylan going electric."

"Why would you want to do that?" I asked.

We were sitting in Mike's basement when Rodney broke the news, our current campaign laid out on his dad's old poker table. An uncomfortable silence had over everyone, and I only said it to break the tension.

"Play football?" Rodney said. "I don't know. Why do you play soccer? Or field hockey?"

"Yeah, but—"

"Football's for jocks," Mike chimed in.

"And soccer isn't?"

"You know what I mean."

"Rodney," I said. "The guys on the football team are a bunch of dumb jerks."

"So? That doesn't mean I'm going to be one."

"Brett Barber pulled Derrick's swim trunks off at the Y when we were in fifth grade, remember?"

"Thanks, Amanda," Derrick said.

"And Thor Tucker elbowed Mike in the face last year in the commons."

"Jeez, Amanda."

Rodney was not to be persuaded.

"C'mon, guys. It's me. It'll be fine."

It wasn't.

Rodney became a jock in the worst sense of the word faster than I think even he believed was possible. One week after his first practice, I saw him standing in the commons talking to Brett. I said "Hey, Rodney!" and he barely returned the greeting. A week after that, Derrick tried to get his attention at lunch, and Rodney ignored him. And a week after that, I was coming out of the bathroom when I saw him and Thor coming down the hallway and Mike and one of his friends from Orchestra heading toward them. Thor whispered something in Rodney's ear, and when Mike and his friend passed, Rodney shouldered Mike so hard that he flew up against the cinder block wall and dropped all his books.

I wasn't going to let that go, no sir. I ran up to him while he and Thor were high-fiving each other, and gave him a taste of his own. I might have been a girl, but I wasn't Derrick or Mike who, between the two of them, probably had never played more than twelve hours of any kind of sport. I'd spent my time going up against girls bigger than Rodney, scary farm girls with horse necks and iron-plated forearms. I squared my shoulders and launched from legs, making sure to catch him in the chest, and knocked him to the ground.

Thor took one look at his fallen comrade, mouth agape, and laughed. Rodney wasn't so happy about it. He scrambled to his feet, yelling, "What's your problem?"

"You're my problem, Rodney! You think you're so big and tough now that you're on the football team. How'd all your football buddies like to know your D&D character's name? Or that you cried at the end of *Watership Down*?"

"Shut up!"

"Screw you, Rodney!"

"Damn, Hotrod," Thor said. "You gonna let some lesbo talk to you that way?"

I pushed Thor so hard in his chest that his voice shook.

"Shut up, Thor."

Thor wasn't no Rodney. He didn't have no compunction about hitting girls. His face went dark and he balled his hands into fists, but before he could do anything, Mr. X appeared and said, "Mr. Vance, Ms. Jett, is there a problem?"

The kids that had gathered around us, eager to see the situation explode, skedaddled immediately. Even Thor, who went from about to hit me to about to cry.

"No, sir," I said. "I'm fine."

"Mr. Vance?"

"I'm fine," Rodney muttered.

"What was that?"

"I said I'm fine."

Mr. X gave him a nice long look. The bell rang, and for once Rodney looked a little anxious.

"Can I go now?"

"Yep. Go ahead."

Can *I* go now. Not 'we,' but 'I'. That told me all I needed to know.

Remember when I said something about a group of plucky nerdlingers taking on the popular kids and coming out ahead? Well, that was a lie. Stuff like that rarely happens in reality. In reality, the bullies and the jocks win. Hands down. At least for a little while. Time wounds all heels. My Nana used to say that. I always thought she was saying "heals" h e a l s but it wasn't until what happened to Rodney made the news (local AND national) that I realized she was using it as an insult.

Almost a year after I took Rodney down in the hallway, he and Thor and a half dozen other meatheads got put in jail for rape. Turns out they'd started a little hazing tradition for the incoming freshman football players. From what I read in *The Free Lance-Star*, it started out innocent enough. Making them do extra laps after practice. Having them ask popular upperclassman girls out on dates.

But boys is dumb. That's science. Not all of them, of course, and of course I've met me some mighty thick members of the female persuasion, but boys' frontal lobes, the part of the brain that's responsible for impulse control and executive decision making, don't normally develop until their early twenties. So instead of doing the responsible thing—keeping the 'hazing' mild and innocent—Rodney (or should I call him Hotrod?) and his idiot friends doubled down and got nasty. The article didn't go into too much detail, but some of the more salacious words I remembered were "digital penetration," "sodomy," and "wooden broomstick."

Man.

For all their talk about how tough and manly they was and how gay people ain't real men, high school football players certainly is the most repressed homosexuals I ever did know. So how did the nerds come out on top? Mike. His little brother, Neil, was one of the kids Hotrod and all his friends assaulted. Tried to commit suicide one afternoon after football practice, but Mike walked in on him and stopped it. When Mike asked him why he done it, Neil spilled the beans about what they did to him.

Mike snapped. I read about most of what happened in the paper, but he told me everything after his parents paid his bail.

"I grabbed this billy club I'd bought at Corky's and headed straight for that asshole's house. I don't know what I was going to do, and about halfway there, I started to calm down a little. I was thinking I could maybe get an apology out of him. But when I knocked on the door and Rodney opened it and saw me, he had this look on his face. This smug look.

"'What do you want?' he said.

"Amanda, other than D&D, my whole life I'd never even thought about hurting anybody. But when Rodney said that, something broke in me.

"I'll never forget the look on his face when he saw the club in my hand. The way that sneer turned into surprise. I'm not going to lie. It felt good."

For someone whose battles occurred with a pencil and twelve-sided die, Mike certainly did him some damage. He broke two of Rodney's fingers, his elbow, and blacked his eye so bad his retina detached. Got himself a trip to the emergency room. When the cops came for Mike, he told them exactly what he'd done and why he done it. After a short investigation, Rodney and Thor and several other kids were arrested and brought up on charges. Ended up serving nine months in juvie and two years on house arrest.

So Nana was right. Time really did wound all heels.

Back to the Hive world, and me and Berenice standing out on the sidewalk in front of St. George's Church while G-men in dark green suits menaced us on all sides. I tried to pull her closer to me, but she started squirming and protesting.

"Missus! I can'ts breathe!"

Where could I run? There were people all up and down the sidewalk and cars choking the street. The G-men started waving people back, yelling "Move! Move! Run! Now!"

I backed up, deciding at that moment to turn and dip back into the church and then . . . what? Hide under a pew? Hope the green mist seeped back up from the basement so we could travel back to our world? It was an idiot plan, but one I didn't have to put into place because before I could execute it, the G-men in green was there. They grabbed me by the shoulder and—holy smokes.

They pushed me away.

"Get out of here, now!" one of them yelled.

Berenice and I stumbled off the curb, and a car honked and swerved to avoid us and, turning back to the church, I saw a kid standing in front of the red double doors. He was dressed all in red. Blood red.

Strapped around his chest was a khaki canvas vest, packed with explosives.

"Divine Wind! Certain death!" he screamed.

The G-men tackled him and they all fell into the church, and then the world exploded and everything went white.

". . . miracle girl."

I opened my eyes. Everything was blurry. I could see figures hovering over me. Smelled smoke. Felt like someone had plugged my ears with cotton. I was in pain, so much pain. My head throbbed like someone had clubbed me in the base of my skull. Trying to move was like swimming in syrup, but I felt the overwhelming need to run, to get out of there, to—

"She's awake."

"Miss? You need to calm down."

I tried to sit up, but the pounding got worse and the dizziness doubled. A gentle hand on my chest held me down. I tried to speak.

"B-Bere—"

"Miss, listen. I'm Joe Kramer. I'm a doctor. Don't try to talk. Just relax."

"Where . . . what . . . ?"

"It's an attack. You've suffered a concussion and some scratches but that's it."

"She's a miracle girl!"

"Ma'am, please step away. We need the space."

"But you saw what happened! Nearly the whole church was blown up, but she's perfectly okay."

"Ma'am, please."

"If that door hadn't landed on her—"

"I'm going to have to insist."

I sat straight up, ignoring the pain.

"Berenice!"

I was laid out flat on the other side of Princess Anne. Smoke clouded the air. Sirens blared all around me. I think I saw an arm in the middle of the street. A green fedora rolled by in the wind.

"Who's Berenice?"

Joe Kramer was young and handsome. He was dressed in a white shirt and wool trousers, and his hair was slicked back and short, and his shirt was covered in blood.

"She's my, my—"

"Your daughter?"

I shook my head.

"Cousin. She's only eight. Where is she?"

A hearse pulled up and out jumped a couple of men carrying doctor's bags. One ran over to a woman sitting on the bank steps and holding a crying baby. Another ran over to a man lying face down on the street. He put his fingers up to the man's neck, looked sadly down, and moved on. I tried to get up, and then another explosion rocked the street. The front of the bank shifted forward, and parts of the other buildings clattered all around. Joe Kramer threw himself over me, grunting as the debris landed on his back. A third bomb went off, this one farther away. The air was thick with smoke, and I could see legs running this way and that.

"You're crushing me," I said

Joe Kramer coughed as he pushed himself off. His hair was white with dirt and dust.

"Sorry."

"I have to find her."

"No. Stay down."

"I'm not staying here!"

"I'll find her for you. What's her name?"

"Berenice."

"What does she look like?"

"Um . . . I . . ."

"Okay. Don't strain yourself. Berenice. Eight-years-old. I'll find her."

Seconds after he dashed off, Berenice called to me from the alley next to the bank.

"Missus!"

Oh, thank goodness.

"Berenice!"

A little blond head poked out from around the corner, her fingers gripping the bricks.

"Missus! Comes and looks! Looks at me!"

"Okay, sit tight. Let me get my legs under me."

It took a solid minute, but I finally got up, my breaths coming in big gulps and gasps. I'd had a concussion before, and I knew that I'd feel bad for the first twenty minutes or so but then it'd get better. I could walk, barely, and I had to lean against the bank to stay upright, all of which was why when I finally made it to the alley corner, I doubted exactly what I was seeing.

The little girl standing in the alley wasn't Berenice. I mean, it was and it wasn't. Gone was the melonhead, gone was the wrinkles, gone was the pointy teeth and the blood red eyes and the stringy, patchy hair, all replaced by the cutest, button-nosed, most beautiful little fairytale elf I'd ever seen in my life.

"Berenice?" I said.

She looked mortified.

"I knows, Missus! I'm hideous am I! But looks! Looks at you!"

She pulled me down the alley to a darkened window where I could see my reflection perfectly. Just like Berenice, I wasn't me and I was me. I was tall and strong, with long, blonde hair and everything right in its place. All of my girlish features had disappeared—the baby fat, the round face, the awkward nose. I'd grown up. I looked like my momma. I was . . . I was . . .

"You're beautiful, Missus! More beautifuller than ever before!"

I had to admit it. She wasn't wrong.

I was startled out of staring at myself by the sound of a truck pulling up on the street. Sirens filled the air, old-timey sirens like I used to hear on *Hogan's Heroes* and *Car 54, Where Are You?*, and I knew it was time to get out of there. The question was, where could we go? A troop transport pulled up filled with boys all wearing the same green uniforms Gomez Gomez had worn months ago when he tried to catch me at the bonfire at Hurkamp Park. That lit a fire under me.

"Come on, Berenice," I said. I started pulling her down the alley in the opposite direction. "We got to go."

"Where, Missus? Where?"

Walking was hard. My lower back twinged with each step, but it felt like if I didn't get out of there soon, one of them Green Shirts was bound to recognize me no matter how much I'd grown up (my face was still my face, after all), and I didn't want to know what would happen if they did.

"I don't know, Berenice."

She trotted behind.

"But what about the handsome man?"

"Handsome man?"

"Oh, he was tall and slim, and he likeded you, he did. I could tell!"

A few of the Green Shirts had occupied the alley, standing with their backs to us.

"I don't know, Berenice. Maybe we'll see him some other time."

"Oh, I hopes so! I hopes so!"

It wasn't difficult avoiding attention. All eyes were on the bombing. I could have taken off my clothes and gone gimping down Princess Anne Street waving a flag and nobody would have noticed. I steered us toward Route 1 without really thinking about it, but when another couple of troop transports unloaded a company of Green Shirts to patrol the north end of the city, I cut for the river.

More posters with my face had been plastered on every light pole. They hung in every storefront window we passed. After the fifth one in as many steps, I thought it wise to keep my head down. I wasn't the only one the Hive was looking for, I guess, because I came across more Wanted Posters for other people, too. Didn't recognize any of them until one of the last store I passed, a junk shop on the corner of Princess Anne and Route 1. The face on the poster shocked me to stillness.

It was Vlad. Vlad Sokolov. The last time I'd seen him, he'd been corkscrewed by Principal Greene, but I guess he got over it. He was older now, his hair long, face worn and grizzled, but he had the same sharp features I remembered. He had a different air about him now, too, and I think it was his eyes. They were piercing, intense, angry. None of that was as shocking as what was written on the poster. WANTED it said. WALDO SOKOLOV for SEDITION.

Waldo Sokolov? Waldo? It was too much of a coincidence to be false. Vlad was Waldo. Waldo was Vlad. Huh.

Berenice came up beside me, rattling the front page of a newspaper.

"Missus! Missus! Looks!"

"Stop, Berenice."

"But looks!"

I took the paper but didn't look at it. I folded it and put it in my back pocket instead. Berenice saw the poster and said, "Who is that, Missus? A friends?"

"Yeah. A friend. A real important friend."

A siren ramped up in the distance, and I think I heard a gunshot. Berenice tugged on my hand.

"No time to look, Missus. We must flees! You saids so."

"I know, I know, Berenice."

I had a hard time getting down the hill from River Road to the bank, and climbing over the rocks wasn't a treat neither, but it was worth it when we finally made the water's edge. It was quiet down there. Peaceful. Hobos or high school kids had set up a bunch of logs and stumps around a fire pit, and I took my ease on one of them, sitting down with a grateful groan."Missus is hurts, she is," Berenice said.

"Yeah. I'm surprised you ain't."

"Oh, no no no! Missus falls on me, protects me from the boom."

"Oh, I see now. Maybe you was the miracle girl that lady was talking about."

It was colder down there by the water, and I wrapped my arms around myself, thinking maybe I should put that fire pit to use. But I worried about the smoke and them teams of Green Shirts. Would they see it and investigate? Berenice kept a steady eye on me. She sat down on a log to my left and mimicked my posture. Stuck her leg out. Wrapped her arms around herself.

"What are we going to do for supper, Missus?"

"I don't know, Berenice."

"I could hunts a critters!"

Thinking about the kind of critter she'd bring back made my stomach flip.

"I don't think that'll be necessary, Berenice."

"But what wills we eats? I'm's starving!"

"I don't know, Berenice. Let me think for a minute."

And just like that, her whining turned into a full-on fit. She threw herself to the ground, crying and moaning and slamming her fists into the dirt.

"Berenice, shut up!" I hissed. "You'll draw attention to us."

"But I'm's hungry, hungry, hungry!"

I squatted over and patted her on the back, trying to get her to be quiet, but nothing would work. Then something started to thrash around in the woods, something big and heavy. It thrashed and thrashed, finally punctuating it all with a feral snort. Berenice stopped her crying and snapped her head in the direction of the noise.

"A foods!" she cried.

Then she popped up and ran into the brush, sending up her signature ululation in her wake.

I watched her go, muttering "good goodness" under my breath. She crashed around a good bit, oohing and aahing and "Missus"ing at who knows what, and I couldn't help it. I laughed. If she was in any danger, I'd know about it by now. Hanging around Berenice was like hanging around a talking cartoon animal. I sat down on the log and watched the water slide by and listened to the sounds of nature. It was calming, sitting there, even with all that commotion going on behind me. A bird called upriver, and a stiff breeze ruffled the water, reminding me that it was November.

If things was normal, if aliens hadn't invaded the world and killed my Daddy and at least a billion others and turned everybody else into Macks, we'd be getting ready for Thanksgiving. My teachers would be putting up posters with turkeys on them or handing out connect-the-dots worksheets that, when we solved for x, ended up looking like leaves or gourds or pilgrim hats. Every weekend there would be some kind of celebration or another. A pumpkin festival. A maize maze. A hayride. Wine tastings. Oktoberfests. Cookouts.

The weekend before the holiday, Daddy and his friends used to build themselves up a big old bonfire out in the west field, said he needed to do it to clear out the dead wood and scrub, and as much as that might have been true, he also did it as an excuse to hang out with his friends and drink beer and smoke joints and cook steaks and have himself a grand fall bash.

We didn't do a whole bunch to celebrate Turkey Day specifically, which was why it was one of my favorites. Some people invited tons of folks over and cooked way too much food and didn't even eat half of it. We didn't know that many people, not people that was close to us, and even if Daddy was still in contact with his brothers and sisters, I don't think they'd have come out. Ya'll already know enough about Uncle Zeus to understand why he'd never show up, but there was a reason his sisters didn't just leave the farm but the entire state—heck, one even lived overseas.

So rather than worry the issue, we did our own thing. We slept in and had coffee out on the back porch, and sometime around noon he'd start cooking the turkey. I was responsible for the mashed potatoes and green beans, and in between minding the meat, he heated up the rolls and worked on his famous mac and cheese. We ate at three or four and then tucked ourselves in for a full evening of football. Later on, we ate leftovers and had ourselves a hot buttered whiskey. Well, Daddy did. I had me a hot chocolate.

As I was thinking about all this, letting my mind wander (dangerously, I should say, given my current predicament), I remembered the newspaper Berenice so desperately wanted me to read before. I pulled it out of my back pocket and unfolded it. The headline screamed "MASSIVE MONSTER MENACES MULTITUDES!" over a grainy picture of what looked like a horned ape stuck to a kanga . . . Oh my gosh. That was a kangape! But how did it get here?

Suddenly, I came around to the fact that I hadn't heard nothing but the shushing wind and the chuckling water for at least a minute. Normally, that would have been a nice thing, but anybody who'd ever been around a person like Berenice knew that her kind don't agree with quiet, and the only reason for her to give the world the slightest respite from her voice was because she was injured, dead, or disappeared. I stood up and turned my back to the river.

"Berenice!" I called.

She didn't respond.

Two steps forward.

"Berenice? Don't you go messing around, now. This ain't the time."

Still nothing. I waited a tic before picking my way through the brush and found myself in a little clearing. The ground had been trampled, and fur littered the area. I squatted down and picked up one of the hairs. It was thick and coarse and black.

"Berenice!"

She was gone. Without a peep. Vanished.

Now I was really lost. Stuck in the Hive world without a clue as to what to do next. So Waldo was Vlad, but where how was I supposed to find him? What would I do if I got lucky enough to find him? And what was going on with that Divine Wind nonsense? Suicide bombings? Certain kill? And if St. George's Church was the conduit through which I was supposed to get back to my world, how was I going to do that now that it was all blown up? Was I stuck here for good? Would Dr. H get his machine set up? Would my friends come to rescue me?

It was a lot to unpack.

I don't know how long I sat there. An hour or two? The sun settled high over the river. Must have been gone noon. At the very least, I was going to have to find a place to hide out. My stomach rumbled. And I guess I was going to have to steal some food, too. A thought scratched the surface my mind, the briefest edge of an idea, and I rejected it almost as soon as it came. But more I sat there, the more I realized it was the only answer. I had no other place to go, no one else to rely on, and even though even entertaining the idea sent electric pulses of anxiety up my legs, and even though my belly flipped and went cold, another feeling overrode both of those, and that feeling was anger. It was hot enough to stand me up and carry me away from the bank and up into the neighborhood on the other side of Route 1. I was going back to the house where my "family" lived. Momma and Ruth Grace might have been dead, but there was one person left I think I needed to have some words with.

The neighborhood was dead quiet. No kids playing out in the streets or on their lawns, no dogs barking. Made me think that maybe something unspeakable had happened, that somehow my presence almost a year before had caused some kind of crackdown or purge. Sirens blared in the distance, and when I turned around, I saw black smoke smudged against the blue sky.

As empty as everything seemed to be, none of the houses were in bad shape. Lawns had been mowed, gardens weeded. I even saw a trickle of smoke filtering out of a chimney. But THE house, the one those things that looked like my parents lived in, or used to live in, looked haunted. Vines wound up the overflowing gutters. Leaves piled up in the driveway. One of the chains that held the swing hanging from the magnolia on the front lawn was broke, leaving the seat dangling like a loose tooth. A metal hanger squeaked in the breeze.

I paused on the sidewalk, trying to gin up enough courage knock on the door. It should have been easy. Them things didn't scare me. I'd faced Macks and tentacles, death balls and murderers, polar crabs, magic girls, melonheads, mad scientists, hybrid monsters, and even though they was all scary enough on their own, and even though I'd got myself cut, cracked, and concussed in the process, I always managed to come out on top. Ya'll know that. But each time I thought about taking that first step toward the front door, I kept seeing Ruth Grace's brains spilling out on the carpet, or Momma's mouth filled with wiggling tentacles.

It was the tiniest of things that goosed my wagon. My stomach. It rumbled as loud as an earthquake. No matter how old anybody gets or how important they are, bodily functions were always funny, period. If you expected a Spotsylvania girl, and a Spotsylvania farm girl at that, to be well-acquainted with a panoply of them kinds of things, from farts to queefs to burbles and squelches, you'd be right. But this particular Spotsylvania farm girl was still only a teenager, and I snorted at the ridiculousness of it all. There I was, stuck in an alternate reality with no hope of escape, having just barely survived an attempted suicide bombing by some kind of anti-episcopalian terrorist organization, and all my stomach could think about was EAT.

Well, old stomach of mine, if EAT was what you wanted, EAT was what you'd get.

The inside of the house was no better than the outside. It was dark, for one, and it smelled like mold, which made sense because black patches of the stuff kaleidoscoped all over the walls and ceiling. The carpet squished when I walked on it, not too deep with moisture but deep enough. The kitchen tile was dusky with dirt and dust.

I found some canned soup in one of the cupboards. Chicken Noodle. Tomato. Beef Stew. The cans weren't dented or bloating, and the Chicken Noodle didn't hiss when I cracked it in half on the counter. No gas for the range, so I held the can over my mouth and gulped it down cold and my goodness did that taste good! Some of it spilled down my cheek and I scooped it back in with the palm of my hand, moaning as I chewed the noodles. I picked up a can of tomato and was about to bash it on the counter when Daddy appeared in the doorway.

"You're not going to heat them up?"

I froze. A huge part of me wanted to chuck that can of tomato soup at his head, but just as large a part of me wanted to cry again. Tears welled up in my eyes and my face flushed and . . . Dang it! When was this going to stop? When was I not going to react to him like I was a kid? And it wasn't even him! It was a fake, a copy, some disgusting monster that'd taken on his skin.

That helped. Thinking of him as an 'it'. And the 'it' was the Hive, the same thing that killed my real daddy, the same thing that killed millions and millions of real daddies all over the world. I made the choice. Right then and there, I made the choice. I had to grow a shell, make it hard. He wasn't allowed in no more.

"You're not him."

"I know."

"Then why do you keep wearing him like he's yours?"

He looked down at his arms as if seeing them for the first time. He was still wearing the same clothes I last saw him in, when I was running from that very house, trying to find some way to escape back to my world.

"It isn't my choice."

"Oh yeah? Why not?"

He looked at me, really looked at me, like he wanted me to understand, like he needed me to take his side. I felt myself soften but stopped it.

"It isn't right," he said.

"What isn't right?"

"What's happening. To you. To your people."

"Yeah. I get that."

"You've got to understand. Not all of us want it."

"All of us? All of who? All I've ever seen is them damn hives and tentacles and Macks and —"

"Macks?"

"The dead people. The dead people you use to kill us. To eat us."

He looked down and pressed his lips together, and at first, I thought he was smiling. My blood began to boil.

"You think that's funny?"

"No. No. I didn't know what you called them. We called them something different. When the *kushrach uchūbisch* invaded us."

"Invaded you?" I barked out a laugh. "Baloney. How dumb do you think I am? Invaded you."

"It's true."

"Alright. Whatever."

He took a step for me, and I held up the can of soup. Felt kind of dumb doing it.

Without the element of surprise, a can of soup was about as useful as a lizard in a boxing match, but he stopped. Then he held out his hand.

"Let me show you."

"You've got to be kidding me."

"I was only a child when they came and took my planet. We don't have . . . families, not like yours. We have tribes. And when the *uchūbisch* landed, they wiped mine out. Every single one."

"Okay. So what. Now you work for them, right?"

"You don't understand!"

"Oh, I think I understand plenty."

"It was horrible."

"I know. I've seen it."

"Not like this."

He was faster than I thought, and he reached out and grabbed my wrist, and then I wasn't in the kitchen anymore. I was in a jungle somewhere, surrounded by strange, purple trees. The ground was dark, rich brown, and huts made out of the red roots of the trees formed a village in front of me.

At my feet lay dozens of bodies. They were people, maybe not human, but close enough. Men, women, children. Mostly children. All of them done the same way they tried to do me and Daddy (my real daddy). Chests with holes the size of basketballs, their bodies drained from the inside out.

"Dammit!"

I pulled my arm out of his grip and I was back in the kitchen again. I didn't even think. I reacted. I slugged him in the jaw with the can of soup, sent him reeling back.

"Don't you ever do that to me again, you hear?"

His face was covered in red, and I thought I'd broke him until I realized it was the tomato soup. It was also running all over my hand. I cussed and threw the busted can in the sink. One of Momma's (not Momma. She was not Momma) . . . a dish towel hung from the stove handle, and I used it to wipe the soup off. After second, I threw it to him. He caught it and gave me a slight nod.

"Those were your people?"

"Yes."

"You're not a part of the Hive?"

"They force me to be."

"What's the difference?"

"The difference? Don't you get it? You're still fighting. You—"

"Damn right I'm fighting. You're going to blame me for that?"

"You got lucky."

"Lucky? Did you really just say that."

"Your planet. It—"

"My Daddy is dead. My friends are dead. Everybody I ever knew is dead. Vlad. Ray. Maggie May. Even Uncle Zeus. Tell me I'm lucky again."

"And if your planet didn't change seasons the way it does, you'd be just like me right now."

"So what. It does. And I'm not."

"And that's the difference. That's why we're doing it."

"Doing what?"

"Fighting back. The bombings this morning? Those were us."

"You mean the one that almost killed me?"

"That wasn't on purpose. There will be more."

"Already has been."

"More than that."

I let that sink in. If what he was telling me was true . . . a motion in the doorframe caught my attention, and my eyes shifted over his shoulder.

"Oh, hell," I said.

It was Joe Kramer. He wasn't wearing his day clothes no more though, no sir. He was dressed in full Hive regalia. Gray-green overcoat. Officer's hat with a black leather brim. Death's head insignia underneath a strange looking badge: a hive encircled by squirming tentacles.

"I knew I recognized you, Ms. Amanda," he said.

The thing that looked like Daddy closed his eyes. Then he opened them again.

"Run," he said.

He jumped on Joe Kramer. There was a door off the kitchen that led to the backyard, but it opened up right when I moved for it, and three green-shirted kids about my age burst in. I tried to skirt around the kitchen table, but Joe Kramer lurched in from the living room entrance and threw me up against the wall, holding me there with a Kansas City forearm. I gagged.

"Do you know how many people you killed?"

He was choking off my wind, but I was angry enough to rasp an answer.

"Wasn't me."

"There were children in that church."

"Didn't do it."

"Murderer."

I spit in his face and he head-butted me. I felt my nose crunch and one of the Green Shirts sidled up next to him.

"Want us to take her out back, Mr. Kramer?"

"No," Joe Kramer said. "Take her and that traitor to the stadium. Time to get rid of this scum once and for all."

I'd been knocked out plenty enough over the last twelve months to know that I didn't like it, but that didn't mean I wanted to be conscious while the Green Shirts dragged me out the door to what was almost certainly, once again, my certain doom. And it didn't mean I wasn't scared, neither. A body don't never get used to facing its death no matter how many times it happened.

Not that the Green Shirts cared one bit how I felt about things. They clapped a pair of handcuffs on me and shoved me out the door. When I struggled, they punched me in the stomach. I saw it coming and I flexed and what not, but as physical as I'd been for the past few months, I hadn't been doing sit-ups and crunches and torso twists and all the other things that would have made my abs stronger, and I felt that punch all the way in my back. Felt like one of my ribs snapped. I tripped on the way to the hearse they had parked in the driveway and my old break flared up.

I was a proper mess. Crunched nose, bruised ribs, and a leg that didn't feel right. They shoved me in the back and piled in next to me, making sure to put at least three of them between me and the man or thing or alien that looked like my daddy. None of them said a word as we pulled out of the driveway and aimed for downtown.

The roads was clear as we crossed Route 1, steered past the hospital (which was on Fall Hill), and onto Washington. The stadium. The stadium. Kramer must have been talking about Maury. Wasn't no other nearby. We paused at the corner of William to let an ambulance scream by, and I thought, "Good. Another one of them bastards is hurt or dead."

"You don't have to do this."

That was Daddy. Or the thing pretending to be him.

"Shut up," one of the Green Shirts said.

"There is another way. The Divine Wind will help you—"

One of the boys next to him raised his elbow and crashed it down on his nose. Blood poured down his face.

"We said shut up!"

Daddy didn't say nothing more. His chin hung on his chest and his head bobbed with as the hearse swept us toward our fate.

The stadium was lit up as they pulled around to the gate. More Green Shirts, armed, guarded it. One approached the driver, who rolled down the window, and they exchanged something in a language I didn't know, and Green Shirt signaled back to the gate guards and they pulled it open and the hearse drove onto the field.

The stadium was packed. Men, women, children, all dressed in green, all cheering and jeering as the boys pushed us out of the hearse and marched us to the middle. It as deja vu all over again. Remember back in October last year when Seb Mack lured me and Daddy out to his momma's broke down old trailer under the guise of rescuing his sisters but instead his momma breathed that green poison into Daddy and me and they drug us out into the country and tied us down in a field of dead bodies to have our chests get stove in by a killer tentacle? Multiply that by five, and that's what was going on in the middle of Maury Stadium.

Everyone let up a horrible cheer when they seen me. Dead bodies lay strewn all over the field forming a semicircle around a great big hole in one end zone, all of them done the same way Seb Mack wanted me done. The stink made me want to puke, and I do believe I gagged and dry heaved my fair share, and my broke rib screamed with each one, adding more misery to my already sorry condition. After they pinned me to the ground and posted a Green Shirt at my head, and after they'd done the same to Daddy, another hearse drove up with more prisoners, and they frog-stepped them out and threw them to the ground, too. All total, there must have been twenty of us out there about to die.

The boy they put next to me looked familiar. Like, *familiar* familiar. Even though my brain wanted to panic and scream and cry, and even though it was tough to concentrate with all the yelling and booing and cat-calling coming from the stands, I forced myself to get a closer look and good googly moogly. I couldn't believe it.

"Vlad?" I said.

He was in the midst of a full-blown panic attack (stating, not judging), eyes rolling around in his head, chest pumping like a steam train. My feet was tied to a stake in the ground, but just like before, they bound my hands together on my chest (some people never learn), so I raised up my arms and half-rolled to the side and slugged him in the face.

"Vlad!"

He stopped freaking out for a tic and looked at me, and his already wide eyes went wider, and he said, "Amanda?"

"Hey."

"What are . . . how . . ."

"It's a long story. I might ask the same of you. Last time I saw you, they'd drugged you simple. I thought you'd turned."

"Yeah, they tried." He held up his own bound hands. "It didn't take."

"Well, that's good news. I've been looking for you. What's with all this Waldo stuff?"

"That's a long story, too."

"You can tell me when we get out of here."

The Green Shirts posted to us each took a step forward and kicked us in the head.

"Shut your mouths!" they barked.

The crowd hushed and sat down, and then, as if bidden by some invisible clarion, they started to sing. It was that same atonal melody from the first time that happened to me, only worse, and louder, twenty, thirty, forty times louder than before. It sounded like a truck crash or worse, screeching whining, creaking metal on metal, major and minor keys mixed with some I ain't never heard before.

The ground rumbled and shook, and at our feet crowned the egg dome of a hive, THE Hive, it would seem, judging by its size. It rose high above the stadium, pushing dirt and rocks out of the ground, dozens of tentacles pushing out of its skin. The people in the stadium began to sway and moan, sick with ecstasy, and the Hive responded, vibrating its own deep, bass frequency, a frequency so low that I couldn't hear it, but I felt it—in my chest, in my bones, in my bowels. My head filled with fear.

Then the killing began.

This time the tentacles were speedy and purposeful as they plunged down through the air and into the chests of the victims tied to the ground, starting on my right, and heading, one by one, chest by chest, for me.

Here's the thing about dying. It ain't like in the movies. When I think about what happened out in that field, me lying in the grass at the fifty-yard line, I think of pictures I seen in history books. Jews in half-dug ditches staring up at kids playing soldier in black uniforms. Hutus on front lawns with machetes. Mass graves in Srebrenica. When I read about those things, I . . . I don't know how I felt. I dramatized it. Made it feel real and unreal at the same time, like it was in a movie. But that wasn't the truth. In reality, yeah, sure, it was scary and horrible, but it was also numbingly normal. There was the sky and there was the ground. Trees ringed the stadium. And after I was gone, after the Hive had sucked the blood from my body and the marrow from my bones, the sky would still be there, the ground would still be there, and the trees would still be there. It was a proper existential crisis, I'll tell you what, and even though I didn't know it then, I'd pretty much defined nihilism.

Here came the tentacles, one by one.

Thud to my right, down the line.

Oh well. It was my turn next.

I looked at Vlad. His eyes were closed tight. Part of me wanted to close mine, too. Who'd want to witness their own end so that way? So gross and violent. But I couldn't. I wouldn't. I didn't. I let my head roll to the side, and there were all the people in the stadium, swaying like beasts in their bloodlust, singing their horrible song. Their faces flickered, dropping the human shells, revealing their true selves. Some were not much different from human beings. Maybe they had blue skin or red skin or pale white skin, and maybe they had ridges on their noses or flaps of skin hanging off their necks or heavy-boned foreheads like shields, but they were balanced: two eyes, two ears, a nose and a mouth. Others, though. Shoo-wee. There were bug-looking things, slug-looking things, things with hairy crowns and sparkling horns, things with no faces at all, things with two faces on one side. If puking didn't hurt my ribs so much, I would have emptied all that soup all over the field.

All of the noise disappeared, sucked out of the air like I'd been transported into a vacuum. A tentacle waved over me, its mouth opened up, I saw the rows of teeth. It shot down. I couldn't help it. I closed my eyes.

Then a roar broke through that vacuum, and the world raged back into my head. Chaos and confusion. Bellows and bedlam. Gunfire erupted all around, and something knocked me upside the temple and flipped me over. Boy did I eat dirt. Got it in my eye, my ear, the corner of my mouth. When the ringing stopped, and when I realized that the tentacle hadn't eaten me and that I wasn't dead, I pushed off the ground so that I was on my knees.

All that screaming and craziness? It wasn't death come to me hoofed and horned, it was . . . well, actually, it was horned, just not hoofed. What I mean to say is that it was kangapes. Two of them. One of them thundered through the stands, sending white robes flying. The other one had grabbed the tentacle meant for me by each end of its mouth and broke it open as I watched. It was the most glorious thing I'd ever seen. But you want to know something more glorious than that? Berenice was clinging to its back.

"Missus! Missus!" she cried. "We comes for you!"

"Holy. Moly."

"Missus! This is Cherry! Cherry, say hi's to the Missus!"

One of the Green Shirts unslung his carbine and shot Cherry in the shoulder. Cherry grunted and took a step back, then her eyes narrowed in on the Green Shirt, who fired again, missing this time. She pounded forward, tearing up the grass, but the Green Shirt stood his ground, calmly aiming for her head. *Here's one who'd been in battle before,* I thought. *He won't miss this time.*

I lurched forward and grabbed his foot with my bound hands. It was just enough to send him off balance. The shot went wild, and then Cherry was on him.

But the fight wasn't over yet. Wasn't much two kangapes and a melonhead kid could do against the force the Hive had put together. Once the green robes in the seats got over their initial shock, they banded together against the lone kangape. Some of them leaped on it, others sang a tentacle in its direction, and soon it had been taken down. Cherry roared and beat a path over, pounding the field so hard that she tore up the turf.

"Missus!" Berenice cried. "Wait for me! I'll be back!"

I worked myself free of the ropes that tied my wrists together, then helped Vlad, who was already unbinding his feet. We'd just stood up when the old familiar zing flushed through my body. I could tell by Vlad's expression that he felt it, too.

"She's here," I said.

As if it understood, the Hive kicked into overdrive, sending tentacles whipping through the air. We ducked and dived as they struck the earth, aiming for us. An electric pulse filled the air, like a ball of lightning had settled over the stadium, and a brilliant, white light blasted out the middle of the field. Vlad and I were sent flying backward, and three figures emerged from the fading energy. The first was tall and muscular and carrying an automatic rifle. Another was skinny and wearing a lab coat. And the third was short and stumpy with a swollen head perched above a bright red shirt. Timmy Carter. Dr. H, and Bertholdt. Then the white light dimmed altogether, and the Girl and all her friends came into focus.

"Amanda!" Timmy Carter cried.

"Here!"

His head swiveled around, trying to find me in all of the craziness. Kangapes punching Green Robes, Green Shirts firing at Kangapes. One of them aimed for Berenice on the back of Cherry, fired, and missed. Bertholdt saw it, though, and his red eyes burned redder. The Green Shirt saw him sprinting up on them runty little legs and adjusted his aim. But Bertholdt zigged and juked and spun like Art Monk, and the Green Shirt couldn't keep up. His shot went wild and then Bertholdt was on him. Literally ran up his chest, wrapped his legs around the Green Shirt's neck and sank his teeth into his eyeball. I turned away before I saw what happened after that.

Timmy Carter shot at the tentacles as he sprinted for me, the Girl and her friends close behind. A crack formed in the front of the Hive, and out of the pulsing opening poured polar crabs. Every Green Robe in the stadium zeroed in on us. I grabbed Vlad's hand.

"This is it, Vlad," I said.

"This is what?"

"Follow me."

I pulled him forward to meet the Girl at the middle of the field. She grabbed Brownie's hand, and he grabbed the hand of the girl behind him, and so on down the line until all seven of us were linked. A bolt of energy shot through our bodies, and we went rigid with the power. It poured out of our eyes, our mouths, our limbs, and I let it fill me up, heal my cracked ribs, my mashed nose, my bruised brain. It filled every cell in me with its power, and then I *was* the energy, full and furious, and I set my sights on the thing that had caused me so much pain and sorrow. I narrowed in on the Hive. Before I knew it, the power in me responded, and I sped across the field and slammed into the Hive's skin and ripped and tore and shredded. And it wasn't just me. It was the Girl. And Brownie. And Vlad. And the other four.

I could hear it, the voice of the Hive, screaming in pain as we peeled through layer after layer, spinning around and around like shrapnel, aiming for the only thing that would finally kill it. I bore in, drilling down, down, down, and then there it was in front of me, the black heart of the Hive. I started forward but felt something hold me back. It was the

Girl. She was pure white, all of us were, and we all were floating in the center of the Hive. Her eyes blazed silver, her hair floated above her head, and power bolted through her mouth.

"No," she said. "We have to do it together. All of us."

She and the others fanned out around the heart, holding their arms aloft, and I did the same. Electricity linked our fingertips, a live wire of endless energy. The Girl took a deep breath.

"Now!" she cried.

We shot forward, all seven of us, and crashed into the heart, and in the explosion that followed, I knew myself no longer.

KLAUS

This is the last story I'm ever going to tell ya'll, I promise. Some of you will be disappointed. Some of you won't. But make no mistake about it: this is it. The last lemon. The final french fry. The terminal tomato. Now look, it ain't you. It's me. We've shared some good times together, and I ain't telling you this because I'm mad at you or so that you'll change or do stuff different. I just feel like this is the end of the road for us.

All of which is an expensive way of saying I ain't got no more stories to tell.

Except this one.

Four months toward the end of my sophomore year in high school (a few months before the Hive landed), a boy showed up at school that nobody had ever seen before. His name was Billy Ruger. He was a weird looking little guy, with stumpy legs and a little head and piercing blue eyes that always seemed to be watering. Made him look like he was on the verge of a twenty-four-hour nervous breakdown. If he'd showed up when we were in elementary school, our teachers would have made a big deal out of it, you know, "everybody welcome the new kid because he's new and ain't got no training yet" and such. But high school was a different animal completely, and teachers didn't have time for that kind of mess. They taught over one hundred kids a day, most of whom didn't give two shakes for school, their education, and the people around them. Introducing a new kid to everyone in that situation was bound to make a bad day worse, so usually they just said "sit over there, shut up, and get your work done."

That's exactly what Billy did. Well, the first two days, at least. Over the next couple of weeks, it became alarmingly clear to the rest of us that he was a bit touched. He looked like he was paying attention in class. His eyes followed the teachers as they taught. He took out his books and paper and pencils when he was told. But nothing else. If a teacher called on him, his eyes would dart to the blank page in front of him. If they told him to get his work done, he put his head on his desk and covered it with his arms.

As many of you who've been to high school know, that ain't the kind of behavior that made a body a hit with the other kids. Not in the way that was beneficial to said body. Billy got his pretty good. Started out innocent enough. Lunch money stole. Tripped in the commons. Kick me signs. Each time he was mugged, each time he found himself flat on his face, each time they humiliated him, he didn't retaliate. He went hungry. He lay still until they left. He let them laugh.

I tried to talk to him about it. One morning I seen some football player take his breakfast bun from him, and I made up my mind to try and help. We got let go early because a snow storm was coming, and Spotsylvania wasn't particularly known for its winter weather preparedness, so if it even smelled like snow, the whole county shut down for a month. I caught him up as he was heading to the bus. Wasn't easy. Billy Ruger loped and ducked and ran through the crowd like he was trying to win a race. I had to put on my soccer legs, and I still didn't catch up to him until he was almost on the bus. Had to jump out in front of him to make him stop

"Hey, Billy Ruger! Hold up a sec!"

He skidded to a halt and hung his head and looked at the ground. I was breathing pretty heavy.

"Dang, you're fast! You ever think of joining the track team?"

He shook his head hard and fast, and that's when I noticed his bare arms. It was the middle of January, but he didn't even have a long sleeve shirt on let alone a jacket. And his shoes were all ratty and his pants had holes in them.

"Look, Billy," I said. "I gotta tell you something. I saw what that football player done to you this morning." I didn't know a person's head could have hung even lower than his already was, but it did. He seemed to shrink, grow smaller. "You can't let those guys get to you. You gotta stand up for yourself, or it'll just get worse."

Billy's lips started moving but I couldn't hear anything he said.

"You listening to me?"

Nothing.

"Okay. Well, look, Billy. Be careful, okay?"

I went to clap him on the back, and he flinched.

"Sorry. I didn't mean—"

"Don't touch me!" he snapped, and he dashed away.

I watched him bobble up to his bus, his backpack three times bigger than his whole torso. He had to use the railing to pull himself in, and when he did, the bus erupted in jeers.

The next two days, a blizzard dropped over twenty inches of snow on us. We were out for two weeks. When we got back, I saw Billy Ruger get off the bus and run into school looking as tiny as ever. Even though the snow had melted considerable, it still hadn't warmed up more than over forty degrees, but Billy Ruger wasn't wearing nothing more than his usual ensemble: a ratty t-shirt, worn Wranglers with holes in the knees, and a pair of Converse sneakers that might have been white at some point. It occurred to me that he moved like a shadow, slipping in and out of the columns that lined the entrance, hiding in the wake of the larger groups of kids. I watched until he disappeared into a side door, and even then I didn't actually see him go in, just the flick of a single dirty shoe before the door clicked shut.

I wouldn't see Billy Ruger until fourth period, right before lunch. Or I wasn't supposed to. In the middle of second period (World History with Mr. Johnson—yuck), Vice Principal Olney stuck his head in the door and said, "Mrs. Johnson?"

We all giggled.

"Mrs. Johnson's my wife," Mr. Johnson said. "Or my mother."

Olney didn't even skip a beat.

"Can I see Jett for a moment?"

I started to get up when he added: "You can bring your things with you."

If it was dead silent when I left the room, it was even quieter as I walked down the hall. I didn't really ever get in trouble, so I didn't really know what do to or what to say. Mr. Olney sauntered in front of me, his heels clicking on the tile. He and I knew each other okay. His daughter was on the field hockey team and he was often one of the chaperones.

"What's going on, Mr. O?"

"It's a sensitive matter, Jett."

"Can't you tell me even a little bit?"

"I'm sorry, I can't."

"But what'd I do?"

He didn't answer, and I racked my brain.

"Is this about the tampons in the girl's bathroom?"

"What?"

"Never mind."

He led me down the hall and into the office and told me to sit down in the chair outside Principal Lee's door before he went inside. Not two seconds later, he poked his head back out and said, "come on in, Jett."

Daddy was in there, looking about as awkward as a forty-year-old pot farmer who barely graduated from high school could look.

"Hey sugar bean," he said.

"Don't call me sugar bean."

"Okay."

A police officer scowled in the corner behind the principal's desk. I didn't think he was scowling at me necessarily, but that was just what his face did. I unslung my backpack and put it on the carpet next to the seat next to Daddy.

"What's this all about?"

Principal Lee cleared his throat.

"Ms. Jett. I want to begin by telling you that you're perfectly safe here. Nothing bad is going to happen to you."

I laughed and looked at Daddy, but he didn't seem to find it amusing.

"I know. Daddy, what's going on?"

"'Manda, just answer his questions, okay?"

"What questions?"

"Ms. Jett," Mr. Lee said. "Do you know a student here by the name of William Ruger?"

"Billy? The new kid?"

"Yes, that would be him."

"Sure, I know who he is. We're not friends or nothing. What happened? Is he okay?"

Suddenly every adult in the room looked interested. The cop even added a frown to his scowl. Principal Lee leaned forward and templed his hands on his desk.

"Why do you ask that?"

"I don't know. Other kids like to bully him is all."

"Bully him?"

"Yeah. He's a little runt and he don't stand up for himself, so they take his lunch money, push him down. The usual."

"And you say other kids do this?"

"Yeah. The jocks and the waistoids and the populars and such."

"But not you?"

"What? No way!"

"Did you ever approach Billy and talk to him?"

"Yeah, once."

"When?"

"Before the break."

"Why?"

I looked at Daddy and he nodded.

"I thought he might have needed a little push is all."

"Push?"

"Yeah. A pick-me-up. Some coaching. I don't know if you noticed, but Billy don't look like he got much going on at home."

"Yes, we know. Ms. Jett, did you tell Billy to 'be careful'?"

I laughed out loud.

"Yeah."

"So you admit it?"

"Why wouldn't I?"

"Because you were threatening him."

"Threatening him? I was worried about him! He was getting beat up every day. I told him to stand up for himself."

Principal Lee was writing on a notepad.

"Stand up for himself?"

"Yeah. I told him it was just going to get worse if he didn't fight back."

"That's what he said."

It got real quiet and tense and I didn't know why. Outside, I could hear the phones ring and the secretaries talking. Mr. Lee was staring at me.

"Mr. Lee?" Vice Principal Olney said. "Do you mind?"

Principal Lee gestured with his hands as if to say, "go ahead."

"Amanda," Olney said. "Can you tell us exactly what you said to Billy that day?"

"Sure. I said, 'You gotta stand up for yourself, or it'll just get worse.' And when he didn't say anything because he don't never say nothing to nobody, I told him to be careful. And that's it. Then he ran to his bus."

The tension in the room collapsed.

"I think I understand now," Principal Lee said.

"Good. You mind explaining it to me?"

He'd already stood up.

"I'll let your father do that on the way home."

"Home? But I got practice."

"Not today, 'Manda," Daddy said. "Come on."

"What? This ain't fair! I didn't do nothing."

"'Manda, I'll explain everything in the car. Mr. Lee? Mr. Olney? Thank you."

He nodded at the cop.

I waited until we got out of the parking lot before I let him have it.

"What was that all about! What's going on! You know I got training!"

"'Manda, that boy Billy brought a gun to school."

"A gun? Like a hunting rifle? I don't mean to bust your bubble, but this here is Spotsylvania County, and—"

"A handgun, 'Manda. Brought it in with him. Hid it in his backpack. Somebody saw him take it out and put it in his locker."

"Oh. So what does that have to do with me?"

"Mr. Lee said that when they questioned him, the only thing he'd say was your name. Over and over. When they pressed him some more, he said you told him it was going to get worse and that he'd better be careful."

"But—"

"Yeah, I know. We know that now."

"Is he—"

"They took him away, 'Manda."

"So why am I in trouble?"

"You ain't. They want you to go home in case something bad happened."

"Like what? Ain't he gone?"

"Yeah, but . . . they're just taking precautions."

I let the information sink in. It was a lot to process. I know I've told ya'll several times that I wasn't a whiner, but this was all new to me, and I was just a kid, and all I could see was the look on Billy Ruger's face when I tried to pat him on the back. Pure terror and hate. And then all I could see was that same face coming up to me in the hallway and me saying, "Hey, Billy Ruger," before he blasted my face off. I couldn't help it. I started to cry. Not out and out bawling, but tears started to roll down my cheeks.

"Daddy, was he really going to kill me?"

"I don't know what he was going to do, 'Manda. I'm just glad they caught him before he did it."

"I didn't mean to scare him. I wanted to help him."

"Oh, 'Manda. This ain't your fault. That boy had a lot of problems. This wasn't the first time he'd done something like this. Apparently, he near to beat some boy to death at the last school he was in."

"Oh."

"Yeah."

Still didn't make me feel better about it.

I never heard a word about Billy Ruger again. It was a relief, I guess, but every now and then I'd think about him and wonder if he was going to come back. It was an unpleasant way to experience life, worrying if some crazy kid would show up and try to kill me. Not many other girls could say that was how they spent their teenage years. Kept me up at night. At least until the Hive showed up.

We spent the first three weeks of January traveling the countryside killing off any Macks and spare hives we came across. Or I should say, we were trying to. Most of the Macks we found were hollow shells of meat and gristle lying in the grass or curled up on the road. We thought they was dead, but of course the Hive couldn't let them go so easy. Dang thing had lost its hold on them but left them alive, maybe even aware somehow. I knew this because more than once I seen their eyes roll up when I straddled their bodies, pleading with me, I hope, to put them out of the hell they were in.

So I did.

It was a brutal, messy job. Didn't help that it was cold out. Colder'n the devil's pecker, as my daddy used to say (pardon my vulgarity). Hard to believe that two months before it felt downright tropical. But I guess killing off the main hive set the world back to rights, and with a powerful sneeze, too.

We returned to the Courtland Colony sore, tired, hungry, and ready for a nice long nap. All except for Timmy Carter. Timmy Carter'd gone and broke his foot. He took it manly enough, even if he did limp all the way home.

"Timmy Carter, you might be big, but you're a fragile little thing, ain't you?"

"Very funny, Amanda."

"No, seriously. Seems like every couple of months one of your bones cracks in half."

He didn't talk to me much after that, and when we got back, it was straight to the clinic for him.

"You take it easy, Timmy Carter," I told him. "Leave the saving the world to the big girls." He gave me the two finger salute. "When are you heading back?"

"Probably tomorrow. I'm going to heal up here tonight first. I'm a little busted up."

"I'm surprised you stuck around as long as you did. You must miss her."

He smiled.

"A little."

"Come get me before you leave. I'll walk you out."

I started to turn away and he grabbed my wrist.

"Yeah?" I asked.

He opened his mouth, seemed to think better of it, and closed it tight.

"Timmy Carter, you going to say something or just stand there imitating a fish?"

He pressed his lips together like what he was about to say was really difficult, but if I'm being honest, he looked like he was trying not to fart.

"I had something planned," he said. "but . . . damn!"

"What's up? Just say it."

"Okay. Okay." He looked me in the eye. "I'm glad it was you, Amanda. I'm glad it was you."

I let that hang in the air for a while, and I couldn't decide whether or not to make fun of him for it, but in the end, I softened.

"Thank you, Timmy Carter," I said, and I went in for a hug. "I'm glad it was you, too."

The very next morning, the second strangest kid I ever met in my life showed up at the front door of the Courtland Colony.

I woke up early because I had to pee, put on my shirt and my jeans and my belt and my knife and the screwdriver I'd taken to carrying around because I liked the idea of stabbing someone with a screwdriver for some reason, and shuffled off to find a suitable place to do my business. I didn't like to use the facilities closest to the commons. Always seemed a mite pedestrian to me. And open. I preferred to take my morning constitutional alone, you see, and there were only two places in the building that afforded that kind of abulatory privacy: the commode in the clinic, and the privy in the principal's office. The commode in the clinic was occupado that morning, but the privy in the principal's office was free and clear.

Ailani didn't like to waste water on something we could have done out in the woods, but when the hives were still out there, nobody wanted to risk copping a squat with all them tentacles squirming around, so she tolerated it. Now the hives were gone, and even though she kept making noise about stopping the practice, we were used to it.

So I did what I needed to do and was walking out into the main office when I saw a figure standing on the other side of the front door. I watched it, wondering if it was one of the guards or someone who'd gotten locked out. It didn't move for a full minute, and darker thoughts came to my mind. Another Mack, maybe? How had it gotten through the gates or the roadblock?

Sighing, I searched my belt for my knife and ambled out of the office. I imagined that I'd have to get used to that kind of thing, stray Macks and all. The fact that this one was still mobile was different, but after the year I had . . . . Let me put it this way: if I was going to have to take out some Macks every now and then, I was going to have to take out some Macks every now and then.

"Alright, dummy," I said, yanking the door open. "You picked the wrong—"

It wasn't a Mack. None of the Macks I'd come across over the past three weeks were as well-put-together as whoever this was—well, well-put-together in relationship to the average Mack. It was a boy. He was short and fat, with a big head and thin hair and stumpy legs. His hands barely peeked out of the cuffs of his wool coat, and his brown pants looked they was made by an angry momma. In fact, now that I inspected him closer, I noticed that his coat had hooks and eyes instead of buttons, and his dusty boots had brass buckles instead of laces, and his pants stopped at the tops of his ankles, and he was wearing a silk cravat, and he was holding a wide, flat-brimmed hat in one hand, and his curly bangs were uneven and the rest cut all wonky and I thought, *what a strange little person this is.*

"Hello," I said.

The boy gave a wary, childish smile but nothing else.

"Are you lost?" I asked.

What kind of question was that? Of course he was lost. Ain't nobody who looked like that really belonged nowhere, not those days, at least. Letting him in didn't seem to be prudent, not if the events of the past year were any barometer. I tried another approach.

"You got any people?"

That seemed to rattle something loose. He patted a fold in his coat and produced two letters that had been pinned to the fabric, holding them out to me like he was offering a million dollar bill. I took it and read the front. The first was addressed to "The Captain of the Courtland Colony," with the heading "From the Blue Ridge border/unknown/date redacted." The second one was blank. The envelopes were old and worn and water stained like he'd been traveling with them for a long, long time.

"Huh," I said. "Did you write these?"

"I don't know."

"You don't know if you wrote these?"

"I don't know."

His voice was neither high nor low, which surprised me. I thought for sure he was maybe eleven or twelve years old, but the tenor of his words revealed otherwise.

"What are you, fifteen? Sixteen?"

"I don't know."

"Is there anything you do know?"

He stared at me, held my eyes, and turned his attention to the space over my left shoulder and left it there. I tapped the edge of the letters against my palm. If I let this little freak in and he ended up being some kind of attack idiot sent by the last vestiges of the

Hive, I'd never forgive myself. But I couldn't leave him standing out in the cold neither, not the way he was dressed, so I led him in and set him down in a chair in one of the offices.

"I'm going to close the door and go get some people. You stay here. Don't move, don't touch nothing, just stay here, you hear?"

"I want to go home."

"Home? Why'd you come here, then?"

"I want to go home!"

"Where's home?"

"I don't know."

"Alright, listen—"

"I want to go home! I want to go home!"

"Holy moly."

Resisting the urge to smack him, I got the heck out, making sure to close the door behind me. I took one more look through the window before I left. He was sitting in the chair, staring off into space.

Ailani read the letters while sitting in the main office. We were just outside the door of the room I put him in. The one without an address simply said the boy's name was Klaus Richter and that he'd been "born strange." The one with the address was from a "poor farmer from Bristol" who apparently found

Klaus on his doorstep sixteen years before and raised him as his own.

"I done my best," the letter read. "He ain't the brightest but he ain't the stupidest neither. He wants to be a magician, just like his father."

"Dang, Ailani," I said. "You think they knew anything about anything that was going on these past twelve months?"

"Beats me."

"What do you want to do with the kid?"

"What kid?"

Crap. Frankie. She must have snuck up on us.

"Hey, Frankie," I said. "You're up early."

She ignored me.

"What kid? What are you two talking about?"

"Amanda found a boy out front," Ailani said.

"*Found* a boy? Where out front?"

"Under the overhang," I said.

"How did he get that far?"

"How am I supposed to know?"

She came over and peered in the window.

"Why did you let him in?"

"I couldn't let him stay out there, Frankie."

"He could be a spy. Or a plant. Or . . ."

"Spy for who? The Hive is dead."

"We don't know who else is out there, Amanda. People are desperate. We have resources."

I opened my mouth to argue, but she was right. I clenched my jaw. Ailani tried to cut the tension.

"Calm down, Frankie. We're only trying to figure out who he is and what to do with him."

"I know exactly what to do with him. Set him loose."

"We're not going to do that," I said.

Both Ailani and Frankie said, "We're not?"

"No! He ain't right. We might as well kill him."

I held out the letter for Frankie to read. She scanned it and shook her head. Then she thrust it back at me.

"Exactly. He ain't right and we have a pile of problems of our own to deal with here without adding him to it."

"He's right there, Frankie," I said, glancing at the office door.

"I don't care. He could be dangerous."

That went on and on, all three of us making good arguments and bad arguments, and then it got old and nobody was backing down, so the discussion kind of petered out and we stopped.

"So that's it?" Frankie said, staring hard at Ailani.

"Nothing's been decided, Frankie. We should bring it up to everyone else. Take a vote."

"A vote?" I said. "We going to vote every time someone finds this place?"

"That's not what I meant."

"Good because that would be crazy. We've got to come up with something for when this happens again. A rule or a law."

"I agree," Frankie said.

Now it was Ailani and me who both said, "You do?"

"It's a good idea. We can't let everybody who stops by in. I say let's lock the doors for good."

"That's not what I meant," I said.

Not everybody agreed with her. At least not at first. We held a vote with all of the adults left in the colony. In regards to letting people in, the vote went 50/50. Half of us said no more, the other half said we need to build our ranks. In regards to Klaus, I won fifteen to six. He was allowed to stay, but only if we had another vote in the spring. Until then, he had to prove he wasn't a drag on our resources. If he was, he'd be kicked out. If he wasn't . . . I don't know, maybe he could stay? We weren't clear on that point, even though it was implied.

There was one condition, though. He had to stay in that room for a week so we could observe his behavior. I thought that was too much but didn't really have a choice. The people who voted in favor of giving him a chance wouldn't have voted in favor of giving him a chance without it.

"It's only a week, Amanda," Ailani said.

"A week locked in a tiny office."

"Can I ask you something?"

"Sure."

"Why do you care so much? You don't even know this guy. Frankie isn't wrong. He could be dangerous."

"I know."

"From what you told me about what happened on your farm—"

"What about it?"

"I guess you'd be more likely to agree with Frankie."

I thought about it. Then I chuckled.

"It's spite, isn't it?" I said. "It's hard to agree with someone like her."

"You don't like her. I get it."

"But she's right." Ailani raised her eyebrows. "What Uncle Zeus did was wrong. He was the worst kind of man, and if them hive balls hadn't come along when they did, he'd of killed us all. I should have shot him dead the moment I saw him." Ailani nodded as if she knew what I was talking about. "But I don't want to be like that. We got a chance here. We got a chance to decide who we want to be. I don't want to be like Uncle Zeus. I won't be like him."

"Even if it means some of us will suffer?"

"Who said that's for certain?"

"It's a possibility."

I shrugged and started off for the kitchen.

"Maybe it is, maybe it isn't."

"Where are you going?"

"I'm going to bring him something to eat. Poor thing looks half to starving."

I fixed him up a plate of corn on the cob, a cut up pepper, and one hardboiled egg. When I opened the door to the office, he was asleep on the floor, curled up like it was the most comfortable thing in the world. I put the tray down next to him and shook his shoulder.

"Wake up, Klaus."

He stirred and eyed me. Then he sat up and put his back against the wall and stared at the ground at his feet.

"You hungry?"

"Yes."

I toed the tray toward him. He looked at it.

"What is that?"

"What, this? Corn and peppers. An egg."

He picked up the egg and sniffed it. Put it down. Did the same with the corn and the peppers.

"I thought you said you were hungry."

"I am."

"So eat."

He stared at the corner.

"Well, here's the deal, Klaus. You can stay for a while. But you got to prove yourself, okay?"

He stared at the corner some more.

"I ain't going to lie to you, neither. There's some people who don't want you here."

"Frankie?"

"How'd you know her name? I mean, I ain't saying it's—"

"She's the one."

"What's that supposed to mean?"

"Frankie reminds me of a man."

"What man?"

"I slept in a cell with no window. The floor was straw. Every morning, I woke to a plate with bread on it and a glass of water. Sometimes the water was bitter and made me sleep. When I woke up, my hair was shorter."

He looked wonderingly at his fingers. I didn't know what to say.

"Alright then, Klaus," I said, backing to the door. "Somebody'll be by later to take you the bathroom."

"Bathroom?"

"Yeah, one of the guys will—"

"Not you?"

"No. I didn't think you'd be comf—"

"You can go now."

"Alright."

I closed the door and locked it. When I looked in the window, he was still staring at his fingers.

Since it was only a few weeks past our last hive hunt, Ailani still had us on war protocol. Nobody out of the building after dark. Nobody out of the fence line ever (unless on a raid). Doors locked at night. And my favorite: twenty-four-hour guards, inside and out. With our manpower non-existent, that meant everybody had to take a turn.

She doubled us up for safety. I would have preferred partnering with Timmy Carter, but Timmy Carter was laid up with that broken foot, so I got . . . well, I didn't get Frankie, so you don't need to worry about that. If Ailani had been dumb enough to make that decision, I would have flat out refused. No way I was going to be anywhere with that snake rolling around in the dark with a gun.

No, instead I got some old hippie who called himself Burroughs. I don't know if that was his real name or not. Probably wasn't. Burroughs was tall and stooped and had short hair and a clean shaved face and a lot of luggage under his eyes. And he was tall. So tall. His legs looked like they was all knee and shin.

And he loved guns.

I wouldn't have thought a self-professed hippie would've loved firearms so much, but Burroughs's affection for them could have been immortalized by William Shakespeare. "How do I love to blow heads off with thee? Let me count the ways."

Burroughs loved guns more than he loved anybody, even himself. It's weird to say this out loud, but I think that he loved guns even more than Daddy did. Daddy thought of them as tools. He used them to hunt or to put down a dying animal or for personal protection. Burroughs though . . . his feelings for his arsenal (because that's what he had, his own private arsenal) bordered on obsession. It's all he ever talked about, which was why I didn't talk to him all that much. If I did, he didn't even pretend to try and carry on a conversation, he'd wait until I was done with my end, and then he'd start talking about the difference between an automatic and a semi-automatic, or why there was no such thing as an "assault rifle" or why, in his opinion, the M16 was a vastly underrated weapon in comparison to the AK-47.

Once, when I pointed out that the AK had a kind of exotic appeal, Burroughs cut me off and said: "Never underestimate the ignorance of an American."

Timmy Carter was standing next to me when it happened, and when he saw my mouth working but no words coming out, he burst out laughing. Burroughs plowed forward regardless.

"And before you call me a right-wing nut job, know this: if you call me so much, I'll introduce you to Louise. I'm as pink as a fellow traveler as you'll ever meet."

"Who's Louise?" Timmy Carter asked.

I was too late with my "don't ask."

Burroughs was one of the few people who dared to stand eye to eye with Timmy Carter, and right then, stand eye with him he did.

"Come by my room later on tonight, big boy, and I'll give you a personal introduction."

Timmy Carter watched him walk away, a curious expression on his face.

"Did that old man just come on to me?"

"Don't take it personal, Timmy Carter. He says that to everybody who asks who Louise is."

Burroughs and I had a deal. He took the first half of the night and I took the second, that way we didn't have to spend any more time around each other than absolutely necessary. Ailani would have threw a fit if she found out, but she never did because she was asleep.

I don't know what Burroughs did when it was my turn to wander around the school and pretend like it was important, and I didn't want to know. When it was his turn to do it, I holed up in the school store, locked the door, wedged a chair under the knob, and decked out on a double-wide sleeper couch I confiscated from the football coaches office.

That's exactly where I was the night of the day I found Klaus, snoozing comfortably in my regular position: flat on my back, hands clasped over a pillow on my chest, right leg bent out with the bottom of my foot against my left knee. Sometime real late, I startled awake in pitch black, certain I'd heard the report of a gun.

I was on my feet and out the door lickety-split, stumbling around in the commons, trying to get my bearings and draw my gun without running into one of the cots we'd left out or a lunch table or one of the columns. By the time I remembered I had a flashlight, I'd already banged my shin twice and tripped over something hard and knobby sticking out of the floor. I snapped my walkie-talkie out of my pocket and said, "Burroughs? Burroughs? Was that you?"

Shouts rang out upstairs, doors slammed, and beams of light skittered all over the walls. Ailani's voice came over the walkie-talkie.

"Amanda! What's going on?"

"How the heck should I know? Burroughs must of shot at something."

"Where is he?"

"That's what I'm trying to find out."

"Why aren't you two together?"

"We split up."

It wasn't necessarily a lie.

"Where are you?"

"In the commons heading toward the main gym."

"Stay there. Wait for me."

Another shot rang out and I involuntarily half-crouched. Sounded like it was coming from the gym.

"The hell I will," I said, and I jogged toward the noise. When I turned the corner with the trophy case on the wall, my light flashed across a figure standing near the lockers, and my heart stopped as fast as my feet.

"Who is that?" I barked, training my light and my gun the way I'd seen it done on television, and . . .

Holy moly.

"Klaus?"

I inched forward, keeping the light and gun on him. He stood there, hands in the air, squinting.

"How'd you get out?"

"The man."

"What man?"

He pointed at the doors to the main gym.

"Something's happening."

The doors had been propped wide open, another strange development. We usually left them closed. It was a safety thing, fires and invading aliens having a harder time getting around and all. The gym was even darker than the commons, a great big, black void. Sure I'd spent the last year hunting and killing the kinds of things that would hide in the shadowy folds of that void, waiting to suck me in or arm-bar my throat or remove a limb, and sure it had been weeks since I'd seen something like that, but that didn't mean I wasn't a little afraid, and it didn't mean that there wasn't one hiding in there, not in light of weird old Klaus's cryptic syllables. I stepped through the door like I was stepping into a bear cave.

The beam of my flashlight cut a feeble ray in the dark, and the relative quiet of the hall outside was replaced by a yawning hush. I suddenly felt like I understood what it might have been like to be shot out of a spaceship and into the cold terror of the universe. I heard a gagging noise, a huffing and grunting, and I immediately regretted every single science fiction movie or television show I'd ever watched.

"Hello?" I called.

The gagging and grunting got louder, and I fought the urge to run. I had a gun, I kept reminding myself, a gun and a full year of experience hunting and killing and surviving situations exactly like the one I was in. How horrible would it be, I thought, to make it all this way only to be killed at the very end? Killed *after* we'd defeated the bad guys? It had to have happened, right? Those were the deaths that never made the history books. The splinters that ended up gangrene. The rotten tooth that turned into an infection. The forgotten tentacle monster that didn't know the war was over.

I inched forward until I was about forty feet in, standing around where the basketball hoop should have been. The gagging got louder, more desperate.

"I ain't in the mood for this!" I yelled.

"Help!"

It was raspy help, the kind that sounded like a windpipe slowly being crushed. And it was right above me. I shined my light and my gun straight up.

A pair of feet dangled in the air, kicking and peddling in the air. I took a single step out toward the middle of the court and aimed the light higher, and there swung Frankie, hanging from a noose. She was clawing at the rope, trying to pull it away from her throat, but it didn't seem to help none. I jammed my gun in my pocket and ran underneath to try and help her. Maybe I could push up on her feet and relieve the pressure? But I was too short and she was too short and my arms wouldn't reach.

Klaus was a dark form in a dark door. I shined the light on him.

"Klaus, go get someone!" I yelled.

He didn't move.

"Klaus!"

"I want to go home!"

I guess I had my walkie-talkie, but I was in a panic. The first thing to go in stressful situations and all that. So instead of calling for help, I looked around for something I could use to get higher up. There had to be a piece of equipment or a bench or . . . the weight room! I ran in, found a stand-alone bench and hauled it back out onto the hardwood.

"Don't you worry, Frankie!" I cried as I plunked it down.

I got up on it and found her feet.

"I got you! I got you!"

I pushed up but didn't feel any weight. She must have been bending her knees.

"You got to stand on my shoulders, Frankie, come on!"

"Amanda!"

It was Ailani.

"Ailani, help. She's hanging from the hoop."

I kept pushing up on Frankie's legs but she wouldn't lock her legs. Ailani shined her light over my head.

"Amanda—"

"Don't just stand there!"

"Amanda, stop."

"But—"

Ailani grabbed my belt and pulled me off the bench.

"What the hell, Ailani! Frankie's—"

She pointed her flashlight in the air where I had just been.

"Look!"

I did.

Nobody was there.

"But . . ."

"What's going on, Amanda?"

"It was Frankie. I . . . I . . ."

"Amanda, nobody's there."

"Where's Klaus."

"What?"

"You didn't see him?"

I pointed my flashlight at the door, but he was gone.

"No," Ailani said. "Isn't he locked—"

"He was right there. He told me something was wrong, then he pointed in here, and . . . Frankie . . ."

Ailani took her walkie-talkie off her belt and spoke into it.

"Frankie you there?" She waited. "Frankie? Come in." Still nothing. "Fra—"

"What?"

It was Frankie's voice, alright. Irritated as usual.

"Just checking to see if you're alive."

"And kicking. What's going on on your end?"

"Nothing. Looking for Burroughs. I'll check back soon."

"Got it."

"Ailani, I swear she was up there. And Klaus was out there."

"It's okay. I believe you."

"You do?"

"Yeah. Come on. Let's find Burroughs."

It didn't take long.

He was crumpled up at the end of the hall that led to the auxiliary gym with a bullet in his brain. His gun wasn't nowhere in sight.

We found Klaus sitting in the office with his back to us. He was playing with something in his lap. I took a single cautious step in. Ailani positioned herself in the jamb.

"Hey, Klaus," I said. "Whatcha got there?"

He held it up and twirled it around on his finger. It was Burroughs's gun. Ailani hissed and drew her weapon. I took a step back.

"Toy," Klaus said, smiling.

"Jeez Louise, Klaus. Where'd you get that?"

"The man."

"Burroughs?"

"The man."

He hunched back over and continued flipping the gun in his hands. I exchanged a look with Ailani.

"Klaus, you know that's a gun, right?" I asked.

"Toy."

"No. Gun."

"Gun toy."

"Klaus, I think you need to give that to me before someone gets hurt."

"No."

"Seriously, Klaus. I don't know how you—"

He twisted quick as a fox and pointed it at me.

"Pow! Pow!"

If I hadn't done all I done, seen all I seen, killed all I killed, and if my belly was full and my bladder fuller, I might have soiled myself. I did freeze, though. I closed my eyes. I ain't proud of it, but it happened. How else is someone supposed to act when a weirdo like Klaus pulled a stunt like that? I exhaled when I realized nothing happened, that my face or my chest or my neck or my stomach or some other important part of my anatomy hadn't painted the wall a bright shade of red. Klaus had gone back to playing with the gun in his lap again, and Ailani, who was now beside me, her own gun pointed at his head, said, "Amanda—"

"Yeah, okay."

We barricaded him in using whatever furniture we could find that hadn't already been scavenged and repurposed. The copiers were heavy, and the mobile chalkboards were good to jam up under the knob. We backed it all up with my special couch and a couple of pieces of cargo furniture. Then we went to break the news to the others.

The next morning, I stood in the parking lot staring up at the flagpole. A tattered American flag flapped in the breeze above the flag of Virginia. Below them both swung Klaus. A crow called in the distance. The rope we used as a noose bit into his neck, and I wondered aloud if we left him up there too long whether it'd cut his head off.

"We'll fix it when that happens," Ailani said.

"Good. I want to give him a proper burial."

"That's not what I meant." I gave her an astonished look. "People need to know, Amanda. Not to mess with us."

She looked up at him one more time and shook her head. I couldn't tell if she was angry or sad or disgusted. Then she walked back into the school.

I stayed out there for a little while longer. Part of me wanted to cut the rope and bring him down right then and there without nobody knowing. Drag him out into the woods and bury him somewhere they'd never find him. I didn't want to be the kind of person who would do something as terrible as what Ailani had implied. I didn't want to live in a place where kids saw something like that every day and thought it was normal.

In the end, I didn't do anything.

I knew that no matter how honest and moral and kind I wanted to be, convictions like those were a luxury, a thing of the past. Maybe someday we'd get comfortable enough to think of the world in quaint terms, but it wouldn't be any time soon.

So I left him up there.

I walked back into the school, the knell of the snap hook clanging behind me.

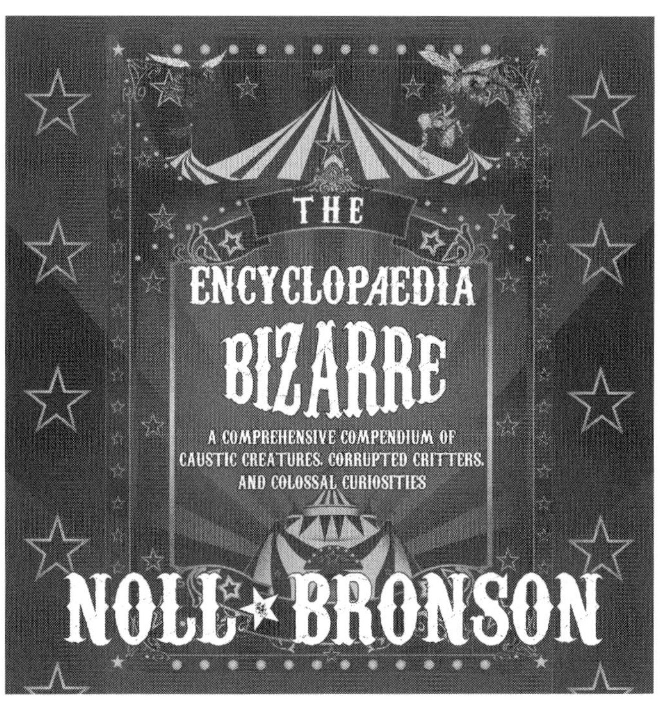
THE
ENCYCLOPAEDIA
BIZARRE
A COMPREHENSIVE COMPENDIUM OF
CAUSTIC CREATURES, CORRUPTED CRITTERS,
AND COLOSSAL CURIOSITIES
NOLL BRONSON

THE SQUIRSQUITO

The first documented encounter with a feral squirsquito can be found in Sir Robert-Forbes-Buckingham-Keys-Oswolf-Heathecote-Kingsley's seminal account of his years exploring the jungles of South America, Journey Into The Abyss: Bot Flies, Gangrene, Scurvy, and Starvation, or, Good God That Was a Horrible, Horrible Mistake.

After describing a peaceful encounter with a tribe that was rumored to be cannibals but which only turned out to be rabidly fanatical chicken and pork enthusiasts, Forbes-Buckingham-Keys-Oswolf-Heathecote-Kingsley narrates the following tale:

. . . relieved the night's watch, Jones-Kay-Lloyd-Stewart, a ruddy lad with a shock of red hair. Good boy. Useful in a fight. Hands like a gorilla. I found him asleep on his feet and was formulating a sharp rebuke when I saw the pale face, the wide eyes, and the slumped carriage I had all too readily come to recognize as the pose of death-by-crazy-monster. My native attaché appeared out of the bush and shewed

me what ended poor Jones-Kay-Lloyd-Stewart's life. It was a puncture wound in his chest, easily the size of a fist and perfectly round. At first I thought he'd been run through with a spear, but then my attaché drew attention to the pallor of the skin, and I realized that he'd been completely exsanguinated. Fearing some kind of jungle vampire, my compatriots and I decided that the most civilized response would be, as writ in Amendment 14, Section 3 of our bylaws, ritual decapitation and wet disembowelment-by-spork, followed by sexual corpse desecration and cold-fire immolation.

Two weeks later, and I had my first encounter with the creature that killed poor Jones. We were hacking through a swath of particularly thick bush near the poisoned marsh on the eastern side of the village, looking for the lost city of pewter that was rumored to be buried was rumored to have been buried there, when out of the bog burst the most hideous creature I'd ever encountered.

It was at least six feet long, with an insect's thorax that ended in a delightful, fluffy tail, and slick, glistening, gossamer wings. Its face, while admittedly cute (resembling a child's stuffed toy) was marred by a three foot long, spear-like proboscis, and though its rear paws were mammalian, its forelegs were thin, spindly, and jointed.

The beast harpooned my trusted manservant, Jonathan Cave-Smith-Tempest-Smith, in the stomach and bore him to the ground a corpse where it proceeded to siphon the blood right out of his body. It drained every drop before I could even think to remove my sidearm and sword. We hacked and shot the thing for at least two minutes before the brute met its end, but at the last moment, it pierced Davis-Webly-Gough-Willoughby through the thigh with its terrible bayonet. While Davis-Webly-Gough-Willoughby did not succumb in the manner of poor Jonathan Cave-Smith-Tempest-Smith, he developed a high fever, and his leg swelled up to the size of an elephant's; by morning an infection had spread, inflating his entire body until his head popped—a terrible turn of events for Davis-Webly-Gough-Willoughby to be sure until one stops to think about those who cleaned up after the tragedy!

Oh, what a miserable idea it was to ever explore this horrific place! Would that I could travel back to the moment when the idea first struck and throttle myself unconscious.

Even the cursine, though it can easily dispatch a squirsquito with a single swipe of its claws, will avoid any encounter with the beast. There are only two other natural predators of the squirsquito: the allicopter and the rhinodactyl.

Put Some BEEF in your Beauregards!
with
BARREL
ARM
BICEPS

Did You Know?

Most people think that the Aztec race died off in the 16th Century, but in reality, many lived on well into the 20th. In fact, one particular sect escaped the destruction of their race and migrated north to what is now known as Kinderhook, NY, where their descendants made a fortune in the pork industry and became linked with the Van Buren family.

The ties between the Aztecs and the Van Buren family were so strong that President Martin Van Buren relied extensively on their financial advice, which unfortunately consisted of a policy of the near-complete deregulation of financial institutions. The resulting recession lasted much of his first and only term.

In 1839, the financial crisis still bottoming-out the American economy and his presidency threatened by the Whigs, Van Buren once again turned to his Aztec friends for advice. Their solution resulted in the single most horrific episode of human sacrifice on American soil since The Salem Witch Trials.

Although nearly 50,000 people had their hearts ritually ripped from their chests on the lawn of the White House, the economy did not recover, and Van Buren went on to lose the next election to William Henry Harrison, whose campaign slogan, "I will not tear the beating hearts out of the chests of your loved ones" is the first recorded instance of an American president denying the long-accepted benefits of human sacrifice.

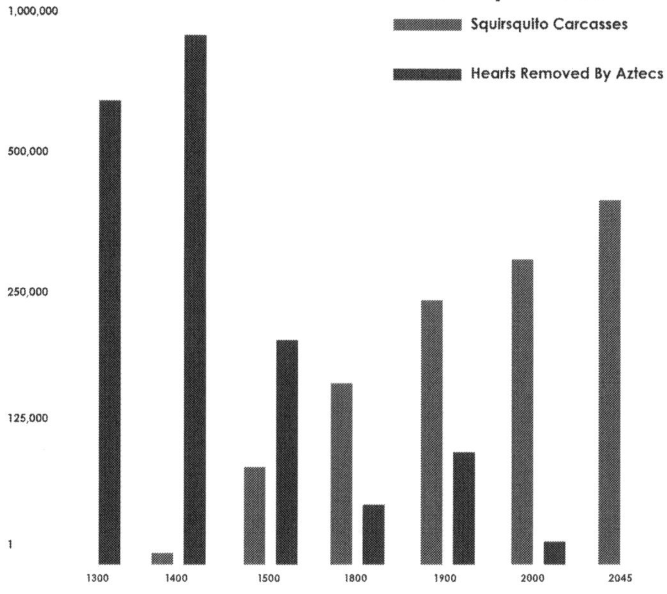
Number of Squirsquito Carcasses Compared to Hearts Removed From Chests By Aztecs
1,000,000
500,000
250,000
125,000
1
Squirsquito Carcasses
Hearts Removed By Aztecs
1300
1400
1500
1800
1900
2000
2045

Featuring the lore, mythology, and illustrations of never-before seen hybrid creatures such as Sniders, Sceels, Squirsquitos, and other beasts whose names do not begin with the letter 'S,' THE ENCYLCOPÆDIA BIZARRE is better than *The Sun Also Rises, Tender is the Night, Don Quixote, Anna Karenina, One Hundred Years of Solitude, The Iliad, 1984, Candide,* and every issue of Playboy from 1964-1972.

THREE HIGH SCHOOL ENGLISH TEACHERS who work with the author agree:

"*The Encyclopædia Bizarre* is the most exciting encyclopædia I've ever read, and I read A LOT of encyclopædia."

—Sarah Pendleton, English Teacher

"This book is so good that I fell down and broke my foot."

—Leslie Stretton, English Teacher

"I hate James Noll and everything he stands for."

—Kevin Johnson, Social Studies "Teacher"

THE ENCYCLOPÆDIA BIZARRE is one of the strangest, most engrossing and entertaining books TO EVER EXIST.

A NOTE FROM AMANDA

Hey ya'll! It's Amanda. Amanda May Jett from Spotsylvania County, Virginia. Hopefully you're doing well. Better than us, I guess.

While I got you here, do you think you could do us a teensy favor? The guy who was kind enough to write my story makes a living off these kinds of things, and it really helps if somebody who read his books left a review. Even if they didn't like it.

So if you could find a way to leave him one, that'd be great!

ABOUT THE AUTHOR

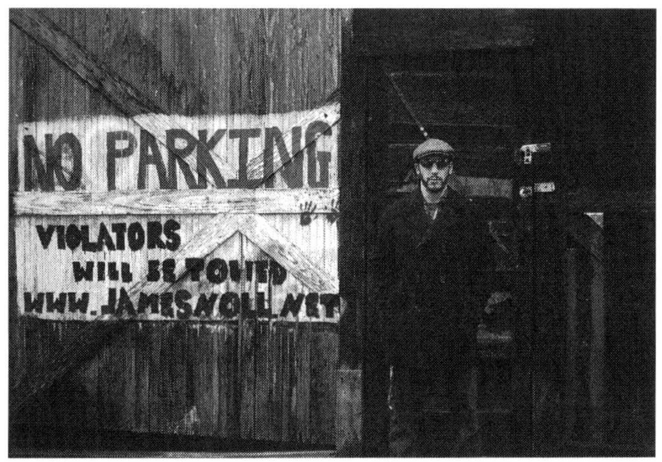

James Noll is a freelance writer, an educator, a musician, and a novelist from Fredericksburg, VA. He's published four other books: The Mad Tales Trilogy: *A Knife in the Back, You Will Be Safe Here,* and *Burn All The Bodies,* and the first book in The Bonesaw Trilogy: *The Rabbit, The Jaguar, & The Snake. The Hive* is his first serialized novel. Seasons One through Three are here. Look for Season Four (the final season) of *The Hive* winter 2018!

Check out his work at www.jamesnoll.net

Made in the USA
Middletown, DE
18 September 2024

60547384R00368